Born to Love STACKS

Born to Love

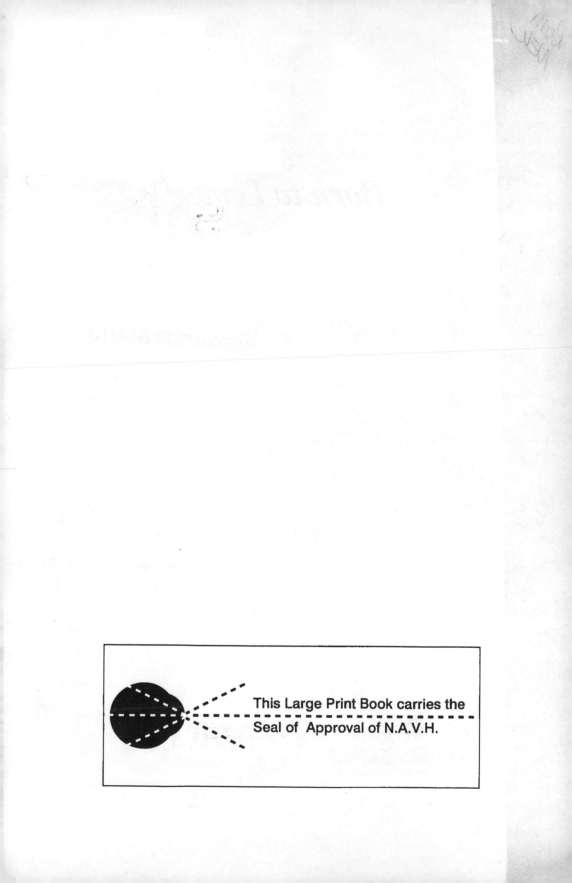

Born to Love

Leigh Greenwood

WHEELER
PUBLISHING

Published in 2003 by arrangement with Leisure Books, a division of Dorchester Publishing Co., Inc.

Wheeler Large Print Softcover.

The text of this Large Print edition is unabridged.
Other aspects of the book may vary from the original edition.

Set in 16 pt. Plantin by Myrna S. Raven.

Printed in the United States on permanent paper.

Library of Congress Cataloging-in-Publication Data

Greenwood, Leigh.
    Born to love / Leigh Greenwood.
       p. cm.
   ISBN 1-58724-513-2 (lg. print : sc : alk. paper)
     1. Galveston (Tex.) — Fiction. 2. Large type books. I. Title.
PS3557.R3976B67 2003
  813'.54—dc22
                                              2003057576

To Dr. Brett Christoffersen.
I hope I got all the medical stuff right.

National Association for Visually Handicapped
-------------------- serving the partially seeing

As the Founder/CEO of NAVH, the only national health agency solely devoted to those who, although not totally blind, have an eye disease which could lead to serious visual impairment, I am pleased to recognize Thorndike Press* as one of the leading publishers in the large print field.

Founded in 1954 in San Francisco to prepare large print textbooks for partially seeing children, NAVH became the pioneer and standard setting agency in the preparation of large type.

Today, those publishers who meet our standards carry the prestigious "Seal of Approval" indicating high quality large print. We are delighted that Thorndike Press is one of the publishers whose titles meet these standards. We are also pleased to recognize the significant contribution Thorndike Press is making in this important and growing field.

Lorraine H. Marchi, L.H.D.
Founder/CEO
NAVH

* Thorndike Press encompasses the following imprints: Thorndike, Wheeler, Walker and Large Print Press.

Chapter One

Galveston, Texas, 1867

Holt Price didn't like the look of the crowd gathered down the street. It had the distinct appearance of passersby gathered to gawk at some tragedy. He brought his horse to a standstill while he considered finding another way through town. Despite the medical bag he carried with him, he didn't think of himself as a doctor anymore.

But he couldn't turn away. It could be a serious accident with no doctor to help the victims. He'd always wanted to help people in trouble. That was why he'd wanted to be a doctor in the first place. He approached the crowd slowly. From astride his horse, he could see there had been a carriage accident. He took his medicine kit out of his saddlebag and dismounted. He rarely used it anymore, but he couldn't make himself leave it behind.

"Is anyone hurt?" he called out.

The gawkers, none of whom turned around to see who was speaking, were slow to move aside, so Holt pushed his way in. The sight that met his eyes reminded him forcefully of scenes he'd witnessed during the war. Two people, one a man, the other a boy, apparently more battered than broken, were covered with blood, their clothes badly torn. The third man had the shattered spoke of a carriage wheel sticking out of his upper left thigh. He lay in a large pool of blood, his skin a nickel gray. Three men leaned over him, all talking, none doing anything.

"I'm a doctor," Holt said as he approached the group. "Can I help?"

"He's a doctor, too," one of the three said as he pointed to a middle-aged man with untidy clothes and a balding head.

Holt nearly sagged with relief. He wouldn't be needed.

But his first look at the doctor's upturned face shocked him. It didn't take a physician to know the man had been drinking. What was worse, from the look in his eyes, he didn't know what to do. Holt was dragged back into it. It was his duty to help.

"What have you done for this man?" Holt asked.

"Nothing yet," the doctor replied, his words slow and slightly slurred. "I'm Paul Moore. I wasn't in my office. I don't have my bag."

There was no law that said a doctor couldn't have a drink, especially when he wasn't seeing patients, but Holt felt a doctor was honor-bound to keep himself in such a condition that he could function in an emergency any hour of the day or night. Holt would wait and see if Dr. Moore was more capable than he appeared. If not, he'd take charge.

"He has a wheel spoke sticking out of his leg," the doctor said.

"We can all see that," Holt said. "What are you going to do about it?"

"Pull it out, I guess," Dr. Moore said, sounding uncertain.

"You can't just *pull it out*," Holt said. "It's probably hit the femoral vessels, by the look of all the bleeding. He may have injured a vital internal organ. He could bleed to death before we get him to a hospital."

"We don't have a hospital," one of the onlookers said. "It got blown up during the war."

"Then we have to get him to the nearest doctor's office. If he doesn't receive attention immediately, he'll die."

"He looks dead already," someone said.

"How's his pulse?" Holt asked Dr. Moore.

"I don't know. I haven't checked it yet."

"See how badly the others are hurt," Holt said as he knelt down beside the motionless man. He picked up the man's arm — it was broken — and managed to find a weak, thready pulse. The chances were very good the man would die, but if he was to have any chance, they had to remove the spoke and stop the bleeding.

"Where is the nearest surgery?" Holt asked.

"Doc Moore's the nearest," somebody said.

"You two get me a wagon or a cart, something flat we can carry this man on," Holt commanded as he pointed to two onlooking men.

9

Holt then pulled out a rubber strap from his bag and slipped it under and around the bleeding man's upper thigh. He looped it twice and with a firm pull cinched on a tourniquet.

"How about the buggy seat?" an onlooker said. "It ain't no use in that buggy now."

"Fine. Help me get this man on it. Move him as gently as you can."

"We moved enough men during the war to know how," said a young man who'd stepped forward. "Don't look like Durwin's gonna make it. You ever taken a spoke out of a man's leg?" he asked Holt.

"No, but I've taken just about everything else out. I was a surgeon during the war. I've treated bayonet stabs that looked like this."

"You mean you butchered men," someone heckled. "It was doctors like you who cost me my leg."

Holt had always done his best, but during a battle so many horribly wounded men came so fast, there was seldom time for much more than desperate measures.

"Doctors did not fire the bullets that killed and wounded so many," Holt shot back. "That was nice young men like you. It was doctors who kept you from bleeding to death or rotting with gangrene. Now, are you going to help me move this man or are you going to just stand there feeling sorry for yourself and let him die?"

The ex-soldier moved aside, and several of

10

the onlookers helped move Durwin to the buggy seat.

"Make sure the other two come to the office," Holt said. "They'll need attention."

"I can take care of them," Dr. Moore said.

"Right now you can serve us best by leading us to your office as quickly as possible."

Holt guessed the doctor didn't like having Holt take over, but as far as he could tell, the doctor had been unable to make up his mind about anything. Holt didn't know whether he'd been incapacitated by alcohol, shock, or something else, but they had to act quickly.

"Doc lives real close," one of the men carrying the buggy seat said. "We all know how to get there."

"Then let's go. I need to operate."

"That's Doc's job," one of the men said. "He's the doctor around here."

"I'm a doctor, too," Holt said.

"That still don't mean you can come in here and take over."

Holt thought loyalty to friends was a fine trait, but not when it put a man's life in jeopardy. "With three men hurt, two doctors are better than one," he said.

"Maybe we ought to let the new doc see to Durwin," one man said, lowering his voice. "Doc Moore's been drinking again."

"Ain't nothing wrong with him," another said. "A little bit of whiskey never hurt nobody."

"I'd appreciate your help," Dr. Moore said to Holt. "That spoke worries me. I've never done that kind of surgery."

"I did it for four years," Holt said. "I'll be glad to do it for you."

"You can help if you want, but you let Doc take care of Durwin," a man said. "He knows what to do."

"Don't you listen to him," the cautious man said to Holt. "Everybody knows Doc ain't as good as he used to be."

It was clear that Dr. Moore didn't know what to do and couldn't have done it if he had. But it was also clear that these men weren't going to accept Holt's taking over. Deciding it was better to leave things alone until they reached the doctor's office, he dropped back to the wounded man and his son. "How are you two doing?" he asked.

"I sure am bloodied all over, but I'm doing better than Durwin," the man replied. "I think my boy here broke something."

"It's his collarbone," Holt told the father after a brief examination.

The small procession traversed the sandy streets of a town grown up on what had once been a windswept barrier island covered with sea grass and gnarled sea oaks. Fueled by a busy port, Galveston had expanded rapidly in the postwar years, transforming the island into the largest and most important city in Texas.

It didn't take them long to reach the doctor's

house. The procession entered a yard surrounded by a low picket fence that needed paint and slats replaced. The yard showed signs of neglect.

As the men carrying Durwin on the buggy seat climbed the steps to the porch, the door to the house swung open and a young woman came to hold the door. She was of average height, had a nice figure — what Holt could see of it — and was very pretty, but she wore a dress that could never have been more than plain and now showed wear.

Yet there was something about her that immediately caught his attention. Maybe it was her intensity. She seemed keyed up — worried, frightened, defensive, he couldn't tell — but there was a nervous energy about her that was unmistakable.

"What happened to Durwin?" she asked.

"He was racing down the middle of the street like the damned fool he is," the wounded father said. "He tried to run over me and Evan. Nearly killed himself instead."

"Bring him in. I'll show you where to put him so Papa can get that spoke out of him. Henry, I'll get to you and Evan in a minute. Who are you?" she demanded of Holt.

"My name is Holt Price, ma'am. And you?"

"Felicity Moore. The doctor is my father."

"You'd better call your mother. Your father is going to need help."

"My mother is dead. I can provide all the

help my father needs."

Holt didn't know her age, but he was certain she didn't have the knowledge and experience needed to help her father. Not many women would.

"Then I guess I'd better wash up. He needs trained help."

"What makes you think you can do a better job than I can?"

"I'm a surgeon. I spent four years trying to patch together boys that other boys had tried to kill. There's little that's stupid, senseless, and a criminal waste of bright, young lives, I haven't tried to fix." He hadn't meant to spout off at her. It had been two years since the war ended, but he hadn't recovered from the shock of the senseless slaughter or his own helplessness.

His answer appeared to upset Felicity, but he got the feeling her reaction had nothing to do with the horrors he'd witnessed. It was almost as if she wanted to get rid of him.

"I told your father I could take the spoke out of Durwin's leg. If he doesn't need me to do that, I can take care of these others. The boy has a broken collarbone. His father doesn't appear to have any broken bones, but both could have serious internal injuries. It was a very bad accident."

"Do you think you can get that spoke out of Durwin without killing him?"

"I don't know, but if somebody doesn't try soon, there won't be any need."

14

"Maybe you could take care of Durwin. Papa hasn't been feeling well lately."

Holt couldn't imagine she was naive enough to believe her father's condition was due simply to feeling unwell. She had placed herself between Holt and her father as though trying to protect the older man.

"Papa doesn't do much surgery. When he does, it's mostly simple stuff. He can take care of Henry and his son."

"I can't do this by myself," Holt said. "Your father will have to help me."

"I'll help you."

"I need someone who knows how to assist in an operation," Holt said as he moved quickly to try to save the man's life.

Felicity's chin jutted out and she got that unmistakable look of a woman who'd just been insulted. "If you know enough to get that spoke out of Durwin's leg without killing him, I know enough to help you. Who do you think helps Papa when he's working, or does the ether when he's got to put somebody out?"

"How would I know?" Holt asked as he opened his medical bag and began to lay out his instruments.

"You don't, any more than I know you can take that spoke out without killing Durwin. Do you think you can save him?" Felicity queried after a short pause.

"I don't know. I hope his internal injuries aren't too severe."

While they talked, she'd been moving about the room, taking out bandages, bottles with labels he couldn't read, washing her hands thoroughly. That impressed Holt. He'd been introduced to the germ theory in medical school. Though he'd explained it at length during the war, he hadn't been able to convince more than a few surgeons to wash their hands and their instruments between operations. Most thought he was a young fool with a new-fangled theory. The notion that invisible *germs* were to blame for infections was too far-fetched for most to accept.

"What are you doing?" Holt asked. He wanted to know whether she was washing on purpose or out of habit.

"Washing my hands," she said. "There's a theory that germs cause infection. If you wash before every —"

"I know about the theory," Holt said. "I'm surprised you do."

"My father studied medicine in Edinburgh. They believe —"

"I know what they believe. What do you wash with?"

"Carbolic."

"Wash my instruments while I prepare the patient."

Holt knew he sounded abrupt and unfriendly, but he was appalled that a man who'd had the advantage of a superior education should render it virtually useless because he preferred to pickle his liver in alcohol. He wondered if Dr. Moore remembered enough to set Evan's broken collarbone.

Holt wrenched his thoughts from the doctor and his daughter and directed them to the man lying on the buggy seat. He dreaded removing the spoke. Once it came out, Holt's speed in repairing the damage would be critical. He tried to ignore the sick feeling in his stomach. He'd have to use ether, but he still had his doubts about Felicity. Ether could kill if not used properly.

"Okay," he said to Felicity. "I'm ready."

The surgery lasted only a few minutes. Holt's fingers flew from instrument to instrument: clamps, suture, gauze, more suture. Once the femoral vein was repaired, Holt placed a few strategic sutures to hold the deeper flesh together and began giving instructions in how to bandage the still grisly wound. It would have to heal by growing in from the edges.

Felicity watched as Holt stepped back and slumped against the wall.

"That's the best I can do," he said. "From now on it's up to him."

She didn't answer. She didn't know what to say. She'd never seen anyone operate like that. It must take unbelievable courage to rip into a man's leg like one was cutting into the carcass of a steer. She knew her father could never have done it. She didn't know many doctors who could, and none could have done it with the confidence, the sureness, that Holt Price had just demonstrated.

"Where did you learn to do that?" she asked.

"On the battlefield."

"You didn't hesitate. You acted like you knew exactly what you were doing."

"I didn't in the beginning. None of us did, but we couldn't hesitate with the poor devils they brought to us. And they brought us so many. Sometimes the sheer numbers were frightening. No matter how little we knew, how poorly we could operate, we were their only chance, and everybody knew it."

He didn't appear to take pride in his skill. Rather, he seemed weary of it, or of the circumstances by which he'd acquired it. Or maybe it was the necessity to use it. She knew doctors of less than half his skill who were too full of pride to admit they had any limitations. For herself, she'd always thought the ability to save people's lives, to make them well again, was the most wonderful gift anyone could have.

"Where did you study?" she asked.

"The University of Virginia. Why do you ask?"

"Your accent. I don't know many Virginians, but you don't sound like they do."

"That's because I come from Vermont. I'm a Yankee."

She practically recoiled. He smiled when he saw her reaction.

"My friends told me I'd better learn to talk like a Southerner if I wanted to keep my head."

"What are you doing here?" Felicity asked. "The only Yankees in Texas are soldiers come to trample in the dust what little pride we have left, or carpetbaggers come to steal our money."

"I'm neither," Holt said. "One of the men I served with during the war invited me to Texas to help him round up his cattle and put his ranch back into working order. I might still be there, except I'm not cut out to be a cowboy."

"So you've come to Galveston to set up a medical practice." As the biggest and most important city in Texas, Galveston was the logical destination for a talented surgeon.

"No. I came to Galveston to search for the woman I love."

Felicity didn't like it when she had reactions she didn't understand. She had too many uncertainties in her life to be undecided in her own mind, but her reaction to Holt Price confused her. At first she'd been afraid of him. She didn't know if he was a good doctor, but even a bad one would know her father had drunk too much to be treating patients. She wanted Dr. Price out of the house and out of her life before he could do anything to endanger her father.

At the same time, she'd been hopeful he could save Durwin. Everybody knew Durwin had no sense, but he was such a sweet man, everybody liked him. Holt's skill had impressed her. She had to admire anyone who could do what he'd just done. But that made him even more dangerous to her father. Sending Holt off to look for his long-lost sweetheart seemed the perfect way to get him out of her life.

So why didn't she want him to leave?

Felicity had no business letting herself think about him, but she couldn't stop. She had a perfectly stupid feeling that she wanted to keep him near, to protect him. That upset her. There was no rational reason for her to feel as she did.

Except that he looked like the man of her dreams.

Holt didn't look like a cowhand. Undeniably handsome, he dressed like a Southern planter — black frock coat, blue embroidered silk vest, a white linen shirt and cravat, gray pants that clung to muscled thighs, and black shoes. He was tall, more than six feet. His body was lean, but the muscles in his chest, shoulders, and forearms indicated considerable physical power. The fact that she found that exciting worried her. Her mother had said she was born to love. This man could be the man of her dreams.

Yet he was the man of her nightmares. He was the one man who could ruin her father's life.

"What's the name of the woman you're looking for?" Felicity asked. "Galveston is a large town, and lots of new people have moved here in the last few years, but I might know her."

"I doubt it. Her family is part of society."

His response annoyed her. She wasn't part of society anymore, but Holt made it sound as if she wasn't good enough to belong.

"You might find it difficult to meet society people," she said, determined to be helpful. "They don't like Yankees unless they can find a way to make money from them."

"Her name is Vivian Stone. She married Abe Calvert and moved to Texas, but he was killed in the war."

"I don't know any Calverts, but that doesn't mean there couldn't be plenty of them around. There are more than ten thousand people in Galveston." The city had recently passed San Antonio in size, with newcomers arriving every day. But she knew little of these new arrivals. Ever since her father lost his money, society had turned its back on him. "How do you plan to go about finding her?" Felicity asked. "Put an ad in the paper?"

"I haven't decided, but I won't place an ad. Vivian wouldn't like that."

"But it would be the quickest way to locate her."

"I've waited two years. A few extra months won't matter."

He didn't sound like an impatient Yankee. Being willing to wait was a characteristic that made him almost Southern.

"I'd better see how your father is getting along with Mr. Black and his son," Holt said.

"I'm sure he's taken care of them already. Father deals with cuts and broken bones all the time."

"He was drunk."

She knew her father drank too much, but his drinking was not a problem as long as she was there to watch out for him. "He had something to drink — everyone does — but that doesn't mean he was drunk."

"He was confused, unable to make up his mind what to do."

"The accident was unexpected."

"All accidents are. That's why they're called accidents."

"There's no need to be rude. I'm not stupid."

"No, and because you aren't, I expect you to recognize drunkenness when you see it."

"He hasn't been well recently. The war —"

"You can't use the war to excuse drinking."

"Why not? Everybody else uses it as a reason to lie, cheat, and steal."

"That doesn't make it right."

"Nor does it give you the right to come in here and make judgments concerning something you know nothing about."

"I know when I see a medical emergency. Durwin was in need of immediate help, and he wasn't getting it."

Holt Price might be low-keyed in his efforts to find this long-lost sweetheart, but he gave Felicity the impression he would insist that every doctor hold to his own high standards.

That made him even more dangerous to her father. The sooner he started looking for Vivian, the better.

"My father is not a surgeon. He can take out tonsils and gallbladders, but he was glad to have you operate on Durwin."

"There must be other doctors in Galveston who could have done it."

"As you pointed out, we had to operate immediately."

"So he would have tried to operate himself and bungled it."

"He wouldn't have tried to operate," Felicity said, putting her hands on her hips.

"How do you know?"

"Because if he had wanted to, I would have stopped him." She hadn't planned to admit that, but telling the truth was better than letting him believe her father would have been reckless.

"Why should he listen to you?"

What could she say that wouldn't sound like she was making medical judgments? "My father takes his work seriously. As a consequence, he sometimes becomes too emotionally involved. He depends on me to tell him when that's happening."

She couldn't tell if he believed her. His expression made it abundantly clear he didn't like the situation, but just then her father entered the room.

"Is Durwin still alive?" he asked.

"For now," Felicity answered. "If he survives, he'll owe it entirely to Dr. Price. I was just telling him there isn't anyone in Galveston who could have performed that operation as well as he did."

Her father walked over to where Durwin still lay on the buggy seat. Much to Felicity's relief, he seemed much steadier. Maybe he hadn't drunk very much. "Anything broken besides his arm?" he asked Holt.

"No. Considering the state of his buggy, it was a miracle he didn't break both legs and arms."

"Durwin's like rubber," Dr. Moore said. "You wouldn't believe the accidents he's survived with barely a scratch."

"Well, the law of averages caught up with him today."

The doctor finished his inspection of Durwin and turned to Holt. "Do you think he'll live?"

"I don't know. The next couple of days will tell. He's in as much danger from infection as anything else."

"Was there much internal damage?"

"No, so I guess Durwin's luck is holding. The spoke nicked the femoral vein but missed the artery and nerve."

"You had no trouble closing him up?" Bandages covered Durwin's leg.

"I closed up hundreds of soldiers during the war."

Felicity wished Holt hadn't mentioned the

war. The effect on her father was immediate. The energy and confidence he'd displayed when he entered the room began to fade. "Dr. Price wanted to know how Henry and his son are getting along," she said, hoping to distract his thoughts.

"Fine," her father said, momentarily side-tracked. "Henry's got nothing more than cuts and scratches. I set Evan's collarbone and sent them home." He turned back to Durwin. "It was a good thing you turned up," he said to Holt. "I couldn't have done anything like that."

"I'm glad I was able to help."

Felicity could tell that Holt was studying her father closely. She was relieved that he looked almost sober.

"What do we do now?" her father asked Holt.

"We wait. The next few hours will be critical. I'm hopeful he'll be okay."

"What brings you to Galveston?" her father asked.

"I'm trying to find someone I knew before the war."

"Got any place to stay?"

"Not yet. I just rode in today."

"Good. You can stay with us."

Chapter Two

Felicity barely stopped herself from rescinding her father's offer. She couldn't believe he would do such a thing. He *knew* better.

"I'd feel a whole lot better if you were here until Durwin recovers," her father said. "After all, it was your operation. I don't know what you did."

She couldn't prevent herself from looking at Holt to see how he'd taken the offer. Westerners were very hospitable — inviting strangers to stay wasn't unusual — but it didn't happen so often in cities. It wasn't as if there were no hotels available.

"I couldn't impose," Holt said.

"You won't be imposing," her father said. "There's just Felicity and me in the house. There's plenty of room. You could bed down in the room next to Durwin. He's not going home just yet."

"We shouldn't impose on Dr. Price," Felicity said. "I'm sure he would prefer to get on with his business."

"I'm just offering him a place to sleep for a couple of days," her father said. "There's nothing in that to keep him from getting along with his business."

He looked at Durwin's still form, and Felicity

saw fear in her father's eyes. He didn't feel capable of handling this situation. She also saw the look that meant he was seeing the past — seeing sights only whiskey could drive out of his mind.

Felicity felt caught. She had to protect her father. He hadn't been badly drunk in more than a month, but having to deal with a situation he couldn't handle might drive him over the edge. Having Dr. Price here would take the responsibility off his shoulders.

Yet she was afraid of Dr. Price. How could she expect him to understand why her father drank?

"Are you sure it won't be a bother?" Holt asked Felicity.

"If you'll take care of Durwin, you'll actually be a help," she said. "That way Papa can focus all his attention on his regular patients."

Holt didn't look convinced. For a few moments she was sure he was going to refuse. Much to her dismay, she found herself growing tense waiting for his response, hoping he would stay when she ought to be wanting him gone.

"If you're sure I won't be a bother." He didn't look happy.

"Hell, no," her father said, breaking into a big grin. "I haven't had anybody worth talking shop with for a long time."

"You're sure?" Holt asked Felicity.

"If my father wants you to stay, it's okay with me."

She didn't want him to think *she* wanted him to stay. Even though Holt had shown no signs of being susceptible to her charms, she was used to men being attracted to her. However, their interest seldom developed into anything stronger. For Felicity, love was the goal, the only kind of relationship worth striving for.

"Nothing ever bothers Felicity," her father said. "And you won't have to pay anything. We should be paying you for taking care of Durwin. Are you planning to stay long in Galveston?"

"I don't know," Holt replied. "I'm looking for someone I knew before the war. She may have come here. If not, I'll have to continue my search."

"Ask Felicity. She knows everybody in Galveston."

"I don't know the woman he's looking for."

"Then she's not in Galveston," her father declared.

"I wouldn't give up yet," Felicity said.

"I tell her she stays cooped up in this house too much," her father said. "She takes good care of me, but she ought to get out more, meet some young men. She'll never get married hiding in the house."

Felicity hoped she wasn't blushing, but she always did when her father acted as if being twenty-six meant she'd never find a husband. He was convinced she would die an old maid. Her mother had married at sixteen.

"I'm not hiding," Felicity said. "I'm just not willing to marry the first man who walks through the door."

"First man!" her father snorted. "You don't let them hang around long enough to know if you like them or not."

"I'm sure Dr. Price doesn't want to hear about every man who's ever crossed our threshold."

"Wouldn't take long. Danged few get that far."

There were times when Felicity wanted to shout at her father that he was the major reason she wasn't married, with a husband and family of her own to love. Neither did he seem to realize that true love was worth waiting for. Maybe it had come too easily to him.

"Have you had breakfast?" her father asked Holt.

"No. I didn't like the looks of the food where I stayed last night."

"Felicity, take him into the kitchen and give him something to eat."

"You don't have to do that," Holt said. "I'm sure there are plenty of places I can buy a meal."

"Plenty that will take your money and not feed you half as well as Felicity. If you're going to stay and help me, you'll eat with us, too."

"It's too late for breakfast," Felicity said, "but you can join us for lunch."

They were interrupted by a banging at the

front door. Durwin's brother practically hurtled into the room.

"Where's Durwin?" he demanded. "They told me he finally killed himself."

"He's right over there," her father said, "but he's not dead."

Darcy Sealy crossed straight to his brother. "He looks dead."

"He probably would be if Dr. Price hadn't happened by," her father said, crossing to join Darcy, who put his ear to his brother's nose. Apparently, he could feel enough breath to reassure himself.

"What's he doing bandaged like a mummy?"

"He had a carriage spoke in his leg," her father explained. "Dr. Price took it out."

Darcy looked up, turned around, and stared at Holt. "You the doc he's talking about?"

"Yes," Holt answered.

"Why didn't you do it?" Darcy asked her father.

"I had to take care of Henry and Evan."

"They weren't hurt bad. You should have taken care of Durwin."

"Dr. Price has a lot more experience doing this kind of operation than I have," her father explained. "He —"

"Durwin wouldn't want no stranger cutting on him," Darcy said.

"I helped Dr. Price with the operation," Felicity said. "I can promise you no one could have done a better job."

Darcy still looked unhappy, but apparently as long as somebody he knew had been in the operating room, it was all right. "He'd better not die."

"I can't make any promises," Holt said. "Nine times out of ten an injury like that would have killed him instantly."

"Why didn't it kill Durwin?"

"He managed to escape any major internal injury," Holt said. "As long as infection doesn't set in, he's got a chance to recover."

Everyone knew the danger of infection and what it meant.

"What are you doing to keep out the infection?" Darcy asked.

"Watching the wound and keeping it clean," Holt said.

"I'm asking the doc," Darcy said to her father.

"Exactly what Dr. Price said," her father replied. "That's all we can do now."

"Who's watching him?" Darcy asked.

"I am," Holt replied. "Dr. Moore has offered to put me up for a couple of days."

"I want the doc watching him," Darcy said. "You talk funny. I can tell you're not from Texas."

"I've got other patients to take care of," her father said.

"Let him do it," Darcy said, indicating Holt.

"They won't want to see a stranger any more than you do," Felicity said. "Now stop making foolish objections and go tell your mother Durwin's doing as well as can be expected. I know she's worried about him."

"It would be better if he killed himself," Darcy said. "Then at least Ma wouldn't have to worry herself sick every time he sets out from the house." He looked back at his brother. "He sure looks like he's dead."

"He probably wouldn't regain consciousness for some time yet," Holt said. "The wound was serious and caused considerable trauma to the body."

"What does that mean?" Darcy asked, suspicious.

"It means he nearly died," Holt explained, "and the body has shut down everything it can to concentrate all its effort on healing the wound and preventing infection."

"But how can he eat if he doesn't wake up?" Darcy asked.

"He'll wake when he needs to," Holt assured him.

Felicity left the room, stopped on the other side of the closed door, her mind grappling with the situation. Holt was going to stay. He was going to be around at night and in the morning. He was probably going to watch her father work. It wouldn't be any time at all before he knew everything about her father.

She was confident her father was the best physician in Galveston. He had the best education, wide experience, and he really cared about his patients. He drank too much, but that wasn't a problem as long as she could watch him to make sure he didn't get into trouble. She was sure Holt wouldn't agree.

That was why she didn't want him around. He was no fool. He knew her father had been drinking and couldn't cope with the accident. Despite his fancy education, her father was a country doctor at heart. He liked to visit his patients, know their families, discuss their care with wives, mothers, and daughters. He delivered their babies, set bones and cured fevers for their children, and helped them enter old age comfortably. He would probably go the rest of his life without having to face another accident as grave as Durwin's. As long as nothing really serious happened, she could keep him safe.

She had to make sure Holt understood that. It was her duty to make sure he didn't do anything to harm her father.

"Where are you from?" Dr. Moore asked Holt after Darcy had left.

"Vermont."

Dr. Moore whistled. "How did you end up this far from home?"

"A great-uncle offered to pay for my education if I'd come to Virginia. I thought he was being generous because he was rich and didn't have any children. I didn't realize until he promised to leave me his farm that what he wanted in exchange was for me to take care of his ward Vivian. But I fell in love with her, so everything worked out for both of us."

"Folks aren't going to like that you're a Yankee."

"Why not? Almost everybody in Texas came from somewhere else."

"Most of them came from the South. The only Yankees we have here are the Union Army, the Reconstruction, and the carpetbaggers. That doesn't put you in very good company."

Holt already knew that, but there was nothing he could do about it. Besides, he didn't plan to stay in Texas after he found Vivian.

"I have nothing to do with the Army, Reconstruction, or people trying to pick the bones of the defeated. I only want to find Vivian."

"You won't get any argument from me," Dr. Moore said. "I was just trying to let you know what you were up against."

"I already knew."

But maybe he didn't. Living on Cade Wheeler's ranch, he'd been surrounded by friends, protected by Cade's reputation and success. People accepted him because they accepted Cade and Pilar. In Galveston he was on his own.

"You'd better have your lunch," Dr. Moore said. "Felicity hates to wait once she's got it ready."

"Aren't you coming?"

"I'll stay with Durwin. I don't think he ought to be left alone."

Holt didn't think Durwin was in any immediate danger. It was the possibility of infection that worried him. Once the body was open to the air, it was nearly impossible to prevent infection from setting in. Modern medicine had discovered germs and determined that clean hands and instruments would help prevent infection, but doctors had no effective means of fighting an infection once it set in.

"Don't worry about Felicity," Dr. Moore said. "She's not a bad girl once she gets to know you."

Holt decided not to tell Dr. Moore that he had no desire to get to know his daughter. She was attractive and far more skilled and knowledgeable than he would have imagined, but she appeared to dislike strangers — or at least this particular stranger — even more than Darcy Sealy did.

"Where's my father?" Felicity asked when Holt strode into the kitchen.

"He wanted to stay with Durwin."

"I'll take his lunch to him."

"He said he'd eat after I finished. That way I could watch Durwin for him."

Felicity had been dismayed to see Holt enter the kitchen alone. She couldn't understand her reaction to this man — she understood even less *why* she should be reacting to him in such an unexpected manner — but she was certain she wanted to keep plenty of distance between them.

"I apologize for serving you in the kitchen," she said, "but it's easier with only Papa and myself. Besides, it's the warmest room in the house in the winter."

"You don't know what cold is until you've lived through a Vermont winter," Holt said. "Snow arrives in October, and we don't see the ground again until April."

"I've never seen snow."

"Count yourself lucky. I remember one year when we had to tunnel to the barn before we could milk the cows."

"You had that much snow?"

"We had to melt ice so the livestock would have something to drink."

"I've never seen ice, either. It never gets that cold around here, not even in the winter."

Her mother had contracted a wasting illness when Felicity was very small. Her father had decided to become a doctor so he could cure her. He'd left them to go to Scotland, never thinking of the hardship of a woman alone managing a plantation.

Her father had told her stories about winters in Scotland — he liked to tell them to equally amazed patients to take their minds off their suffering — but not even her father's vivid imagination had been able to conjure in her mind the reality of frozen water that could float down from the heavens like so many tiny white chicken feathers.

"Tell me about it," she said.

36

She didn't especially want to hear any more stories about snow, but it was safer than letting the conversation drift toward medicine. She didn't want to know what he thought of her father's appearance this morning. He'd had a drink of whiskey early. He had sobered up very quickly, but she was certain Holt wouldn't take that into consideration.

Holt had very good manners. She didn't know why she'd thought a Yankee would be some kind of barbarian, but Holt was an attractive, well-educated man who spoke intelligently and knew not to talk with food in his mouth or pick his teeth with his fork. She kept looking for imperfections but couldn't find any. Whether she wanted to admit it or not, Dr. Holt Price was just about the closest thing she'd ever seen to the man of her dreams.

Felicity had reached the age when she was considered by many to be past being able to contract a suitable marriage, but she hadn't gotten there because she was indifferent to men. Running the plantation when her father was too drunk to care, helping him in his practice, and spending the war in Andersonville prison had kept her from having any time for herself. The only man who'd ever proposed to her backed out when her father lost his money after the war. It seemed that no matter what she did, her chance for love continued to elude her.

Still, she wasn't willing to give up hope. Her

mother had said she was born to love, had named her Felicity because she was destined to be happy. She had promised Felicity that one day she would find the kind of all-consuming love her parents had. So she had waited for a man to come along who would cause her to think of him whether she wanted to or not, to be interested in everything he did, to notice all the little changes or differences in him from day to day, to want to know even the smallest details about him, to feel a physical attraction that pulled as strongly as a sturdy rope.

It worried her greatly that Holt appeared to be that man.

"I can't believe that," she said, suddenly focusing on what he'd been talking about. "How can anyone have icicles in their nose? Wouldn't it hurt?"

Holt laughed. "You're too numb to feel much of anything."

"But how . . ." She didn't even know how to ask what she wanted to know.

"When it's thirty or forty degrees below zero and the wind is blowing so hard you have to lean into it to stand up, moisture freezes instantly."

"Why would anybody want to live in a place like that?"

"Because they're born there."

"But they could move to places where it's warmer."

"Vermont is beautiful in the summer. The

days are warm and bright, the evenings perfect for sitting on the porch and talking with the neighbors."

"You can do that here practically all year long."

"Spring in Vermont is magical. It's like a birth every year when the snow melts and the earth bursts forth with its green mantle. The birds return, the animals dig out of their burrows. Everything virtually explodes with energy. It's as if the world is rejoicing to have escaped the iron grip of winter once more."

"It sounds like a hard life."

"It is, but it's a healthy one. It's not unusual for people to live into their nineties."

Felicity didn't know anyone over seventy-three. "I guess it's not as healthy in Galveston," she said, "but it's a whole lot more comfortable. I'm sure you miss your home a lot."

"Not much."

That answer surprised her. "Do you plan to go back when you find the woman you're looking for?"

"No."

Chapter Three

Felicity didn't know why his comment should have caused her to start inwardly, but she was beginning to accept that anything this man did would have an unexpected effect on her. She couldn't imagine not wanting to be near one's family. She'd devoted her life to her parents. She expected to be even more devoted when she had a husband and family of her own. There could be lots of good reasons for Vivian to disappear, but Felicity was certain of one thing. If a man loved *her* as Holt appeared to love Vivian, she'd never have let the war separate them.

"What is this I'm eating?" Holt asked.

"It's sweet potatoes."

"What's that?"

She couldn't believe that anybody didn't know what a sweet potato was. How could she describe it? "It's like a potato, only it's orange and sweet. It tastes better with spices and nuts."

"It reminds me of squashes my mother used to cook, only she didn't put nuts in them. We didn't have pecans."

Something else she found hard to comprehend. Pecan trees grew wild in Texas. There was hardly a stream that didn't have a grove clustered along its banks.

"Did your mother teach you to cook?" Holt asked.

"No. She died when I was thirteen."

"I'm sorry. It must have been hard on your father raising a little girl by himself."

"When my mother died, my father sold his plantation and moved to Galveston."

"Who taught you to cook?"

"A nice lady from Mobile, Alabama. She lived with us until my mother died."

"So why aren't you married?"

"I haven't found anybody worthy of me."

She didn't know why she said that. She'd never said anything like that in her life, but something about this man irritated her as well as attracted her. An uncomfortable combination. She was pleased to see that her answer surprised him. She wasn't as pleased when a slow smile spread across his face.

"That's candid. I'm sure many women feel that way, but I've never met one brave enough to say it."

"I never have before," she confessed, "but you irritate me."

"Why?"

"Maybe it was your assumption that I didn't know enough to assist you in your operation."

"I apologize. You did very well. What else do I do that irritates you?"

"Nothing."

"There's got to be more. You got your back

up the moment you set eyes on me."

"What else could I object to? I don't know you."

"You're irritated your father asked me to stay here for a few days."

It was fear, not irritation, but she couldn't tell him that. "It wasn't exactly irritation. His inviting a stranger into the house, someone he'd never seen before . . ."

"And a Yankee, to boot."

"I didn't expect it. Papa hasn't done such a thing before."

"I'm sure it's only because I'm a fellow doctor. This is really good," he said, indicating chicken in a cream sauce poured over a cornmeal shortcake. "I never would have thought of putting chicken and corn bread together."

"That's not corn bread. It's a cornmeal shortcake."

"It tastes like corn bread to me."

"It's half cornmeal, half flour. What have you been eating?"

"Nothing like this. The man I worked for married a wealthy woman of Spanish and French heritage. The food was very good, but it was different from this."

"I'm sure it was," she said, feeling slightly defensive. "I can't afford to cook like that." *Anymore*, she added silently.

She hadn't meant to sound defensive, but he'd already made it plain he thought the woman he loved was so high in society, Felicity wouldn't have met her. Now he was telling her he'd been dining at the table of a woman who was practically an aristocrat. She didn't know why he'd accepted her father's invitation. He must think they were beneath him.

"No need to get your back up," he said. "This is more like the food I grew up eating. After what we had in the war, anything that isn't spoiled or burned tastes great."

"Did you do any fighting in the war?"

"No. What did you do?"

"I worked with my father."

"Doing what?"

"Taking care of prisoners."

"What prisoners? Where?"

"Several places. The last and worst was Andersonville."

"I never heard of it. Where was it?"

"In Georgia."

"What was it like?"

"To quote my father, it was like being in hell."

Holt had finished his meal. He folded his napkin and settled back in his chair. "Tell me about it."

She didn't want to talk about it. She didn't want to remember, but she knew that sooner or later he'd learn where her father had worked. When he did, he'd ask questions. Everybody did.

"I'll tell you on condition that you never mention it to my father."

"Why?"

"He's never recovered from having to watch so many men die — some from starvation but most cut down by disease he was powerless to prevent or do anything about."

"Why not?"

"They wouldn't let him. But they wouldn't let us leave, either. They made him stay there day after day, month after month, watching those poor men die like penned animals. It bothered him so much, he attacked the commanding officer. They locked him in his house for nearly a month. I could see him suffering more each day. You could see the camp from our house. On days when the wind was in the wrong direction, you could smell it."

"I get the feeling you haven't told anybody else about this. Why are you telling me?"

"Because you've already decided my father is incompetent and a danger to his patients. That's why you decided to stay here. Your friends are society. We're not. You're watching Durwin because you don't trust my father to do it without killing him."

She wasn't sure what kind of reaction she expected — she would have to know him better for that — but she had expected *some* reaction. Instead he just sat there, watching her out of hooded black eyes. He wasn't her idea of a typical Yankee. She saw them as blond, blue-eyed predators. Holt had dark brown hair parted on the side and combed neatly into place. His skin was fair and clean-shaven, but she could see the outline of his beard. Neither was he the short, stocky, powerfully built bully she'd envisioned from the tales she'd heard. Until he opened his mouth and spoke, she could have believed he was a native Texan. His tall, slim, broad-shouldered body was that of a cowboy.

"Your father had been drinking when I saw him this morning."

"How do you know that?"

"I'm familiar with every aspect of what alcohol can do to a person. I couldn't miss the signs."

"Papa had just one glass of whiskey. Just about everybody in Galveston does."

"Just about everybody is not a doctor."

"He doesn't have any patients until the afternoon. He had plenty of time to enjoy a drink if he wanted."

"A doctor can never confine his work to a few hours of the day," Holt said. "He may be called upon at any time."

"So you're saying he can never take a drink. I suppose you never take a drink."

"No, I don't."

She wasn't sure she believed him. She didn't know any man who didn't take a drink on a regular basis. She knew far too many who took *a great many* drinks on a regular basis.

"I never knew a man who didn't drink at all."

"You know one now."

"My father likes a glass of whiskey, but he doesn't have it to get drunk."

45

"I don't know your father, but my impression is that he's serious about his work. That's why I don't understand why he'd risk making a mistake by being drunk."

"He wasn't drunk."

"Are you going to explain that?" he asked after a short silence.

She rose. "Do you want some coffee?"

"Yes, thank you."

She took her time pouring it. "Cream?"

"Black. Cade wouldn't let me back on the ranch if I took to drinking it with milk."

"Not something a cowboy would do?"

"His wife likes it just as strong as he does."

"All that French and Spanish blood."

"I guess so." He took a sip of his coffee. "Not quite as strong as Pilar makes it, but it's good. Now tell me why your father wasn't drunk, even though he gave every appearance of it."

She was reluctant to begin. She could tell from the jut of his chin that he wasn't going to believe her. But he didn't know that her father had lost a wife he loved so passionately he still spent hours staring at her portrait, or that he'd watched thousands of men die, knowing he was responsible for them but unable to do anything about it.

"I'm not sure Papa was a good planter. Becoming a doctor was probably the best thing he could have done. He moved to Galveston because he wanted to be a doctor for the people, not just the planters who had money. We lost everything when Confederate money became worthless, including our position in society. This house is all we have left, but he doesn't mind, because he prefers caring for ordinary people. He'll never make a lot of money, but he makes enough for us to get by. When people can't pay with money, they leave something else in return."

She was sure Holt knew all about that. She'd been told that country people in New England distrusted paper money and depended on the barter system.

"Did somebody leave this chicken?"

"No, but a patient left the flour. We get butter and eggs all the time. Sometimes we get so much, I have to sell it or it would spoil. Papa would prefer that I give it away, but we need the money."

"Okay, so your father's generous heart will keep you poor. That still doesn't explain his condition this morning."

"In a way it does. Papa gets so upset when he remembers what happened in Andersonville, he gets sick. Not that he gets a fever or has to go to bed, but he feels unwell, won't eat, and can't rest. The malaise saps his strength so much that in a few hours he can't walk steadily. He takes a drink to help steady his nerves."

"I don't believe you."

"And to help him forget."

"I can't accept that."

"I'm not asking you to believe or accept anything. That's what happens. He was much worse right after the war. He would be out of control for days at a time."

"What did you do?"

"I took care of the patients until he recovered."

She really succeeded in upsetting him this time. He probably wouldn't have looked any more aghast if she'd said the patients died and they buried them in the root cellar. Only nobody had a root cellar on Galveston Island. The highest point was only seven feet above high tide.

"You're not qualified to treat sick people."

"I'm far more qualified than a mother or father, and they treat their children all the time. Why is it worse when they come to me?"

"Because you're not a doctor."

His words made it clear exactly what irritated her about him. He could be a doctor because he was a man. Her knowledge was useless because she was a woman.

"What makes a doctor?" she asked.

"Training, study, knowledge, experience."

"I have training. I've worked next to my father for as long as I can remember. I have studied his books. And I have knowledge and experience because I've worked with patients, made diagnoses, determined cures, and put them into effect. That's how doctors are trained."

"We have medical schools now."

"But not every doctor goes to a medical school. Most still train through apprenticeships."

"But that doesn't make you a doctor."

"What does? A piece of paper from some medical school? Putting a sign up on my door? Men do that all the time. But they're men, so it's all right."

"It's not all right for men of conscience."

She rose to her feet. "Are you implying I have no moral sense?"

"Of course not. Sit down. You look like a hen about to pounce on a snake."

"What an appropriate metaphor."

"Will you sit down?"

She didn't want to sit down. She didn't want to remain at the table. She didn't want to listen to a word he said.

"I need to clear away the dishes. Papa will want his lunch soon."

Holt stood. "I'd forgotten. I'll tell him to come eat. But don't think we're through talking."

"You don't have any right to tell me what to do."

"I have a moral right, and you know it." He turned and left the room with a long, quick stride that signaled his irritation. Maybe even anger. His expression alone had made it abundantly clear that he believed she was doing something very wrong.

And though she tried not to think about it,

she'd never been able to banish a vague feeling of guilt about the way she was protecting her father. But she didn't know a single doctor who didn't take a drink from time to time. Holt was right that a doctor could be called to care for the sick or injured at any time, but nobody ever said he had to deny himself sleep or relaxation. Besides, every man considered it part of his right as a free citizen to drink when he wanted.

Still, her conscience bothered her.

When it came to her practicing medicine, her feelings were different. Having been around her father her whole life, she'd seen more than most doctors when they went into practice. She kept journals of every case and studied them to see what she could learn. She felt certain her knowledge was sound in many areas.

But that was the crux of the problem. *In many areas.* There were some things she could only learn by attending medical school. But she didn't want to be a doctor. She never had. She wanted to be a wife and mother. She *longed* for that, but she also had to protect her father. So while she was waiting for the perfect love her mother had promised, she would continue to take care of her father.

"What did you say to that young man?" her father asked the moment he entered the kitchen. "He's as cross as a water moccasin that's had its nest disturbed."

"We had a disagreement."

"Do you have to have a *disagreement* with

every man you meet? He seems like a fine man, one who —"

"Would make me a fine husband," she finished for him.

Her father looked slightly abashed. "I wasn't going to say that, but yes, I think he would make some woman a fine husband."

"Some woman, but not me. He's got too many hidebound ideas." Besides, the man she married would have to love her as much as her father had loved her mother. She couldn't imagine Holt loving anyone more than his sense of duty.

"He's a good man. You shouldn't mind his hidebound ideas."

"The same way I shouldn't mind if you get drunk before mid-morning."

He looked up, hurt in his eyes. "I only had one whiskey, and it wasn't a very big one. I wasn't drunk."

"I know that, and you know that, but your *ideal husband* in the other room thinks you were drunk and unfit to handle your responsibilities as a doctor."

"That's nonsense." Righteous indignation changed abruptly to chagrin. "We both know I've taken care of people when I was in much worse condition." He reached out and took his daughter's hand. "I know I have you to thank that you never let me work when I was truly not capable. You're a wonderful daughter to have taken such good care of your papa."

Felicity tried to pull away, but he wouldn't release her hand. "Could you have managed Durwin's operation?" she asked.

"Not with Dr. Price's skill, but that would have had nothing to do with my having had a glass of whiskey. I don't have much experience with that kind of operation. It's time you started thinking of yourself, of your future. Staying here cooking for me, helping me in the office, watching to see that I don't treat anybody when I'm unfit — that's not what you ought to be doing with your life."

"It's my life, and I'll be the one to decide what to do with it."

"Why don't you marry one of Durwin's brothers? They've been after you for years."

Felicity took her hand away to bring her father his coffee. "I wouldn't marry Darcy. He's handsome and sweet, but he's nearly as stupid as Durwin. And while Dermot is smarter and more dependable than his brothers, I can't stand his repeating everything he says because he thinks women are too stupid to understand the first time."

"Okay, the Sealy boys aren't ideal, but there's no point in ignoring this man. I'm not saying you should marry him. Neither of us knows him very well yet. I am saying you shouldn't get your back up every time a man says something you don't like. You're going to make me sorry I brought you up to be so independent."

"I like being independent."

"I know. I'm just afraid you're going to be independent right up to your grave."

Felicity thought of all the men who'd shown her attention. In addition to the Sealy brothers, she'd been approached by a barber with bad teeth and ill-fitting clothes, a farmer who thought she'd make a good mother for the six sons he intended to father, a couple of men working for hourly wages — one on the docks and another as a clerk in a feed store — one land speculator she wouldn't trust not to lie to God, and a handsome young wastrel who thought it would be wonderful to live in her house and be supported by her father while she catered to his every want. There were a few more who would probably have shown interest if she hadn't convinced them almost immediately it was useless.

"Unless I have different choices from what I've had already, I'd prefer to go to my grave an old maid."

"Felicity, you can't —"

"Maybe I'll marry a cowboy and take to doctoring cows," she said. The thought that followed those unthinking words brought a flush to her face. The only cowboy she knew was Holt. "Eat your dinner and stop teasing me. I'll marry if the right man comes along. Otherwise, I'll plague you the rest of your life."

Her father reached for her hand once more. "You're not a plague. You're a blessing and you know it. Sometimes you look so much like your mother, I think she's sitting with me again." He laughed without humor. "It's a good thing she's not sitting where you are. She wouldn't recognize the sad wreck I've become."

Felicity cherished a daguerreotype of her mother and father taken shortly after their wedding. They had been a handsome couple, her mother beautiful, slim, and round-cheeked, her father tall, thin, and sporting a full head of nearly unmanageable hair. Now the little hair he had was white — Felicity didn't remember it being any other color — and he had gained considerable weight through the middle. His posture was bent, his body slumped forward as though weighed down by the burden of life.

"Mother would be proud of what you've done," Felicity said, squeezing her father's hand. "Not many men would give up the comfortable life of a wealthy planter to doctor people who pay in barter more frequently than money."

"And she'd be very proud of a daughter who stood over her foolish old papa, protecting him from himself."

"And from people like Dr. Price," Felicity added.

"Why should you have to protect me from him?"

"Because he's one of those rigid moralists who never does anything wrong and doesn't allow anybody else latitude to make mistakes."

"You're too hard on him."

"No, I'm not. You didn't have to sit with him while he preached about how a doctor owed it to his patients and his profession to be in the best possible condition to deal with sickness or injury at every hour of the day."

"He's right."

"Within reason. Nobody expects you to deny yourself pleasure and recreation, not to mention indulging a man's ordinary appetites, just because you're a doctor. That's almost as bad as saying that if I were a doctor, I couldn't have a baby because someone might need me while I was in labor."

"Now you're being ridiculous."

"I know that's an extreme situation, but that's what I'm trying to tell you. Your marvelous Dr. Price believes in extremes. He doesn't allow any room for extenuating circumstances. I don't know who this woman is he's trying to find, but I wonder if she ran away because she knew she'd have to be a paragon to live with him."

"That's unkind, Felicity. You don't know this young woman. There could be many reasons why she hasn't found him again."

"Mainly because she's afraid."

"That's a possibility, but it's more likely she doesn't know where to find him. Why are you so set against him?"

"Because I don't trust him not to hurt you."

"He only wants the best for patients."

"And he doesn't think you can deliver it."

"I couldn't have done the operation on Durwin. I said as much."

"Now you've invited him to stay here to look after Durwin. I can't throw him out, but until he leaves you're not to swallow a single drop of whiskey."

"Felicity, you're putting yourself in a bother for nothing."

"I hope so, but we can't afford to take the chance. We can't have anybody broadcasting it about that you're too drunk to take care of your patients."

She didn't tell him — she hoped he wouldn't know — but people already whispered behind his back about his drinking. The men didn't seem to think it mattered, but some women had started to go to other doctors. It was hard to hold her head up when she knew that people pitied her, but she was proud of her father, too proud to let anyone suspect she felt even one moment of shame.

"My patients are loyal."

"I hope so, but Dr. Price is very good. He's also a zealot. That's a combination I don't trust."

The opening of the kitchen door interrupted their conversation. Holt stuck his head in. "Durwin is awake and demanding to go home."

Chapter Four

"I thought you said he was awake," Felicity said. Durwin was unconscious.

"He was. I gave him some laudanum," Holt said. "He's in no condition to be moved, much less go home."

"I don't like giving my patients opium in any form," Dr. Moore said. "It sometimes masks symptoms I need to see to treat them properly."

"I don't like it either," Holt said, "but he showed signs of becoming unmanageable. I thought sedating him was the best thing to do for the time being."

Holt was already wishing he hadn't agreed to stay with the Moores or look after Durwin. The war had deprived him of his innocence and a large part of his sympathetic responsiveness. He'd had to harden himself to what he was doing, force himself to forget that the bodies he operated on belonged to people just like him, or he wouldn't have been able to endure.

And Felicity Moore's attitude heightened his desire to leave.

She looked at him like he was a Judas just waiting for an opportunity to betray her. He wasn't fool enough to think no doctor ever drank, but he distrusted anyone who drank in the morning. Because of his own father, his stance on drunkenness was uncompromising, but he had great sympathy for anyone who suffered from the horrors of the war. He'd been troubled by nightmares himself.

"You should have called my father," Felicity said. "Durwin would have listened to him."

"I considered it, but by then he was struggling so hard, I was worried he'd tear something loose."

Even though she knew a great deal more about medicine than he'd supposed at first, he didn't understand why Felicity tried to second-guess him at every turn.

"Laudanum might slow his breathing and heartbeat," Felicity said.

"I didn't give him much. I prefer to administer a few small doses rather than one large one."

"Did you use it a lot during the war?" Dr. Moore asked.

"What little we had was exhausted at Bull Run. After that, we could never get more than occasional small amounts. Most of the poor devils had to suffer their pain with nothing to dull it."

He didn't tell them that many doctors didn't believe in giving anything for pain. They took it for granted that patients would suffer until they became unconscious, got well, or died.

"How long do you think we'll have to keep Durwin immobilized?"

"At least two days."

"How long could he be in danger?"

"A week."

"Will you stay that long?"

It was on the tip of Holt's tongue to say that he wouldn't stay beyond the two days, but he hesitated. This was the first time he'd operated since the war. Though he didn't want to remain in medicine, he wanted to be the one to monitor Durwin's recovery.

And he felt a kinship with Dr. Moore. He meant to be ruthless if he found the doctor treating patients when drunk, but he could sympathize with the old man's condition. People said doctors had had it easy during the war — all they had to do was cut on people who were going to die anyway — but Holt knew better. Every doctor he knew had been scarred for life by what he'd seen and had to do.

Then there was Felicity. He couldn't decide whether he hesitated because he was attracted to her or because he was angry at her misinterpretation of his intentions and wanted a chance to prove her wrong. He didn't usually pay much attention to what people thought of him. He'd developed a thick skin growing up, but Felicity had managed to get under it.

"I can't promise," Holt said, "but I won't disappear without warning. I've got some decisions to make about my future. Working with you for a few days will give me some time to think about my choices."

"I thought you had dedicated your life to taking care of the sick and infirm," Felicity said, not without a note of sarcasm in her voice.

"I thought I had, too, but that was before the war."

"You can't give up medicine," Dr. Moore said. "You're a brilliant surgeon."

"Your daughter tells me you had a difficult time getting over your experiences during the war. I have, too. I've spent the last two years working as a cowhand so I could put medicine behind me."

"You didn't hesitate with Durwin."

"I guess I was like a horse suddenly back in harness. There he was in desperate need, and I couldn't find a single excuse not to help."

"What else are you considering?" Felicity asked.

Holt had no idea. He'd never enjoyed being a merchant, but it didn't matter, because his father has lost their store. Holt had quickly discovered he had no desire to be a farmer. The war had spoiled medicine, and he wasn't cut out to be a cowboy. He felt restless, unsettled, unable to concentrate.

"I've got nothing particular in mind at the moment."

He'd fallen in love with a Southern aristocrat who'd married someone else, then disappeared, leaving him a letter saying she'd always love him. Holt was determined to find her. He'd also come to Galveston looking for Laveau diViere. He had an old score to settle.

"I'd say you have a lot of deciding to do," Dr. Moore said. "I can't think of a better place to do it than right here. You can help me while you look for this young woman, and I won't charge you room and board."

"Don't be putting pressure on him, Papa," Felicity said. "He might not need to save money or want to help you with patients."

"He's not pressuring me," Holt said. "I think it's a very good solution. I'm just not sure it's the solution for me. Could you give me a day to think about it?"

"Sure. In the meantime, you can explain to Durwin's mother why she can't take him home."

Dr. Moore pointed to the window. Looking out, Holt saw a woman and a young man approaching the house at a purposeful gait.

"You're lucky she didn't bring her daughters," Dr. Moore said. "We would have had to lock the door and make a run for it."

"You're sure you won't leave him until he's better?" Mrs. Sealy asked Holt for at least the fourth time. "He is my son, but I wouldn't be telling the truth if I didn't say he doesn't always do what's best unless he's got somebody standing over him."

Felicity thought Durwin was a charming fool who never had a lick of sense and didn't seem to care that he stumbled from one life-threatening situation to another.

"Dr. Moore has invited me to stay until Durwin is out of the 'woods,' Holt said.

Mrs. Sealy cast a startled glance at Felicity's father.

"Dr. Price is much more up-to-date on wounds like Durwin's," Dr. Moore said. "He was a surgeon during the war."

He'd said that at least three times as well, but although Mrs. Sealy had accepted the news that she couldn't take Durwin home, she wasn't entirely comfortable with having a stranger taking care of him. And unless Felicity was mistaken, the woman had detected the accent Holt had tried so hard to disguise. Much to her surprise, she had an impulse to defend him. She didn't like foreigners, and anybody from Vermont was about as foreign as you could get, yet she had to admit Holt didn't seem foreign.

"I heard about them surgeons," Mrs. Sealy said. "Butchers is what some people call them."

"I'm sure some doctors amputated because it was the fastest and easiest way," Felicity said, "but Dr. Price isn't like that. If he had been, he wouldn't have stopped to help Durwin."

"I'm sure I don't mean anything personal," Mrs. Sealy said. "It's just a mother's concern, you understand."

"Of course," Holt said.

But Felicity thought she could detect a hint of strain, maybe anger. She guessed he'd run into this kind of prejudice a lot since he'd been in Texas. Feelings were just too strong after the war. And now with the Reconstruction government making things even worse, people weren't in any mood to consider a Yankee innocent until proven guilty. Seeing Mrs. Sealy's reaction made her feel guilty about her own prejudice. She ought to know better.

"There's no question of amputation with Durwin," Felicity said, "unless he gets in another accident. Dr. Price can watch him while he's here, but once he leaves, it'll be up to you and his brothers to make sure he doesn't do anything foolish."

"The only way to keep Durwin from doing something stupid is tie him to his bed," Dermot said. He'd accompanied his mother instead of Darcy.

"I won't have you talking about your brother like that," his mother said.

"No use pretending Durwin's got good sense," Dermot said. "He's been trying to kill himself since he learned to walk."

"Then it's up to you and Darcy to see he doesn't. Your pa and me can't know what he's doing all the time."

"You sure you can't find an excuse to fit him with one of those artificial legs?" Dermot said to Holt. "I seen a couple soldiers stumping along with them. Slowed them down real good. Maybe it'd work for Durwin."

"Your brother has had a very serious accident," Holt said. Felicity thought she saw amusement dancing in his eyes, but she didn't know him well enough to be sure. "I think his long period of recovery will give him time to reflect on his ways."

"You don't know Durwin," Dermot said, sounding disgusted. "The only way he's gonna reflect is if he sees himself in the mirror."

"Stop talking about your brother like that," Mrs. Sealy said again. "He's just high-spirited."

"And low-brained," Dermot muttered.

"I'll come back this evening to bring him supper," Mrs. Sealy said. "Durwin is particular about what he eats."

"Yeah, he eats anything he can reach," Dermot said.

"I'm talking about when he's sick," his mother said. "He likes my special bean and ham hock soup. I'll bring him a pot."

"That'll be fine," Holt said. "He appears to have a healthy body."

"See there?" Mrs. Sealy said to Dermot, giving him a thump on his shoulder to emphasize her point. "The doctor says he's mighty healthy. He'll be home and well before you know it."

"I hope you'll send him to Uncle Hobart this time."

"I don't want him working around wild longhorns. I wouldn't get a night's sleep for worrying about him."

"You ain't getting any sleep now."

She thumped her son again. "That's from worrying about you and Darcy. It's time you both settled down. Your pa and I have been wanting a couple of grandbabies." She cast an arch look in Felicity's direction.

"If you want grandbabies, you ought to find somebody to marry Durwin," Dermot said. "Then we can stop worrying about him and let his wife take over."

"I think we ought to leave Durwin to rest," Holt said.

"I want to talk to this new doctor," Mrs. Sealy said. "Alone, if you please."

Felicity had to stifle an impulse to object. She knew Mrs. Sealy was aware of her father's drinking. The last time she'd needed a doctor, she'd gone to someone else. Felicity was afraid of what Mrs. Sealy might tell Holt. She searched her mind for a way to prevent the tête-à-tête.

"We'll all be looking after Durwin at one time or another," Felicity said. "If you have any special instructions, we all need to know."

Mrs. Sealy looked slightly uneasy. "I don't have any special instructions, but you can't expect me to leave my son in the hands of a doctor I know nothing about."

"You can ask me anything you want to know in front of Dr. Moore and his daughter," Holt said.

"I insist upon speaking to you alone," Mrs.

Sealy said. "I really don't understand why you don't want me to."

"Mother, nobody said that," Dermot said.

"You stay out of this," her mother snapped. "The way you talk about your brother, I might think you didn't want him to get well."

"I'll be happy to speak with you privately," Holt said. "We can go into the parlor."

When they entered the parlor, Mrs. Sealy didn't sit down. "Do you drink?" she asked Holt the moment the door closed behind him.

"No," he replied. That was the last thing he'd expected her to ask.

"No need to lie," Mrs. Sealy said severely. "I just want to know how much."

"I don't drink at all."

She eyed him suspiciously. "You're not some kind of religious fanatic, are you?"

Holt relaxed and smiled. "No. I just don't drink."

Mrs. Sealy didn't look as if she believed him entirely. "I had to know. Dr. Moore is unsteady these days. Darcy and Dermot tell me I'm being foolish, but I don't like leaving Durwin here. I especially don't like leaving him with a Yankee. It seems like treason."

Holt would have thought he'd be angry at her remark, but instead he found it amusing.

"Felicity is a wonderful girl," Mrs. Sealy said, "but she can't watch her father all the time." She fixed him with a hard eye. "You

66

sure you won't leave Durwin?"

"Yes."

She looked relieved. "I feel sorry for Felicity, and I feel like a traitor, but a mother has to look out for her children."

"You seem very adept at dealing with mothers of patients despite your accent," Dr. Moore said to Holt after Mrs. Sealy left, smiling.

"I learned to do that as a child."

Felicity was starting to be very curious about Holt Price. There was a great deal more to him than she expected.

"Well, if you decide to stay in medicine, that ability will be invaluable," her father said. "Half of getting a patient well is convincing the nurse she has to follow your orders exactly."

"That'll take some getting used to," Holt said. "I'm used to soldiers doing it."

Felicity couldn't imagine men taking care of patients. Most of them didn't know how to feed themselves. And as soon as they had the slightest thing wrong with them, they thought they were dying.

"Women do all the nursing," Felicity said.

"You shouldn't have any trouble if you ever get sick," her father said to Holt, and winked. "A handsome young man like you has only to smile and they'll fall over themselves trying to please you."

Felicity hated it when her father acted as if a

woman would make a fool of herself just because a man was pleasing to look at. Holt certainly qualified as good to look at, but she wasn't about to let him make her act like a fool. Not that he was trying. He was just about as cool to her as she intended to be to him. He thought she was a person with no ethics. She thought he was a snob and a self-righteous moralist. She was sure he'd stumbled sometime in his life.

In the meantime, though, she didn't like the fact that her body seemed to be developing a life of its own when it came to Holt. She felt slightly tense, vaguely uneasy, a trace of panic. Nothing pronounced, just the feeling of being slightly unwell. She didn't like that either. She'd never had this kind of reaction to a man, and she didn't want it now. What did it mean that she felt slightly queer all over? She knew it had something to do with Holt.

"I'm certain Dr. Price believes the strict practice of medicine is all a conscientious doctor need rely on," Felicity said.

"If he does, he's not the man I take him for," her father said with a rude snort. "Everybody knows women pay more attention to a good-looking man, and Holt here certainly fits the bill."

"It's equally true that men pay more attention to attractive women," Holt said. "I'm afraid both sexes are equally guilty."

Okay, so maybe he wasn't as cocksure as

she'd thought. Still, honesty made her admit he had reasons for his confidence. She was attracted to him and she didn't even like him.

"It's a characteristic of people at all ages to like pretty things," she said. "Now let's stop talking foolishness and set up a schedule for the two days Dr. Price will be here."

"Don't go limiting him to two days," her father said. "He might want to stay longer."

"We can change the schedule any time it's necessary."

The discussion was brief. Both men accepted her suggestions without dissent.

"You don't really have to take a turn sitting with Durwin," Holt said to Felicity. "That's the way I'm supposed to earn my keep."

"My father's hoping to have time to talk to you," she said. "If you're going to learn your way around Galveston, you couldn't find a better guide. He knows the location of every hotel and restaurant in town."

She knew what Holt would be thinking when she said that, but she said it as a challenge and dared him to make anything of it.

"Except for waiting for Pilar to have her baby, I haven't had to sit with anybody since the war. That's my friend's wife," Holt said in response to Dr. Moore's blank look. "A perfectly ordinary childbirth, except that her grandmother kept screaming that men shouldn't have anything to do with birthing babies, that it was women's work."

"Midwives deliver most of the babies in Galveston," Felicity said. "Some don't even want my father to help."

"Felicity delivers more babies than I do," Dr. Moore said.

"There's no end to your talents, is there?"

Holt's response reminded her of his earlier reaction to hearing she'd helped her father.

"I haven't had the opportunity to explore them all yet," she shot back. "But I expect I can do anything anybody else can do."

He appeared to take that as a direct challenge. Good. That was how she'd meant it.

"It'll soon be time for Papa to start seeing patients," Felicity said. "We'll leave you with Durwin. Let us know if we can be of any help."

She exited the room before he could make a comeback.

"Wonder what Mrs. Sealy wanted to talk to him about," her father said.

"Probably inquiring about his ancestors," Felicity said. "You know Mrs. Sealy. If Holt can't trace his family back at least two hundred years, she probably thinks he isn't good enough to take care of Durwin. She ignores the fact that two hundred and fifty years of Sealys have culminated in three sons with barely enough intelligence for one."

But after her father entered his office, Felicity's cheerful demeanor fell away. She was sure that Mrs. Sealy had talked to Holt about her father's drinking. He had been smiling when he returned, but she could see the tightness around his eyes.

She sank down at her desk. She was so very tired of the battle to keep up the pretense, to act as though she didn't see the pitying looks, didn't know what people were saying about her father behind his back. She was tired of pretending that nothing was wrong, that his practice was thriving and she didn't have to scrimp and cut corners and sell extra produce.

She couldn't pretend with Holt. He wouldn't let her. She had a momentary desire to throw aside all pretense and ask for his help. He was strong enough to face anything. He would know what to do. He would . . .

She was a fool. That's what she got for thinking he looked like her dream man. Holt was not interested in her or her father. He was only here as long as it took him to find Vivian or satisfy himself she wasn't in Galveston.

Why did Mrs. Sealy have to be so defensive of Durwin? she wondered. She hovered over him as if he were still a small child.

Felicity found herself feeling jealous. She'd never had a mother to hover over her, to protect her, to fight battles for her. From the time she was small, her mother had spent most of the day in bed. Felicity had had to take care of her mother because her father couldn't do anything but cry. After he left for Scotland to study medicine, Felicity had had to shoulder the running of the household. Later, when her mother grew too ill to leave the bedroom at all, Felicity had to take over the management of the plantation.

She'd never had the chance to be a child. She'd never known what it was like to be carefree, to have time to play with dolls, to wade in the creek after a summer rain, to dress up in her mother's hat and shoes and play make-believe. She'd never had the time to whisper secrets and giggle with other little girls. She'd never even had time to have a crush on a boy. Now she was so tired, she wondered how long she could keep going.

Despite herself, her thoughts turned back to Holt. A man with courage, integrity, and the strength to stand behind what he believed. She didn't want to throw all her worries in his lap. She just wanted to feel that she could talk to somebody, that somebody cared about her.

Felicity told herself to stop thinking about Holt. He was all the things she'd said he was, but he was absolutely the wrong man for her. However, she couldn't shake the feeling that she'd never find one who was more right.

"The kind of people you're talking about are building houses along Broadway," Dr. Moore said in response to Holt's description of Vivian. "You ought to see some of them. Mansions, that's what they are."

"I thought everybody's fortunes had been wiped out by the war," Holt said.

They had finished office hours and had eaten dinner. Mrs. Sealy had brought her bean and ham hock soup for Durwin. Holt had to admit he'd acted the coward and fled with Dr. Moore, leaving Felicity to deal with Mrs. Sealy.

Felicity had been reluctant to let them go out together. Holt was certain she was worried that he'd get the old man drunk and charge him with being incompetent. Holt didn't drink and had an aversion to drink in general, but he wasn't a fool. Nearly everybody drank. The trick was to judge the appropriate amount in accordance with one's responsibilities. He'd be interested to see how Dr. Moore acted when he wasn't under the eagle eye of his daughter.

"It's a little nippy out tonight," Holt said. The breeze from the Gulf of Mexico was strong and smelled of salt. He'd never lived close enough to the coast to smell the ocean.

"Be glad it's not coming from the land side," Dr. Moore said. "It would be hot, smell of rank vegetation from the coastal marshes, and carry mosquitoes and flies."

"You're not trying to run me off, are you?"

"No. We get a gulf breeze most of the time. There's a whole bunch of places down here where society fellows come to eat, drink, and chase women," he said, referring to the street they were approaching. "I don't come here myself. Can't afford it, for one thing."

"Don't worry. I'm paying tonight."

"It's not that. I don't feel comfortable. That's

odd, since I was born a planter's son and grew up wealthy. But these folks aren't like planters."

"They're businessmen," Holt said. "I probably have more in common with them than you do. Nearly all of my family are in some kind of business. Most of them aren't very good at it, but it's hard to be a successful businessman in Vermont. Not many people need anything they can't make for themselves."

"You can sell just about anything here," Dr. Moore said. "With the army and the carpetbaggers flooding in, there's plenty of money."

They were walking through what was coming to be known as the business district. Lights shone from inside hotels, restaurants, saloons, taverns, business offices. It seemed the town didn't close down. The breeze sent a few scattered clouds scurrying across the moonlit sky. It felt good to be outside, almost like Vermont in the summer.

"Where do you intend to start looking for this woman you're hunting?"

"Where the rich men gather. Vivian is a beautiful woman. Men congregate around her."

"Then we ought to start at the Galveston Hotel. Everybody of importance goes there sooner or later."

It looked like the kind of place Vivian would like. Brand spanking new, it stood three stories of red brick. The woodwork gleamed with white paint. Once inside, Holt knew he'd stepped into a place of luxury. The spacious entrance was arranged with groupings of comfortable chairs along wainscoted walls hung with paintings in heavy gold frames. The sound of their heels on the black-and-white marble floor echoed in the large space. The main lobby was even more impressive. White columns circled the room. Decorated with gold garlands and topped by gold Corinthian capitals, they rose from the first floor past balconies on the second and third floors to a ceiling at least thirty feet above. Small trees in large pots were positioned around the room. Groups of men gathered on long sofas, sat in deep chairs, reading or talking.

"This looks like a men's club," Holt said.

"It practically is most evenings. But the ladies who are guests here like to join the men."

Unlike the entrance hall, the lobby was covered with carpets which softened sound. An occasional laugh interrupted the quiet of the room. Waiters moved among the guests taking orders for the bar.

"How do I begin meeting these people?" Holt asked. "I have some letters of introduction, but —"

"Nobody stands on ceremony in Galveston," Dr. Moore said. "We get a drink from the bar, then move around the room. If I see somebody I know, he'll call me over, and I'll introduce you."

Almost immediately a man hailed Dr. Moore. "Heard Durwin Sealy tried to kill himself again," the man said even before the doctor had had a chance to introduce Holt.

"He would have succeeded if this young man hadn't been on hand to take that spoke out of his leg," Dr. Moore said.

The man looked surprised. "I thought you took care of the Sealy boys."

"Dr. Price happened on the accident just after I got there. Turns out he was a doctor during the war. He's a whole lot more used to operating than I am."

The man turned to Holt and extended his hand. "Clyde Prentiss is the name. Are you planning to stay in Galveston long?"

"We got us a young romantic here," Dr. Moore said, giving Holt a little nudge in the ribs. "Seems he fell in love with a young lady before the war. But he was a penniless medical student and she a young beauty." Dr. Moore turned to Holt. "You didn't tell me all that, but everybody knows all medical students are poor."

"My great-uncle was paying for my education," Holt said.

"But the young beauty married another man," Dr. Moore continued, "only to be widowed by the war. She decided to come to Texas to live with the family of her departed husband. Maybe even to have his child."

It was a possibility Holt had tried to ignore.

"But the handsome young doctor never forgot his beautiful love," Dr. Moore said.

"After the war ended, he came to Texas to look for her."

"When did you get here?" Mr. Prentiss asked.

"I arrived two years ago," Holt said. "I've been working for a friend."

"All the while searching San Antonio and Austin for his beloved Vivian," Dr. Moore said.

Holt was beginning to be a little embarrassed at the melodramatic manner in which Dr. Moore was telling his story. It made him sound like a brainless saphead.

"I'm sure nothing is the same as it was six years ago," Holt said, "but I would like to see her again. I've lost so many friends during the last few years, I've become eager to hold on to the ones I have."

His comments caused Mr. Prentiss's jovial mood to flag. "We all lost a lot in that war," he said.

"We all know how much you thought of young Tom," Dr. Moore said. "His death was a terrible loss."

Tom Prentiss! That name was like a bolt out of the past. There was a Tom Prentiss in the Night Riders. He died the day Laveau diViere betrayed them to the Union Army.

Chapter Five

"Where did your son serve?" Holt asked.

"In Virginia. He was in an elite cavalry troop called the Night Riders." Clyde Prentiss smiled briefly. "He begged me to send him money for a better horse. He said he was ashamed to ride a Texas mustang when everybody else's mount had thoroughbred or Morgan blood."

"He bought a handsome chestnut gelding," Holt said, remembering Tom's great pride in his horse. "It had four white stockings and a blaze. He was almost as good-looking as Tom."

Clyde Prentiss lost all color. "You knew Tom?"

"I was in the Night Riders, too."

"Tell me about him," Clyde asked. "Tom wasn't much for writing unless he wanted something."

Holt didn't want to remember, but Clyde Prentiss's hunger to hear about his son was clearly a vital need. So Holt spent the next thirty minutes talking to Clyde about the son who'd been the light of his life. As he talked, he remembered the other men as well, most of them barely more than boys — young, enthusiastic, burning with determination to protect their homes from the invaders. He remembered Laveau diViere, the horror and cruelty of his betrayal.

And he remembered his vow never to rest until they brought the traitor to justice.

Talking about Tom made him feel guilty that he'd momentarily forgotten Laveau in his desire to find Vivian. Laveau had managed to elude them twice. The Union Army's protection would make bringing him to justice extremely difficult, but Holt renewed his determination to get back into the hunt.

"You'll have to stop by the house one evening," Clyde Prentiss was saying. "Once my wife knows you're in Galveston — hell, it would be the same if you were anywhere in Texas — she won't rest until she pries out of you every detail you can remember about Tom. His sisters'll be just as bad."

"I'll be happy to talk to your family," Holt said. "All of us thought a lot of Tom."

Clyde rose. "I gotta be going. I can't wait to tell my wife. Where can I find you?"

"He's staying with us for the next few days," Dr. Moore said.

"Don't be surprised if Mrs. Prentiss shows up at the doc's place tomorrow. I don't know that she can hold off her questions long enough to feed you first. Who did you say you were looking for?" Clyde asked.

"Vivian Calvert," Holt told him. "Her husband was killed in the war, and she came to Texas to live with his family."

"I don't know any Calverts," Clyde said, "but I'll ask my wife. She and the girls know a lot more about the womenfolk in Galveston than I do."

"I'd appreciate it," Holt said.

It had gotten rather late, and Holt was feeling guilty about leaving Felicity in charge of Durwin for so long, so he and the doctor followed Clyde Prentiss when he left. Holt was relieved that Dr. Moore had had only one whiskey all evening.

"Clyde's a great fella," Dr. Moore said after they parted from Prentiss, "but he has never gotten over his son's death. Fair doted on that boy, he did. We all tried to keep Tom from going off to war — you didn't have to be a fortune teller to know how his death would affect his family — but nobody could change his mind. It was his duty to defend Texas, just as his father had done in '48 against Mexico."

Holt remembered Senora diViere's lament that the two wars with Mexico had cost her a husband and a son. He wondered if people would ever stop using wars to settle disputes.

Occupied with his own thoughts, he let the doctor talk on unheeded about families who'd lost someone in the war and how the losses had devastated those left behind.

"I'm glad you got to talk to Clyde," Dr. Moore said, "but it didn't help you much in your search for your young woman. Clyde doesn't move in the right circles. I'll have to see what I can do another night."

Holt wondered what Vivian would look like.

The last six years must have changed her from the girl he'd known into a mature woman, a wife and possibly a mother. He was almost certain he would find her in Galveston.

If she was still in Texas.

Pilar, his old boss's wife, had reminded him that an unmarried woman without family was at a severe disadvantage. Vivian's position would be even more difficult if she had a child. Wartime conditions would make it virtually untenable. It was possible the Calvert family hadn't welcomed her, that she'd had to learn to support herself. But Holt doubted that could be true. Vivian had no talents except being beautiful. She'd been brought up to believe she didn't need any others.

He couldn't begin to count the number of times he'd asked himself why he couldn't forget Vivian. The most obvious reason was that Vivian was the most beautiful woman he'd ever seen. Thick, golden blond hair framed a face of creamy complexion and perfectly formed features. Pursed red lips and bright green eyes resulted in an enchantress who had all the allure her Irish ancestry could give her. She had a way of making a man feel he was ten feet tall and capable of heroic feats. When a man was with Vivian, he felt invincible.

Vivian had always worried about money. She'd been brought up in great wealth, but her father had gambled it all away. When her parents died, she was left on the charity of Holt's

Uncle William. Vivian quickly took to Holt because, as she told him quite candidly, he was too old to be husband material — as well as being too poor — and she was going to treat him like a big brother. Holt hadn't minded but he hadn't been smitten then. Merely intrigued that this precocious young beauty would treat him like a brother.

He'd lost his heart later, gradually, before he knew what was happening. She had been a delightful elf, a cheerful companion, slightly irreverent. He told her quite often she was being naughty when she teased the men who followed her like panting puppies, but he nearly always laughed with her, because her youthful acuity enabled her to see through people's defenses. And her intelligence enabled her to turn their weaknesses into a wicked joke. Holt had to admit that his remonstrances often lacked conviction.

Then one day after about five years, he looked at her and saw an entirely different person. She was no longer a child, an enchanting, delightful pixie. She was a woman, beautiful and desirable. It had taken him a week before he could trust himself to see her again.

Holt had been so caught up in his thoughts, he hadn't realized Dr. Moore had fallen silent until they were nearly home.

"I'll sit with Durwin first," the doctor said. "That'll give you and Felicity a chance to talk a bit before we go to bed."

"What do we have to talk about?" Holt asked.

"I'd like for you two to get along. There's something wrong between you. I'd like to see you work it out."

"Why?"

"I like you. Don't know when I've taken to a young man so quickly. Maybe I'm hoping you'll stay in Galveston. If you decide you want to stay in medicine, maybe we can work together. Or it could be none of this. But if we're going to be living in the same house, it'd be nice if you two could get along better."

"I can leave."

"I don't want you to do that. I don't know what ails Felicity, but I'm sure you can fix it. Will you talk to her?"

"Sure."

The doctor didn't know that what ailed Felicity was the doctor himself. But Holt meant to keep his own counsel on that score.

"Your father wants us to talk," Holt said to Felicity when she came into the kitchen.

"Why?"

She pulled away from him sharply. He could understand her disliking him because she was afraid he would expose her father. Or because he could do something her father couldn't. Or because she feared he would horn in on her father's practice, then push him aside. But those

83

things could be dealt with in a businesslike manner. Her aversion to being anywhere close to him was personal. He wasn't the most wonderful person in the world, nor the best looking or most charming, but he'd never before encountered anyone who formed an aversion to him the minute they met.

"I don't think he likes living in an armed camp. I know I don't. It reminds me too much of the war."

She seated herself in a chair across from him. He decided to remain standing. He'd sat too long at the hotel.

"You'll have to forgive me if I'm unable to muster the proper enthusiasm to welcome a stranger into my home."

"I'm told Southerners are famous for their hospitality, especially Texans."

"We are, but that *hospitality* is most often extended to family, travelers looking for a place to stay for the night, or someone in need or danger. You don't qualify as any of those."

"So you automatically don't like me."

"I don't like or dislike you. I don't know you well enough."

"I don't believe you."

She looked slightly taken aback, but she quickly recovered. "I do know several things about you I don't like." She cast him an annoyed glance. "I'm getting a crick in my neck staring up at you. If we have to talk, please sit down."

"Nobody ever complained about my height before."

"That doesn't surprise me. Big men, especially those who are good-looking, are allowed to grow up thinking they're special."

"You think I'm good-looking?" He liked that. After years of being around Owen Wheeler and Broc Kincaid, he'd come to think of himself as practically ugly.

"It has been my experience that doctors and military officers are the worst offenders," Felicity said, pointedly ignoring his question. "They appear to think the power of their rank and their right to order people around makes them more deserving than anyone else."

"And since I'm big, a doctor, and served in the military, I've managed to offend you in every way possible."

She waited a moment. "Are you going to sit?"

"I'd rather stand. I've been sitting all day."

"Then I'll stand, too."

"Okay, I'll sit. There's no point in both of us striding about the room. We're liable to collide."

The thought of his body touching hers had an unexpected effect on him. While he'd thought her attractive from the first, he hadn't felt this before, what he could only describe as a physical tug between them. He'd only met her this morning. She shouldn't have any effect on him at all.

But she *was* having an effect. Just thinking about touching her caused his body to stiffen. He seated himself. The last thing he wanted was for her to realize she'd caused this reaction. She'd probably throw him out of the house right away.

"You haven't offended me in any of those ways, though I expect you'll manage it before long," Felicity said.

"Okay, so I made you mad because of what I said about your father."

"You certainly did."

"You think it's okay for him to treat patients when he's drunk."

She waited before she answered, as if she were counting to ten, or twenty-five. "I've tried to explain that, which was more than you deserved. You saw him for the first time today. I've seen him every day of my life. I know him in ways you never can. What bothers me most is the incredible arrogance that allows you to march in here and make a judgment about people's actions. I find that reprehensible."

Felicity Moore was obviously a young woman used to plain speaking. Well, he was from Vermont, and his folks weren't too bad at plain speaking, either. Doctors had to hold themselves to a higher standard. The public offered them blind trust. They couldn't betray that trust by ignorance of medicine or any form of self-indulgence. As limited as their abilities were, the ability to prolong life was an almost

86

divine quality. They were honor-bound to do nothing to dishonor it.

But even as the words sprang to his lips, he hesitated.

He remembered the cruel, vicious things people had said about his father. The fact that many of the things were true only made their words cut more deeply. He'd been scarred so deeply that even the promise of a successful career couldn't lure him back to Vermont. He knew he couldn't face the people he'd known since birth without remembering things they'd said.

About his father. About his mother. About himself.

"Is there anything else you'd like to add?" he asked.

"Nobody made you the supreme authority on what a doctor should do, how he should live his life, or conduct his practice. Or whether his daughter knows enough to help him without jeopardizing the health and well-being of his patients."

He knew she'd get to that sooner or later.

"And I find your attitude that women shouldn't have anything to do with medicine positively barbaric."

"Whoa there a minute. I didn't say *women* shouldn't have anything to do with medicine. I merely questioned *your* qualifications to do so."

"Only because I haven't been to medical school."

"That's one reason."

"What's another?"

"That's the only one I have so far."

"But you expect to add more tomorrow or the next day."

"I expect I'll find you have a competence in a lot of areas. As you say, doctors are still learning by apprenticeships. You've had a better opportunity to learn than most."

He couldn't decide if she was slightly mollified or just stymied for the moment. "You were a great help when I was operating on Durwin. You seemed to know what I wanted before I asked. That's a special talent." That had impressed him, but it hadn't changed his mind about the ethics of her taking care of her father's patients when he was too drunk to do it himself.

Holt watched Felicity as she sat without speaking, looking down at her hands. He didn't understand why she refused to meet his gaze. He wasn't angry. He didn't dislike her. They just disagreed on a few things. Okay, a few *important* things. Still, that didn't mean she had to act as if she wished he'd never set foot in Galveston.

He realized the true reason he was so annoyed was that he wanted Felicity to like him.

"I didn't want my father to invite you to stay here," she said, then lifted her gaze to his. "I have no doubt you're a fine doctor — I know you're an excellent surgeon — but he doesn't need you. I hope you'll go as soon as Durwin's out of the woods." She started to get up.

"Stay a minute," he said. "We might as well get the *real* things straight. You want me out of the house, and probably out of Galveston, because you see me as a threat to your father's reputation and ability to earn a living."

She nodded her head.

"You don't dislike me for any other reason?"

"As I just said, I don't know you well enough to like or dislike you."

"But you could like me if you weren't afraid of what I might do to your father."

She was slow to respond.

"Yes, I could. You have good manners, can carry on an intelligent conversation, and aren't unpleasant to look at."

He controlled the strong desire to use one of Cade Wheeler's favorite curses. "Talk about being damned by faint praise." He thought Felicity almost smiled.

"I suppose it sounds that way, but I don't trust you."

"What would I have to do to gain your trust?" Why was he asking that question?

"I doubt you'll be here long enough for it to matter."

Exactly what he thought. She stood to go, but his next statement caused her to pause. "Let's assume I was going to be here for months, even years. What would it take?" Now he was getting argumentative, asking questions merely to prove a point.

"I suppose you'd have to believe my father was a good doctor who doesn't treat patients when he's drunk."

"And?" He knew there was more. She hadn't gotten to his attitude about women, or her. "You haven't mentioned yourself."

"What you think of me doesn't matter."

"Of course it does. People dislike those who don't respect or value them."

That remark seemed to interest her. "You sound like you're speaking from experience."

"I am. Now answer my question."

"You would have to believe I have the intelligence to know just as much about medicine as any man."

"And if I did?"

"You would have to demonstrate that by trusting me."

"How?"

"By working with me as you would my father. Not by operating, of course. I don't think I would like surgery. I prefer diagnosing a problem and devising a cure to make the patient feel better."

"And if you can't?"

"I defer to my father."

"Even when he's drunk?"

"Even then he knows more than I do. More than you, too, I expect."

His impulse was to dispute that, but he decided to wait. He couldn't deny that experience could teach a man things a book never could.

"Okay, I accept your conditions." He stood and extended his hand. "Let's shake on it."

Startled, she regarded his hand like a snake that might bite her. He let it fall to his side. "How do women seal a bargain?" he asked.

"Mostly they hug each other."

He didn't know what impulse seized him, but before he knew it, he'd stepped forward, put his arms around Felicity, and drawn her to him.

Chapter Six

Everything in Felicity's world seemed to come to an abrupt halt. Her brain stopped thinking. Her body stopped feeling. Her heart stopped beating. Her lungs stopped breathing. Her vision blurred. She couldn't be sure the world hadn't suddenly stopped spinning. Just as abruptly, everything swung into motion, moving so fast she felt she couldn't breathe, that she might faint at any moment.

And Holt's face above her came into absolutely clear focus.

She tried to speak, but she couldn't utter a sound. Her throat felt dry, paralyzed, her wits in equally dire straits. She tried to form words, but messages from her body destroyed her thoughts before they could be completed.

She felt betrayed by herself. There were suddenly two of her, each of radically different minds. And the part of her that liked Holt's arms around her was more powerful than the part that wanted to order him never to touch her again.

She'd been attracted to several men during the last ten years. But not even her teenage crushes had affected her like this. Before, her mind and body had been in the same place. If she'd been reluctant, her body had been cool and calm. If she'd been anxious or unsure, her body had felt the same way.

She didn't know when her arms moved to encircle his waist. She didn't know why she leaned toward him. She couldn't explain the feeling that began to stir deep in her belly. It all happened by itself, as if she were a puppet and someone else was pulling the strings.

"I think I like your way of sealing a bargain better than ours," Holt said.

"I wouldn't recommend it. You'd have a hard time explaining why you were hugging a man."

Holt chuckled. "Or kissing him on the cheek. Women do that most of the time, don't they?"

"Yes." The word escaped before she could capture it and force it back down her throat.

"Another good idea." He brushed her cheek lightly with his lips. "Your turn."

She couldn't move.

"You have to agree, or it's no bargain."

She couldn't command her body to move at all.

"Okay, I'll bend down."

Holt lowered his head. When she remained stock-still, he moved his cheek against her motionless lips. She knew a man's cheek didn't feel like a woman's. She'd kissed her father hundreds of times, but it had never felt like this. The contact sent shivers though her entire body. The reaction had nothing to do with the roughness of Holt's beard. It had everything to do with his nearness.

Felicity had allowed very few men to kiss her, even to brush her lips, but not even the most fervent kiss had affected her as powerfully as Holt brushing his cheek against her lips. It wasn't that her lips felt different. It was that the rest of her was experiencing feelings unique in her experience. She'd been excited before, but not like this. She'd felt light-headed but never dizzy. There'd even been brief moments when she'd been unsure of what she wanted to say, but she'd never been rendered speechless, her mind left blank.

No, it wasn't a blank. It seemed that hundreds of words whirled about in her head, some in phrases, some unconnected, all of them incapable of expressing what she was feeling.

What was she feeling?

Panic. Things felt so strange, she was frightened. Excited. Hopeful. Anything that affected her so strongly must be good. But she was confused. She had no idea what to do about what she was feeling.

"I don't think brushing my cheek against your lips counts as sealing the bargain," Holt said. "I believe it's necessary for you to *do* something."

His voice wasn't quite as clear and steady as it had been moments earlier. She wondered if her nearness was affecting him as forcefully as his was affecting her.

She managed to say, "A verbal agreement is all that's really necessary between adults."

"But wouldn't you agree this signifies a deeper commitment than a few words?"

"Yes." She couldn't recall any spoken word that had rattled her right down to her foundation.

"Agreeing to work together is an important decision. It has to be based on a strong commitment to fair play and cooperation. Don't you agree?"

She nodded.

"Then you'd better kiss my cheek, or I'm not going to have much faith that you'll uphold your part of the bargain."

There didn't seem to be any way she could get out of it now. He'd made it an issue of trust. She might not want to work with him, but she did want to protect her father.

It couldn't be so hard. All she had to do was lean forward a few inches and brush his cheek with her lips. She had done it to babies and children hundreds of times. She'd even done it to women she didn't know and would never meet again. Surely it wouldn't be difficult to kiss this man.

Kiss. She shouldn't have used that word. That wasn't what she was doing. She was merely sealing a bargain with a relatively harmless gesture.

Gathering her courage, she leaned forward and brushed her lips against Holt's cheek.

"That's not a kiss," he said.

She was so worked up, she spoke without

thinking. "That's what you did to me."

"I can fix that," Holt said in a voice that sounded less like him than ever.

Before she could protest that she hadn't meant it like that, he pulled her to him and planted a lingering kiss on her left cheek. It wasn't a light buss. It wasn't tentative or carefully polite. She could feel the pressure of his lips against her cheek, hear the slight smacking sound as he completed the kiss. It was a *real* kiss.

"Your turn," he said.

She felt her strength draining away. She knew that if she didn't do something now, this very moment, she'd soon be incapable of doing anything at all. Summoning all her willpower, Felicity leaned forward and planted an audible kiss on Holt's cheek.

"Good. That wasn't so hard, was it?"

He still didn't sound like himself, but he didn't look as if he'd been shaken right down to his toes. He even grinned as though he thought the situation was amusing.

"It's not a matter of being hard," she said, calling upon the last of her mental and emotional reserves. "After all, kissing someone's cheek requires only a minimal amount of physical energy."

"There are kisses that require a lot more than that."

She refused to allow that thought to stir her imagination. He was trying to provoke her.

"I'm not used to kissing strange men, even to seal important bargains."

"I'm not strange. You've known me for nearly a day."

"It's more common to know a man for years, not hours, before allowing him to kiss you, and then only under certain circumstances."

"You'd have a lot more fun if your rules weren't quite so strict."

"Do men in Vermont go around kissing women they've known only a few hours?"

Holt surprised her by laughing. "New England men are awful. It's considered bad form to kiss your bride before the wedding, even to hold hands. I know some husbands and wives who've never kissed at all."

"What made you different?"

"I came South. Maybe it was the warmer climate, maybe it was the cavalier tradition, but men in Virginia are quite fond of kissing. I decided I liked their traditions better than my own."

"If you change too much, you won't fit in when you go back."

Then she remembered he wasn't going back.

He released her, stepped away a few paces. She had ventured into sensitive territory. His teasing smile had been replaced by a neutral expression. But the tension in his eyes and the set of his mouth indicated that Holt's feelings were anything but neutral.

"There are parts of growing up that most of

us want to forget," Holt said. "That's always easier in a new place."

"But becoming an adult changes everything. You're able to look past childhood memories and put them in perspective."

"Have you looked past yours?"

"All except my mother dying."

His silence made it clear he wasn't going to share his experience with her.

"I guess I'd better check on my patient. It's getting late."

"I made up a bed for you in the next room," Felicity said. "You can leave the connecting door open. That way Dad can wander in during the might to check him and not wake you."

"He doesn't have to do that."

"Dad doesn't sleep well. It will give him something to do when he's up."

"Does he wake up a lot?"

"Not as much as he used to."

"Andersonville?"

"The moans and cries of the prisoners used to keep him awake. Sometimes he thinks he still hears them."

"Every doctor who lived through the war has endured the same thing."

"Maybe," Felicity snapped, "but not all doctors are equally able to forget it." How dare he minimize her father's suffering? Not everybody was insensitive.

"I wasn't trying to belittle your father's feelings," Holt said. "I was just trying to say I understood."

"Sorry. It's just that I know how much my father has suffered. I can't bear to have anybody make light of it."

"Our differences aren't in the suffering. It's in the way each of us chooses to deal with it."

"Not everybody is as strong as you," she said, wondering how she could feel even a small bit of attraction to such an inflexible man. And she *was* attracted to him. That kiss on the cheek had demolished any foolish attempt to deny it. "My father's getting better. One day he'll be able to handle things just as well as you, though not with as much indifference."

She didn't like the look Holt sent her. Okay, she shouldn't have said that, but he didn't understand that her father had a sensitive soul. He'd become a doctor because he wanted to help people. In some ways he was like a child, suffering along with his patients. It wasn't that he wanted to. He couldn't help himself. She was the one who could put things out of her mind, who could do her work without becoming overly emotional. She should have become the doctor instead of her father.

"You'd better go before you goad me into saying something else I'd rather not," she said. "You're an outstanding surgeon, but I find it difficult to swallow your perfection."

Holt's smile was crooked, apparently self-mocking. "I'm far from perfect. You'll find that out very soon."

"I don't plan to know you that well."

He actually smiled. "My imperfections are right on the surface. Now, before I expose all of them tonight, I'd better check on my patient. See you in the morning, and don't forget our bargain."

How could she forget? She wouldn't have a moment's peace until he was out of her house and gone from Galveston. Professionally, he was a threat to her father. Emotionally, he was a threat to her.

"What did you say to Holt?" her father asked as he entered the kitchen.

"You seem to have made him so mad he wants to leave."

"Leave?" Her reactions to that word were wildly contradictory, but she didn't have time to sort them out. "We made a bargain."

"What kind of bargain?"

"He wanted to know what he had to do to gain my trust."

"What did you tell him?"

"That he had to believe you were a good doctor who didn't treat patients when you were drunk."

"What else?"

"He has to believe I could work with you just as effectively as he can."

"You don't know half of what he knows."

"How do you know?" she said, hurt by her

100

father's rush to defend a man who was still a virtual stranger. "All we know is that he can cut people open without batting an eye."

"He's had some excellent training. I don't say you couldn't have learned just as much if you'd had the opportunity, but you didn't."

"He agreed to everything I said."

Her father looked surprised; then a slow grin spread across his face.

"What are you grinning about?" she asked.

"If he agreed to those outrageous demands, then he must really like you. If you'll just stop fighting with him at every turn, I might finally have a son-in-law."

But Felicity knew better. Holt had agreed because he intended to prove her wrong. Despite all his good points, he was not the man to give her the kind of love she'd waited so long for.

Holt forced himself to concentrate on Durwin, making sure the man was as comfortable as possible. The laudanum appeared to be holding. It was important that the patient remain quiet until his wounds began to heal. He seemed to be a very healthy young man, but it would be a long time before Durwin Sealy drove a buggy again.

Satisfied, Holt moved to the adjacent room. It was obvious at a glance that the room had been decorated by a woman. Flowers seemed to be everywhere, on the wallpaper, on the curtains, the bedspread, even the slipcover of a wing chair. The room had clearly been set aside for female relatives. Felicity would probably be delighted to know she'd managed to make him uncomfortable. It was obvious she didn't hold him in high regard. That was okay. He wasn't exactly enamored of her. Every time he felt the attraction between them start to grow, she ruined it by bridling at virtually every word that came out of his mouth.

He opened his suitcase and began to lay out his clothes. Without thinking, he looked around for a chest of drawers. What he found was a wardrobe. He'd heard about them, but he'd never seen one. Everyone in Vermont used chests of drawers. He opened the double doors to find an empty cavity on the left side. Viewing the empty hangers, he decided that something must have been meant to hang here.

The other side offered a wide selection of drawers from shallow to deep. He didn't realize the significance of what he was doing until he'd filled a second drawer. He didn't need to unpack more than a few items if he intended to stay only a day or two. A single change of clothes would be sufficient.

He continued filling the drawers with the contents of his suitcase.

Did this mean he wanted to stay? Was he filling the drawers with his clothes because of his concern for Durwin, his concern for Dr. Moore's patients, or his attraction to the man's daughter?

If he was staying because of any attraction to Felicity, he'd been out in the Texas sun too long. He was in Galveston to find Vivian, wasn't he?

He looked at the hangers and one of his coats. He wondered if it would look better hung up instead of folded carefully. Why not try it? The South had lost the war, but no one could dispute that Southerners knew a lot about clothes.

Holt was coming home from his third time dining out in a week. It seemed the people of Galveston used any excuse to throw a party. Or maybe with his jaundiced New England view of useless frivolity, he was overcritical of the way they enjoyed spending their evenings. They ate too much, drank too much, and flirted too much.

The night was balmy, the heavens brilliant with stars. He could just make out the faint sound of waves beating upon the shore. The slightly rank odor of the harbor competed with the smell of some tiny white flowers that reminded him of the sweetness of honeysuckle. He'd decided to walk the several blocks to Dr. Moore's house. He'd allowed himself to be talked into drinking half a glass of wine with his dinner. He'd flatly refused the many offers of brandy. Even though the wine didn't appear to have had any effect on him, he felt guilty for letting himself be coerced into doing something he'd never done before. And all because he didn't want people to stop inviting him out, thereby inhibiting his search for Vivian.

His capitulation left a bad taste in his mouth. Reason told him a half glass of wine wasn't a problem. Reason also told him any possible effect had already worn off. His wits were in more danger of being dulled by the rich food and smoke-filled atmosphere than a few swallows of wine.

But he felt like a hypocrite. He'd told Felicity he never touched spirits. He'd made a self-righteous son-of-a-bitch of himself over her father's one glass of whiskey, declaring with pious authority that a doctor who took his calling seriously never allowed the sins of the flesh to keep him from being ready to do his duty at all times. He didn't know what had caused him to act like such a narrow-minded, unbending zealot. No one could live up to the standards he'd set forth, not even himself.

And he'd proved it this evening because he was afraid he'd lose his chance to keep looking for Vivian.

Mrs. Prentiss's daughter, Charlotte, had been more than true to her word that she would see he was invited out practically every evening. She had introduced him as the man who'd saved Durwin Sealy's life and the doctor who'd taken care of her brother during the war. But no matter how many people he met, no one knew of a Vivian Calvert. They really wanted only to hear about the war. So he told them stories, borrowing from others when he ran out of his own, determined to continue being invited out until he found someone who could tell him how to find Vivian.

He paused on the road before Dr. Moore's house when he saw light coming through a window. He'd hoped to find the house dark. Durwin was making so much progress, Holt had told his mother she could take him home in a day or two. That would bring Holt to a point of decision. What would he do then? He didn't have any excuse for staying with Dr. Moore, but he didn't really want to leave. The man might be too sensitive — he hadn't been able to grapple with what life had handed him — but when he didn't drink, he was an excellent doctor. Holt no longer felt the calling to medicine he'd once believed he had, but working with Dr. Moore fascinated him. The man knew an incredible amount and loved to share what he knew. But being around the doctor, seeing his love for medicine and devotion to his patients, made Holt painfully aware of his own emptiness, his own lack of direction. The need to find his own path in life tugged at Holt to move on.

Then there was Felicity. Whether he wanted to admit it or not, she knew a great deal about day-to-day medicine and practical remedies. His experience on the ranch had reminded him that most people didn't have access to a doctor.

And many who did couldn't afford one. Teaching those people how to take care of themselves was extremely important. That was another thing he couldn't do.

He hesitated to go inside. The night reminded him of the summer evenings he'd spent at his Great-Uncle William's home. He knew Uncle William had wanted him to marry his ward, Vivian Stone, to make his home at Price's Nob. But Vivian had married someone else, and Price's Nob had been destroyed.

He wondered what Felicity would have done if she'd been in Vivian's place. Vivian had wanted to get away from the isolation of Price's Nob. She'd wanted to go to parties, enjoy herself, be courted by the young sons of wealthy families. Vivian had been determined to marry well.

Had she been in Vivian's place, Holt was certain Felicity would have stayed with Uncle William, working in any way she could to help with the plantation. She'd have stayed during the war, feeling she owed Uncle William any help she could offer since he'd taken care of her most of her life. She would even have refused to marry a man like Abe Calvert, because it would take her away from what she felt were her responsibilities. Felicity wasn't one to shirk her responsibilities.

Holt told himself to stop wasting time thinking about Felicity. He needed to find Vivian and make a decision about what to do with his life.

Having shaken off useless memories of the past, Holt walked up to the house and let himself in the front door. At first everything was quiet. Then he heard voices coming from the doctor's office. Felicity's voice, her father's, and the voice of a man Holt didn't recognize. He turned toward the office. He opened the door to find Felicity sewing up a cut in the arm of a man he didn't know. Both the man and her father were soaking wet.

Felicity knew the moment Holt walked through the door that he had misunderstood the situation. She didn't give him a chance to speak.

"I'm glad you're back," she said. "Orson fell into Galveston Bay and Papa had to fish him out."

"What are you doing sewing up that gash in his arm?" Holt demanded. "That's a doctor's job."

"It usually is," Felicity said, turning her attention back to the wound in Orson's upper arm, "but Papa's too exhausted to hold a needle steady. Besides, women are much better at sewing than men."

"That's not a petticoat or a pillowcase," Holt snapped. "It's a man's arm."

"If you think you can do better, you're welcome to try." Felicity started to get up.

"I ain't letting no army sawbones get hold of my arm," Orson cried. "He's liable to cut it off."

"He'll do no such thing." Felicity knew Orson's accusation was unfair, but it had the effect of deciding Holt to turn his attention to her father. "See if you can get him into some dry clothes and convince him to go to bed," she said. "He may be suffering from hypothermia."

"I had to stay here to make sure nothing was wrong with Orson," her father said.

"He's fine now. Or he will be when he sobers up."

"Sober up, hell!" Orson said from between clenched teeth. "I'm going to get drunk. That damned needle hurts."

"It can't hurt as much as the rudder."

"Didn't feel a thing," Orson said.

"Then it's good Papa was there to fish you out before you bled to death."

"You don't have to go with me," her father told Holt when he started to leave with him. "I can still dress myself."

"I was just going to help you up the stairs."

"I'm not decrepit. Stay and help Felicity."

"You got anything to get rid of the hurt?" Orson asked. "I could use a drink right about now."

"Once I get this bandage tied, you can get as drunk as you want," Felicity said. "But you should go home and go to bed. You'll probably have a low-grade fever. You don't need to put any extra strain on your system."

"Drinking's no strain on me."

"Yes, it is," Holt said. "The more you drink, the harder your body has to work to handle the alcohol. Let me see your wound."

It didn't bother Felicity that he wanted to inspect her work. She knew the value of her skill. Once, a patient had asked her to take out stitches put in by one of Galveston's best doctors and stitch up the wound again. She'd been amazed the man could endure that kind of pain, but the wound had been so badly sewn up, it would have left a horrible scar.

"You have a close network of fine stitches," Holt said.

"It takes longer and hurts more to do it like this —"

"You're damned right," Orson interjected.

"— but the wound heals faster and the scarring is less."

"Hurry up," Orson pleaded. "Much longer and I'll pass out."

"At least then I won't have to put up with your whining," Felicity said. "I've seen kids show more courage."

"It hurts," Orson said.

"Maybe next time you want to go for a swim, you'll try the gulf instead of the harbor," Felicity said. "You're less likely to cut yourself on a ship's rudder."

"How was I to know it was so close? Some fool painted it black."

"Is he as drunk as he looks?" Holt asked.

"Unfortunately, no," Felicity replied. "If he were, he wouldn't be whining so much. Are you going to look after Papa, or do you want to finish Orson?"

"You bandage it up," Orson said.

"I want to see if Dr. Price has any instructions."

"You finish up," Holt said. "I'm sure you believe women are better at bandaging, too."

"They usually are, but I expect you've had a lot of experience."

"Bandaging bleeding stumps," Orson said under his breath.

"And chests I've cut open. Not to mention having to stuff a kid's guts back in before I could sew him up."

"Shut up," Orson said. "You're making me sick."

"You can't expect the doctor to be careful of your feelings when you've been so hard on his."

"Everybody knows —"

"Everybody doesn't know. Keep still. I'm almost through."

"I don't like the way he's looking at me."

"I think we ought to bleed him," Holt said. "He looks overexcited to me."

"You're not bleeding me," Orson said, backing around Felicity and making it much harder for her to secure his bandage.

"It won't hurt much. Just a couple of tiny incisions."

"You come near me with a knife, and I'll set the law on you."

"If you'd prefer leeches, I'm sure we can find some."

Orson grabbed up the end of the bandage strip Felicity was attempting to tie. "My wife can do that."

"About payment —"

"I'll settle with you tomorrow," Orson said,

making his escape through the door her father had left ajar.

"I hope you're satisfied," she said, turning back to Holt. "Now I'll never get the money out of him."

"If I go around to his house with a jar of leeches, I expect he'll pay up quick enough."

Felicity tried to keep a straight face, but she couldn't. "I know he shouldn't have said those things about you, but now you've confirmed his suspicions."

"At least I'll never have to worry about his being my patient."

"He'll probably run if he sees you coming toward him on the street."

"Maybe I should carry a jar of leeches with me when I go out."

"You wouldn't." She was trying not to giggle.

"Why wouldn't I?"

"Because you're much too serious."

"Think of it as preventive medicine. If Orson thinks he has to come to me if he gets cut again, maybe he won't drink so much. And if he doesn't drink so much, he'll be in better health."

"Is that what they taught you in medical school?"

"I've learned to take advantage of all kinds of superstition. You can't imagine how much fun you can have."

She tried, but she couldn't stifle the giggle. "Yes, I can. If you only knew some of the things people believe. Do you know you should tie an onion behind your ear to cure an earache?"

"If you want to get rid of warts, touch each with a separate pebble, put the pebbles in a bag, drop the bag on the way to church, and the finder will receive your warts," he countered.

"To get rid of mumps, put the patient in a donkey's halter and lead him around the pigsty four times."

"Why four?"

"I don't know. Maybe it takes that long for the stench to overcome the mumps. How about this one? For whooping cough, drink water from the skull of a bishop," she added.

"Poor bishop. For a cold, hang a stocking filled with hot potatoes around the neck or rub a roasted one on the head."

"A raw potato in the pocket prevents rheumatism."

"For sexual stamina, crush raw potatoes, carrots, cabbage, and mint."

"Shame on you. Just for that, you should know the surest cure for a man's hernia is castration."

That was too much. They both began laughing uncontrollably.

"What are you two laughing about?" her father asked when he returned to the office.

Felicity sobered quickly. She wished her father hadn't come back. He wasn't drunk. If he had been, he wouldn't have been able to pull

Orson out of the water, but now he looked drunk. She knew his staggering gait was from exhaustion, but she was sure Holt would only see that he'd been drinking.

"We were exchanging medical superstitions," Holt said. "I was trying to top Felicity, but I think she won."

"Where's Orson?" Dr. Moore asked.

"He ran out before Felicity could finish tying his bandage," Holt said. "He thinks all army doctors are butchers. He was afraid I'd amputate his arm rather than stitch it up."

"That's foolish."

"I also offered to bleed him," Holt said.

Her father looked from her to Holt and back again. "Why would you want to bleed him?"

"He didn't," Felicity said. "He was just baiting him because of his foolish beliefs."

"You shouldn't do that," her father said. "Some people are fools, but they're innocent fools."

Felicity thought she should have told Holt that her father had no sense of humor about medicine. But then, she hadn't expected Holt to have one, either.

"I ran into a lot of them during the war," Holt said. "It seemed better to laugh at them than take them seriously."

"Doctors should work to eradicate superstition," her father said. "People need to learn to believe in science."

"Holt was only joking," Felicity said. "You

ought to be in bed. If you're not careful, you'll get chills."

"I can treat myself, daughter. I don't have chills, but I am going to bed. I'll see you in the morning. Thank you for taking care of Orson."

Felicity could sense the change in Holt even before the door closed behind her father.

"He's been drinking again," Holt said.

"He went to the Galveston Hotel to have a drink with some friends," Felicity said, trying hard to act calm. "Not even you could disapprove of that."

"I do disapprove of it."

"What have you got against my father that makes you determined to deny him the pleasure of even one drink? You've done nothing but criticize him and question his medical abilities ever since you got here."

"I've only questioned his ability when he's drunk."

"My father is not drunk!"

"How do you know?"

"Because I've seen him drunk."

"Okay, then I question whether he's had too much to drink to be able to function as a doctor."

"He couldn't have hauled Orson out of the water if he had."

"You sure someone else didn't have to haul both of them out?"

"What are you insinuating?"

"Maybe Orson fell in the bay, your father

jumped in after him, and some ship's crew had to pull both of them out. Or maybe your father fell in and Orson jumped in to pull *him* out."

"My father wouldn't lie."

Holt wanted to tell Felicity how many times his father had lied, how he'd had to learn to question everything he said. She didn't know what it was like to see the father you loved destroy himself right before your eyes, piece by painful piece, year by agonizing year, in full view of the whole town.

"People who drink too much don't like what's happening to them, but they can't stop it, so they lie. People who don't stop them just contribute to the problem. Rather than believe what you see, you come up with reasons why the truth is really something else."

"You don't know what you're talking about."

"Yes, I do. My father was an alcoholic. I grew up watching him slowly destroy himself. I know every stage there is, because I've been through all of them." He could see surprise in her eyes, maybe even shock, but no backing down.

"My father has a drinking problem, but he's not an alcoholic."

"Maybe not yet, but he will be soon. And you're allowing it to happen."

"The biggest problem is your puritanical attitude toward anything you consider a vice."

"I wouldn't care about your father's drinking habits if he weren't a doctor. Because he is a

116

doctor, he has to hold himself to certain standards."

"What standards — the ones you've established? My father has always believed in the highest standards of medical practice."

"Yet he can come home drunk after falling — or jumping — into the bay and be perfectly content to let you take care of Orson."

"I could do what needed to be done for Orson."

"You're not qualified to function as a doctor."

"I wasn't functioning as a doctor. I just sewed up Orson's wound."

"Because your father was too drunk to handle a needle."

"Because he was too *exhausted.*"

"Couldn't you smell the whiskey on your father's breath?"

"I could smell whiskey," she admitted, "but Orson had been drinking, and I was closest to him."

"You're not going to admit your father was drunk, are you?"

"Why should I admit what I don't believe?"

"Because you're too intelligent not to *know* it's true."

Holt couldn't see any reason to prolong this discussion. Felicity had taken her position and didn't mean to change it.

"I have to leave," he said.

"Where are you going at this time of night?"

"I have to move out of my room, out of this house. If I stay here, I'm giving at least tacit approval to what you're doing."

She looked surprised. "You promised to stay until Durwin got well."

"Your father can look after him."

"How can he when he's drunk half the time?" she said quietly.

"Since you know so much, you can do it."

She reacted as if he'd slapped her.

"My father will be more than glad to assume Durwin's care," she said, sounding as pompous as any doctor. "Although performing that operation might have been beyond his experience, caring for a patient with a life-threatening wound is not. For myself, I will be relieved to have you go. I appreciate the help you offered my father, but I find your constant attempts to characterize him as a drunk and an alcoholic inexcusable. Maybe Vivian knew what she was doing when she chose another man over you. I should imagine it would be very hard to live with a saint."

Many responses teetered on the tip of Holt's tongue, but he uttered none of them. He wouldn't apologize for what he'd said about her father, he didn't regret his attempts to get her to see what was happening to him, but he remembered enough of his own agony when confronted with what his father had become to sympathize with her. She had to be hurting inside, fighting against what she soon wouldn't be able to deny. He didn't want to make it harder on her.

"I'll leave in the morning. I'll check on Durwin before I go."

"Breakfast will be at the usual time."

Felicity wanted to follow Holt out of the room, but she had to tidy up, put things away. But as she rolled up the unused strips she used for bandages, put the equipment into hot soapy water, and cleaned up the damp left by wet clothes, she felt her righteous indignation gradually fade. She knew her father drank too much on occasion, but he seldom got really drunk and she was always there in case he needed help. It was ridiculous of Holt to insist that she couldn't sew up a cut, even a long and deep one, without having a medical degree. Anybody could do that.

She was glad he was going. Her father didn't need his help. Many patients distrusted Holt, some because he was a Yankee, others because he was a stranger, but mostly because he'd been an army doctor.

She scrubbed at the damp that Orson had left in the chair, irritated that the smell of harbor water would remain in the consulting room. What was she doing scrubbing? She was supposed to be drying the chair, not trying to wash it clean.

It was all Holt's fault. He always upset her. She didn't know what it was that made her act so unlike herself when he was around. She even argued more. But what really bothered her was that her feelings seemed to go to extremes; everything was more important now; everything made her happier or more upset than usual. There was just more of everything and no explanation why.

She finished with the chair and turned her attention to the instruments. There weren't many. It would take her longer to clean up the blood that Orson had dripped from the front door to the office.

She stared at the soapy water as her hands searched for the instruments hidden beneath the surface. Why did she feel so depressed? She'd wanted Holt to leave almost from the moment he'd entered their house. He'd questioned her ability and accused her father of incompetence. Nothing had been the same since he'd arrived. She hoped he'd soon find his Vivian and leave town.

But no sooner did she think of Vivian than she wondered again why the woman had left Holt to marry another man. Society women were pretty much like women everywhere. They married either for love or for their advantage. This woman hadn't married for love, or she'd have married Holt. What made him think she would want to marry him now? There were lots of wealthy men in Galveston, and more coming all the time. Vivian could have any number of wealthy potential husbands to choose from. She might have married already.

She felt sorry for Holt. She wondered what he'd do if he found that Vivian had married again, or if she was single and refused to marry him. It was bound to hurt.

She dried the needles and put them away. Then she took a rag, immersed it in the soapy water, and started wiping up the blood on the floor. It was pointless to waste her time musing about Holt's future. After tomorrow morning, she wouldn't see him again.

Yet she couldn't *stop* thinking about him. He had taken possession of her mind, influenced her emotions, and called forth a physical response she was unable to control or deny. He made her aware of the great vacuum in her life.

She had not found love.

For years, when the need — and fear — had come on her so strongly she couldn't ignore it, she'd told herself she wasn't ready. It wasn't the right time. The right man hadn't come along. She couldn't desert her father. All these excuses had helped blunt the pain of being unwanted, the feeling that life was passing her by, the hunger for children, and for a husband to shower with all the love she'd been saving up for the perfect man.

Then the man of her dreams had appeared in the guise of a man who would destroy her father. If her father were denied the right to practice medicine, he *would* turn into a hopeless drunk. She had to protect him from Holt.

But she couldn't drive out the feeling that

Holt not only looked like her dream man. He *was* her dream man.

He made her laugh. No one had ever been able to do that. Laughing made her feel good, more hopeful. It released some of the tension, made it easier to worry less. She had more than enough proof of his high standards and integrity. Holding fast to one's beliefs wasn't all bad. Even when she told herself she didn't like him, she was attracted to him. She wanted to touch him, to feel his arms around her. But she didn't dare. If she ever did, she feared she'd never be able to stop.

She was a fool. Regardless of everything, he would never be the man for her. He was in love with another woman.

Holt stuffed the last of his clothes into the suitcase and looked around the room to make sure he hadn't forgotten anything. It would be a relief to leave all these flowers.

But that wasn't the reason he was relieved. He'd let working with Dr. Moore and sparring with Felicity take up too much of his time. He'd used the excuse that he could save money if he stayed here, that he could help the doctor, that he could use Felicity and her father's contacts to give him entrance into Galveston society.

But the truth was he didn't need to worry about money, and Felicity's barely repressed determination to get rid of him had put a limit on how much he could help her father. And while he had made some contacts, he didn't have much to show for his week in Galveston. He would have made better progress going straight to one of the banks and trying to make the most of his tenuous connection with the Randolph family.

Felicity's accusation still rang in his ears. *Maybe Vivian knew what she was doing when she chose another man over you. I should imagine it would be very hard to live with a saint.*

But he'd never acted saintly with Vivian. She said she had to be so careful around his uncle and aunt that she looked forward to being with him because she could be herself. Holt had excused her occasional lapses in taste as outbursts of youthful high spirits. But she had married Abe Calvert. Had she seen Holt as a paragon rather than a love-besotted young man? He'd never thought of himself as repressive or saintlike.

He tried to recall Vivian to mind. Much to his surprise, her image wasn't as sharp and clear as he expected. He didn't understand. He had no trouble remembering every detail of Felicity's appearance. From her rich, brown hair and deep, soulful eyes to her slim neck and faded dress; her strong hand as she sewed Orson's cut; her firm mouth. If he could remember Felicity so vividly, why not Vivian?

Because he hadn't seen Vivian in six years. Besides, until he'd met Felicity, no other female had interested him enough for him to re-member her. It was a shame that Felicity was so determined to deny her father's problem. She would make some man a wonderful wife. He had no doubt that, once given, her love would never change, never fade, but would grow stronger and deeper with each passing year. That was what he wanted. What he hoped to find with Vivian.

He was wasting time. The sooner he left, the sooner he could find Vivian. And Laveau.

He closed his suitcase and set it out in the hall, then made his way to the kitchen. Felicity and her father were at the table when he entered.

"Felicity says you're leaving us today," Dr. Moore said.

"I need to move on," Holt said. "I really haven't done what I came to do."

"Sorry I couldn't help you more, but Felicity and I don't get out much. Certainly not with the people Adelaide Prentiss's daughter knows."

"You've done more than enough. I've just come to say my goodbyes and then I'll be on my way."

"You can't go without having some breakfast."

"That's all right. I can get —"

Dr. Moore got up from his seat, came over to Holt, and propelled him to a chair at the table. "I couldn't show my face outside my door if I

124

let a guest leave my house without giving him breakfast. You sit right down. We have more than enough. Felicity, get this young man some breakfast."

Holt couldn't miss the fact that Felicity hadn't looked at him since he'd entered the kitchen.

"What are you going to do?" Dr. Moore asked as soon as Holt was seated.

"I haven't decided."

"First you need someplace to stay. What are you looking for? All the best hotels are close to each other."

"I was thinking about a rooming house. I might even consider a rented room if I can find someone who'll provide meals and washing."

"You're in luck," Dr. Moore said, breaking into a smile. "There's a room like that next door. That way you'll still be close enough to come over when you're not busy."

Chapter Eight

The thought of having Holt next door, of having him free to drop in at any time, jarred Felicity so badly she nearly dropped the plate. She barely had time to pull herself together before she set a breakfast of pork chops, fried eggs, and grits swimming in gravy in front of Holt. By the time she poured his coffee, her hand was steady.

"I'm sure Mrs. Bennett is an excellent landlady, Papa," she said, "but you can't railroad Holt into staying next door just because you want someone to talk medicine with."

"I'm not railroading him."

"What do you call taking him over and introducing him? What's he supposed to do after that, unless the sheets haven't been changed and he sees soap rings in the washbasin? And you know he won't, because Mrs. Bennett is an excellent housekeeper."

"Which is exactly why I think he ought to stay with her. Besides, she's a war widow. It's his patriotic duty."

"Now, that's really unfair. Suppose he wants to stay downtown, go to parties, meet other people his age."

"Mrs. Bennett's not a curmudgeon." Her father winked at Holt. "But I don't think she'd approve of you bringing young women home for the night."

"I couldn't possibly consider staying with her then," Holt said, throwing Felicity a grin that told her he knew exactly what she was doing. "I had planned to become a regular Don Juan. After spending so long with nothing but cows, a man needs some diversion."

"From what I've heard, most of them would benefit by being turned into steers," Felicity said.

"Don't listen to her," her father said. "No woman understands men."

"And no man understands women," Felicity said.

Her father sobered suddenly. "I understood your mother. Sometimes I believe we actually shared each other's thoughts."

It was Felicity's privately held belief that her mother had died too soon for her father to realize they were quite different. Her father was a dreamer, an idealist, a person who could live his life without ever truly coming face to face with reality. Her mother had been the one to make sure the plantation ran smoothly.

"I just don't think you ought to take him over to Mrs. Bennett," Felicity said as she seated herself again. "There are other rooming houses in Galveston. I'm not trying to tell you where to live, Holt. I just don't think it's fair of Papa to make it difficult for you to make your own choice."

"Okay, you take him over," her father said.

"It would be exerting the same kind of pressure."

"If I didn't know better, I'd think you were trying to get rid of me," Holt said.

"Felicity wouldn't do that," her father said. "She's very fond of you."

"I didn't know," Holt said, with a grin that made her want to slap him.

"You can stop trying to make fun of me."

"Holt wouldn't do that."

"It's not the normal kind of fun, Papa. It's what men who've spent too many years living with cows think is humorous."

"Ouch!" Holt said. "She has fangs."

"Claws, too," Felicity said.

"I wish you two would stop," her father said. "I don't understand you when you talk like this."

Felicity got up from the table to scrape her plate into the slop bucket. She'd lost any appetite she might have had. She'd spent half the night lying awake trying to figure out why she couldn't stop thinking about Holt. Why she couldn't mark him off her list as a self-righteous know-it-all and put him completely out of her mind. Despite several hours of thought, she couldn't come up with a good reason.

But she had several *foolish* reasons. He was definitely attractive. His dark brown hair was always straight and neat. It looked as if the wind could never muss it. His heavy brows and the shadow of his beard even when freshly shaved gave him a dark, rough, masculine look. His slim build and broad shoulders were more than enough to make a woman feel confident he could protect her. But it was those black eyes that bothered her most.

They seemed to drill right through her. She felt they wanted to strip her of all pretense, to lay bare her soul. But just as disturbing was the invitation he extended for her to do the same to him. He wasn't willing to share with everyone — he seemed too untrusting for that — but he was willing to share with her. She didn't understand why.

This lack of understanding held her captive.

"I'll be happy to have either one of you go with me to see Mrs. Bennett's rooms," Holt said, "but I'm not promising anything."

"If you're going to be here for more than a few weeks, you ought to look at several places," Felicity said as she reached for her father's plate. She turned away to the sink. "If you want, you can stay here while you look."

That last sentence came out unexpectedly. It was sensible, but she knew she said it because she didn't want Holt to walk out the door and vanish forever. It seemed silly to her that she could feel that way under the circumstances, but there was no disputing that she did.

"He doesn't have to leave here at all," her father said.

"I'll leave my suitcase here if you don't

mind," Holt said, "but I'd like to find a place today."

"I'm sorry to lose you," her father said.

The talk turned to medicine while Holt finished his breakfast. Felicity had washed all the dishes except the coffee cups, put everything away, and cleaned up the kitchen when she heard a knock at the back door. It was a local boy.

"Mrs. Farley's not feeling very good," he said, mentioning a neighbor's name. "She wants the doc to come see her right away."

"What's wrong?" her father asked.

"She says the pain is fair killing her."

"I'll be right there. Let me get my bag."

"You want me to go with you?" Holt asked.

"You'd better not. Alice doesn't take to strangers. She's liable not to let either one of us in."

"What's wrong with her?"

"She's got a tumor. It ought to come out, but she won't hear of me cutting her open."

"What are you going to do?"

"There's nothing I can do until the pain gets so bad she can't stand it. I'd better go. Felicity can take you to see Mrs. Bennett."

"He doesn't need me —" But her father was gone.

"I guess you're stuck," Holt said. "Unless you want to go over alone first and poison Mrs. Bennett's mind against me."

"While you're so busy congratulating yourself

on figuring out what I'm doing, remind yourself that I wouldn't feel this way if you hadn't attacked my father."

"Since we've proved we're not likely to reach agreement on that, I don't see any point in talking about it anymore," Holt said.

"Neither do I."

"Good. Now, are you going to take me over, or do I go by myself? It would probably be better if you introduced me."

"Do you really want to stay with Mrs. Bennett?"

"Why not?"

"It's right next door. You'll practically be forced to know everything that goes on in Papa's office. People talk about anything."

"I might not be at home very much. I may soon develop different interests, make new acquaintances."

"That will be best for everybody. Besides, you came to Galveston to find your long-lost love, not to get tied up with an alcoholic doctor and his presumptuous daughter."

What was wrong with her? she wondered. She had reason to want him as far away from her father as possible, but she had no reason to start sounding like a jealous shrew.

"If you're ready, I'd like to meet Mrs. Bennett."

"Give me your cup." She washed it, dried it, put it away, then threw out the dishwater. A quick look about the kitchen satisfied her that everything was where it ought to be. "Okay, let's go."

The two houses were close together, but there were a couple of trees and some shrubs to block the view, one from the other.

Mrs. Bennett's home was a narrow two-story, wood-frame structure with a front porch and large windows facing the wide street. A low picket fence encircled the tiny yard, which someone obviously tended with great care. Bright splashes of color filled the many small flower beds that dotted the yard.

"It must take a lot of work to keep these flower beds so neat," Holt observed.

"Mrs. Bennett loves to garden," Felicity said.

"I hope she doesn't try to enroll me. I have a brown thumb." And absolutely no desire to spend his spare time digging in the dirt.

"She's more likely to have you arrested if you touch anything," Felicity said.

The woman who opened the door to them wasn't at all what Holt had expected. She was so tiny, she barely reached his waist. If she weighed more than ninety pounds, he'd be surprised.

"Morning, Mrs. Bennett," Felicity said. "Are your rooms still for rent?"

"You thinking of moving out of your father's house?" Her expression was one of amusement.

"No, but I'm bringing you a prospective boarder. This is Dr. Holt Price. He's come to Galveston looking for a friend he lost track of during the war."

The tiny woman didn't appear the least intimidated by Holt's size. "Come on in."

It didn't take Holt long to decide that the rooms would have been perfect if they hadn't been so close to Felicity and her father. Mrs. Bennett was remarkably spry for her fifty-five years. She had lost her husband in the war with Mexico. Holt could have the whole upper floor if he wanted — bedroom, sitting room, and his own bath. There wouldn't be anyone in the house to bother him. He could have as many meals as he wanted, and she'd send his clothes out for washing.

"Everything sounds perfect," Holt said, "but I'd like to look round a bit more first."

"Look all you please," Mrs. Bennett said, "but don't come banging on my door after dark. I get up with the sun and go to bed with it."

That wouldn't bother Holt. Cade's longhorns kept the same hours.

"I don't want to take up any more of your time," Holt said.

"Will you be back for supper?" Felicity asked when they were outside.

"I can get something out rather than bother you."

"It's no bother to set an extra plate. Besides, Papa will be disappointed if you leave without seeing him again."

"I can't promise. I might find something I like and move right away."

133

They had reached Felicity's house. They stood there, neither knowing why they were hesitating, but neither of them apparently finding the words to say goodbye. Holt wondered if it was the hot climate that enabled people to get so close to each other so quickly. In Vermont a family practically had to live somewhere for a generation before the locals would do much more than nod in church. He'd spent eight days in the Moore household and he felt like he belonged there. But he really needed to start looking for Vivian and Laveau. He could have done it without moving, but something always seemed to get in the way. He couldn't stay focused. That never used to happen to him.

"If you don't want her rooms, don't wait too long to tell Mrs. Bennett," Felicity said.

"I won't."

"I hope you find something you like soon."

"I hope your father feels better today. You need to watch him more closely. If you see —"

"You'd better get started if you're going to see more than a few places today."

She turned, entered the gate, closed it behind her, and walked up to the house without looking back. Holt turned and walked away, but his thoughts never left the doctor's house; he wondered what was going to happen.

Felicity couldn't control her father's drinking. As far as Holt could tell, she didn't try. But she was fierce in her defense of him, trying to cover for him when he was incapacitated. She thought things would get better, but Holt knew they would only get worse. Maybe she was right that her father had never gotten falling-down drunk or completely beyond his ability to function, but it would happen.

One day he would be so drunk, he'd make a terrible mistake and a patient would die. He would be ruined, and he would ruin Felicity, too. They'd probably be forced to leave Galveston, find another town, one where the people were so desperate for a doctor they'd accept a drunk. Which would only make things worse, because he'd drink more.

Things might not be too bad for the doctor if they headed for the frontier. Men were tolerant of each other's weaknesses there, but it would be devastating for Felicity. She'd end up an old maid or married to someone who'd beat her, expect her to work to exhaustion, and fill her belly with so many children her body would give out.

Holt told himself to stop thinking about anything to do with Felicity or her father. He wasn't responsible for their situation, and he couldn't change anything even if he tried.

A niggling voice told him that because he knew of the situation, he couldn't ignore it. It was his duty to the patients. It was his duty to the profession. It was his duty to himself.

He pushed the thought aside. Until the profession organized itself, until somebody required all doctors to have a uniform education in the basics of medicine, until states established societies to supervise the practice of medicine, there was nothing that conscientious doctors could do.

He told himself that all of this would soon be in the past for him. He had to find Vivian. Before that, he needed to decide what to do with his life. He hadn't found anything to fill the void left by medicine. Nothing had revitalized the core which had been burned out of him by the war. Somewhere, somehow, there was a place for him, a job, a role that would replenish his soul, give him back the man he wanted to be, fill the shell he had become.

He had a terrible feeling that Vivian wouldn't be able to help him find the answer.

"There wasn't much of a choice," Holt told Felicity from where he sat across the supper table. "Not only did Mrs. Bennett have the best rooms, she gave me the best terms."

"Glad to have you close by," Dr. Moore said. "I was missing you already."

"I may not be in much," Holt hastened to say. "I ought to look into making some business investments."

"I didn't realize you were rich."

"I'm not, but there's no point in letting what money I do have just sit in the bank."

"Dad's not much interested in business," Felicity said. "Not that we have any money to invest."

"A doctor shouldn't grow rich on the misery of his patients," Dr. Moore said.

Holt agreed with him in principle, but he didn't see any reason why a doctor shouldn't be paid well for his services. He guessed there must have been some discussion that day over unpaid bills. Felicity must feel put upon trying to run the household without sufficient income. He was glad he was no longer a burden.

Dr. Moore pushed back his chair and got up. "I'm off to see Mrs. Farley. Her pain hasn't let up."

"You ought to talk her into letting you take out that tumor," Holt said.

"She's a very stubborn woman," Felicity said to Holt after her father left. "She said if God put it in her body, then it ought to stay there."

"But God didn't put it there. Something caused it to start growing long after she was born."

"I explained that," Felicity said, getting up to begin clearing, "but she wouldn't listen."

"Maybe I . . ." Holt made himself stop before he finished the sentence. This wasn't his battle anymore.

Holt had spent much of the day looking at hotels and rooming houses. Mrs. Bennett's rooms were superior to all the others. But he knew that wasn't the real reason he returned to Menard Street. He'd come back because of Dr. Moore.

He simply couldn't, in good conscience, leave

him to continue to get drunk and treat patients. As long as he only made diagnoses and prescribed medicine, sewed up cuts, and set broken limbs, he probably wouldn't cause any major damage. Holt was certain that Felicity checked everything he did, and knew enough to guard against a critical mistake. But what if he started to operate? Even if he were an accomplished surgeon, it would be all too easy to make a mistake.

He might as well admit he'd come back because of Felicity, as well. He and Felicity didn't agree often. She certainly wouldn't agree that she was caught in a situation in which she had no life of her own, everything she did was for her father, because of her father, to protect her father. Holt knew he couldn't stop her, but neither could he leave her to do it by herself.

She'd probably learned a great deal working so closely with her father. If she'd read his books, she knew even more. But sooner or later she was bound to face a crisis she couldn't handle. And as long as Holt was in Galveston, he might as well try to help. She wouldn't ask for it, but if he was close by, she probably wouldn't refuse.

Okay, so he was going soft on Felicity. He understood her stubborn defense of her father; she probably felt she couldn't do anything else. He'd felt the same with his own father. Trapped.

"You couldn't help," Felicity said. "Papa was right when he said Mrs. Farley wouldn't let you in the house."

"Well, I'll be glad to help."

"Papa knows how to handle tumors. He's removed them before."

He decided not to tell her he was talking about her as much as her father. He'd never defended his own father as vigorously as he could have. He'd been ashamed of him most of the time, had left Vermont as soon as he got the chance. He'd told himself that he'd done everything he could, that it was time to make something of his own life. And that was true, but seeing Felicity's sacrifice made him feel guilty all over again.

Besides, what had leaving accomplished? He didn't know where he belonged, where he fit, what he wanted to do with his life, how to make a positive difference. After all the death and destruction he'd witnessed, he felt the need to do something important, but nothing he'd tried had felt right.

"I'm sure your father can handle a tumor without my help. I just thought as long as I was here . . . But maybe that isn't a good idea. No point in starting what I don't mean to continue."

"You still intend to leave medicine?"

"Yes."

"What are you going to do?"

"I don't know."

"It would be better if you figured that out be-

fore you found Vivian."

"Why?"

"A man's choice of profession is a very personal thing. If he allows that choice to be influenced by someone else, it can lead to unhappiness and casting of blame later."

"Do you blame your father for choosing your profession?"

"My father had nothing to do with it. It was my decision to —"

"Your father has no ability to manage money or a household, much less a medical practice. He needs a full-time cook, housekeeper, and nurse. He also needs someone to watch out for him, protect him when he's too weak to protect himself. He could hire someone or go into practice with another doctor, but you haven't asked him to do that. Instead, you let yourself be trapped here, turning your back on any opportunity for marriage and a family of your own."

"It's not a trap. It's my duty, my responsibility."

"That doesn't mean you have to give up your own life."

"Several men have wanted to marry me, but I never considered leaving my father."

"That's because you know he can't get along without you."

"That's not true. He —"

"My father couldn't get along by himself, either, but he didn't even try. He did try to make

140

me feel guilty when I didn't put his needs before mine. He could be too drunk to walk a straight line, too drunk to stand on his own, but he was never too drunk to make me feel like a worm for wanting a life of my own, for wanting to have something, *anything,* that wasn't sullied by his drunkenness."

He'd said too much, but he couldn't stand to let Felicity continue telling herself she was devoting her life to her father because she wanted to, that she wasn't making a sacrifice in doing so.

"I'm sorry your life was so unhappy," Felicity said, "but mine isn't like that. Papa would be delighted to see me get married. He wanted me to consider marrying you five minutes after you walked in the door."

"I'm sure he would be truly happy to see you married with a passel of children, but he hasn't made any attempt to free you from your responsibilities. He can wish you marriage and bountiful happiness because he doesn't have the remotest idea what will happen to him if you leave. But you do, and that's what keeps you a prisoner."

"I'm not a prisoner. I —"

Holt didn't know what impulse caused him to spring out of his chair and round the table before either of them knew what was happening. He grasped both her hands. When she tried to pull away, he encircled her waist with his arms.

"What are you doing?" she asked, her eyes wide with surprise . . . and fear.

"I'm trying to show you that you're a living, vital creature. You need love. You need a family. Your own *life*. Your soul will wither if you stay here."

"That's preposterous." She struggled, but he refused to let her go.

"You long for love. You ache for it."

"I do hope to fall in love, but this is not the right time."

"Then why are you trembling like a leaf?"

"I'm not used to being manhandled."

"I'm barely touching you. It's your soul crying out through your body."

"My soul is perfectly content."

"Liar. You don't even like me, yet you're about to jump out of your skin from my touch."

"I do like you. It's just that you won't —"

"If you were content, you wouldn't be trembling. Your eyes wouldn't be wide with apprehension as well as anticipation. Your breath wouldn't be shallow, your heart wouldn't beat so fast, and you would be straining to break my hold."

"I —"

"You'd either slap my face for my boldness or be bored and indifferent. But you're not doing any of those things."

"I —"

"You can't *make* yourself do any of those things because that's not how you feel. Inside,

142

you're dying for the right to be a woman rather than just a daughter, for the right to have a life of your own."

"You don't know —"

"I know because I was there myself. My family cut me off because I wouldn't sacrifice myself for my father's weakness. Your father will have a difficult time, but he'll find a way to survive."

"You can't know —"

Holt put his finger over her lips to stop her protest. "I've seen the way you look at the children that come into the office. The longing in your eyes is so visible I can almost feel it. But it's not just children. You're thinking about the father of those children, the man who would be the center of your life. You're hungry for the chance to become a mother, a wife, a lover. You ache for a man's touch, for a man's love, a man you can see every day, talk to, touch, sleep next to at night."

"I've never heard such deranged —"

He put two fingers over her lips. "You've got to let go, stop denying your feelings, stop letting duty dominate your life. You've got to look inside and find your own source of life before it dries up and disappears." He cupped her face in his hands. "You're a lovely woman, Felicity. You're warm, caring, and fiercely loyal and protective. There must be a hundred men in Galveston who'd fall on their knees for the chance to marry a woman like you."

She tried to back away, but he pulled her toward him until their bodies touched.

"Let me go," she cried, pushing hard against his chest. "I never thought you could be so cruel."

"I'm not being cruel. I'm being honest. I'm trying to make you see what you're doing to yourself. It hurts me to see you cut yourself off from everything that could make your life full and meaningful, from what I know you want so badly it must haunt your dreams."

Her eyes had filled with tears. He felt cruel. What right did he have to force his opinions on her? He didn't know what the hell to do with his own life. How could he dare tell anybody else what to do? Still, he couldn't back down. If no one forced her out of her self-imposed prison, she'd remain there forever. With one hand at her back, he brushed a tear from her cheek with the other.

"I've never met a woman more deserving of love," Holt said, "nor one so determined to hold it at bay."

"How can you say that when you're in love with another woman?"

"It's because I'm disinterested that I'm able to see your situation so clearly. My vision isn't clouded by emotion or lust."

The last word had barely left Holt's mouth when he realized his body was reacting to Felicity's closeness so strongly that in a moment it would be impossible for her to be unaware of it.

She would believe that every word was just an attempt to seduce her. That would drive her even deeper into her prison. He released her and stepped back.

"I didn't mean to upset you, but I couldn't watch you waste away and not say anything."

This wasn't working. He couldn't look at the tears in her eyes without wanting to kiss them away. He couldn't see her unhappiness and not want to do something about it. He couldn't tell her she was beautiful and desirable without desiring her himself. He couldn't let her know any of this without destroying everything he was trying to do. And if he didn't sit down, she'd be able to figure it all out on her own. He rounded the table and took a chair.

"Now let's talk about something else," Holt said.

"What?" She looked stunned at the abrupt shift in topic.

"A party. Adelaide Prentiss's daughter, Charlotte, has invited me to a party she's giving tomorrow night. She says there's a chance someone might know Vivian or know how I could go about looking for her."

"I hope you find her soon." Her voice sounded hollow.

"You can help. I want you to go to the party with me."

Chapter Nine

Felicity was certain she was losing her mind. One moment Holt held her so close her body shook like that of a frightened puppy. The next moment he was inviting her to a party just as though what he'd done moments before was ordinary, everyday behavior.

But she knew it wasn't, and she fought to regain control of her body, her mind, her emotions. Holt had attacked her defenses, shattered them, and left her helpless to deny what she'd tried so hard to hide. She wanted love desperately, and resented the duty to her father that kept her from finding it.

There! She'd admitted she was an ungrateful daughter. She wanted desperately to take Holt's advice and think only of herself. The temptation to imagine herself in the arms of a man like Holt was overmastering. Even now she could feel his arms around her, her face in his hands, his fingers touching her lips, tenderly brushing her ears. Why couldn't this have happened to her before now? Why did attraction have to come in the shape of a man who threatened her father, a man who loved another woman?

So many times she'd cried herself to sleep over the cruel twists of fate that had seemed always to keep love just out of her grasp — taking care of her father, the war, the loss of their fortune — but it had done no good. When she'd dried her eyes and washed her face, she still had her duty to her father. Well, it gave her something to do, was a source of pride, so she could hold her head up despite the whispers and the loss of old friends.

Just once she'd like to feel loved, surrounded by it, smothered by it, completely immersed in it. A love so powerful it rendered all previous loss and hurt meaningless. If she could just taste it once, she wouldn't ask for anything ever again.

But there was no such love. She couldn't understand how Holt could go from speaking of love to inviting her to a party as though both were of equal importance. Of all the things Holt could have asked, that was about the last thing she expected.

"I can't go to Charlotte's party," she said after she managed to collect her wits. "I wouldn't know anybody."

That wasn't true. She knew many people, but she had fallen off the invitation lists when her father lost his money. She felt a pang. It would be nice to be back where she used to belong, but she wouldn't go to be pitied or whispered about.

"You know Charlotte. That's one person more than I'll know."

"You know Charlotte, too."

147

"She only invited me because her parents pressured her into it."

"Taking me wouldn't make things any better."

"At least I'll have somebody to talk to."

"We never talk without arguing."

"I promise to be a charming companion the entire evening."

"No."

"You don't think I can be charming?"

"I believe you could be as charming as a snake-oil salesman, but that's not why I won't go."

"What are your objections? You don't know anybody, but we've already dispensed with that."

Just like a man to ignore any difficulty that wasn't his. "My objection is me. Myself. I wouldn't fit in."

"You're only going to a party, not marrying into the family."

"I still can't go."

"Why?"

"I don't have anything to wear."

"What's wrong with what you have on?"

He really couldn't expect her to go to a society party in a house dress. "If you don't know, you'd better stay away from that party because you'll never fit in, either," she said.

"I don't want to fit in. I just want to see if anyone can help me find Vivian."

"If you don't have the right clothes and don't

know how to behave, they won't talk to you."

Holt laughed, and she felt something catch in her throat when he flashed a smile that was as powerful as the sun coming out from behind a cloud. "I not only have the right clothes, I know how to behave."

"Then you don't need anybody to go with you."

"Maybe not, but I want you to go with me."

"Ask someone who can help."

"I want you to go. Besides, you need to get out once in a while, forget about your responsibilities occasionally, meet some new people, have a little fun. You might even meet someone who would sweep you off your feet."

"I'm too old to believe in fairy tales."

"I just told you how wonderful I think you are. Why shouldn't some nice young man fall in love with you?"

"No reason at all, except if he's rich, sophisticated, and handsome, he'd never be interested in anybody like me."

"You won't know until you give him a chance."

"Well, that's one chance I'm not taking. Even if I wanted to go, I couldn't. Like I said, I don't have anything to wear."

"I'll buy you a dress."

She looked at him as if he had lost his mind. "What do you think people would say about me if they found out you were paying for my clothes?"

"If I asked your help and advice in a business matter, you'd expect to get paid for it, wouldn't you?"

"Of course."

"Well, that's what I'm doing, paying for help and advice. It'll be your decision to use the money to buy clothes. That's what most women would do, isn't it?"

She knew that any woman would jump at the chance for a new dress, especially one pretty enough to wear to a party.

"How much would a dress cost?" he asked.

"I don't know. I haven't bought one in a long time."

Holt dug into his pocket and came up with a thirty-five-dollar gold piece. "Do you think you could buy one dress with this?" he asked.

Felicity hadn't seen that much money in one piece since before the war. "I could buy two."

"Spend it on a really nice dress."

Felicity was tempted. It wasn't as though she wouldn't be doing something to earn the money for the dress. She could think of the dress as a tool she needed to do her job. This was a chance to see old acquaintances again. Maybe she'd judged them too harshly, refused Charlotte's invitations unnecessarily. Maybe people had stayed away to avoid embarrassing her over her recent reversal of fortune. This would give her a chance to get in touch again.

She looked at the gold piece lying on the table between them. She hadn't realized how much she wanted a new dress until she'd been presented with the opportunity to realize her wish. Until now, she had had no place to wear such a dress, so it was foolish even to think about it.

But the money was on the table. It was hers if she wanted it. All she had to do was pick it up. Her acceptance didn't commit her to anything except going to a party.

She practically had to grip her hands together to keep from picking the coin up.

"I really can't," she said, turning away resolutely.

"I'm not trying to seduce you."

"I know that."

"Then why do you hesitate? Do you dislike me so much?"

She turned back to face him. "I don't dislike you."

"Okay, so you're just afraid I'm going to do something to hurt your father. In that case, the best thing you could do would be to help me. The sooner I find Vivian, the sooner I'll leave Galveston."

There went those strange feelings again. She didn't want him to leave. She especially didn't want him to leave with Vivian. She couldn't account for her certainty that Vivian was unworthy of Holt — she didn't even know the woman. But surely if Vivian had loved him, she would have at least tried to let him know where she had gone.

Felicity told herself to stop. She had no business imagining anything about Vivian Calvert. She would have hated it if someone had done that to her.

"Okay," she said, "I'll go. I'll buy only one dress and bring back the change."

"I won't take it."

"Then I won't go."

"All right. Have it your way. The party starts at eight-thirty."

Felicity nodded, but she wasn't really thinking about the time to arrive at the party. She was thinking that for the first time in years she could buy a truly pretty dress. For once, she was going to look beautiful like her mother looked in the painting that hung in the parlor.

Felicity looked at herself in the mirror and smiled at her reflection. She'd never thought of herself as more than passably attractive, but in this bottle-green satin gown with dazzlingly white lace at the throat and sleeves, she looked elegant. It helped that she'd piled her nearly black hair atop her head, with a curl dangling over each ear. An emerald and diamond necklace flashed at her throat in concert with earrings of matching stones, gifts from her father to her mother that had cost him the profits from an entire cotton crop. An ivory comb held her hair in place.

"How do I look?" she asked Mrs. Bennett, who on hearing that Felicity was going to a party had insisted upon fixing her hair.

"Like a princess. You've always been pretty, but that dress and those jewels transform you. I've never seen anything like them."

"My father gave the jewels to my mother on their wedding day. He would never let me sell them."

"I don't blame him. They're breathtaking. You'll be the belle of the ball."

Felicity was filled with anticipation. Though she still dreaded actually walking through the door at Charlotte's party, she was looking forward to seeing the surprised looks on everyone's face.

"I can't wait to see how Holt reacts," Mrs. Bennett said.

"He disapproves of me."

"Men forget things like that when they come face to face with a beautiful woman."

"I'm not beautiful."

"Let's ask your father."

Felicity knew as soon as she entered the parlor that her father had been drinking. She stifled a pang of guilt that she wouldn't be home to watch him, but she wouldn't be gone long. She'd see he went to bed early.

"What do you think of your daughter, Dr. Moore?" Mrs. Bennett asked.

Her father had been staring at her mother's portrait when they entered, but he turned at the sound of Mrs. Bennett's voice. When his gaze landed on Felicity, he went white.

"Are you all right, Papa?" she asked.

His gaze shifted to the picture of his wife and then back to his daughter. "You look so much like your mother, I could almost imagine she'd stepped down from that picture."

"I'll take off the necklace. I didn't mean to upset you."

"No. She wanted you to wear it. That's why I wouldn't let you sell it even when we were short of money."

Felicity hadn't worn the jewels until tonight. She hadn't had a reason.

"Her mother was wearing a gown like that when I met her," her father told Mrs. Bennett.

Felicity supposed that without realizing it, she'd looked for a gown that reminded her of her mother. She had been so beautiful, and Felicity wanted to look as pretty as possible.

"I remember that evening as if it were yesterday," her father said.

"I should never have chosen this dress," Felicity whispered to Mrs. Bennett.

"Nonsense. It looks beautiful on you."

"But look what it's done to Papa." He was talking to the picture now, as if her mother could hear him. "I can't leave him by himself."

"Will he drink?" Mrs. Bennett asked.

Felicity didn't want to admit that anyone knew of her father's weakness, but it was useless to deny it to Mrs. Bennett. "He does when he gets like this."

"Then I'll stay with him."

"I couldn't ask you to do that."

"You're not asking. I'm offering. I'm glad you're finally willing to let me be neighborly. I've been watching you for a long time. You work too hard. A woman needs some joy in her life, even if it's just little things like a walk on the beach. Besides, it would be a crime for you not to go out when you look so beautiful."

"That's not important."

"Why don't you ask Holt?" Mrs. Bennett suggested as her boarder entered the room.

"Don't you think Felicity looks just like her mother?" her father asked, gesturing to the picture.

Holt didn't respond immediately. He looked as if he didn't know what to say.

"The doctor asked you a question," Mrs. Bennett said, smiling and winking at Felicity.

Holt seemed to snap out of his trance. He looked from Felicity to the picture and back. "She looks a great deal like her mother," he agreed. "Mrs. Moore was a very beautiful woman."

"Don't you think her daughter is beautiful, too?"

"Don't put words in his mouth," Felicity said to Mrs. Bennett. "He can't be honest without being rude."

"I think you —"

"My self-esteem isn't so low it needs false assurances," Felicity said.

"What if they're not false?" Holt asked.

"If you don't make them, I won't have to ask that question. I know I promised to go with you tonight, but —"

Mrs. Bennett slipped her hand into Felicity's and squeezed. "I told you I'd stay with him," she whispered. "I'd like it better than sitting at home by myself."

"Are you sharing secrets?" Dr. Moore asked.

"Yes," Mrs. Bennett said, "and don't ask what they are, because we won't tell you."

"That's unfair," Holt said.

"That's because you can't be trusted," Mrs. Bennett retorted. "Now take Felicity off to your party and don't you dare show your faces back here before midnight."

"You take good care of her," her father said to Holt. "She's all I've got."

"Don't be ridiculous, Papa. I'm a grown woman. I can take care of myself."

"No lady can take care of herself," her father declared. "That's a man's job."

"I promise to look after her like she was my own," Holt said.

Felicity knew he was only saying that to please her father, but it caused an uncomfortable reaction somewhere in the region of her belly. She really had to stop reacting to everything Holt said as though it meant something special to her. But after what he'd said a few days ago, she couldn't help it. She couldn't stop wondering if she affected him like he said she would affect other men. She couldn't be sure, but she thought his body had become aroused. If so, all kinds of possibilities were there to be explored. But she didn't want to make any assumptions. The letdown would be too painful.

"If Papa gets too melancholy," Felicity said to Mrs. Bennett, "ask him to take you for a walk. That always makes him feel better."

"I'll do that. Now, don't worry. I'll take good care of him."

Felicity guessed she hadn't really believed she was going to a party with Holt until that very moment. She must have thought — or feared — that something would come along to make it impossible. When she looked up and saw Holt dressed in evening clothes and realized he was only waiting for her to put on her wrap, the full realization hit her.

She was going to a party escorted by Holt Price. Though she knew it was only a business arrangement, the rest of the world would think it was something quite different.

She wished it were something quite different.

That was an unwelcome thought, but she couldn't banish it. She told herself not to be foolish, that while Holt might believe she was beautiful and desirable, he didn't desire her. She'd been telling herself that for days, to no avail. Holt had been the one to say she was beautiful and desirable. He'd been the man who held her and brushed away her tears. He'd been the man who said she deserved love, who promised to force her out of her prison. Surely he couldn't feel all that and be indifferent to her.

She kept reminding herself that he loved Vivian, that he understood her because he'd been in the same situation, but she couldn't banish hope from her heart. Seeing him dressed up didn't help. He looked handsome and extremely elegant in a black suit with a stiff white shirt, black satin waistcoat, and white bow tie, every bit the Southern gentleman dressed for a night on the town on a cool spring evening. She remembered some handsome beaux before the war, but none could compare to Holt.

"Are you ready to go?" Holt asked.

"As ready as she'll ever be," Mrs. Bennett said, draping a capelike jacket over Felicity's shoulders. "Make sure she doesn't get a chill."

"You can depend on it," Holt said.

Felicity didn't dare let herself imagine what Holt meant by that. Considering her present frame of mind, it would be extremely dangerous. And foolish.

When she stepped out on the porch, she saw a waiting buggy. No, it was a carriage. A *closed* carriage, the kind important people used. She felt rather foolish that it took her a moment to realize it was meant for her. She was wearing a king's ransom in jewels but she'd assumed that Holt would expect her to walk through the streets in the dark.

"It was very nice of you to hire a carriage."

"Charlottesville is a small town, but ladies never traveled to a party on foot unless it was next door."

Felicity allowed Holt to walk her to the street and help her into the carriage. He climbed in behind her, and the carriage started forward.

"Now tell me what this is going to be like," Holt said. "I'm so nervous I feel like six vaqueros are doing a fandango in the pit of my stomach."

Felicity decided Holt couldn't have a nerve in his body. He swore he didn't know a person in the room except Charlotte, but you'd have thought he'd grown up with every one of them. The fandango dancers had moved to her stomach. She'd come to the party hoping to be accepted into her former circle. Instead, the sidelong glances from several women convinced her she'd made a mistake. She felt like an interloper, a fraud in a borrowed dress. She was Cinderella at the ball. At midnight she would turn back into a poor doctor's daughter.

"Relax," Holt said. "Every man in the room is anxious to meet you."

"You mean they're wondering where you found me."

"Stop looking so formidable. You'll scare them away."

So much for the ability of a man to understand women.

"I don't know what you're so anxious about," he continued. "Everybody likes you. I heard Charlotte telling one of the men she intended to invite you to her next party, too."

"I won't go."

"You might feel differently after tonight."

She'd been born the daughter of a well-to-do planter who had been on a first-name basis with two English lords when he was in Scotland, but she was an outsider in this gathering. Everybody here was young and vigorous, driven by a ferocious desire to succeed, to acquire the trappings of wealth. These people were determined to recover everything they'd lost because of the war, or to capitalize on any advantages the aftermath of the war might throw their way.

Felicity's one overwhelming desire was simply to be loved.

"Have you met anyone who knows anything about Vivian?" Felicity asked.

"No one knows a Calvert family."

"Maybe she's not in Galveston. She could be in a dozen other places."

"Almost anything is possible, but the Vivian I knew would starve without people, excitement, glamour. She might have to settle temporarily for a small town, even a ranch, but she wouldn't stay there."

"What do you two have in common? When you start talking about medical ethics, you sound like the first Christian martyr."

She shouldn't have said that. He wasn't that bad.

"Vivian was a child whose values were formed by adversity. Once she feels safe, once she knows she's loved for herself, not just her physical beauty, she will become a different person. She'll see that all these trappings of wealth and social success are just that — trappings."

Felicity had never seen Vivian — she was gradually coming to the point that she hoped she never would — but she was certain that any woman who'd grown up valuing money and social position above all else wouldn't chuck those trappings overboard for some hopelessly romantic Vermont doctor. She was much more likely to laugh in his face.

But Felicity wasn't about to say that. Holt believed in Vivian so deeply, it would hurt him tremendously to learn he'd been wrong. She didn't say it because that was how she would want some man to believe in her. For her, the love of a good man *would* be all the security she needed.

"She was open and genuine," Holt said. "She didn't hide anything from me, not even the things she probably should have. There's a lot of good in her if it just had a chance to come out."

Outside of the fact that she would sound like a jealous shrew if she continued to question Vivian's character, Felicity didn't want to jeopardize her position with Holt. His belief in her was extremely important. It helped her face the possibility that her father really was an alcoholic. It also let her hope she wouldn't face that harsh truth alone. Having Holt at her side had become important to her.

"I hope you find her," Felicity said, "for her sake as much as yours."

"Smile. Here comes our hostess."

Charlotte brought with her a woman who was the most expensively dressed, if not the most elegant, person in the room. An attractive man followed in their wake.

"I want to introduce Gloria Webster," Charlotte said to Felicity. "She's just moved to Galveston from New Orleans. Her husband is in shipping."

The man was introduced as Gloria's brother, Beau Stregghorn. He winked at Felicity. She didn't know how to respond, so she simply returned her gaze to her hostess.

"We've just bought a house on Broadway," Gloria said. "We're having an open house next week. I do hope you'll be able to come."

"You, too," Beau said to Felicity.

"Thank you very much," Holt said, showing absolutely no reaction to Felicity's startled look.

"Next Tuesday," Gloria said, "starting at six."

"And it doesn't stop until everybody gets too tired to stay up any longer," her brother said.

"That's usually around ten o'clock in Galveston," Charlotte said.

"In New Orleans, a really good party lasts all night," Beau said.

Felicity couldn't imagine any party being good enough for her to want to stay up all night.

"Gloria's husband and brother plan to help change Galveston from a sleepy village into a truly sophisticated town," Charlotte said. "Isn't that exciting?"

Felicity didn't care what they did as long as they stayed off the streets when they were drunk. She dreaded the thought of more accidents like the one that had befallen Durwin.

"Will it be a large party?" Holt asked Gloria.

"We're inviting everybody who has even the smallest amount of influence," Gloria said. "My husband says Galveston can become the richest and most important city in Texas if all the people with means and intelligence work together."

"He thinks New Orleans is the natural market for Texas beef," Beau added. "He plans to develop a regular fleet of ships to carry cattle to New Orleans, maybe even Mobile."

"Have you met a lot of people since you've been here?" Holt asked.

"Hundreds," Gloria said. "I can't remember them all."

"Do you know anyone named Vivian Calvert?"

163

"No, but Beau is the one you ought to ask about women."

"I don't know anybody by that name," Beau said.

"What about Vivian Stone?"

"Stone is my mother's maiden name. I'd have been sure to remember it."

"Do you know anyone named Vivian?" Felicity asked. And immediately wondered why she'd asked that question.

"Wait a minute," Gloria said, appearing to think very hard. She turned to her brother. "Didn't we meet a woman with very blond hair by that name?"

Chapter Ten

"Vivian has blond hair," Holt said. "And enormous green eyes."

"I don't know if she's the same woman," Gloria said.

"I'll ask around," Beau said. "If she's pretty, someone will know her."

"She was a beauty."

"Then I'll definitely ask about her," Beau said, his grin one that Felicity wouldn't have hesitated to describe as a leer.

"What brings you to Galveston?" Gloria asked Holt.

"He's a doctor," Felicity said. She didn't know why she was fearful that Holt would say his only reason for being in Galveston was to find Vivian.

"Our brother is a doctor," Gloria said. "He's working in Baton Rouge. He wants to move to New Orleans, but I told him to come to Galveston instead. What do you think?"

Beau rolled his eyes and grimaced at Felicity. "Once my sister starts talking business, you can't stop her. Why don't you let me get you something to drink?"

"Yes, do," Charlotte urged. "Beau can introduce you around." She winked at Felicity. "Several men have been asking about you."

Felicity didn't want to leave Holt. He represented safety, but Charlotte hooked her arm in Felicity's and literally pulled her away from Holt.

"How long have you lived in Galveston?" Beau asked.

"My father and I moved here in 1855, but he volunteered for the Confederate Army. We didn't get back until the end of the war."

"Felicity's father is a wonderful doctor who often forgets to charge for his services," Charlotte said.

"Which must make it hard on his daughter," Beau said.

"Papa's patients are very conscientious. When they can't pay with money, they give us what they do have."

"My brother has to put up with the same thing," Beau said. "He can't get it through his patients' heads that it's much easier to buy what he needs with money rather than be given a basket of eggs or a squealing pig."

"That's all some of them have," Felicity said.

"Then let them sell it and bring him the money. Commerce will never fully develop as long as people still barter for what they want." Beau took two glasses from a tray borne by a servant and handed one to Felicity. "Let's forget patients and talk about you," he said, steering her toward doors that opened onto a garden. "How come a beautiful woman like you isn't besieged by suitors?"

"I'm usually in my father's consulting room," Felicity said. She looked for Charlotte, but her hostess had deserted her.

"You're too beautiful to be hidden away. Let's drink to a future full of brilliant parties and impatient suitors."

"I don't want a future like that."

"You're being modest."

"No, I'm not."

"Then drink to my future," Beau said. "May it be filled with beautiful women like you and perfect wine like this."

He raised his glass in a toast, then drank. Felicity couldn't refuse the toast, so she took a swallow of her wine.

"Tell me about yourself," Beau said. His hand on her elbow, he guided her through the open doors into an extensive garden still in the early stages of development. The night air was cool, the gulf breeze laden with the smell of salt. It felt good on her skin. The air inside the house had become overheated with the press of bodies.

"There's not much to tell," Felicity said. "I keep house for my father and help him with his medical practice."

"I should think such duties would offend the tender sensibilities of a genteel lady such as yourself."

"Even genteel ladies are called upon to nurse the sick and wounded."

"If you were my wife, I'd shower you with

beautiful clothes and surround you with servants."

"Well, I'm not, so that doesn't come into it."

Beau exchanged her elbow for her hand. "But it should," he said. "Beauty such as yours should be cosseted."

Felicity tried to withdraw her hand, but he raised it to his lips and kissed it.

"If you saw me coming out of my father's consulting room, or after I'd finished mopping the floors, you wouldn't think I was beautiful."

"That's all the more reason why you should be released from your bondage." Beau gripped her fingers and pressed them against his chest. "Beauty should be nurtured, enhanced, displayed for all the world to see before age steals it away."

Felicity didn't mind being thought beautiful. It was very pleasant after feeling drab for so long. But she wasn't foolish enough to think herself a great beauty like her mother, or to think Beau was doing anything more than filling a pleasant evening with a little flirting. But she didn't like flirting. She also didn't like the fact that Beau seemed to think that having been allowed to possess her hand unchallenged, he could now become familiar with more of her body.

"We ought to go back inside," she said, attempting to pull her hand from his grip.

"Not yet. The night is wonderfully cool and pleasant. Besides, I don't want to share you."

"I didn't see anyone competing for me."

"Now that I've rid you of that doctor, they'll close in like hounds after a fox."

"Then I'd better find my doctor."

"Don't go. He doesn't appreciate you as I do."

Beau placed his hand in the small of her back, preventing her from moving away.

"He appreciates me enough," she said, struggling to get away.

"Then you don't know what it means to be appreciated by a man who knows how to make a woman feel valued," Beau said.

He pulled her closer. Felicity pulled back, but her strength wasn't the equal of Beau's.

"What a good idea to come out here," Holt said. "It's hot inside."

Felicity was so relieved to hear Holt's voice, she could have kissed him.

"That's one of the advantages of living practically on the shore," Beau said. He released her gradually, his body stiff, his expression one of concealed anger. "Even in the summertime, there's nearly always a cooling breeze."

"Is there a breeze in New Orleans?" Holt asked.

"No. We're too far upriver."

Felicity had managed to maneuver until Holt stood between her and Beau.

"If this were Virginia, I'd probably say your sister was asking for you," Holt said, "but it goes against my Vermont conscience."

"What are you getting at?" Beau asked.

"Besides, I find that in Texas they don't much care about etiquette."

"I suppose there's a meaning somewhere in that jumble of words."

"You could say that. If you lay a hand on Felicity again, I'll break it for you. But you're in luck. I'm a doctor, so I could set it, too. If you kiss her against her will, I'm liable to shoot you. But a doctor can't always fix a gunshot wound, so I'm not sure how much use I'd be to you with that."

Beau's reaction suggested he wasn't used to such plain speaking. "I expect my sister *is* wondering what has become of me," he said. "She doesn't like to be left alone when she doesn't know everyone."

He threw Felicity an angry glance, then left.

"Thanks for coming after me," she said to Holt.

"What did you mean by leaving the party with him?" Holt said.

The suppressed anger in his voice stunned her. She hadn't expected him even to be aware she had gone.

"I didn't *leave the party*. Charlotte practically threw me into his arms. I couldn't get away without causing a disturbance."

"You don't have to go anywhere you don't want to go. And if anybody tries to force you, you can kick up a fuss."

She didn't know how they brought up young

women in Vermont, but she doubted it was very different from the rest of the country. Nowhere was *kicking up a fuss* considered an admirable attribute in a young lady.

"I'd never be invited to a party like this again."

"Which is another reason not to run off with strange men."

"I didn't *run off.*"

"You didn't stay with me."

"I didn't think you cared. It took you long enough to notice I'd gone."

"I never thought you'd leave."

"Why? Because it's so fascinating to listen to you asking everybody about Vivian?"

"I have to find her."

"Well, I don't."

"You agreed to help me."

"I agreed to keep you company."

"I expected you to stay close. I can't be chasing men away all night."

She couldn't believe he was scolding her like a younger sister. She was an adult. She could go where she pleased, do what she wanted. She started to go inside. "I want to go home."

"We can't leave yet. I haven't found anyone who knows Vivian."

"You found Gloria."

"What if the woman she remembers isn't Vivian?"

"Then you can keep asking."

She wanted to go home. She needed time to

171

think about Holt being angry with her. It had been unexpected. It had been unfair. But it had also been intriguing.

She hadn't known he cared enough to worry about her. Had he missed her on his own, or had Gloria pointed out her absence? Had he wanted to find her, or was it just what was expected of him? Was he angry because she'd inconvenienced him, or was he really upset that she had been in danger? No one had ever threatened to shoot anyone because of her. Maybe that was what cowboys did. She couldn't be sure. Holt was the only one she knew.

Somehow the answers to all these questions had to fit together, but she couldn't make sense of them with Holt scowling at her. Even as she tried to sustain her anger, she felt it melting away. He had come after her, and he had threatened Beau with physical harm if he touched her again.

She liked that. She'd spent all her life looking after her parents, worrying about them, trying to make certain no harm came to them. She'd had no idea how nice it was to have someone take care of her. Even if it was just for a few hours at a party, it was just nice to know that somebody was making sure she was safe.

"I didn't mean to get caught alone with a man who thinks he's so marvelous no woman can resist him," she said. "Thank you for being concerned about me."

172

His anger vanished.

"You had me worried. It probably comes from spending so many years surrounded by a hostile army or rustlers and bandits, but I started to imagine all sorts of things."

"Like what?"

"Like you'd been abducted by pirates and smuggled out to sea where you'd be sold to a desert Arab chieftain."

"That's impossible. There aren't any . . ." She stopped in mid-sentence. He was making a joke, but this was too important for jokes. "I need to find Charlotte and say goodbye," she said. "I want to leave before I'm exposed to any more pirates."

He put out a hand to stop her. "I shouldn't have made a joke, but I was worried."

"Sorry to snap. I'm still upset about Beau. I suppose a more sophisticated woman would have known how to handle him."

"I like innocence better than sophistication."

Then why was he in love with Vivian? she wondered. From what he'd said, she would be the epitome of a sophisticated woman.

"Well, I don't like being innocent. It makes me feel like a fool," she said.

Later, when she lay awake at home, unable to sleep, Felicity accepted that she'd been disappointed in the party. Somehow she'd expected to be welcomed home to familiar territory, but despite Charlotte's friendship, the women had held back. She'd felt as if she were among strangers. In six years, people had changed. Where were the men she knew before the war, the gallant men like Holt who would protect a woman? How would she ever find love if they were all like Beau Stregghorn? Women kept their distance. Men considered her prey.

Whether she wanted to admit it or not, Holt had awakened a sleeping desire within her — or released it from bondage. She couldn't turn back now. She couldn't get rid of the feeling this was her last chance to find love. She felt guilty about leaving her father, but she also resented his hold on her time. She wanted her own life. If Holt could strike out on his own, why couldn't she?

She needed love. She had to find it.

She refused to think of herself as an old maid. She was still reasonably young. Holt said she was pretty. Her father said she'd make a perfect wife. She only had to wait. The right man would come along. Maybe at Gloria's party. Her mother had promised.

"I want to see the new doctor," the woman said.

"He's only going to be here for a short time," Felicity said. "Wouldn't you rather talk to a doctor you can continue to see?"

"Mrs. Prentiss said I was to ask for the new one. She said he was the best doctor in Galveston."

"He's certainly very good, but —"

"Has he gone away?"

"No, but —"

"Then I want to see him."

Felicity gave in. "I'll check to see if he has time to see you this morning."

"If he can't, I can come back this afternoon."

"Perhaps that would be best."

It was all she could do to keep a smile on her face and her voice calm and pleasant. This was the third person today who'd asked to see Holt rather than her father. She couldn't be angry at Mrs. Prentiss for telling everyone about Holt, but she still couldn't keep from worrying what this would do to her father.

She found Holt reading one of her father's medical books when she entered the consulting room.

"Where's my father?"

"Lying down."

"Has he . . ." She didn't finish the sentence.

"I think so. He didn't object when I suggested he might want to take a nap."

"He doesn't sleep well."

"I know."

"He never has gotten over Mother's death."

"I know."

"If he just hadn't been sent to Andersonville."

"There's nothing you can do about that now."

She wanted to lash out at him, at his complacency, and his never-ending competency, his patience, his unbending standards, but she didn't because she knew that in his own way he was protecting her father just as she was.

"There's another patient who wants to see you this afternoon."

"Good, your father will be down by then."

"She says Mrs. Prentiss told her you were the best doctor in Galveston. She won't see anyone else."

He viewed her with a look that showed so much understanding she got mad all over again.

"Mrs. Prentiss doesn't know anything about my qualifications as a doctor. She's only recommending me because I knew her son."

"I know that, and you know that, but this woman doesn't."

"What's wrong with her?"

"She didn't say."

"Probably some long-standing ailment no one has been able to cure, so she's coming to me in hopes I can do something no one else has. I'll ask your father to look at her with me. Don't let him leave after lunch."

That was another reason she couldn't get angry at him. He didn't blink at the thought of surgery, but when it came to the diagnosis of ordinary medical problems, he lacked her father's knowledge and experience and didn't hesitate to admit it.

"Start talking medicine, and he'll stay here without my having to say a word," she said.

That was something else that annoyed her. He had more influence over her father than she did.

Only it didn't stop the drinking. Nothing stopped that.

"There's a lot I can learn from him," Holt said. "He's generous in sharing his knowledge and experience."

He was generous with everybody except his daughter. She was expected to keep his house, cook his meals, help with his patients, and make excuses for him when he couldn't work. She'd always done those things, and she knew he was thankful.

Only he didn't tell her. He'd never told her. She'd gradually slipped into that role during the last years of her mother's illness. By the time he recovered from the shock of his wife's death, he'd accepted his daughter's role in his life as the way it should be. He depended on her, needed her, so he took it for granted that she would always be there even as he fussed at her about having her own family.

Felicity felt trapped, helpless, and unappreciated, and that made her angry. It was nearly impossible not to be mad at Holt, because he had butted into their lives without so much as a by your leave. But her anger disguised a feeling that had been developing below the surface, out of sight, beyond the edges of her awareness.

She liked Holt. A lot.

"Despite Mrs. Prentiss's enthusiastic recommendations, not all of our patients will want to see you. You're still a stranger."

"Maybe you can convince one of the patients who will see me to swear I don't bite."

She smiled. She liked that he could find humor in difficult or frustrating situations. "It's hard for women to go to a doctor. You're all men. You don't understand a woman's body or how she feels about it. Besides, you're young and attractive. That makes it even worse."

"Do you find me attractive?"

"Don't ask foolish questions." She wasn't about to tell him how she really felt about him. Her feelings would shock him.

"I don't see that it makes any difference how old I am or what I look like. The only question should be whether I'm a good doctor."

"Wouldn't it make a difference to you whether you saw a man or a woman?"

"No."

"I can't understand that. I can only assume you're not interested in women."

His reaction was immediate.

"That's not true, and I can prove it."

Chapter Eleven

Holt hadn't meant to say that. It just came out on its own. It actually amused him that Felicity might believe he didn't like women. Apparently she didn't understand that when it came to working with patients, it was best if the doctor could forget whether the patient was male or female, old or young, attractive or not, charming or abrasive.

"Proving my interest in women would be a lot more interesting than this medical book."

Felicity recoiled. "I didn't mean that the way it sounded. I can presume your interest from your pursuit of Vivian."

"You asked about my interest in *women*. That means I have to prove I'm interested in more than one woman."

"No, you don't."

She looked unsure of what he intended to do. He didn't know either. He laid the book aside.

"How are you going to prove anything? There's no woman here."

"You're a woman, and you're here."

"But you're not interested in me."

He stood. "I'm very interested in you."

She backed away a step. "Only because you think I'm allowing my father to drink and endanger his patients."

179

"This particular interest has nothing to do with that."

"What interest?"

"I'd rather show you than talk about it."

"I'd rather you talked about it."

She looked ready to run out of the room. "Are you afraid of me?"

"No."

"Then why are you backing away?"

"I didn't realize I was."

He stepped forward, and she immediately retreated a step. "See, you did it again."

"It's habit. I'm not used to being alone in a room with a strange man."

"You've known me for two weeks. Your father's patients have an excuse to think of me as a stranger. You don't."

"I'm still not comfortable being in a room alone with you."

"Why?"

How do you tell a man you like him and are attracted to him at the same time as you're angry about what he's doing despite the fact you respect him for standing up for his principles? He'd think she was crazy. Sometimes *she* wondered if she wasn't a little bit crackbrained.

"Are you afraid of men?" he asked.

"No."

"And you do like them."

"Of course I like them. What kind of question is that?"

"The kind you asked me."

"I didn't mean it that way. It's just that you seem so obsessed with Vivian, you don't see other women as women. I mean, not the same way you see Vivian."

He smiled and came a step closer. She held her ground.

"Believe me, I'm able to make the connection."

"I'm glad," she said, wringing her hands nervously. "I was worried."

"In what way?"

He came closer. She desperately wanted to retreat, but she held her ground even though her heart seemed to be beating too fast for her to take a deep breath. "I was afraid you might never find Vivian. Or that if you did, she would be married, or wouldn't love you, or you wouldn't . . ."

She let the sentence die away. He was looking at her in a way that made her temperature rise so quickly she expected perspiration to pop out on her forehead.

"If you couldn't see other women as women, you wouldn't have anybody. I mean, you wouldn't fall in love and get married."

"Why would I need to get married?"

"Every man wants to get married," she said, searching blindly for responses because her brain wasn't working as well as it should. He was too close, and his expression was akin to that of a cat about to pounce on a particularly tasty morsel. If she hadn't known he was obsessed with Vivian, she'd have sworn he was about to pull her into an embrace.

"Some men prefer a mistress," he said. "That way they're not tied to one person for the rest of their lives."

"But what about children?"

"They prefer to devote their lives to pleasure rather than providing for progeny."

"Is that how you feel?"

"I don't know about progeny, but I'm all for pleasure."

"One shouldn't indulge in pleasure without responsibility," she said. Her feet had carried her backward, bringing her up against the wall, her escape cut off by a chair and a table.

"Why not?"

"It's not right." That sounded like the kind of answer a person gave when she knew she was wrong and couldn't think of a reason to support her position.

"What's not right about it? If it involves just two people, whom are they hurting?"

"Nothing can ever involve just two people. Unless it was Adam and Eve. And even they had God and the snake to worry about."

She knew she was sounding like an idiot.

"I guess the two people would have to decide whose needs are more important, their own or those of the people around them," he said.

"They'd be very selfish not to consider other people."

"Satisfying one's needs doesn't mean one

can't satisfy the needs of another person at the same time." He was practically touching her now.

"I think trying to keep everybody's needs straight would be too complicated."

"A very good point. Let's forget everybody else's needs and think only about our own."

"Our own!" Her voice ended in a squeak.

"You need proof I'm interested in women other than Vivian."

"I believe you."

"But I won't be happy until I've banished every doubt."

He reached out and took hold of her hands. She gripped them together to stop their nervous movement.

"Why are you frightened?" he asked.

"I'm not."

"Nervous, then?"

"I don't know what you're going to do."

"Does my holding your hands make you nervous?"

"No." It really didn't. Anybody could hold a person's hand. People did it all the time. He'd pried them apart and now held each of her hands in one of his. It should have been a simple act, a harmless act, even a practically meaningless act, but it wasn't. She felt that something momentous was about to happen. Maybe it already had.

"You ought to be used to men wanting to hold your hand or put their arms around your waist. You're a very attractive woman. Beau Stregghorn saw that right away."

"I don't know any men like Beau Stregghorn."

He placed her hands on his chest, forcing her to come closer to him. The energy pouring out of him rushed through her body, sapping her strength, making it nearly impossible for her muscles to function. When her father was in Scotland, a medical student from South America had told him about catching hold of an electric eel and feeling as if his body was jolted with so much energy, he couldn't control his muscles. That was how she felt now.

"Maybe you ought to meet some new men."

"I'm content with my life as it is."

His smile was almost sly, as if he'd caught her at last with no possible means of escape. "Maybe your mind is content, but your body isn't."

"What makes you say that?"

"You're trembling again."

He'd released his grip on her fingers and was running his hands up her arms toward her elbows. The nerve endings in her skin telegraphed his progress to her brain at a screaming pitch. Not even Beau had caressed her like this.

"I'm just not used to what you're doing."

"What am I doing?"

Driving me crazy, she wanted to shout. She wanted to break contact and run from the room, but something even more powerful prevented her from moving out of Holt's reach.

"I'm just touching you," Holt said.

Now his hands were on her upper arms. Because it was a warm spring day, her arms weren't covered by sleeves. Holt's touch was light, barely skimming the surface of her skin, but her upper arms were even more sensitive than her forearms. The sensations had become so intense, she could hardly remain still. She wondered where he would stop.

She wondered *if* he would stop.

"I've never let a man touch me like this."

"Do you want me to stop?"

She wanted to shout *yes,* but her throat muscles choked the word off before it was born. Unable to speak, she shook her head.

"Has anybody ever kissed you?"

She didn't know why he thought he could ask such a question. She refused to answer.

"The men in Galveston can't be typical Southerners. They'd gobble up a woman like you on first sight."

"I wouldn't like that."

"Then they'd keep persuading you until you did."

His hands had moved to her shoulders, but they weren't still. They roamed about, massaging here, rubbing there, caressing someplace else. It was hard to listen to what he was saying, especially when he began to massage the muscles in her shoulders.

"You're tense," he said.

"I'm worried about my father." She was more worried about Holt.

"You can stop worrying. I'm here to help you."

But it didn't feel as if either of them were talking about her father. Holt's hands moved to her neck. His thumbs slid along her jaw, gently massaging away the tension. His touch was positively hypnotic. With a little encouragement, she could melt right into the floor.

"You've got to learn to relax more," Holt said. "It's not good for you to be so tense."

"I am relaxed."

That was partly true. One part of her felt so relaxed, she couldn't move. The other part felt so tense, she couldn't move.

Holt started massaging the muscles at the back of her neck. It took about ten seconds for Felicity to realize she could fall in love with a man who'd massage her neck. She hadn't experienced anything so wonderful in her whole life. She hoped he wouldn't stop.

"You worry too much," Holt said.

She didn't have anybody to worry for her. It would be nice to have Holt around to help take care of things. She didn't always agree with him, but he was the kind of man you could depend on. He was certainly attractive enough to hold her attention. He was big enough to defend her honor. He was also kind and thoughtful. That was important.

Of course, he didn't think she was qualified to take care of patients, he was inflexible about her father, and he was in love with Vivian. Still, he'd already begun to show more respect for her abilities, and he was helping her with her father, treating him with kindness. He seemed to understand her better than anyone else ever had. No one else cared enough about her to force her out of her rut.

She felt something warm and soft brush her lips. Until her eyes flew open, she hadn't realized she'd allowed them to gradually close. Holt's face was only inches from hers, his eyes wide, trying to read her reaction to his kiss.

That must have been what she'd felt. She'd never been kissed on the lips, but what else could it have been? She wondered if he'd do it again. She hadn't been paying attention the first time. It might never happen again. She wanted to be able to remember what it felt like.

Apparently able to read her thoughts, Holt kissed her again.

His lips were incredibly soft. She didn't know that anything about a man could be that soft. It was like the touch of a gentle breeze on a warm summer night, like when she went down to the beach and turned her face into the gentle wind coming off the Gulf of Mexico.

But his lips lingered, moving back and forth over her mouth, planting tiny kisses along the way. She couldn't move. She didn't breathe. She waited in a state of suspended animation, anticipating something more but not knowing what it might be.

"Now do you believe I like women?" Holt asked. His voice was soft, almost a whisper.

She couldn't answer.

"Do you need more convincing?"

Again she was unable to answer. She continued to look at him smiling down at her, trying to put what had happened to her into the frame of what she called her life. So far it didn't fit. There was no way to explain this experience, no way to catalog how it made her feel. Just now he cradled her head in his hands, turned her face up so that she looked him full in the face. She'd never realized his eyes were so black. They were like onyx, opaque and fathomless. Yet they glistened, drew her into their unseen depths.

"Maybe I've been too tentative," Holt said.

She felt Holt's hands on her face as he leaned down and his lips covered her mouth in a kiss that was as unmistakable as it was riveting. There was no brushing, no gentle wandering, no tiny scattered kisses. This time she responded. She moved into his kiss, gave back the pressure, moved into him until her breasts came into contact with his chest.

She kissed him back.

Shocked down to her toes, certain she'd be so mortified she'd run from the room, she was even more stunned to realize she was kissing him *even more passionately than he was kissing her.* She was out of control, acting so unlike herself she wouldn't have believed what was happening if she hadn't been the one it was happening to.

She couldn't describe the sensations that flooded her body. Her life had been so uneventful, her behavior so circumscribed, her contact with interested suitors so infrequent, she wasn't prepared to have so many feelings and emotions jostling each other at the same time. It was just like —

The sound of a doorknob turning and a door opening caused her to spring away from Holt.

"I'm looking for the doctor," a man said. "Nobody answered when I knocked on the door."

"I'm the doctor," Holt said. "Is it time for your appointment?"

"Yes. I'm Jimmy Powell. I wanted to see you about . . ." He looked at Felicity.

"Miss Moore often assists me or her father."

"Can't I see you alone?" the young man asked.

"Certainly." Holt turned to Felicity, his expression calm despite the extra brightness in his eyes. "We'll finish our discussion later," he said.

"Of course," Felicity said, leaving the room as quickly as possible. She was certain Jimmy Powell knew exactly what had been happening when he opened that door. Whatever had possessed her to let Holt kiss her?

What could have possessed *her* to kiss *him?*

Holt must think her a desperate old maid who would throw herself at any man who showed her the slightest bit of attention. She practically ran up the stairs, tripping on the hem of her gown in her hurry to reach the safety of her room.

How would she ever explain her outrageous behavior to Holt? She certainly couldn't tell him the truth, that she liked kissing him so much, she didn't want to stop.

Well, what was done was done. And in a way, it was all her fault. She'd asked him if he was interested in women. What did she expect any red-blooded male to do but attempt to prove himself on the spot? She'd asked for what she got. There was only one problem.

She liked what she got. And she wanted more. Soon.

"I really appreciate your coming to this party with me," Holt said to Felicity as the carriage bounced along.

"I don't know why you don't go alone. You seem perfectly at ease with strangers."

After the kisses they'd shared, he'd had a difficult time getting her even to look at him. She didn't attempt to back out of helping him with patients or avoid him at mealtimes or at any other time when their paths would normally cross. But she'd kept their meetings to a minimum and had spoken to him only when necessary. Her coolness had been so obvious, her father had asked Holt if they'd had an argument. Never one to back away from the truth, Holt had explained that he'd kissed her.

Rather than get angry, demand an apology, or order Holt out of his house, Dr. Moore tried to pretend he wasn't smiling. Holt was certain she wouldn't have agreed to go with him tonight if her father hadn't practically pushed her out of the house. He said Mrs. Bennett had offered to sit with him, and he wanted the *young people* out of the house so they wouldn't have anybody looking over their shoulders.

"There aren't many really rich people in Galveston," Felicity said. "You become the friend of one, and you'll soon know everybody."

"You're Charlotte's friend. Why don't you know everybody?"

"We move in entirely different circles."

She'd been telling him that all week. He knew she was doing it to put distance between them — she was still upset that he had kissed her.

He wasn't an experienced lover like his friend Owen, but he could tell when a woman returned his kisses, and Felicity had definitely kissed him back. With passion. He'd speculated more than once on what might have happened if Jimmy Powell hadn't shown up early for his appointment. *Nothing* should have happened; he was in Galveston to look for Vivian.

Yet there was something about Felicity that

refused to let him go. He guessed his confusion came from being an inexperienced lover. If he were as skilled as Owen, he'd be able to catalog the different kinds of attraction. He was definitely attracted to Felicity, but he loved Vivian. Somehow one should cancel out the other, but it didn't.

"How long do you plan to stay at this party?" Felicity asked. "If you don't see Vivian within the first half hour, that probably means she isn't coming."

"Let's see how things go. The people are probably nice, and I'm sure the food will be excellent. Gloria said there'd be dancing."

"I don't want to dance."

But he could tell she was excited. She had bought another new gown. *I can't wear the same dress to two parties in a row,* she'd told him, as though to do so would create a scandal. Mrs. Bennett had told him it was made of ecru buff brilliantine trimmed with slate satin-bound scallops. She looked damned pretty all the time, but she was downright beautiful now. He'd have to stick close to her tonight. There were bound to be lots of men wanting to get to know Felicity a little better. Holt couldn't understand why she kept saying men didn't find her attractive. He'd even dreamed about her.

"Try to enjoy yourself," Holt said as the carriage came to a stop before a handsome house made of red brick and rising three stories above the street. "I'm told the house is spectacular inside."

Holt had grown up with a Vermonter's liking for spare and plain. Even some of the farmhouses he'd seen in Virginia's Shenandoah Valley during the war seemed like mansions to him. But this house outdid anything he'd ever seen.

"Papa used to drive by when they were building this house before the war," Felicity said, standing with Holt to take in the expansive exterior with its wrought-iron porches on two floors. "He used to say it took a lot of cotton to build a place like this."

"Have you ever been inside?"

"Of course not. When people in this part of town get sick, they don't call doctors from our part of town."

"Well, you're a guest tonight, so hold your head high."

Holt had to admit to feeling slightly anxious. It had nothing to do with the size of the house or the sumptuous furnishings of the interior. The moment he entered, his gaze swept expectantly from one end of the room to the other. He craned his neck to see every guest as they entered. But after thirty minutes he gave up on finding Vivian. Either she wasn't coming, or the woman Gloria Webster had met wasn't his Vivian.

"She's not coming," Felicity said. "Let's go."

"Why? You've had a steady stream of men

asking you to dance, offering to bring you food, show you the garden, bring you more champagne than both of us could drink. And you've turned them all down."

"I'm not interested in these men. And they're only interested in me for the moment."

"It's not necessary for everything you do to have lifelong significance. Never pass up a chance to have a little fun, even if it lasts only for a moment."

"I'd have thought a person as serious as you would reject such a philosophy out of hand."

"I can't stop wondering how many young men who died in the war passed up a chance for a few moments of fun because it wasn't dignified, grown-up, or didn't have any serious meaning."

"I don't understand you," Felicity said. "Here you are telling me to enjoy some frivolous moments of fun and in the next breath you're talking about death bed regrets."

"Call it my New England Puritan conscience showing through."

"It sounds more like you're looking back on your life and regretting some of the things you did . . . or didn't do. You've got plenty of time. You're still young."

"Even young people can have regrets for moments lost and never to be retrieved. Now stop arguing. I want to dance."

Felicity allowed herself to be led onto the floor with a suitable show of reluctance. Holt could feel the tension in her body, but he had noticed the way she watched the other dancers, as if it was a pleasure she'd enjoyed in the past but didn't expect to enjoy again. She was stiff when he put his arm around her, but it took only a moment for Holt to realize that Felicity danced much better than he did. "You've been holding out on me," he said.

"All Southern girls learn to dance."

"You must have danced a lot."

"We used to have parties all the time before the war."

"We don't dance much in Vermont. It might get young couples too excited."

"Where did you learn to dance?"

"Vivian taught me. We had lots of parties in Virginia, too."

But dancing with a girl wasn't the same as holding a woman in his arms. He found it impossible to pay attention to his feet when he held Felicity so close. He wondered what she was like before the war, before her father's condition got worse, before they lost their money. Did she smile, laugh, flirt with handsome young men? He was certain they wanted to flirt with her.

"You're easy to dance with," Holt said.

"You, too."

"It's too late to start telling me lies, even little white ones. I know I'm a terrible dancer."

Felicity laughed softly. "You're not an accomplished dancer, but my toes are still uninjured."

"Give me time."

"You can only do so much damage in one dance."

"You're going to dance a whole lot more before the evening is over. There are at least three young men here who'd like to know you better."

But he wasn't ready to yield to those eager young men just yet. He liked dancing with her. She felt good in his arms. She didn't resist being close to him, seemed actually to enjoy being with him. For the last few minutes, she had lowered her defenses. She was treating him as a man she enjoyed dancing with. That was a change he found he liked.

"We ought to do this more often," Holt said.

"Then you'll have to find a way to get invited to more parties."

"We can have our own dance."

"Not unless you have a fortune you haven't told me about. It's expensive to hire an orchestra and buy food. If you don't know the right people, nobody will come."

"You don't have to be . . ." He broke off, his thoughts breaking like a fragile thread.

"I don't have to be what?" Felicity asked.

"That woman who just arrived," Holt said. "It's Vivian."

Chapter Twelve

Holt had anticipated this moment for more than six years. He had imagined how he would feel when he caught his first glimpse of Vivian. He'd pictured what she would look like as a mature woman rather than a seventeen-year-old woman-child. He'd rehearsed a thousand different conversations, replaying them in his mind and rewriting them every time. He envisioned the smile that would light up her face when she saw him, the old familiar sparkle in her eyes when she shared a confidence. He'd tried to foresee every possibility.

And they'd all been wrong. He felt paralyzed, unable to move, unable to speak.

Part of him wanted to rush across the room and tell Vivian how long he'd searched for her, how much he'd missed her.

Another part of him wanted to hold back, to be sure of his ground, wanted to know why she'd disappeared without telling him where she was going, why she'd never attempted to contact him after her husband died.

But another part of him harbored totally unexpected feelings. It urged him to leave before she saw him, to disappear and never again attempt to contact her. It whispered to him that her part of his life was in the past, not to attempt to revive it. He wasn't the same man he'd been when he'd fallen in love with a charming pixie. Even if Vivian had stayed the same, *he* had changed.

Felicity's voice pulled him out of his abstraction. "Aren't you going to speak to her?"

"I don't want to go up to her just yet," he said, trying to recover his feeling of calm. "I'll wait until people aren't crowding around her." He tried to continue dancing, but gave up before he did permanent injury to Felicity's feet.

Still another part of him was surprised that Vivian's beauty wasn't as dazzling as he remembered. She was certainly beautiful. Maturity had enhanced her youthful attractiveness, but somehow it didn't grip him as viscerally as he'd expected. He thought she'd be more striking if she had more color, if she weren't so *blond*. Yet it had been her angelic fairness that he used to feel was the most compelling aspect of her beauty. Why should it have lost its hold on him?

"If you wait much longer, the line will stretch out the door."

It was obvious Vivian had made conquests of most of the men in the room.

"She's very beautiful," Felicity said.

"She always was."

"She enjoys being the center of attention," Felicity said.

"I don't know if she enjoys it so much as she knows it's inevitable," Holt said.

"Did your uncle have any daughters?"

"He had no children at all." His uncle had promised him Price's Nob in the expectation he would marry Vivian. The fact that Vivian had chosen to marry someone else wasn't enough to release him from the responsibility he felt to take care of her.

The crowd around Vivian was deeper than ever, but she was moving in their direction. He wouldn't have to compete to capture her attention. She'd see him, and that would be all that was needed. He could already see the look of surprise in her eyes, could see the smile that would curve her lips until it wreathed her entire face. She would hold out her hands to him the way she always did, expecting him to take them in his own, give them an affectionate squeeze.

"I would guess from all the attention she's getting, she hasn't married again," Felicity said.

In the beginning he'd told himself he hoped she had remarried, that she'd found someone she could love, but now he knew that all of that was untrue. He was holding his breath, waiting for her to tell him there was no other man she loved as much as she loved him.

"You don't have to introduce me," Felicity said. "I'll —"

Holt's hand shot out to restrain her. "Of course I'll introduce you. I hope you two will become friends."

"We live in two different worlds."

"You've got to stop saying that. You told me

your father used to be rich."

"My father represented a class that passed out of existence before he was born, people who expected money to be there because they were born with it, who would work very hard for others but had no idea how to work to support themselves. The people crowding around your friend are very different. They know what they want, and they know how to get it."

Vivian was getting so close, Holt expected to see her look of recognition at any moment. He could hear her voice when she answered one of the men surrounding her. Her laugh was the same soprano trill he remembered from afternoons sitting together on a bench behind the serpentine walls that surrounded the gardens of the University of Virginia. She was so close he could see the candlelight reflected in her eyes, hear the whisper of her petticoats as she walked, so close he could reach out and touch her.

She walked past him without any sign of recognition.

Holt felt the blood slow in his veins, the breath still in his lungs. The moment he'd looked forward to for so long had passed without anything happening.

"She didn't recognize you," Felicity said.

Holt felt the energy drain from him, leaving him with an unfamiliar feeling of weakness. It took a great effort to answer Felicity. "It's been a long time. I guess I've changed more than I thought."

"She was too busy flirting with all those men to notice anybody who wasn't directly in her path, or to pay attention to a man who appeared to be taken already."

"What do you mean?" But he knew before the words were out of his mouth. Vivian would take it for granted that any man standing with another woman was married. "She has no reason to think I'm within a thousand miles of Galveston. Even if she noticed me, she'd think I was some stranger who just looked a lot like a man she used to know."

"You can make excuses if you want, but I think she was too busy to notice anyone who wasn't standing next to her."

Was he making excuses, or was he just being realistic? People change a lot in six years, especially if they're young. He'd have recognized Vivian anywhere, but four years of war and two years of working cattle under the brutal Texas sun had changed him inside as well as out.

"Are you going to speak to her?" Felicity asked.

"In a minute."

"What are you waiting for?"

"Until she's not surrounded by men."

"She'll never be without a circle of men around her."

Why did he feel so reluctant to speak to Vivian? He *was* certain she'd be glad to see him. He *was* certain her feelings for him hadn't changed. He'd been trying for years to find her.

There was no reason for him to hesitate a minute longer.

Still, the ambiguity of his feelings held him back. He'd expected to approach her as a lover reunited with a long-lost love, each yearning for the other. But Vivian didn't appear to be pining for him or her husband. And he had been shocked to discover that the reality of her wasn't the same as his expectations. What was so different? *Why* was it different?

"Go talk to her," Felicity said.

"It's not the right time."

"If you don't speak to her now, I'm going home."

"Why?"

"Helping you find that woman is the only reason I'm here."

"Okay, I'll speak to her."

"I'll wait for you here."

Holt reached for her hand, grasped it firmly. "I won't let you hide behind the furniture."

Felicity resisted the tug on her hand.

"If you don't go, I won't go either," Holt said.

"You're the one Vivian remembers. Why should she want to meet me?"

"Because you're my friend."

"I'm not your friend. You don't even like me."

That statement shocked Holt. He was certain she knew he liked her. He'd told her she was extremely attractive in her new gown. He'd been proud of her tonight, proud of the interest the men showed in her.

"That's ridiculous," Holt said. "I've always liked you."

"You have not."

"Stop being coy. You know you're extremely attractive in that gown. If you don't believe me, you can at least believe all the other men who've told you so."

It was hard to tell in the uncertain light, but he thought she blushed slightly.

"Do you mean to say your opinion of a woman could be changed because of her looks?"

"No, but that doesn't alter the fact that you're very pretty."

Now he was certain she blushed. "It's just the dress."

"It's a pretty dress, but it merely complements your looks. In fact, I'm not sure but what it's only pretty because you're wearing it."

"Something's wrong with your eyesight. Maybe you spent too much time in the sun when you were chasing those cows. How can you look at Vivian and still say I'm attractive?" she asked, gesturing to where Vivian stood surrounded by a half dozen men.

"People are attractive in different ways. Owen Wheeler was the best-looking man in our troop, but Pilar thinks he's not half as handsome as his cousin Cade. Everybody likes something different. I happen to think you're extremely attractive."

"You'd better go talk to Vivian before your brain goes soft," Felicity said.

"Only if you come with me."

"Why do you want me to meet her?"

"Like I said, I want you two to be friends."

"That's impossible, but I suppose the only way to convince you is to show you."

Holt was unprepared for the anxiety he felt as they made their way toward Vivian. It didn't make sense that he should feel perfectly comfortable one moment and just the opposite the next. It wasn't as though he were approaching a woman he didn't know, a woman whose reaction to him he couldn't predict. It wasn't as though his whole future rested on what happened in the next few moments.

It didn't, did it?

"Excuse me," he said to one of the men standing between him and Vivian. "I'm an old friend. I haven't seen Vivian in years. I want to say hello."

The man seemed inclined to refuse, but his expression changed once he saw Felicity. Holt could practically hear his thoughts. *Married man. No competition here.*

"Hello, Vivian," Holt said when the man moved aside. "I've been looking for you since the war ended. Why didn't you let my uncle know where you'd gone?"

Holt had no difficulty identifying Vivian's expression. It was obvious she had no idea who he was. He had remembered everything about her, down to the shoes she wore the last time he saw her. Yet she didn't remember him at all.

Holt felt like a fool. The men probably thought he was too drunk to know that Vivian wouldn't be interested in a married man, even if she had known him sometime during her childhood. Holt knew he ought to give her his name, give her a chance to remember him, but he was too proud. If she didn't remember him, he'd turn and walk away.

"Holt Price!" Vivian exclaimed, animation turning her expression from quizzical surprise to a dazzling smile of welcome. "Is it really you?"

Holt felt the tension inside break and a well-spring of relief surge upward. Vivian *did* remember him.

"Have I changed that much?" he asked.

"Completely," Vivian assured him. "I wouldn't have recognized you if you hadn't spoken. What are you doing in Galveston?"

Looking for you. But he couldn't say that. The words wouldn't come out. "I've been working on a friend's ranch for the last two years. Right now I'm working with a doctor here in Galveston."

"I met Holt when he was studying to be a doctor," Vivian said to the impatient men gathered around her. "I was a foolish girl and he was my wise big brother." She reached out,

205

took one of his hands in hers, and brought it to her cheek. "I couldn't have survived growing up without him. Whenever I needed someone to talk to, he would always listen." She dropped his hand and smiled brilliantly at him. "I can't believe I've found you again. You've got to introduce me to your wife."

"We're not married," Holt said.

Vivian's laugh sounded like a soprano cadenza, rising and falling without effort. "Sorry. I just assumed —"

"Holt works with my father," Felicity said.

"Then — ?"

"There is no *then*," Felicity said. "I'm only here because Holt is new in town."

"I know what you mean," Vivian said and turned to Holt. "I've felt like a stranger almost my whole life."

"You were never a stranger to me," one of the swains around her said. "I feel as if I've been waiting for you my whole life."

Holt didn't know how the man could make such a statement without gagging. Not only that, the idiot looked as if he believed his own words.

"You're sweet," Vivian said, giving him a smile. "I love Galveston. I can't imagine living anywhere else."

"I'm going to do my best to see you never leave," another suitor said.

"We've got to talk," Holt said to Vivian. "I want to know everything that's happened to you since you left Charlottesville."

Vivian's brilliant smile clouded. "When my husband was killed, I was certain I would lose my mind with grief. I had nowhere to go, no one to turn to."

"You could have come to me," Holt said. "You know I would have taken care of you."

Vivian reached for his hand once more, clasped it in hers, and drew it to her breast. Holt heard gasps from at least two of the men gathered around her. He was sure they would have endured privation to be in his shoes at this moment.

"I never doubted that," Vivian said, looking up at him as though he were some stone saint rather than a flesh-and-blood man. "But I felt I had to make it on my own."

"Maybe you should save the rest of this until you can speak privately," Felicity said to Holt.

"Felicity's right," Holt said. "I'm so glad to have found you, I forgot your friends."

The several young men immediately looked less bored, ready to compete for Vivian's attention once her intrusive *big brother* moved away.

"I'll call on you tomorrow afternoon," Holt said.

"I can't. I'm to ride in Randall's boat," she said, indicating a slim dandy with reddish-brown locks plastered to his scalp.

"Yacht," Randall corrected. "It's too big to be called a boat."

"I'm shaking already," Vivian said. "Boats

scare me half to death."

"Yacht," Randall repeated.

"Then I'll come in the morning," Holt persisted. "Where are you staying?"

"With poor Abe's sister and her husband," Vivian said. "They have a brand-new house on Broadway. Don't come too early."

Holt couldn't understand why he didn't mind letting her go. After waiting six years, these few minutes should have been far too few to satisfy the emptiness that had built inside him. He didn't blame Vivian for wanting to turn her attention to the young men gathered around her. She must have suffered during the war. Her beauty would fade. Let her enjoy it while it lasted.

"It was so good to find you after all this time," Holt said.

"I'll look forward to tomorrow," Vivian said. "I can't wait to sit with our heads together as we used to do, sharing secrets and laughing at people behind their backs."

Holt had enjoyed sharing the secrets. He'd long since regretted the laughs.

Vivian leaned forward on tiptoe and planted a kiss on Holt's cheek. "I really did miss you," she whispered.

Then with a laugh and a wave of her hand, she was borne away by her covey of young men. He had thought that separation would be like pulling out his guts. Instead it was something of a relief. He didn't understand that.

"I didn't realize she was so young," Felicity said.

"She's twenty-two," Holt said. "She was much too young to get married."

"I know women who got married two or three years younger," Felicity said. "Are you ready to go?"

Much to his surprise, he was. He retrieved Felicity's cloak, and they left. He expected Felicity to ask whether finding Vivian again had turned out to be what he'd hoped for, but she didn't say anything at all until they reached her house.

"She really is a very beautiful woman," Felicity said as Holt helped her down from the carriage. "I'm surprised she hasn't married again. I'm sure she's had many offers."

Holt paid the driver and followed her up the walk to the house. "Vivian won't marry just anyone."

"She must be a very strong and resourceful woman. It's not easy to be unmarried and without family."

"She's been without a family since she was a little girl."

"Then her success is even more remarkable." Felicity turned at the door. "Will you eat breakfast here or with Mrs. Bennett?"

She sounded very cool, very businesslike. "Here, if it won't be any trouble."

"It's just as easy to cook for three as two. See you in the morning." Without waiting for a response, she opened the door and disappeared inside the house.

Holt didn't move down the steps. His mind was busy trying to gauge Felicity's reaction to Vivian. No matter how beautiful a woman might be, she couldn't be expected to enjoy meeting a woman who was even more beautiful, especially a woman so beautiful that men automatically gravitated toward her. But Felicity's only reaction seemed to be indifference.

He went down the steps and walked toward Mrs. Bennett's house.

It would be a better use of his time to try to figure out his own reaction. There wasn't any doubt about his initial response. After the first shock of seeing her, realizing it really was Vivian, that he had truly found her after all this time, he'd been filled with relief. The unnamed fears that had clustered at the back of his mind for so long could be banished. She was alive and safe.

Next came a kind of euphoria. His long search had come to an end. All he had to do was speak to her and the past six years would roll away. Naturally, it would take time to catch up on their lives, time to reestablish the intimacy they'd shared. In some ways it would be like getting to know each other all over again, but he was certain they could regain their old relationship.

But even as the thoughts formed in his mind, he wondered if they could be true. Neither he nor Vivian was the same. They'd experienced a lifetime of change during the past six years. The carnage of the war had left him certain he didn't want to be a doctor. She'd been married and widowed, had grown into a woman who'd learned to take care of herself.

And then there was the problem that he didn't really know what he wanted to do with his life. How could he even think of a wife and children? The idea of so much responsibility hung heavy around his neck. He'd spent his childhood being responsible for his father. And feeling a failure. He'd joined the army to help his friends, but his skills hadn't been sufficient to save many men from death. He'd spent years feeling he was responsible for Vivian, that he'd failed again. Marriage and children would merely add to the possibility of more failures.

He still couldn't understand why he didn't mind leaving Vivian, why he felt more comfortable with Felicity. He liked Felicity a lot, but he'd loved Vivian for years. Felicity was pretty, but Vivian was beautiful. Yet he felt more at ease with Felicity talking about Vivian than actually talking *to* Vivian. Did he resent her calling him her big brother? Could it be that he didn't love her as much as he'd thought, that his attraction to Felicity was eating into his feelings for Vivian? Could his reluctance be fear that she didn't love him anymore?

He pushed that aside. She'd been happy to see him again. Their feelings for each other were still intact. It only remained to revitalize them.

Then why had she married Abe Calvert after knowing him only a few weeks? It had taken Holt months to absorb the fact that she really had gotten married and really had disappeared from his life.

It didn't matter that he probably didn't — couldn't — love her the way he used to. They were both adults now. They would start over again. Not from the beginning, but getting to know each other, learning the true nature of their feelings for each other. The shock of seeing her tonight, the real Vivian, forced him to realize he'd spent six years building a fantasy in his mind. If his feelings were not what he thought, it was just as likely that Vivian's feelings for him weren't the same. They couldn't have been, could they? After all, she'd married another man.

There was no point in torturing himself with these questions tonight. He'd soon have the answers to all his questions. He'd waited six years. He could easily wait a couple of days.

He had walked up the steps and reached for the knob on the front door when he heard a door open and Felicity's voice calling his name.

"What's wrong?" he asked, moving quickly down the steps and across the yard separating the two houses.

"Papa's operating on Mrs. Farley's tumor, but he did something wrong. I'm afraid she's going to die."

Chapter Thirteen

The scene in the office reminded Holt of the tent hospital where he'd performed so many operations. Dr. Moore and the patient were covered with blood. Holt shed his coat, rolled up his sleeves, and plunged his hands into some soapy water. "What have you done?" he asked Dr. Moore as he dried his hands and doused them with alcohol.

"She came in complaining of bleeding."

Holt cut him off. "What did you do after you cut her open?"

"I was just going to remove the tumor."

"What happened?"

"Blood started oozing everywhere."

"Didn't you stop it?"

"I can't. Every time I move my hand off the wound, it bleeds again."

Dr. Moore had somehow cut a vein or an artery.

"I've got to sew it shut and hope it doesn't leak," Holt said. "I need the smallest needle and finest silk thread you have."

Felicity must have analyzed the situation as quickly as he had. She placed the threaded needle in his hand only moments after he asked for it.

"Don't let go," Holt told Dr. Moore. "Hold it closed while I sew."

Holt had done this many times before, but knowing that his patient could die made every time feel like the first. Each tiny stitch, each nearly invisible knot was a victory. By the time he'd finished, he felt exhausted from the struggle.

"That's it," Holt said as he straightened up. "Now let's clean out the cavity and see if the stitches hold."

Dr. Moore, looking very old and tired, stumbled as he backed away. "You do it."

It was impossible to tell what was affecting him most — alcohol, fear, or exhaustion.

"I can't do this operation alone."

"Felicity can help you," her father said.

Holt wanted to argue, but he didn't have time. Besides, he remembered how efficient Felicity had been when he operated on Durwin. "Can you do this?" he asked Felicity.

She nodded.

"Okay, let's clean her up and remove this tumor."

By the time he'd removed all the blood from the abdominal cavity, Holt was more worried. The patient had lost a lot of blood, more than he'd thought at first. The artery seemed to be holding, but her pulse was weak. He didn't know if she could endure the operation, but he had to remove the tumor. It was foolish to leave it.

"That's all I can do," he said, after he'd removed the tumor and sewn up the cavity.

"We'll have to depend on Mother Nature now."

He stepped back. His patient didn't look good. Her breathing was shallow, her color almost gone. It would be touch-and-go, but she had a chance. He hoped her constitution was strong enough. No one spoke while he cleaned up and Felicity put all the instruments into hot, soapy water.

"We have to talk," Holt said to Felicity.

"You'll want to do it in here so you can watch Mrs. Farley," Felicity said. "I'll make some coffee while Papa goes over her case history with you."

Holt spent the next ten minutes questioning Dr. Moore about Mrs. Farley. But as soon as Felicity entered with the coffee, he brought the discussion to an end. Dr. Moore slumped in a chair, his head in his hands, but Felicity faced Holt.

"Talk," she said.

"I feel uncomfortable talking in front of your father."

"It's his career you're talking about. No one has a better right to hear what you have to say."

"That was a simple tumor," Holt said, "only two inches across, barely under the skin. Your father should have anticipated it would bleed. Yet all he was doing was applying pressure. He didn't even try to ligate a single blood vessel. Can't you smell him? He's been drinking."

"I know he drinks more than he should, but —"

Holt cut her off. "But what? He's a threat to patients. He did more harm to Mrs. Farley than help her. She might die from blood loss because of his carelessness."

"What are you going to do?"

"Notify his patients, other doctors."

"And what do you hope to accomplish by that?"

"To protect his patients."

"Suppose the patients don't listen to you. You're a Yankee, and they don't trust Yankees."

"They'll listen after I explain what happened."

"Can you prove it? Mrs. Farley only knows that my father operated on her. Unless my father or I corroborate your statement, you have no proof."

Holt couldn't believe his ears. Felicity couldn't mean she would endanger the lives of innocent people just to protect her father's reputation.

"How do you know other doctors in Galveston aren't incompetent?" Felicity continued.

"I don't, but I know Dr. Moore is. I might have to go to the police."

"The police will only be interested if somebody dies. Nobody has. Besides, half of the police force come to my father. He's always taken good care of them."

"Your father is an alcoholic," Holt said, unable to keep from throwing at her the one word she refused to hear. "Do you understand what that means? I do, because my father was an alcoholic. It means he can't help himself. He has to have a drink. And once he starts, he can't stop."

"I do drink too much," Dr. Moore said, "but I'm not an alcoholic."

"See. I told you —"

"No alcoholic recognizes his condition," Holt said, cutting Felicity off. "My father would come off a three-day drunk and tell me he could stop any time he wanted. But sooner or later he always gave in to the temptation to have just one drink."

"My father has never come home falling-down drunk, and he's never been drunk for days on end."

"No, he just drinks too much, then thinks he can operate without anyone to assist. Alcoholics are incapable of thinking through problems and weighing the risks. They think they can do anything they want. We can't keep this quiet any longer."

"So you're going to ruin my father."

"I don't make him drink. You can't blame this on me."

"If you ruin his career, his reputation, I surely will blame you."

"So you prefer to let him keep operating until he kills somebody."

"No."

"Then what do you propose we do?"

Felicity turned from him to her father. "I don't want to do this, but I must. You understand, don't you?"

He nodded.

"Have you talked about this already?" Holt asked Felicity.

"You told me before what you would do if anything like this happened," she said. "I couldn't just wait around and do nothing, so I talked to Papa."

"And what did you two decide?"

"That you should take over Papa's practice until he's better."

Holt looked from one to the other, but it was clear that Dr. Moore wasn't surprised by his daughter's proposal.

"My taking over won't change anything. It will only hide the problem temporarily."

"So you'd rather destroy my father."

"I'd rather not let him kill any patients."

"Then take over the practice."

"For how long? A month? Two months? What happens then? I just turn my back and walk away?"

"He'll be recovered by then."

"No, he won't. I know about alcoholics. They don't get better. They remain alcoholics forever."

"Then tell me what to do."

"He has to stop drinking completely. Not even one drink."

"He will."

"You can't watch him all the time."

"I will."

"This is a ridiculous conversation," Holt said. "You've got to recognize the situation for what it is."

"My father lost everything when the war ended. Without his practice, he has no way to make a living."

"That's not my problem."

"You think Vivian is your problem because your uncle left you his estate. Yet you intend to deprive my father of his living and you don't think you're responsible. Forgive me, but I can't follow that."

"Vivian couldn't help her situation. Your father can."

"Vivian *did* help her situation. She got married. She has family. That dress she was wearing cost three times what I paid for mine. We have only what my father earns taking care of the poorest people in Galveston. If you deprive him of his practice, we'll be destitute."

"So what do you propose?"

"As I said, that you take over his practice."

It was on Holt's lips to refuse. He wasn't interested in being a doctor, but he'd always wanted to know more about family medicine. After all, he'd have a family some day and he would want to know if they were getting the best medical treatment.

"Okay, but only on three conditions." What was he talking about? There weren't any conditions that would make this a good idea.

"What are they?"

"First, your father can't sit in his room brooding. I'm not a general practitioner. Your father knows twice what I know. The two of us will see every patient together. We'll consult on every decision. We'll operate together."

"Is that okay, Papa?" Felicity asked.

He nodded.

"My second condition is that your father *never* take even one drink. Not with dinner, not with friends, at a party, or at the hotel bar. Even one drink and the deal is off."

"Everybody has a right to have a drink sometimes," Felicity protested.

"Maybe, but that's my second condition."

"I can do it," Dr. Moore said. "I'm not an alcoholic. I'm just weak."

Felicity gave Holt a hard look. "What's your third condition?"

"That I move back into this house so I can keep an eye on your father."

"Next door is close enough."

"Those are my conditions. They're not up for discussion."

Felicity looked furious. For some reason, that made him feel better. He was glad to know he could shake her iron control.

"It's all right, Felicity," her father said.

"It's not all right with me."

"If he's staking his reputation on my behavior, he has a right to make sure I'm holding up my side of the bargain."

"It'd be like living with a spy in the house," Felicity objected.

"Try thinking of me as a friend and supporter," Holt said. "I'm doing this to help your father, not ruin him."

"You've threatened to do it often enough."

"In case you haven't noticed, you keep talking me out of it."

"Because you know it's not right."

"It's letting you talk me out of it that's not right," Holt said before turning to Dr. Moore. "You understand that even one drink and our agreement is off, don't you?"

He nodded.

"I'll do what I can to help, but I can't do it for you. You've got to do it for yourself."

"I'm not an alcoholic."

Holt didn't believe that, but he wasn't going to argue. "You two can go to bed. I'll sit up with Mrs. Farley."

"When are you moving in?" Dr. Moore asked.

"First thing in the morning."

"Good," he said. He got up and left the room.

"I ought to thank you for giving him another chance," Felicity said.

Holt smiled despite his irritation with himself and the whole situation. "Not if it's going to be given so begrudgingly. You sound as if saying the word would cause real pain."

Felicity's expression softened. "I suppose I do sound ungrateful, but you forced this on me."

"No, your father forced it on all of us. If you don't accept that, you won't be any help to him, and you'll just keep being angry with me."

"Why shouldn't I be angry with you?"

"Defending your father, protecting him, is just enabling him to continue drinking. He won't get better until you accept that he has a problem that's not going to be fixed by denying its existence."

"You've made your point. Now may I go to bed?"

"Sorry. I didn't mean to keep you, but I wanted to talk to you."

"Why?"

"We can't go on living as if we're in an armed camp. I want us to be friends."

"Is that your fourth condition, that I pretend we're friends?"

"No. It's just a wish. Try. Other people seem to like me."

"I could like you very well if it weren't for what you're doing to my father."

"Try to think of what I'm doing as helping him. His life and yours will be better."

She didn't look convinced.

"At least try," he said.

"Okay, but I don't guarantee I'll succeed."

"You may not have to do it for very long."

"Why not?"

"If I ask Vivian to marry me, I won't be in Galveston much longer."

He couldn't interpret Felicity's expression. Her gaze swung from him. "You haven't even talked with her yet. Her feelings might have changed. *Yours* might have changed."

"They haven't." But even as he said that, he knew it was not true.

"If that's what you want, I hope you'll be happy." Felicity started to leave, then turned back. "Thanks for helping with Mrs. Farley. I'd never have been able to live with myself if she'd died."

She left the room abruptly.

Holt's body sagged against the back of his chair. He hadn't realized he was so tired, but it had been an eventful evening. He'd found Vivian, performed an emergency operation, and come to an agreement to take over Dr. Moore's practice.

What could have possessed him to agree to take on responsibility for another alcoholic? It was like dealing with his father all over again. And Felicity was like his mother, denying her father was an alcoholic, protecting him, unable to see that her complicity was hurting him rather than helping him. She was also unable to see that she was cutting herself off from any chance of finding love.

She couldn't meet any man without being afraid he would discover her father's secret. So she would continue to keep everyone at a distance, denying herself any hope of a normal life.

Holt decided he had to do something to keep that from happening. She was too pretty to hide herself away. But that wasn't the real reason. He liked her. When she wasn't angry with him — and that wasn't very often — he enjoyed being with her. She was intelligent, energetic, and charming. That she was hardworking, loyal, and dependable went without saying.

Her capacity for love was without question. Her love for her father was so great she was willing to sacrifice her own interests for his.

But that was where Holt parted company with her. He believed there came a time when everyone had to take responsibility for himself. His mother didn't agree and had never forgiven him for leaving. When his father died a year later, she laid the blame on Holt, saying his father would still be alive if Holt had stayed.

She hadn't written again.

His father's death still haunted him, but Holt knew he had had to make the decision to leave. Not just for his career. For his own sanity. He'd had to put himself first.

And that was exactly what Felicity needed to do. She was too good to waste.

She was not for him. Though he wanted to be friends, any closer relationship was out of the question. He and Felicity would be badly mismatched. He was certain they could be lovers under the right circumstances — the tug of attraction between them had been growing stronger — but it would be impossible for them to live together. She would always resent the fact that he had forced her to accept the truth about her father.

Still, the idea of being married to Felicity wasn't disagreeable. He had to smile at the thought of what she'd say to the idea of marrying him. She certainly wasn't a woman to keep her opinions to herself. Not that he minded that. He'd never been around women who were short of opinions or the courage to express them.

He looked over at Mrs. Farley. He wondered why nobody had come with her. Didn't her family care that she was ill and had nearly died? He asked himself whether anyone would care if he died.

He refused to be morbid. Mrs. Farley would get well. He would do his best to help Felicity and her father. He had found Vivian and would take care of her. He had friends in Texas who would help him if he needed it. He wasn't alone and friendless. He was just tired. That was why he wasn't thinking rationally. Everything would feel different once he got some rest.

But even as he turned his mind to deciding which of Dr. Moore's books he'd read, he had the uneasy feeling he really was alone in the world. He had friends, but no one who loved him.

★ ★ ★

Felicity looked at her reflection in the mirror. *You know it's your fault Mrs. Farley almost died, don't you? Holt tried to tell you your father would make a mistake someday and kill someone, but you were so sure you could watch him and make sure it never happened, you wouldn't listen. It didn't matter what anybody said. You could handle any situation.*

But she hadn't been here when her father needed her because she had gone to a party. She couldn't excuse herself by blaming it on Holt. She knew her responsibilities, but she'd let the excitement of wearing a new dress and dancing with a handsome man make her forget her duty.

She had promised her mother she would take care of her father. And for thirteen years she had. But now she had no choice but to concede that that agreement, too, had been a mistake. She'd protected her father because she loved him, but protecting him had enabled him to keep drinking, to keep endangering his health, to come close to destroying his life. She had been hurting him while trying to help him.

She had fallen short of her duty to her father, her promise to her mother. She had failed because she didn't have the courage to do what was right. She had always known deep down that her father needed to stop drinking, that he couldn't keep on this way without hurting himself. But when it came down to it, she didn't have the courage to make the right decision. She'd opted for the easy answer, rather than the right answer.

Holt was right. Her father was an alcoholic, and she had allowed it. Holt had had the courage to say so regardless of what she thought of him.

Felicity felt worthless. Taking care of her father was the one thing she'd done in her life, and she'd done it wrong. How could she have been so blind? How could she be sure that any of her other decisions were right? Maybe she'd been wrong all across the board.

Suddenly it was all too much. Her mother's death, her father's drinking, her lonely, unfulfilled life. Tears overcame her, and she buried her head in the pillow. When she finally stopped crying, she dried her eyes and made herself a promise. She was never going to take the easy way out again. She would do what was right. If it hurt, she'd learn to live with the pain.

"You know you can't take another drink," Felicity said to her father. "Holt won't hold back next time."

"I know. He's been very understanding."

She refilled his coffee cup. "Finish your breakfast," she said. He hadn't eaten much. She wasn't hungry at all. "I'm worried about you."

"It's time you stopped. You've got to think of yourself for a change."

"Don't start in on how you've kept me from finding a husband and having a family."

Her father reached out and grabbed her hand when she started to turn away. "I've kept you closed up in this house cooking and cleaning, helping me in the office, and taking care of me when I drink too much."

"I want to take care of you."

"I want to see you married, settled, with children of your own."

"I'm not sure I want a husband."

"Of course you want a husband."

"Mrs. Bennett has been widowed for years and she doesn't appear to be the slightest bit interested in getting another husband."

"She was married and had children. You haven't done either."

"Let's not talk about it anymore."

"We have to talk about it. What are you going to do if I take another drink? If Holt does what he said, I won't have any patients."

"You're not going to take another drink."

"I know what I told Holt, but I'm not sure —"

A knock on the back door caused her father to break off his sentence. When she opened the door, she found Mrs. Bennett on the back stoop. She came inside without waiting for an invitation.

"I hear you've stolen my lodger away," she announced. "How is a poor widow woman to make a living when her neighbors plot against her?"

"I didn't want to steal him away," Felicity said.

"Maybe he wanted to be stolen," Mrs. Bennett said.

"Not if you're thinking what I *think* you're thinking. We can't be together for more than five minutes without arguing."

"That's not always a bad sign."

"It is in this case."

"He seems to be a really nice man."

"He is," Dr. Moore said. "I'm the trouble."

"How's that?" Mrs. Bennett asked.

"Papa, you don't have to —"

"If I'm going to lick this thing, I've got to bring it out in the open, admit I have a problem."

"You talking about your drinking?" Mrs. Bennett asked.

"How did you know?" he asked.

"Don't you think I know what a man's been up to when I see him stumbling down the street long after he ought to be in bed?"

"Do other people know?" her father asked.

Felicity knew they did, but she'd never told her father.

"Can't speak for anybody but myself, but I expect they do," Mrs. Bennett said.

"Then why do they keep coming to me when they're sick?"

"Because you're good, you're convenient, and you're very understanding when it comes to payment."

"You mean I'll take a few chickens or a stack of kindling wood as payment instead of money. You've never come to see me."

"I've never been sick."

"But if you had been?"

Mrs. Bennett's gaze didn't falter. "I'd check to see if you'd been drinking first. If I suspected there was anything seriously wrong with me, I'd see someone else."

It hurt Felicity to see the stricken look on her father's face, but it was time they both faced the truth. He was an alcoholic.

"Thank you for being honest," her father said. "And I have to be equally honest with you. Holt is moving back to keep an eye on me. I started an operation last night that I couldn't finish. If he hadn't come home when he did, the patient would have died."

"*Might* have died," Felicity said. Habit. She had to stop.

"Stop trying to protect me, Felicity. Thank God Mrs. Farley is doing well this morning. You and I both know Holt saved her life. He only agreed not to expose me because I promised never to take another drink."

"That won't be easy," Mrs. Bennett said, "but I'd like to help."

"How?"

"There'll be times when you can't stand staying in the house a minute longer. You'll want to go somewhere, *anywhere*, just to see people. If you go to a saloon or a hotel bar, you'll take a drink as sure as you live and breathe. So whenever you get to feeling desperate, you come over to see me. I'm not a man, but I'm better than no entertainment at all."

Felicity was surprised to see her father smile.

"Do you really mean that?" he asked.

"I'd be a fool to offer if I didn't. I could end up with you on my hands every night of the week."

"I hope you're not talking about me," Holt said as he entered the room. "I thought you liked me."

"I don't know," Mrs. Bennett said. "You turned your back on me as soon as you got a better offer from a younger woman."

Felicity felt her face grow warm. She'd been so concerned about her father, she'd never stopped to think how Holt's presence in her father's house might be viewed by an outsider. It was clear that Mrs. Bennett thought Felicity liked him. Her stomach began to churn. Did she like him? Had she wanted him to move back?

"Don't you know you can't trust a Yankee?" Holt said.

"My family came from Kansas," Mrs. Bennett said. "We were taught to make up our minds for ourselves."

Holt walked over and put his arm around Mrs. Bennett. "I'll fight you for her," he said to Dr. Moore. "Do you want swords or pistols?"

"I know better than to come to blows with a younger man who's used to fighting long-horns," Dr. Moore said with a smile. "I'll plead old age and retire with my dignity still in one piece."

"Where's all this Southern chivalry I've heard so much about?" Holt asked.

"It died with all those fine young men in the war," Felicity said.

"You sure know how to put a damper on a conversation," Holt said. "I'd better leave before I make things worse."

"Where are you going?" Immediately the heat of embarrassment flooded her whole body. It was a totally inappropriate question, and everybody in the room would know it. "I need to know if you'll be back for dinner," she said. It was a feeble attempt. If that was all she'd wanted to know, she'd have said, *Will you be back for dinner?* Asking *where* he was going implied something else entirely.

"I'm going to see Vivian," Holt answered.

Felicity felt the pit of her stomach contract into a hard knot. That was where she was afraid he was going.

Chapter Fourteen

"I was worried about you when I heard your husband had been killed," Holt said to Vivian when she showed him into the parlor of her brother-in-law's mansion. "I wanted to let you know I would help you, but I didn't know where to find you."

"Abe's family insisted I come to them," Vivian said. "They treated me like a princess when they found out I was going to have a baby."

Vivian retained the boundless energy and optimism, the bright eyes and flawless skin of her youth, combined with the fullness, the sensuousness of maturity. Yet Holt was surprised to find he preferred the memory of that young girl. There was something about her that the more mature and poised Vivian lacked.

"The war ruined them just like everybody else. They died and left me a plantation I didn't know how to run, so I sold it and came to Galveston."

"So you're not broke."

"Not yet, but I soon will be if I don't find a husband."

"I can help you," Holt said.

"How?"

He'd been waiting to ask her to marry him

for so long, he'd forgotten when the idea first came into his mind. Yet now that the moment had arrived, he couldn't say the words.

"Uncle William left me Price's Nob," he said. "We can go back to Virginia."

Vivian's eyes flashed. "I'll never go back there again. It was like a prison. I hated it."

Even though he knew Vivian had never liked the isolation of Price's Nob, the vehemence of her words surprised him. He couldn't understand how she could compare his great-uncle's guardianship to being confined in prison. "Uncle William loved you. He meant for you to have Price's Nob." He saw momentary interest.

"Is there any money?" she asked.

"The Union Army burned the house and salted the land."

"Then there's nothing to go back to. I intend to stay right here in Galveston. It's full of rich men getting richer, and there are parties every night. Why would I want to bury myself in Virginia?"

Holt could think of several reasons, but Vivian answered before he could.

"I spent my childhood bored to distraction. I only felt alive when I escaped to Charlottesville. Your uncle would let me do anything as long as my *big brother* was with me. Then after Abe died, I was shut up on a plantation. In Galveston I finally feel alive, like I can breathe." She positively beamed. "You always said I was made for gaiety and laughter."

"But nobody can live on gaiety forever."

"Maybe not. But after a lifetime without it, I won't have my fill for a long time."

The door opened and Vivian's sister-in-law entered the room. "Carl and Edward called, but I told them you were with an old friend."

Vivian jumped to her feet. "Where are they?"

"I told them to come back tomorrow."

Vivian ran to the window. "They're still in front of the house. Have somebody run and stop them."

"They didn't mind," her sister-in-law said.

"I don't want them tomorrow," Vivian replied, her face tight with anger. "I want them today. Send someone . . . I'll do it myself." She darted out of the room.

Lillie Hart turned to Holt. "I'm sorry," she said. "I thought she'd want . . ." Her voice died away.

"Vivian has always craved company," Holt said. "The more, the better."

"But you're her oldest friend."

"Which makes me practically a brother." He hadn't waited six years to be a *brother*. But even as he said the word, it took away some of the tension, the sense of unease he hadn't been able to explain. He'd had the sensation of being closed in. Now he felt relieved, didn't feel guilty for wondering if he really loved Vivian as passionately as he had thought.

"Then I guess that makes you an uncle," Lillie Hart said.

"Huh?" Holt said, startled.

"An uncle to her son, Abe. He was named for his father. Want to meet him?"

"Sure."

Holt let himself be led away, wondering how his role of suitor had been transformed to that of brother and uncle, wondering even more why the transformation didn't upset him.

"You've got to eat something," Felicity said to her father. "You've hardly eaten anything all day."

"How can you say that after practically stuffing me with food?" her father asked. "I'm not hungry now because I've eaten enough for two people already."

Holt was going out to a party, so she had fixed an early dinner for her father and herself. Even in the confines of their small kitchen, Holt's absence made the room seem empty.

"Holt said the best thing you could do for yourself was eat."

"Yes, but he didn't say you had to stuff me like a Christmas goose. Now eat your own dinner and relax."

"I'm worried about you."

"Don't be. I'm not an alcoholic. I just drink too much."

She didn't agree with her father, but she couldn't make herself use that awful word, *alcoholic*. "Holt doesn't take anybody's word for anything."

"Don't you go being too hard on the boy. He's right about my not seeing patients when I've been drinking. Let's face it, Felicity. I drink too much all the time."

"I know, and that's why I'm determined you won't drink anymore. I want you well as soon as possible. Then there'll be no reason for Holt to stay here."

"Don't you like him?"

She couldn't say no. It was too much of a lie to pass her lips. Yet she wasn't about to tell her father her real reason for wanting Holt to leave, her fear that she was starting to like him too much, that she was hoping he would want to kiss her again. She'd never tell anyone she'd started to dream about him.

"It has nothing to do with whether I like him," she said. "I just want things to go back to the way they used to be."

As soon as the words were out of her mouth she knew that wasn't true. She didn't want Holt to leave. She just didn't like the fear, the uncertainty, the feeling of being constantly on edge.

What was she afraid of? Holt exposing her father, ruining his career? He'd had several chances already and hadn't done it. She *was* afraid Holt would leave. She was afraid he would marry Vivian without realizing she didn't love him. She was afraid that now that he'd found Vivian, he would never want to kiss her again.

"I don't want things to go back to the way they were," her father said. "That would be bad for both of us. Holt's being here may be my only chance to stop this feeling of helplessness, of despondency, of not wanting to get out of bed."

"You will get better, I know you will. You only need —"

"And things aren't right with you," her father continued. "You don't go anywhere, don't see anybody, never have any fun. At least with Holt here, you're acting like you're alive."

Her father's words shocked Felicity. "What do you mean?"

"I mean I'm tired of watching you watching me. I'm tired of you never leaving the house, of looking worried all the time. I'm tired of you acting like your life is over and this is all you'll ever have to look forward to."

"But I don't feel like that."

"You should be furious at me, resentful as hell. At least now that Holt's here, I've seen some light in your eyes. You don't look *resigned* anymore."

"Resigned?"

"Given up. Lost hope."

"I know what it means. What are you talking about?"

"About you liking Holt. You could fall in love with him if you gave yourself half a chance."

"I don't want to fall in love with him."

"Yes, you do, but you're afraid. I should be

taking care of you. And the first thing I should do is find you a husband."

"You can stop thinking about Holt. He's in love with someone else."

Her father pushed his plate away untouched. "I'm not so sure of that. He thinks he's in love with her because he ought to be, but I think he's more interested in you."

"You wouldn't say that if you'd seen Vivian. She's very beautiful. He's always wanted to marry her."

"He's believed that for so long, it'll take him a while to realize he's changed his mind."

Felicity gave up trying to convince her father. "Let's not talk about this anymore." She got up to start clearing the table. "What are we going to do this evening?"

"You're going to the party with Holt."

"I'm not leaving you alone on your first evening."

"Why? Are you afraid I'll have a drink as soon as you're gone?"

"Of course not." But wasn't she? Didn't he drink every night? And if he had so much as one drink, she was certain Holt would leave just as he threatened. Good Lord. Was she more worried about Holt's leaving than about her father getting well? No man had ever had such a hold over her.

"We always spend the evening together," she said.

"All the more reason you should go with Holt."

"I'm not leaving you. Now, what do you want to do?"

"Mrs. Bennett invited me to visit her. I think I'll ask her to come on over."

"She was just being polite."

"I like Ellie. It's about time she stopped being a widow. I think I'll tell her so."

Felicity was so shocked, she couldn't think of anything to say.

Felicity had been in many beautiful homes, but none of them approached the splendor of the one she was in tonight. She found it difficult to believe that even a cotton fortune could have built such a magnificent house. The sixteen-foot ceilings were decorated with intricate plaster moldings. In the huge reception room — referred to as the Gold Room — a thick carpet covered heart-of-pine floors. Ornate gold cornices crowned every doorway and window. Silk curtains hung at the windows, and paintings in gold frames covered the walls.

Despite her sumptuous surroundings, Felicity was angry at herself for agreeing to go to the dinner party with Holt. She was more angry that Holt couldn't seem to see that Vivian didn't return his feelings, that she felt about him the same way she would a brother — or some sort of male satellite she didn't see as a worthy object of her affections. Maybe Vivian's dress had something to do with that. After the horrors of the war, sober fashion dictated high necklines and full skirts. Since nearly everyone had lost a father, husband, brother, son, relative, friend, or neighbor, most women wore black. Vivian's gown was a bright lemon yellow, the neckline so shockingly low and her skirt so tightly fitted, you could see the outline of her hips. Her whole body might as well have been exposed to view.

Felicity was scandalized. The male guests appeared mesmerized. Felicity knew that married women had more license, but for a respectable woman, this was carrying things too far. Especially for a woman with a fatherless five-year-old son.

"Other than her beauty, why do you admire her?" Felicity hadn't meant to ask that question. She was certain she wouldn't like the answer, but she was too angry to control her tongue. It was foolish of her to accompany Holt when she knew exactly how things would be.

But they weren't, not exactly. Though Holt's gaze frequently strayed to the part of the room where Vivian was holding court, he had stayed at her side the whole evening.

"I admire her for the courage it took to grow up living on the charity of her father's best friend. She did it with a great deal of cheerfulness, never feeling sorry for herself."

Felicity couldn't quite credit Vivian with the same degree of courage. It had to be hard knowing you were beholden to a stranger for the food you ate, the clothes on your back, and the roof over your head, but she'd never known any woman as beautiful as Vivian who couldn't bend virtually any man to her will. She'd bet her two new dresses that Vivian had only been waiting for a rich man to come along before she threw over the traces.

Abe Calvert's father had been very rich until the blockade of Southern ports kept him from selling his cotton. Felicity wondered where Vivian had found the money to support her expensive way of life if all she'd had to sell was a useless plantation. Money from such a sale could only last so long. She was certain that although Vivian welcomed Holt's attention, she wouldn't marry him, because a mere doctor couldn't provide her with the style of living she felt was necessary for her happiness. Far greater fortunes were being made in Galveston than even the most successful doctor could accumulate.

"Before you get lost in Vivian's court, you ought to pay your respects to your hostess," Felicity said.

"Why are you so down on Vivian?" Holt asked. "You don't even know her."

Felicity could feel Holt's temper rising. She *didn't* know Vivian, but her instincts screamed the other woman was dangerous and insincere. "It's not really Vivian," Felicity said, bending the truth a little. "I just don't want you to get hurt. I don't believe her feelings for you are as strong as yours for her. I think she's enjoying all the admiration too much to settle down."

"Considering what you think of me, I'm surprised you aren't secretly hoping she will throw me over."

"I've never felt that way." Felicity was shocked at Holt's words. But she realized she had felt protective of him from the moment she'd set eyes on Vivian. No, even before that. From the moment she'd heard of Vivian. She hadn't thought much of a woman who could leave a man like Holt for some young man whose primary recommendation was that his father was rich.

"You could have fooled me," Holt said.

"Just because we don't always agree, that doesn't mean I'd wish any misfortune on you." Surely he couldn't think she was that awful.

"It's because you want me out of your house as soon as possible."

She couldn't believe they were standing against the wall, like a couple of outcasts, engaged in a discussion that should have taken place anywhere but here. She couldn't believe he cared what she thought. She didn't even know why he was still at her side, especially if he thought she was so anxious to get rid of him. Didn't the man have enough sense to know she wouldn't have accompanied him if she disliked him so much?

Why *had* she agreed to come with him? She didn't like parties where she didn't know people. She didn't like feeling out of her element. She didn't like feeling she was being invited out of pity — or merely because Holt wanted someone to talk to.

"I'm so glad to see you. I was hoping Holt could talk you into coming tonight."

Relieved, Felicity turned to see Charlotte Albright approaching. Her husband lagged a few steps behind, his attention caught by Vivian's trilling laugh.

"It wasn't easy," Holt said with his warm, welcoming smile. "She seems intent upon hiding away at home."

"I'm not hiding," Felicity said. "I have more than enough work to keep me busy."

"You have too much," Charlotte said. "It's good for you to get out once in a while. It'll give you a chance to make new friends. You might even meet a man you'd like."

"That's what I've been telling her," Holt said.

"Why is everybody trying to marry me off?" Felicity asked, exasperated.

"Because they think no woman can be truly happy unless she's married," Charlotte's husband said. "But look at that woman over there," he said, indicating Vivian. "She's not married, and she appears to be extremely happy."

"That's Vivian Calvert," Holt said, an edge to his voice. "Her husband was killed during the war."

"She appears to have gotten over her grief," Albright said. "I've never seen a dress like that in my life."

"And you won't on a woman with proper sensibilities," Charlotte said, her disapproval obvious.

"What's wrong with a beautiful woman wearing a beautiful dress?" Holt asked.

"There's a time and place for everything," Charlotte said. "Wearing such a bright color flies in the face of the grief of women suffering from the loss of loved ones. After losing Tom, my mother will never wear colors again. Then there's the question of the propriety of wearing a dress that's so revealing. No real lady would want to be stared at in such a fashion, to have herself perceived in such a way by any man who wasn't her husband."

Felicity couldn't help feeling sorry that Holt had to hear criticism of the woman he loved, but she was glad someone had been willing to say the words she'd been reluctant to voice. Before he asked Vivian to marry him, he needed to know that the woman of his dreams had some serious character flaws.

But rather than looking at Charlotte, Holt was looking toward the door with a look of shock followed by one of growing fury.

"What are you looking at?" Felicity asked.

"That man who just came in."

She turned in the direction of Holt's gaze, expecting to see something outrageous. What she saw was a tall, handsome man speaking to their hostess. Except for slightly pinched features, an aquiline nose, and intense eyes that in combination gave him the appearance of a hawk, she saw nothing out of the ordinary about the man.

"I don't know him," she said.

"His name is Laveau diViere. During the war I took an oath to hang him."

Chapter Fifteen

Holt could hardly have shocked Felicity more. He was passionate about a doctor's duty to save lives. How could he have taken a vow to kill someone?

"Why would you do a thing like that?"

"He betrayed my troop during the war. Twenty-four men died when Union soldiers ambushed us, one by Laveau's own hand."

"Surely that can't be true," Charlotte said.

"He works for the Reconstruction government," her husband pointed out. "That means the Union Army. They'd consider anyone who betrayed a Confederate troop a hero."

"Lots of people know him," Charlotte said. "He's invited everywhere."

"Nobody cares about the war anymore," her husband said. "People are interested only in making money."

"But if he works for the government, how can he be wealthy?"

A thoughtful expression crossed her husband's face. "I don't know that he is, but if he is, that's a good question."

DiViere's eyes had swept the room as he moved away from his hostess. His gaze came to a halt when it reached Holt. "I think he's seen you," Felicity said to Holt. "Do you think he'll come over?"

"No."

But Holt was wrong. DiViere started toward them, a thin smile gradually curving his lips into a look that showed neither welcome nor pleasure. Putting her hand on Holt's arm, Felicity was surprised to find it as rigid as an oak beam. She looked up at him, but his gaze was riveted on diViere.

Holt was stunned by the violence of the emotion that gripped him the moment he set eyes on Laveau. He hadn't seen the man in three years, yet seeing him walk toward him with that well-remembered smirk on his face was like being flung back in time. He'd never liked Laveau. The man acted too much like a privileged aristocrat to fit with Holt's egalitarian New England upbringing.

But he wouldn't have believed that Laveau could take the life or cause the death of a companion and fellow soldier. Having committed such a hellish crime, how could Laveau show absolutely no feeling of guilt or embarrassment? Cade Wheeler always said Laveau had no sense of right or wrong, only what was of advantage to himself. Holt guessed that was how Laveau excused what he did. He wanted to change to the winning side, and the best way to win the trust of the Union Army and gain a high position for himself was to betray his troop.

Holt couldn't think of anything more contemptible.

"I never expected to see you in Galveston," Laveau said when he reached Holt.

"I expected to see *you*," Holt said, "lying and cheating as usual."

Laveau went white, his features coalescing into a rigid mask. "The war is over. I advise you to take advantage of being born a Yankee instead of standing alongside people whose beliefs you don't share."

"I wasn't aware I was standing alongside anyone."

"What do you call helping Cade steal *my* cows?"

"I know Cade sends you your share of the income from the ranch every year."

"So that's where you get your money," Charlotte's husband said to Laveau.

"My *money* comes from a ranch Holt's friend stole from me," Laveau said, his black eyes afire with hatred.

"Is that your excuse for trying to kill Cade and his cousin?" Holt said.

"I don't know what you're talking about," Laveau said, his smile back in place, his eyes clouded. "I haven't seen either man in years."

"Not since you betrayed them to the Union Army," Holt said.

"Laveau! Where have you been? I was beginning to think you didn't mean to come." Vivian burst into the midst of the small group, apparently oblivious to the tension. She smiled radiantly at Laveau while offering her hand for a kiss. "I didn't know you were acquainted with Holt."

"I met him during the war," Laveau said.

"How? You weren't on the same side," Vivian said.

"We were in the beginning," Holt said. "Laveau changed sides when it was clear the Union was going to win."

"I'm sure that was all very painful at the time, but the war is over now," Vivian said. "We can all be comfortable again now."

"Not all of us," Holt said.

"I refuse to talk about the war," Vivian said, her smile crumpling. "It reminds me too much of poor Abe."

Holt felt guilty for having called to mind a painful memory.

"Come meet my friends," Vivian said to Laveau. "You and Holt can catch up with each other later."

"That's unnecessary," Laveau said. "I'm entirely at your disposal."

"Did he really betray Confederate soldiers to the Union Army?" Charlotte's husband asked as soon as Vivian had carried Laveau off.

"And stole his best friend's money," Holt said. "But I'm sure he didn't consider it stealing, since he was sure Ivan would be dead and somebody else would get the money if he didn't get it first."

"Nobody's going to believe you," Charlotte said. "He's accepted everywhere."

"Not everywhere," Felicity reminded him. "Some people still believe loyalty is more important than money."

"Not in Galveston," Albright said. "And if I expect to keep making money, I can't start attacking a member of the Reconstruction government, especially one the Union Army considers a hero. Come on," he said to his wife. "We have a lot of people to speak to before we sit down to dinner."

Felicity watched Holt watching Vivian and Laveau in the center of a laughing group at the other end of the room. "It looks like Charlotte's husband isn't anxious to believe what you said."

"I expect he's one of the new breed, men who can see opportunity in the face of even the greatest tragedy."

She didn't know what to say. Nothing could change the fact that some people were more interested in money than integrity. Neither could she change the fact that some women were more interested in money than love. He would certainly accuse Charlotte's husband of the former, but she was certain he would acquit Vivian of the latter.

"I didn't know you and Holt were going to be here."

Felicity turned at the sound of Vivian's sister-in-law's voice. Lillie Hart smiled broadly. Her husband was talking to their host.

Holt turned to Lillie with a welcoming smile. "She wouldn't have been if I hadn't practically twisted her arm."

"That's not true," Felicity said. "I just don't happen to like parties like this very much, especially when I don't know many of the guests."

"I feel the same way," Lillie said, "and I know practically everybody. But if you want to be successful in Galveston, you have to be seen everywhere."

"Your husband's home is in Mobile," Holt said. "I would have thought New Orleans was a more likely place to go."

"That's where we were going until Vivian convinced Clifford to come to Galveston," Lillie said. "I didn't want to come, but things have gone very well for us the past three years. I have to thank Vivian for that." Lillie paused, seemingly undecided whether to go on. "I didn't really trust her at first. Her son inherited the family plantation, but Vivian hated living *in the sticks* as she put it. She sold the plantation first chance she got and moved to Galveston. We thought we'd seen the last of her, but she started encouraging us to move to Galveston and didn't stop until we did. She never stops trying to talk people into sending their business to Clifford. She's a wonderfully loyal sister-in-law."

That's what you get for making up your mind about people before you know them, Felicity said

252

to herself. *You were determined Vivian was an awful woman who would break Holt's heart. You even imagined her marrying just for money, then being relieved her husband was dead so she could enjoy all the attention her beauty could bring. Serves you right to have to listen to her sister-in-law paint an entirely different portrait that shows Vivian's loyalty and willingness to share her success with her new family. She may not be a paragon of virtue, but she is probably worthy of Holt's admiration.*

But try as she might, Felicity couldn't bring herself to believe that Vivian was worthy of his love. She decided Vivian's character was hopelessly flawed. She couldn't make herself believe that Vivian was the kind of woman to do anything out of charity for others. She didn't like the fact that Vivian was so beautiful, and she didn't like the fact that Holt was in love with her. There was no other explanation for it. She was hopelessly jealous. And she was jealous because of Holt.

"After all Vivian's kindness, I feel guilty that I can't like Mr. diViere," Lillie said. "I feel especially guilty because he's recommended my husband to some of his best clients."

"Why do you dislike him?" Holt asked.

"I have no real reason," Lillie said. "Clifford has forbidden me to mention it to anyone. I wouldn't have said anything to you except that I knew you felt the same way."

"How?" Felicity asked.

"I saw the way he looked at Mr. diViere," Lillie said. "That's as close as I've ever come to seeing hatred in anyone's eyes. I was afraid you might fight him."

"I have good reason to dislike Laveau diViere," Holt said, "but you don't have to worry I'll start a fight."

"It is a nice party," Lillie said. "Clifford says we were lucky to be invited. We wouldn't have been if it hadn't been for Vivian."

"That's the only reason we're here," Holt said.

Lillie turned to glance at Vivian, then turned back. "I wish she weren't so friendly with Mr. diViere. I've heard whispers that he knows things he shouldn't and takes advantage of them. Some people will not invite him into their homes anymore."

"I would find it very difficult to be civil to anyone who works for the Reconstruction or the army," Felicity said.

"That's not the worst of what he's done," Holt said.

"What do you mean?" Lillie asked.

"I don't think you ought to tell her that," Felicity said. She didn't doubt what Holt said, but she didn't want him spreading the story all over Galveston. She worried what the Reconstruction government or the Union Army would do. They allowed no opposition from any quarter.

"Why not?" Holt asked.

"It could get you into serious trouble."

"Is it that terrible?" Lillie asked.

"He betrayed his troop to the Union Army," Holt said.

"Are you sure?" Lillie asked.

"I was part of that troop. I saw men murdered while they slept."

Lillie looked stricken. "Vivian can't possibly know that. She wouldn't have anything to do with him if she did."

"I don't expect she does," Holt said. "It wouldn't be to Laveau's advantage."

Felicity couldn't imagine what it was like to see friends killed before your very eyes, men you'd ridden with, joked with, fought with, eaten with and slept next to. For a man like Holt, the worst part must have been knowing he could do nothing to help them.

"Do other people know what he did?" Lillie asked.

"You'll just start trouble if you tell people," Felicity said to Holt.

"Only if I make a public accusation," Holt said.

"What can we do?" Lillie asked.

"Nothing yet," Holt said. "Seeing Laveau here tonight surprised me into speaking without thinking. I need to consider what to do next."

"I have to tell Clifford," Lillie said.

"I expect seeing me was an equally nasty surprise for Laveau," Holt said. "I'm sure he's already concocting some story to make me look like a fool if I start spreading rumors against him."

"It's more probable he's trying to work out a way to have the army put you in jail," Felicity said.

"They don't have to have a real reason," Lillie warned. "They'll hate you just because you fought on the Confederate side."

"But he's from Vermont," Felicity said.

"It won't make any difference," Lillie said. She looked over at Laveau, her glance now fearful. "I don't know what I'll do if he speaks to me."

"Act as you always have," Holt said. "If you don't, your family could suffer."

"Maybe I could ask Vivian —"

"Leave that to me," Holt said.

"Are you sure you ought to tell her?" Felicity asked.

"She has to know."

"If she doesn't believe you, it'll damage your relationship with her. If she does believe you, it'll put her in a difficult position. She can't suddenly stop seeing a man everyone knows is her friend without people wanting to know why."

"I can't let her continue thinking Laveau is a man of character. Now, if you ladies will excuse me, I want to speak with Vivian before we sit down to dinner."

"I like him," Lillie said as Holt moved to join the group around Vivian. "I hope you marry him."

"Me! Marry Holt!" Felicity exclaimed.

"You like him."

"He's in love with Vivian. He came to Texas just to look for her."

"He may have, but he likes you."

"He loves Vivian."

"No, he doesn't. He's just infatuated with her."

"Why do you say that?"

"The first time he came to visit, Vivian ran off and left him. He talked with me a long time. He probably doesn't realize it now, but the idea that he wants to marry her is so ingrained, he hasn't given it any real thought. When he does, he'll realize he would be miserable married to her."

"Why would he be miserable?"

"I don't like to criticize Vivian after she's been so good to us, but she won't settle for anyone who isn't rich. She likes gaiety, parties, admiration."

"Holt isn't like that."

"I know. He'll marry you if you want him."

"But I don't. I mean, I have all I can do to help my father with his medical practice. Besides, I'm too old to be thinking about marriage."

"Nonsense. Holt must be over thirty. You're perfect for each other."

"I agree he shouldn't marry Vivian," Felicity said, "but I wouldn't want a husband I had to *compete* for."

"All women compete for their husbands. We just compete in different ways. Now I need to find my husband before they announce dinner. I suggest you insinuate yourself into that circle around Vivian. It would do her good to realize she has some competition."

"I'm not competition for Vivian! She's extraordinarily beautiful."

"You're quite lovely yourself." Lillie patted Felicity's arm. "I'm putting my money on you."

She's crazy, Felicity thought as she watched Lillie leave to find her husband. There wasn't a person in the world — certainly no man — who would say she was attractive enough to receive a second glance when Vivian Calvert was in the room. Clothes, jewels, makeup, and hairstyles could do a lot to compensate for the lack of natural beauty, but Vivian had the advantage in those areas as well. In addition, she was vibrant, sparkling, probably witty, and had an entrancing smile. You only had to look at the men surrounding Vivian — and the lack of men paying *her* attention — to know who would win any tug of war.

Still, this wasn't about her or Vivian. It was about Holt. She wasn't sure she believed Lillie was right when she said Holt's desire to marry Vivian would change. But she was sure that Vivian would be the absolute worst wife for him. She would be doing them both a favor if she could make them realize that before they made a commitment they couldn't change.

She was certain that nothing would come of it, but she would join the circle around Vivian. But before she could follow through with her intention, two women she hadn't seen in several years approached. Felicity greeted them with a smile of welcome. It would be nice to renew acquaintances.

"We haven't seen you in *years*," Megan Fraser said. She didn't give Felicity the expected hug or buss on the cheek.

"I thought you'd left Galveston," Carleen Phillips said. She inspected every inch of Felicity's person, apparently looking for something to comment on.

"I've been very busy helping my father with his medical practice," Felicity answered.

"I didn't know your father was still a doctor," Megan said.

"He can't have a big practice," Carleen said. "Nobody we know goes to him."

The cattiness of Carleen's remark surprised Felicity. "My father hasn't been entirely well since the war," she said. "He accepts only a few patients."

"I heard some doctors have had to accept a side of bacon or a bag of nuts for payment," Megan said.

"Some people are lucky to have that much since the war," Felicity said.

"Tell your father to insist on gold," Carleen said. "If he doesn't, you'll never be able to buy another dress, not even one like that."

Felicity's dress was quite nice, but it wasn't sumptuous like Carleen's. She'd married a shipping merchant whose business was booming.

"I don't go to many parties," Felicity said.

"Neither do we," Megan said. "It seems one of my children is always coming down with something. I tell them they fall sick just to keep me home."

"I don't know how she keeps looking so young," Carleen said of her friend. "She's got five children."

"You've got four," Megan replied. "Sometimes I think we're both slaves to our husbands' desire to replace all the men who died in the war. Be glad you'll never have to worry about that."

"I hope to marry and have children," Felicity said.

"Sorry if I've put my foot in it," Megan said with a labored attempt to laugh. "I assumed you were still single *at your age* because you didn't want to get married. You are a year older than I am."

"I haven't yet met anyone I want to marry," Felicity said, shocked and hurt that two women she'd considered friends would say such things.

"We lost so many fine young men in the war," Carleen said. "It's inevitable that many women will end up old maids."

"Have you heard anything from Ben Odum?" Megan asked Felicity.

"I forgot to tell you," Carleen said to her friend. "My husband ran across him in Houston a few months ago. He married a nice little girl from Dallas. Her father does something there that makes a lot of money. I think he hopes to move to Galveston as soon as his wife has her baby. It's their first," she said to Felicity. "They're very excited."

Ben Odum was the man who'd asked Felicity to marry him. He'd disappeared when her father lost all his money.

"Please ask your husband to extend my congratulations to Ben and best wishes to his wife and my hopes for a safe delivery," Felicity said. "I'd love to catch up on all the latest news, but my escort has been motioning for me to join him for the last several minutes. Please come visit sometime. We live at the same address."

Felicity escaped before either woman could respond. She refused to let them even guess she was upset or hurt. It was clear she would have to banish any hopes she might have had of picking up with her old friends. That avenue was closed, but she wouldn't let anyone see her hurt. She'd learned to hold her head high and ignore whispers and gossip years ago. She could still do it.

"She didn't believe me," Holt said. "She didn't say I was lying, but she didn't believe me."

They were on their way home, the clip-clop

of their horse's shod feet on the sandy street falling like dull thuds in the quiet of the night. The weather had been so warm, Holt had chosen to rent a buggy rather than a closed carriage. Felicity had looked forward to the drive home, to leaving a party she hadn't enjoyed. However stupid it might have been, she'd hoped they might find a way to reach a better understanding between them. The moon was bright, the stars twinkled, only one cloud marred the perfection of the sky, and the breeze from the sea made it the perfect temperature for snuggling.

Only Holt couldn't think of anything but Vivian's not believing him.

"You can't expect Vivian to believe what you said about Mr. diViere without giving her some time to think about it," Felicity said, sighing in defeat. "After all, you were accusing one of her friends of a heinous crime."

"I've known Vivian since she was eleven years old," Holt said. "She ought to realize I would never lie to her."

"It's hard for someone to believe a friend could be capable of such a crime," Felicity said. "She probably just needs time to grow used to the idea."

"She said it didn't matter now if it was true — people did all kinds of awful things during war."

"She was probably just too shocked to be able to accept what you said."

"Why are you defending Vivian?" Holt asked. "I know you don't like her."

Felicity was thankful the darkness shielded her expression from Holt's gaze. She knew she blushed. She could feel the heat in her skin. She was relieved that Holt was occupied with encouraging the particularly stubborn hired horse to turn the corner toward her house rather than go in the direction of his stable.

She wasn't defending Vivian so much as she was trying to soften the blow to Holt. He wasn't just surprised. He was hurt. It was a virtual attack on his character, his integrity, from the one person he'd never expected to doubt him. He didn't always say what people wanted to hear, but he didn't varnish the truth.

"I don't know Vivian well enough to dislike her," she said.

"That's not the feeling I get."

Okay, it was time to tell him what she thought. She didn't expect him to listen to her — he never did — but it didn't look as though he was going to figure it out for himself. "I know it's none of my business, but it worries me that you believe she still loves you. She was a young girl when you knew her, you a wise older man who befriended her. When it came time for her to choose a husband, she chose another man. After he died, she didn't try to find you. She obviously still likes you and values your friendship, but I worry that her feelings for you don't match yours for her."

"You think I'm a romantic fool who's let himself be dazzled by the beauty of a younger woman."

Not quite. He was a rigidly principled idealist who held his beliefs so strongly, he couldn't believe a person he liked could hold a different set of values.

"Any man would be dazzled by Vivian's beauty. I'm continually astonished by it myself," Felicity said.

"But you're not so astonished you're unable to dislike her."

"I'd rather say I don't know her well enough to trust that she wouldn't unknowingly hurt people who invest more importance in her words than she does."

"Did anyone ever tell you that you're very good with words?"

"I'm usually told that I'm much too blunt."

"Why are you changing now?"

That was a question Felicity needed to answer for herself before she could explain it to him. Why was she trying so hard to protect him? Not because he was weak or prone to getting his feelings hurt. In fact, for a time she believed he didn't have any feelings. Maybe finally accepting what he'd said about her and her father had enabled her to think about him differently. She only knew that while she wanted to shake him for not seeing what was obvious, she wanted just as much to spare him the hurt of what she was certain would be

Vivian's ultimate rejection.

"Maybe because I can understand how she could feel so threatened, so insecure, so frightened, that she would refuse to face reality. I can understand how she would build protective walls around herself because I did it myself."

"But you were protecting your father and your means of support. Laveau is practically a stranger to Vivian. He means nothing to her."

"That's not the impression I got."

"What do you mean?"

Chapter Sixteen

Felicity could have bitten her tongue. When would she learn to shut up before she got herself in so deeply her only option was to plunge ahead and hope to escape without too many wounds?

"I don't mean Vivian has done anything wrong," Felicity said. "Mr. diViere is an attractive man. I imagine he can be very charming."

But for the life of her, Felicity couldn't see how Vivian could possibly think Mr. diViere was more handsome than Holt. Laveau was handsome in an aristocratic way that lacked warmth and humanity. His aquiline features appeared predatory rather than merely lean and clean of line. Holt was entirely different. His dark brown hair was straight and neatly combed into place without looking as if it had been lacquered until it shone in the light. Laveau's eyes were cold, flat, emotionless. Holt's black eyes, usually so intense, could sparkle with amusement. They could also glow with warmth. His mobile eyebrows were nearly as expressive, drawing close together when he was displeased, rising when he was on the verge of laughter or teasing her. They could also lower ominously when he was angry.

Laveau was tall, but his complexion was

sallow and his body soft and paunchy. Holt reminded her of a lithe wild animal. His skin was tanned from working in the sun. His broad, muscled shoulders and long, sinewy arms were the result of compelling cantankerous longhorns to do what they were determined *not* to do. Felicity couldn't imagine how Vivian could prefer Laveau or any of the other shallow young men who clustered around her. Just thinking about Holt caused Felicity to go all hot inside.

Which wasn't something she wanted to happen. She was acutely aware of every quality that made Holt superior to Laveau and every other man she'd met, but she was determined these qualities wouldn't affect her judgment. Holt might be the perfect man, but he wasn't the man for her.

"Laveau is a devil," Holt said.

Holt's words jolted Felicity out of her thoughts. "You know that because you witnessed the terrible consequences of what he did," she said. "Vivian didn't see that, didn't know anything about it until you told her. He's obviously cultivated a persona that will make it difficult for people to believe your allegations."

"Do you believe me?"

"Yes," she said without hesitation. "I've seen the evil that men can do. I've also seen the evil they can overlook."

"What are you saying?"

"Vivian doesn't have the same knowledge of Mr. diViere as you do. So she'll never feel the same way about him. She obviously likes him or she wouldn't have come in search of him the minute he entered."

"Unlike me whom she didn't even recognize."

"She hadn't seen you for a long time," Felicity said. "Besides, she had no reason to expect you to be in Galveston. But she was watching for Mr. diViere's arrival tonight."

"I think she was only trying to make him feel welcome."

"They seem very comfortable together."

"You can't be thinking she's in love with Laveau?"

"I have no idea what her feelings are for anybody," Felicity said, wishing fervently she'd never opened her mouth. "Their familiarity implies she considers Laveau a friend."

"I've known Vivian since she was a child," Holt said. "She could never be a friend to a man like Laveau."

Felicity was relieved when they finally reached the house.

"It looks like Papa is still up," she said, seeing a light through the window. "I wonder what he's doing in the parlor. He never sits in there."

"Maybe he's trying to avoid old associations," Holt said. "There were certain times, places, or situations that always made my father reach for a bottle."

"Since we've been in Galveston, he's rarely had much to drink at home, so I never thought about it like that," she said as she let herself into the house. "I guess I blamed his drinking on going to bars and the company he kept."

"It's much more enjoyable to drink with people who aren't condemning," Holt said, closing the door behind them. "If your companions are drinking, too, then you can rationalize that it must be all right."

Felicity stepped into the parlor and came to an immediate halt. Mrs. Bennett was sitting on the sofa next to her father, patting his hand and talking softly to him. She looked up and smiled when she heard Felicity and Holt enter the room. "Did you have a good time?"

"What's wrong with Papa?" Felicity asked, going straight to her father.

"Nothing's wrong with him," Mrs. Bennett said, continuing to pat her father's hand. "He's just a little tired." She gave his hand a final pat and got to her feet. "Now that you're here, I'll be going home."

"Thank you for sitting with him," Felicity said mechanically. She was looking at her father, who seemed dazed and disoriented. She'd seen him look like this many times before, but it was always after he'd had too much to drink. She didn't know what it meant when he hadn't had anything at all.

"Has he been like that long?" Holt asked Mrs. Bennett in a soft voice.

"Only just the last little while. I think he's exhausted. Take care of them both," she said to

Holt. "They'll need you."

"Stay a bit," Holt said. "I'll walk you home in a minute."

"Are you tired?" Felicity asked her father. He seemed to be more alert.

"A little. I'm not as young as I used to be."

Felicity figured fifty-three wasn't all that old. Besides, he hadn't looked like this yesterday. She noticed he had to keep his hands clenched or they shook uncontrollably.

"You shouldn't have waited up for us," Felicity said. "You know you're always in bed by now."

"I wanted to know if you enjoyed the party," he said, looking a little more like himself. "It isn't often my favorite daughter gets invited to dinner at the home of the richest man in Galveston."

"I only got invited because of Holt," she said.

"And I only got invited because of Vivian," Holt said.

"It doesn't matter why you got invited. You did."

Her father looked more animated, but Felicity continued to examine him closely. She was sure he didn't want her to know how much he was suffering.

"Is the house as elegant as everybody says? People haven't stopped talking about it since they laid the foundation."

"It's beautiful," Felicity said.

Her father attempted to get up but failed. He

waved away her offer to help him but accepted Holt's. "I'm too fat for a little thing like you," he told her. "I'd pull you over on top of me."

Felicity wasn't used to her father spurning her help for Holt's. She felt ousted from her position, a foolish and unworthy response she immediately tried to repress.

"You've got to be tired, too," she said to Holt. "I can help Papa."

"Let it be, child," her father said. "No man wants to be put to bed by his own daughter."

She wanted to remind him she'd put him to bed before, but she said nothing as he walked out of the parlor leaning on Holt. She turned to Mrs. Bennett. "I've been taking care of him since Mother died."

"He feels guilty about depending on you so much."

"But I want him to depend on me."

"He worries that he's dominated your emotions so much, you don't have room for a husband and family."

"He can't know that."

"It's how he feels."

"But he doesn't mind letting Holt help him."

"There are some things a man takes better from another man. Help is one of them."

"But to take it from a stranger rather than his own daughter . . ."

"He doesn't consider Holt a stranger. And neither do you."

Felicity felt heat warm her skin. "He's not family."

"I think your father is beginning to see him as the son he never had."

Felicity felt as if someone had physically hit her.

"That hurts, doesn't it?" Mrs. Bennett asked.

Felicity nodded.

"Don't let it. Your father wouldn't trade you for all the sons in the world. He just wanted a son who could be a doctor with him. Now he feels he has both."

That didn't make Felicity feel any better.

"Don't you like Holt?" Mrs. Bennett asked.

"I guess so."

"That's a strange reaction for a young woman to have toward a handsome young man."

"Holt's not your ordinary *young man*."

"That's all the more reason why your reaction is unusual. I'd have thought you'd have welcomed his attentions."

"Do you call forcing his way into our home and telling us what to do *attentions?*"

"He's done a great deal more. Besides, he's taken you to several very nice parties."

"Only because he wants to see an old girlfriend and doesn't want to go alone."

"I never knew any man to ask a woman to go out with him if he didn't want to be with her. Men aren't subtle about things like that."

"I did it only because he practically forced me."

"And maybe to protect him?"

Felicity decided Mrs. Bennett had to be a witch. She knew too much.

"Men are such fools when it comes to a beautiful woman," Felicity commented.

"Do you think Holt is a fool?"

"Not about other things. But he's known Vivian since she was a child. He feels protective of her. Worse still, he thinks he's the only man who can love her for herself rather than her beauty."

"And you're afraid he can't see that she doesn't love him."

"I don't know. At times I get the feeling he thinks he's obligated to marry her regardless of how either one of them feels about the other."

"Have you asked him about it?"

"I couldn't ask him anything like that."

"Then you'll never know the truth."

Felicity fidgeted under Mrs. Bennett's penetrating gaze.

"Has he ever been reluctant to ask you questions about yourself or your father?"

"No."

"Has he thought less of either of you as a result of your answers?"

Holt had certainly condemned her father's seeing patients when he'd been drinking and her for helping him conceal his problem, but he was helping her father now, and his relationship

273

with her was more comfortable than it had ever been.

"I guess not," she replied.

"Then I doubt he'd be upset if you asked him a few penetrating questions, or if you happened to disagree with him."

Felicity was willing to give Holt credit for being fair-minded, but she wasn't ready to ask him personal questions. Mrs. Bennett took Felicity's hands in her own. "Trust him. I think you'll find him worthy of your confidence. And don't worry about your father. He's going to be all right."

"I want to help him, but I don't know how."

"Just keep letting him know you love him."

"He already knows that."

"Sometime it's necessary to hear the words. Men aren't very different from women when it comes to that. Now I hear Holt coming back. Put your dependence in him. And if I can do anything to help, let me know."

"You've done so much already. I don't know how to thank you."

"Don't. I was fed up with being a lonely old widow. It's fun to feel useful again. Now, be really nice to that young man. You might be surprised at what will happen."

Felicity reminded herself that Mrs. Bennett didn't know of the angry words that had passed between her and Holt. Her attitude toward him had changed a lot, but he'd been too preoccupied with Vivian to think of her. She didn't want to admit that caused her a pang of jealousy.

"Has Mrs. Bennett left?" Holt asked when he entered the front hall.

"Yes. How's my father?"

"I left him sitting up in bed. I'm going to give him a dose of laudanum."

"I don't want you giving him drugs."

"I'll only give him a small dose, and then only for a couple of nights to get him through the worst of the withdrawal symptoms."

She followed him into her father's office where he kept his medicines. "What are the symptoms? How bad will they be?"

"That depends on how much he's used to drinking, how long he's been drinking, and how his body reacts to being deprived of alcohol."

Felicity experienced a sinking feeling. "He started drinking heavily after my mother died. That was thirteen years ago, but it got really bad when we were at Andersonville. I thought it was better after we returned to Galveston, but I guess Papa was just better at hiding it. What symptoms is he showing?"

"His hands are shaky. I doubt he could hold a cup of coffee. He looks tired, but he won't sleep well."

"Anything else I should watch for?"

"His eyelids might flutter and his tongue quiver, but that's not too serious. The symptoms ought to disappear in a day or two. He may also crave sweets."

"This will be hard for him, won't it?"

"No harder than it'll be on you."

"Why do you say that?"

"I've noticed that any kind of suffering upsets you."

"Isn't that true of all doctors?" she asked. "And the reason they become doctors?"

"No. To some it's the science that attracts them. To others it's just a way to make a living. Making people well is what they're supposed to do, so they do it."

"How do you feel about it?"

"When I discovered I would make a lousy farmer, I decided to be a doctor. I knew I was partly motivated by guilt over my father, but I really wanted to be a family doctor. The horrors of the war changed all that. I became a good surgeon by practicing on people who had no hope without my limited skills. By the war's end I hated what I was doing. Since I've started working with your father, I've discovered there's another way to practice medicine. Being able to help people without cutting off limbs is like being given a whole new way of seeing medicine. I'm learning so much I never knew, things I wanted to learn. I may decide to stay until he's well. Maybe by then I'll know how I feel about making people well."

"Papa became a doctor to save Mama."

"It's become his reason for living now," Holt said. "He has a wonderful ability to inspire confidence in his patients. That's why it's essential that he never do anything to compromise his ability."

"Well, he's doing everything he can now," Felicity said. "How much laudanum should I give him?"

"I'll give it to him. You need your sleep."

"You don't think I'm going to bed while my father is suffering like this, do you?"

"You can't stay up all the time. We'll take shifts."

That surprised her. "You don't need to do that."

"I'm the one who forced this on him. Besides, I wouldn't leave you to go through it all alone. You don't know what to expect. I do."

"Thanks, but just tell me what to look for and what to do about it. I won't be able to go to any parties for a while."

"I'm not going either."

"What about your invitations?"

"I'm not leaving your father until I'm sure he's past the worst of the withdrawal period. I intend to help, so give in gracefully."

Felicity didn't know what to say. It had never occurred to her that Holt would give up a chance to be with Vivian so he could sit with her father.

"I'll go first," Holt said. "I can sleep late."

"You have to see patients all day. And you need your breakfast."

"We'll work something out," Holt said. "Now off to bed. And don't worry." With that he put his hand under her chin and kissed her lightly on the lips. "I intend to take very good care of Dr. Moore because I like his daughter a great deal."

Felicity stood rooted to the floor as Holt turned and left her. That kiss wasn't at all like the first time he kissed her. There was no challenge, no threat, no intimidation. Just a nice, sweet kiss from a man who liked her.

But she wished it had been more. Or less. She didn't believe for one minute, as Mrs. Bennett did, that Holt was romantically interested in her. It was her feelings that caused her to wonder.

Was she falling in love with him?

She didn't think so. It was hard to figure out just what she did feel about Holt when she was so busy worrying that Vivian would turn her back on him and break his heart again. She wanted to reach out and put her arms around him, partly to protect him from Vivian, partly to assure him that some woman in the world would love him. Of one thing she was certain. Even if Vivian did love Holt, she was far too self-centered to be the kind of wife he deserved.

She realized she was still standing in the hall, exactly where Holt left her. She quickly blew out the lights and picked up the lantern Holt had left for her.

As she climbed the stairs, she told herself Holt's future wasn't any of her business. And even if his decisions were terribly wrong, she couldn't do anything but watch.

Holt woke out of a dead sleep to the muffled sound of gunfire and the screams of men and horses. He couldn't understand. The troop was spending the day sleeping at a farm in one of the many small, unmapped valleys in the Shenandoah Valley. The Union Army didn't know where they were, and their raid wasn't scheduled until the next day. Why should it sound as if they were in the middle of a battle?

Having grown up in Vermont and being unused to the hot summer weather in Virginia, he'd found himself a quiet corner in the cool, dark recesses of the root cellar under the outbuildings. It took several moments before he could remember his surroundings, find the ladder, and climb up to the main floor of the building. There had to be a door to the outside, but he didn't know where it was and didn't want to take the time to find it. By the time he found his way out of the cellar, the noise had ceased. When he opened the door, he expected to find it was nothing but a bad dream.

What he found was a nightmare.

A pall of acrid-smelling gun smoke hung in the air, closing out the sunlight, turning midday into dusk. Beneath that somber blanket the dead and dying, Confederate and Union soldiers alike, lay scattered about the farm like so many broken and discarded dolls.

As suddenly as it had fallen silent, the tableau

came to life. The moans and cries of the men mingled with the screams of wounded horses. Like a mindless drunk, Holt staggered from the building, then raced forward. He slowed as he reached the first man. Ed Purdy. A grinning imp from Tennessee who loved a joke more than whiskey. Phillip Wilson. A farmer from Georgia with a wife and two kids back home. Alan Burton. The only son of an old Virginia family. All killed where they lay, sleeping in the shade of a maple tree. A Union soldier, his face made unrecognizable by the impact of a rifle bullet.

"What happened?" he asked Cade Wheeler, his commander and the first man he saw on his feet and unhurt.

"We were attacked by a Union cavalry unit." Cade looked down at another fallen comrade, a young man from Louisiana. "Most of them died in their sleep." He turned his gaze back to Holt, his blue eyes blazing with a fury that chilled Holt to the marrow of his bones. "Someone betrayed us. One of us is a traitor."

"But who?"

"I don't know, but whoever it was must die." Cade gazed once more at the bodies of his fallen men. "He must die!"

He must die! He must die!

The phrase echoed in Holt's head, growing louder with each repetition, until he felt he would go insane. He had to go to the men, help everyone with a chance to live, but he couldn't think, couldn't act, with that phrase banging against his

skull like the clapper of a steeple bell.
   He must die! He must die!

Holt woke with a start to find Felicity gently shaking him.

"Who must die?" she asked.

Chapter Seventeen

The look of concern on Felicity's face made Holt feel guilty, doubly so because he'd fallen asleep when he should have been watching her father. "It was just a bad dream," he said. "It's what I get for falling asleep." He glanced toward Felicity's father, but the doctor was sleeping peacefully.

"You were dreaming about Laveau, weren't you?"

He nodded.

"You know you can't do anything about him, don't you? The Union Army controls Texas."

"He's not in the army anymore."

"They won't care about that. They won't let anybody hurt one of their own."

Holt didn't explain that no one ever really trusted a traitor or why the nature of Laveau's crime made it impossible for the survivors to forget. If Felicity thought he was going to take revenge against Laveau, she would worry.

"Your father has had a surprisingly quiet night," he said, changing the subject. "He grew restless several times, but he didn't wake up."

"Does that mean he's over the worst?"

"We'll have to wait and see. Everybody reacts differently."

"You'd better go to bed," she said. "You've

got a busy day ahead of you."

"What time is it?" It was still dark outside.

"Four o'clock."

"You didn't sleep very long."

"You're the one who's seeing patients. It's more important that you're rested."

"I've had a head start," he said, feeling guilty again for falling asleep.

"I'll wake you at nine. That'll give you time to dress and have breakfast before your first appointment."

"If anything happens —"

"I'll call you. Now go to bed."

He rose to his feet. "Your father is very fortunate to have such a devoted daughter." He leaned over and kissed her on the forehead. "You'll make some lucky man a much better wife than he deserves."

She didn't reply, just pushed him out of the room with orders to go to bed. But once he'd undressed and gotten under the covers, he found his mind was filled with too many thoughts to allow him to go to sleep. He couldn't forget Laveau just because he was protected by the Union Army as well as the Reconstruction government. It was impossible to see the man, even think about him, without thinking of the twenty-four comrades who'd died because of his treachery. He would write Cade tomorrow. Laveau had already escaped them twice. Maybe the third time would be the charm.

He didn't plan to let Cade or Owen endanger themselves now that they were married. Cade had a son, and Owen's wife was expecting their first child. It would be up to the rest of them to bring Laveau to justice.

Holt had no doubt that Laveau was involved in something illegal. Owen had broken up a cattle-rustling operation just last year. He remembered Lillie Hart saying Laveau seemed to know things he shouldn't and took advantage of them. That sounded like blackmail, something Laveau had already tried with Owen's wife. Holt had heard another guest mention some recent thefts of jewelry and paintings. Laveau had stolen cattle — why not jewelry and paintings? If Holt could prove Laveau was a criminal, maybe the Yankees would take care of him for them. But it wouldn't be easy to find out what Laveau was doing or to prove it. He was a very clever man. But if he was as attracted to Vivian as it appeared, maybe she could help Holt come up with the information he needed.

Holt had always known that Vivian liked attention. He excused it because she had no family, but that could not excuse her friendship with Laveau, especially not after he'd told her what Laveau had done.

What bothered him most was her statement that everybody had done terrible things during the war, that the war was over and it was time to forget. Maybe he could have forgotten if

284

Laveau had merely changed sides. It was the death of men who would have risked their lives to protect Laveau that Holt could never forgive. He couldn't understand why Vivian couldn't see that.

Felicity had seen it immediately. He wondered what made people turn out differently. Felicity hadn't changed when her father lost his money. She was pretty enough to draw attention from many men, yet she hadn't taken advantage of her beauty to look for a rich husband. She'd devoted all her time to protecting her father even though it meant she was giving up her own chances for happiness.

Laveau, born into money and an aristocratic family, had become a traitor and a thief rather than work to regain what his family had lost. Vivian had pursued gaiety and extravagant praise rather than settle down to make the most of her son's inheritance. Knowing he could make no difference in his father's life, Holt had turned his back on his family rather than sacrifice his own future. Yet Felicity had sacrificed her future to protect her father.

Did he feel Felicity was throwing her life away?

Yes.

Did he feel guilty for leaving even though he knew there was nothing he could have done to help his father?

Yes.

He wondered what Felicity really thought of

him. Her good opinion was becoming more and more important every day. He'd even begun to think he might like a longer partnership with Dr. Moore. The more he learned, the more his interest in medicine revived.

Holt tossed restlessly. He needed sleep, not the nagging feeling that he was wrong about nearly everything. But Vivian's defense of Laveau had shaken him badly. He could no longer avoid the conclusion that his feelings for Vivian weren't the same as before the war. His need to find her had been driven in part by his uncle's expectation that Holt would take care of her. But Holt expected more of a mature woman — quality of character, courage in the face of adversity, standards of conduct by which she measured others as well as herself. Though he tried not to do it, he found himself constantly comparing Felicity and Vivian.

And Felicity always came out on top.

Was he beginning to fall in love with Felicity?

Exhaustion must be the reason he was having such crazy thoughts. He couldn't be falling in love with Felicity. Even though he felt his love for Vivian draining way, he was still too emotionally involved with her, felt too responsible for her, to be able to love another woman. But could that happen *after* he'd sorted out his relationship with Vivian? Did he *want* it to happen?

Maybe he ought to go back to Cade's ranch until he could figure out what he really wanted. But he wouldn't. He would stay here as long as it took for Felicity's father to conquer his addiction to alcohol. He'd failed his own father. He wouldn't fail Felicity's.

"Let me help you," Felicity said to her father.

"No." His refusal was emphatic and fretful. "If I can't get it to my mouth without spilling it, I won't have any."

"Holt said shaking hands was one of the classic signs of withdrawal." Her father's attempts to eat breakfast had been a disaster. His entire body shook uncontrollably. He'd already spilled two cups of coffee. "At least you got a good night's sleep."

"Only because of the laudanum. Admit it, Felicity, I'm a hopeless wreck. I might as well take a drink and forget the whole thing."

"No!"

"It would only take a little bit to calm my nerves."

"You know you can't drink anything at all."

"I promise I won't take more than one swallow."

"You've tried that before and failed."

"I won't fail this time."

He got up from his chair, but Felicity blocked his path. "There's no whiskey in the house."

"I always keep some hidden in case of emergencies."

"I know your hiding places. I've emptied the bottles."

He dropped back into his seat. "I can't do this," he said.

"You have to for your own self-respect," Felicity said. "You know you don't like it when you drink. Besides, Holt said he'd walk out the door if you ever took another drink."

"Fine. Let him take over my practice. He's a much better doctor than I am."

"Thanks for the compliment," Holt said as he entered the kitchen, "but I'm only good at cutting people open. I'm depending on you to teach me how to make them well without a knife. This is a much too serious conversation to have on an empty stomach. Do you think I could get something to eat?"

Felicity tried to calm her feeling of panic. How much had Holt heard? Did he know her father was considering giving up? "I wasn't going to call you for another fifteen minutes."

"Couldn't sleep."

She wondered if he'd had more bad dreams. Or if thinking of Vivian had kept him awake. "Sit down. I'll have your breakfast ready in a minute."

"How are you feeling this morning?" he asked her father.

"Your father was an alcoholic, so you probably know exactly how I feel."

"My father liked being drunk. You've been trying to numb the pain of some terrible memories."

"It's still a coward's way out."

"I see your coffee cup is empty. I'll get you some more. Wouldn't want Felicity to take her mind off fixing my breakfast."

"Felicity's a good daughter."

"You feel that way because she likes you. You should hear some of the things she says about me."

"She likes you, too."

"That's what she wants you to believe, but she really just wants two doctors working to support her. That way she'll have twice as much money to spend on fancy gowns." Holt bent closer to her father. "She pretends she doesn't like parties, but you ought to see her when she gets there. I practically have to drag her home."

Felicity was feeling more and more as if she wanted to put metal filings into Holt's biscuits and gravy. She couldn't imagine what possessed him to tell her father such ridiculous tales. When he reached the part about her dancing with every man in the room, she couldn't take any more. But before she could voice a protest, she realized his ridiculous tales had kept her father so amused, he had allowed Holt to hold the coffee cup for him while he drank.

Her irritation disappeared, replaced by a feeling of embarrassment that her defensiveness caused her constantly to misjudge him. She was suddenly grateful that he understood her father so well that he could find a way to help him without causing embarrassment. She felt herself being flooded by feelings much warmer than embarrassment or gratitude. She warned herself not to lose her head. Holt might be exactly the kind of man she wanted for a husband, but he was already taken.

"I know Felicity is your daughter, so I hate to criticize her to you," Holt was saying, "but you shouldn't have let her serve you a cold breakfast."

She turned to see Holt looking at the plate of food before her father. He had refused to touch any of it.

"It wasn't cold," her father said. "I just wasn't hungry."

"It's just what a loving father would say," Holt said, "but my grandmother would rise out of her grave to haunt me if she knew I let anybody eat a cold breakfast. You can have some of mine. But check for pepper first. Felicity told me last night she was going to *spice things up for me* if I didn't pack my bags and head back to those stubborn longhorns I liked so much."

"That's the only animal I know that's as hardheaded as you," Felicity said.

"They're tough because they have to live on a diet of thorny plants," Holt shot back. "A lot like living with you."

"So far I haven't been able to find a barb sharp enough to penetrate your thick hide."

"Why do you think I spent two years living with longhorns? I was just getting ready for you."

While they exchanged retorts, Holt gave her father half of everything on his plate and warned him to eat it quickly before Felicity took it back and made them both go hungry. By gentle badgering, Holt got him to eat most of his food and drink another cup of coffee. By the time they had finished breakfast, the desperate look that had always been a harbinger of a bout of drinking had disappeared from her father's face.

With Holt's help, her father had gotten past his first real crisis of willpower.

"It's time we got ready for our first patient," Holt said. "We have to get spruced up. Must make a good impression. If we look successful, they'll be sure we're giving them the best possible advice."

Her father hadn't finished dressing or shaved. The two men left the kitchen together, Holt in the midst of an earnest monologue about what kind of clothes created the best impression with patients — black because the color created a sober and responsible appearance, or fancy dress because it indicated the patronage of wealthy patients who could afford to pay for the very best.

If it hadn't been for the dirty plates, Felicity might have thought she'd imagined the entire last hour. She never would have dreamed Holt could be so sweet, kind, thoughtful, and masterful in getting her father's mind off whiskey, getting him to eat food he didn't want, making him feel like an equal partner in dealing with the patients. She could never have managed it by herself.

She experienced another surge of that much-too-warm feeling for Holt, but this time it didn't catch her by surprise. She refused to let it give rise to thoughts — or hopes — she knew to be impossible. She would be grateful for what he had done for her father, but that would be the extent of it. Anything else would be dangerous.

"I didn't expect to be seen by two doctors," the elderly female patient said. "It was quite confusing." Felicity was seated at her desk in the wide central hall where she greeted patients and they waited for their appointments.

"It's not at all unusual," Felicity replied, trying to sound as reassuring as possible. "That way both doctors will be familiar with your history, so either one will be able to treat you the next time you come in."

"I hope I won't have to come again," the woman said.

"That's always our hope, too," Felicity replied, "but it's best to come in regularly so we can head off problems before they happen."

Her father had always expected people to wait until they had a problem, but Holt said it was advisable for all patients, especially the elderly, to come in for regular checkups. She didn't know if any of her father's patients would cotton to that newfangled idea, but it seemed like a reasonable precaution. She had to admit that a lot of Holt's ideas seemed reasonable once you got past their unfamiliarity.

"Dr. Price is a very young man," the old lady said.

"I believe he's in his early thirties," Felicity said.

"And very attractive."

"Most of our patients think so."

"It makes a woman uncomfortable to have such an attractive young man poking around."

Felicity had heard that before, but as yet no one had refused to see Holt a second time. "We must have young doctors, or there won't be any doctors in a few years."

"I suppose so, but I don't think your father needs this Dr. Price."

"Why do you say that?"

"Every time he told me something, he turned to your father and asked if he was right."

"Was he?"

"Yes, but if he had to ask, your father doesn't need that young man's help, even if he is so attractive you'll probably have every young female in Galveston coming here within the month."

"I believe it's a common practice for young doctors to serve a period of apprenticeship with an established physician," Felicity said.

"I don't intend to pay double just because there are two doctors in the room," the woman said.

"The charge remains the same."

The woman paid in cash, something Felicity was seeing more frequently since Holt had begun working with her father.

"I suppose I should come again in six months," the woman said. "I am getting up in years."

Felicity thought seventy-two could definitely be considered *up in years.*

"Will the young doctor still be here?" the woman asked.

"I don't know," Felicity said, but she found herself feeling rather uneasy at the thought that Holt might not be there.

"I wouldn't think he could learn enough in six months to go out on his own, do you?"

"I really can't say," Felicity replied, "but he seems to be a very bright young man."

"Yes, but he'd want to make sure he had as much experience as possible before setting up his own practice, wouldn't he? There must be a great number of things they don't teach doctors in schools." She leaned forward as though sharing a confidence. "I'm told that some people who set themselves up as doctors don't even go to school."

"I can assure you Dr. Price has had the finest education available."

"I'm sure he has, but the experience of a man like your father would be invaluable to a doctor just starting out."

"I'm sure Dr. Price would agree with you."

Felicity nearly lost the struggle to keep from smiling until the woman left. She wasn't the first woman to pretend indignation when confronted by a handsome young doctor, then want assurance that he would be here when she returned. Felicity supposed she should be annoyed that women could behave so foolishly over a handsome man, but men behaved just as foolishly over a beautiful woman. It seemed a failing shared by both sexes.

And she was honest enough to admit she suffered from the same tendency. Despite her best efforts, she could not banish her feelings for Holt. It didn't help that he had been a perfect angel during the last week.

She laughed at the image in her mind of Holt as an angel. It amused her even more to think of Holt's reaction if he knew what she was imagining. He would look perfectly ludicrous wearing long, flowing white robes, standing under a halo, holding a harp, and singing some heavenly song. The more she thought about the picture, the funnier it became until she started laughing helplessly.

"Anything wrong?" Holt asked, sticking his head out the door.

"No," she said. "That's what's so funny."

"It was very nice of you to invite me to dinner," Mrs. Bennett said to Felicity. "It's a treat not to have to cook for myself."

"It was the least I could do after you helped so much with Papa."

They were in the kitchen washing the cups and saucers from their after-dinner coffee. Despite her worry about her father, the evening had been fun.

"Sitting with your father was a treat rather than a chore," Mrs. Bennett said. "It can get awfully lonely staying at home alone night after night. I enjoy listening to him, especially when he talks about the time he spent in Scotland."

"Papa enjoyed going to school. Between classes and studying, he didn't have much time to drink."

"I know this sounds hard-hearted to you, but it's time your father stopped torturing himself about his past. What's done is done and can't be changed. A body has to go on."

Felicity wanted to say it wasn't as easy as all that, but she bit back the words. "That's what he's trying to do now."

"You're a smart young woman," Mrs. Bennett said, putting away the last cup and looking around the kitchen for any stray task left undone. "You don't need me telling you what you already know. Now I'd better be getting on home, or you'll start thinking of charging me rent."

"You could move in if it would help keep Papa's mind off whiskey."

"Then I could rent my whole house and become a rich widow," she said with a bark of laughter. "Enough foolishness." She leaned over and kissed Felicity's cheek. "It's always darkest before the dawn. I know everybody says that, but you're stronger afterwards."

Felicity wasn't sure she believed that. Her father had struggled for years only to grow weaker. Holt was so taken up with Vivian, he hadn't noticed that Felicity had changed her mind about him. Not that it would make any difference. He wasn't interested in an average-looking old maid who had made it plain from the first that she wanted him out of her life as soon as possible.

"Are you all right?" Mrs. Bennett asked.

Felicity jerked her thoughts back to the present. "Why do you ask?"

"You didn't answer when I spoke —"

"I'm sorry. Sometimes my thoughts take over, and I forget where I am."

"Worrying never makes things better." Mrs. Bennett patted Felicity's hand like she had her father's. "Just do what you can and turn your mind to other things. I can tell you don't believe you can do that — or even that you should — but you'll change your mind one of these days. Don't waste your life worrying or you'll reach my age and realize you've missed everything that made the worrying worthwhile. Now no more lectures. What time do you and Holt plan to leave tomorrow?"

"I don't know."

"He's got invitations for nearly every night.

Your father is delighted with the prospect of your getting back into your old social circles."

"I'm not."

"Give yourself time. Despite being rich and beautiful, they're people just like the rest of us. I imagine some of them are quite nice."

"I'm sure they are, but I'm perfectly happy with the friends I have now."

"Don't cut yourself off from opportunity," Mrs. Bennett said. "You never know what might walk through the door. Oh, dear, I promised no more lectures, and here I go again. I'd better leave before I break my word again."

She left the kitchen at a brisk walk, said her brief goodbyes to the men, and was gone in less than a minute. The parlor seemed suddenly devoid of half its energy.

"I guess I'd better be getting to bed, too," her father said. "Holt says we've got patients scheduled for practically the whole day."

Her father got to his feet with difficulty. He was shaking worse than ever. She wanted to help him, but Holt shook his head. She wasn't sure her father could make it upstairs without help, but obviously he intended to try.

"Having a handsome young doctor is good for business," her father said with a shaky chuckle. "Much more fun to be poked and prodded by him than by a fat old man."

"They're coming for the quality of the medical advice," Felicity said, "not for what you look like."

"I may be an alcoholic, but I can see what's plain as the nose on my face," her father said. "Now I'll leave you two to scheme about how to keep me sober for another day." His progress from the room was uneven but steady. "I liked talking to Ellie. Amazing how you can live next to a woman for years and not know anything about her."

"I want to talk to you," she said to Holt as soon as her father was out of the room.

"I want to talk to you, too," he said.

Chapter Eighteen

"You go first," she said.

She'd been poised to tell him she didn't intend to go to any parties while her father was suffering. He hadn't told her about any invitations — probably because he didn't intend to ask her to go with him — but Mrs. Bennett had. He was getting to know people, feeling more at ease in Galveston society. He could be charming when he wanted. Plenty of women would be pleased to keep him company while Vivian held court. Felicity couldn't really expect him to stay home. He was doing more than enough by making it appear that he was there only to learn from her father.

"No, you go first," Holt said.

She didn't want to go first. It was hard to admit she had misjudged him. She was grateful to him, but it was hard to acknowledge it after she'd said such terrible things. It was also hard to concede that she'd continued to behave badly even after he proved her first opinion of him was unfair.

"I want to thank you for pretending to be my father's student," she said; "for letting the patients think Papa is the doctor making the diagnoses. I know that must be hard on your pride."

"Why would you think that?"

"Papa says you're a fine doctor in your own right. I know you're a brilliant surgeon."

"I just got more practice than most."

She wasn't going to let him minimize her apology. He'd been acting like a saint, and she was determined he would know it.

"I also wanted to thank you for having Papa see every patient with you. I don't think he would have managed to keep from drinking this long if he hadn't had something to do. Considering how you feel about alcoholics, that must have been hard for you."

"Whoa," Holt said. "What kind of person do you think I am?"

"A very kind and thoughtful one."

"No, you don't. You think I'm a conceited, hard-nosed, self-righteous know-it-all who's certain he has all the answers and is going to fix everybody's lives whether they want him to or not."

She had thought so at one time but not anymore.

"You don't have to answer. You've said it all before. First, I *am* your father's student. He knows a great deal more about medicine than I do. My knowledge is very limited, gained from book-learning and being a battlefield butcher. I could remove Alice Farley's tumor, but I've never had to diagnose one, monitor its development, or decide when and if to operate. We talk about every consultation in detail. I pick his brain for everything I can learn."

He'd said that before, but she hadn't believed him.

"I don't hate alcoholics. I hate *alcoholism,* the disease, and what it does to people. My father was once a good man — friendly, dependable, honorable, ambitious. Alcoholism turned him into a useless, selfish, cruel man who would lie, cheat, and steal. I sometimes thought he would have sold his wife or son for a bottle of whiskey. I like to think he tried to overcome his addiction but it was too strong for him. It destroyed his body and my mother's life. I had to turn my back on him to keep it from destroying me as well."

Felicity had thought his inflexible stand on drinking and medicine was primarily an idealistic concept, but now she realized it was much more. He hadn't left his home voluntarily. Alcoholism had driven him out, and the wound was still open and hurting. She was certain he believed that doctors shouldn't drink when they had to see patients, but the vehemence of his position had its roots outside medicine.

"I'm sorry for the things I said," Felicity said. "I didn't understand."

"You're like my mother," he said. "She was so busy protecting my father, she never realized she was hurting him."

"It's hard when you love someone so much and you know he's hurting so badly he can't help himself."

"That's the very reason your father has a good chance to recover. My father wasn't trying to blot out painful memories. He'd become addicted to alcohol and didn't have the willpower to help himself. Your father has used alcohol to forget, to ease the pain. It's time he faced the tragedies in his life, accepted them, and moved on."

"You don't understand. He lost the woman he loved, saw thousands of men die right before his eyes."

"I watched my father slowly kill himself for ten years, grew up being known as the son of the town drunk, watched my friends get blown apart or cut to pieces. What don't I understand?"

She didn't know why she always felt he hadn't experienced loss. "I'm sorry. You seem so unaffected by things, I tend to think you don't care. That's not fair of me."

"No, it's not. It would be the same as me thinking you're weak because you care so much."

"Maybe I am. I can't watch my father suffer and not want to do virtually anything to bring it to an end."

"I wouldn't expect you to feel any other way. Let me be the one to enforce the limits."

Why was he putting himself into a position where both she and her father could resent him?

"You've done enough already. I want you to

know I appreciate what you're doing even when I don't act like it."

"I figured you did, or you wouldn't have gone to that last party with me."

"That reminds me. Mrs. Bennett said you have invitations for the whole weekend. I hope you'll understand that I won't be able to accompany you."

"I already told you I wouldn't be going to any parties, either."

"I thought you meant just last night."

He looked peeved. "I won't be going anywhere until your father is over the worst of the withdrawal. Look, we're all in this together — you, your father, and me. We'll work together until it's over."

"I know what my father and I have at stake, but why should you care what happens to us?"

His look of surprise and hurt made her quickly rephrase her question.

"I mean, why should you sacrifice time with your friends for us?"

"Setting aside the fact I happen to like you and your father and care what happens to both of you, I'm the one who forced you into this. In my mind, I'm obligated to do everything I can to see that you succeed."

If she didn't do something quickly, she was going to cry. For years she'd felt completely alone, with no one she could talk to who understood or who would help. She hadn't realized until now how truly alone she'd felt, how much her fears had forced her to cut herself off from anyone who might become close enough to discover her secret. Now Holt intended to help, even when she insisted she didn't need help. The tension had been so great, the relief was so enormous, she felt almost too weak to stand.

"Are you all right?" Holt asked. "I know you didn't get much sleep last night."

"I'm fine."

"You don't look fine." He took her by the hand and led her to a chair. When she stumbled, he put his arm around her. "You'd better sit down. I'll get you something to drink."

She didn't want to sit down. His arm around her, supporting her, comforting her, was heavenly. She wanted to take hold of his arm so he couldn't remove it. Ever! She allowed him to settle her into a chair. He sat down beside her, her hands still in his grasp.

"I really am all right," she said. "I guess it's just the tension and worry."

"The lack of sleep and lack of food. I haven't seen you eat more than a bite all day."

"I'm too keyed up to be hungry."

"You won't do you or your father any good if you get sick."

"I promise I won't. I guess it's relief, too, having you and Mrs. Bennett to help." She had to keep including Mrs. Bennett. If she thought of just Holt, she'd start thinking thoughts that would lead to trouble.

"I'll be here as long as you and your father need me. You'd better get some sleep. And I do mean sleep. I don't want to find you've been pacing your room or lying in bed wide awake."

She smiled. "I'll do my best." She tried to stand, but her body wouldn't cooperate. Holt stood and pulled her to her feet.

"Are you sure you're all right? I can carry you upstairs if you want."

That thought nearly caused her muscles to go out from under her. "That won't be necessary."

"You don't have to reject every offer of help, you know. It's what friends do."

She felt herself flush. "I guess I'm not very good at accepting help. It always makes me feel I'm somehow inadequate."

"Who told you you had to be able to do everything yourself?"

"I was so afraid of what people would say if they knew, I kept refusing their help until they stopped offering. Then I assumed they didn't offer because they didn't want to."

"You've got to believe that people *like* you and your father, regardless of any imperfections."

This was more than she could assimilate now. Everything had gotten more difficult since Holt had forced his way into her life. At the same time, she had a feeling that his presence would make things better. That thought didn't make any sense, but she was too tired to attempt to figure it out.

"I'll go straight to bed. Be sure to call me when it's my turn. And don't try to be noble and let me sleep an extra hour," she said when he started to reply. "I can fall asleep over my coffee and no one will be the worse for it."

"I don't need much sleep."

"You said we were in this together, so that means we share equally."

"Okay. I'll wake you when it's your turn." He leaned down and kissed her gently on the lips. "Sweet dreams."

They would be. She'd dream of his kiss.

Felicity woke to the sound of voices. Her first thought was that Holt had come for her because it was time to get up, but as soon as the sleep cleared from her brain, she realized the voices were coming from somewhere outside her room. Was there an emergency? Deciding not to take the time to dress, she threw on a robe and left her room.

She didn't expect to find the hallway in darkness. Nor did she expect to discover that the voices were coming from her father's bedroom.

It was just Holt and her father talking. Her father frequently woke in the middle of the night. She turned back to her bedroom. But even as she started to close the door behind her, she paused. Something about the voices wasn't right. Holt spoke in a calm, measured voice, but her father's words sounded rapid and excited, his voice rising and falling in a totally unfamiliar fashion.

She stepped back into the hall and approached her father's bedroom door. She couldn't understand what he was saying because Holt was talking at the same time, but her father was obviously upset. Holt would have called her if he needed help, but this was her father — she couldn't go back to bed knowing something was wrong. She opened the door quietly.

Her father was sitting up in the bed, his hands waving in the air, facing Holt with an expression that was full of pain. At first Felicity couldn't tell what he was saying, but then she caught the word *Andersonville.*

"I can hear them," he was saying to Holt. "I know you can hear them, too. They're just in the next room."

"Andersonville was long ago," Holt said. "There are no people there anymore."

"That's what they tell you," her father said, suddenly dropping his voice, "but it's not true. They're sick, but they won't let me help them. Can't you hear them calling?"

"There's nobody here," Holt said again. "It was just a bad dream."

"It's not a dream. I can hear them now. Why can't you?" He covered his ears. "Their screams are horrible. I can't sleep."

Fear gripped Felicity. What was wrong with her father? He'd never heard voices that weren't there. "What's wrong?" she asked Holt.

"I'm sorry we woke you," he said without turning around. "You should go back to bed."

"What's wrong with Papa?"

"He's having hallucinations. It's not uncommon with people who stop drinking all at once."

"You can hear them, can't you?" her father said, turning to her. "The voices, the men down in the prison yard."

"Answer him," Holt said.

"There's nobody here, Papa," she said. "I don't hear any voices."

"They're worse than they used to be," her father said. "There are more of them."

"There's nobody here," Holt said. "Keep telling yourself it's just your imagination. Help me hold him while I give him some laudanum," he said in a lower voice to Felicity.

"I feel like a traitor conspiring against him."

"You'll be thankful you did once this is over."

"You intended to give it to him all along, didn't you?" she said when he reached for a glass on the bedside table.

"I prepared it in case I needed it. I didn't expect you to be up to help."

It was one of Holt's more annoying traits, always having a reasonable answer whenever she objected to something he wanted to do. She'd taken care of her father for more than half her life, and she'd done just fine without Holt's help.

No, she hadn't. She'd been successful at the

job she was doing, but she was doing the wrong job, trying to hide the problem rather than face it. She didn't know if she was too kindhearted or just weak, but it had taken Holt to make both her and her father face up to the problem.

"You've got to hold him steady," Holt said. "He's moving so much, the laudanum will end up on his nightshirt rather than down his throat."

"I'm doing the best I can."

"Use your body weight against him."

"How?"

"Lean on him."

She laid her father's left arm across his chest, then draped her body across him. Her father was still talking about the dying prisoners, but the laudanum choked off the words. He sputtered, coughed, then swallowed.

"Just a little more," Holt said. "Whiskey acts like a sedative on people. When they stop drinking, their systems can become overactive for a period of time. Laudanum can help them get over the worst of it."

She didn't really care about a medical explanation. She just wanted it over and her father back to normal. *Their life had never been normal. What would the future be like? She didn't like the unknown. It frightened her.

"You can release him now," Holt said. "I think he swallowed enough."

Felicity didn't want to look her father in the face, but she couldn't stop herself. It was worse than she expected. He looked confused. Worse, he looked hurt, as though she'd betrayed him.

"Why did you do that?" her father asked.

"Holt says you're hallucinating. He says you're so keyed up, you can't sleep."

"I can't sleep because of the voices," he said. "I can even recognize some of them."

"There aren't any voices," Holt said in his calm, quiet voice. "The alcohol withdrawal is causing you to hear things that aren't there."

"Can you see anything?" Felicity asked.

"Sometimes," her father replied. "But mostly it's the voices."

"What are they saying?"

Holt shook his head. She knew he wanted her to convince her father the voices weren't real. Gradually the laudanum took hold and her father's voice lost some of its volume and his gaze some of its intensity. Finally his hold on her loosened and he relaxed enough to lean back against his pillow. By small increments his eyelids began to droop and his words to come more slowly.

Then he was asleep.

For a moment, Felicity thought the pressure inside her would explode. She had the sensation of having to hold on tight or she'd start screaming or throwing herself about the room. Then just as suddenly the tension broke and she felt too weak even to sit up. She sagged against her chair, dropped her head into her hands.

"Tired?" Holt asked.

There wasn't a word to describe how she felt. She was empty, physically exhausted, unable to understand the flood of conflicting emotions that washed over her.

"I know it wasn't easy to do what you just did, but this way is much easier on your father."

She knew that, but that didn't stop her from hating it, from being angry with herself for being part of it.

"You can go back to bed now. You've still got time for another hour of sleep."

She couldn't possibly go back to sleep. The shocked, hurt look of betrayal in her father's eyes would keep her awake for weeks to come.

"You go," she said without moving any part of her body except her lips. "I'll sit up with him."

"You're exhausted."

"So are you." She heard his chair creak. He must have gotten up. Maybe he'd accepted her offer to relieve him early. She heard his footsteps, but she didn't have the energy to look up.

"You'd be asleep in fifteen minutes," he said softly.

He'd come around the bed to stand close to her. She opened her eyes to see him staring down at her, a worried expression on his face. She didn't know how it was possible, but even now there was something seductive about him. She felt something stir within her, a response, a reaction. It was clear that neither worry nor fatigue had the power to cancel out the effect of his physical presence. Even now she could feel energy beginning to return to her body, feel the tightening of muscles, the surge of warmth in her belly, the awakening of thoughts she'd tried hard to banish from her mind.

"I'll be fine," she insisted. "I just need a few minutes to recover."

The nervous energy came flooding back, tightening her nerves, awaking her senses, threatening to put her on edge once more.

"Give me a few minutes to put on some clothes," she said.

"You're going back to bed," Holt said. "Even if you can't sleep, you can rest."

She wasn't going to argue with him — he never listened to her — but she wasn't going back to bed. She heaved herself out of the chair, took one step, and her legs went out from under her.

Holt caught her in his arms, pressing her body tightly against his.

"Now will you go back to bed like I asked?" he said.

"No."

She wanted to explain, but that was the only word she could manage. Being in Holt's arms completely destroyed her ability to think about anything else. Even after he'd kissed her that time in the parlor, she'd considered her reaction shock more than attraction. Now there was no question in her mind. She was powerfully attracted to Holt, and the attraction was very physical.

"I could carry you back to your room."

"I'd come back immediately."

"Not if you can't walk."

"It was just a momentary weakness. You can let me go. I'm fine now."

"You're not fine, and you know it."

"You still don't have to worry about me."

"I can't help it."

"Why?" People had managed to keep from worrying about her all her life. She didn't know why he should be different.

"You've been struggling alone for years, doing far more than any one person ought to do, especially a young girl."

"I'm not a young girl anymore."

Everything about her body, his closeness, made her acutely aware of her maturation, of the fact that her needs were entirely different from those of a young girl.

"But you were when you started taking care of your father."

"That was a long time ago."

"For far too many years you didn't think of yourself, what you wanted, what you *needed*."

She trembled, wondering if he knew what she needed, what she wanted at this moment. She was afraid to articulate her needs, even to let them form into coherent thoughts. She knew that once she did, she'd never be able to deny them again.

"I know what it's like to feel there's nobody you can talk to," Holt said, "nobody who can understand that you have dreams of your own, that you feel like you're sacrificing your life and nobody appreciates it. I know how it feels to wonder if there'll be anything left for you when it's all over, and I know what it's like to come face to face with the certainty that there will be nothing left for you — *nothing at all.*"

She didn't know where the sobs came from, but once they started she couldn't stop them. Holt had pried the cap off her fears, and the pressure that had built up over the years boiled over. But even as she started to push away from Holt, she felt an even greater need to be close to him, to cling to him, to lean on his strength. The fact that he *did* know what she'd been through made her feel she was sharing with him rather than depending on him. When she felt Holt's arms tighten around her, she abandoned all resistance.

She didn't know how long she cried. It seemed like hours, yet Holt never moved his arms, never eased his hold on her, never let her feel she wasn't welcome to stay as long as she wanted. But even a well that has taken years to fill will eventually run dry, and finally her tears stopped.

"I'm okay. You can let me go," she said, keeping her gaze on the floor. "I won't fall down."

"Do you mind my holding you?"

The question surprised her so much, she almost told him she liked it very much. She stopped her treacherous tongue just in time. She looked up at him. "There's no need."

"Do you only do the things you *need* to do? What about the things you *want* to do?"

"What about you?" she asked, turning the question back on him. "Did you always get to do the things you wanted to do?"

"No, but I'm about to take care of one thing right now."

Then he kissed her.

Chapter Nineteen

The shock of feeling Holt's lips on her own rendered Felicity nearly incapable of thought as well as action. Any strength that remained to her simply drained away. She wanted to respond, but she couldn't. She felt paralyzed. Holt broke the kiss.

"Sorry. I shouldn't have taken advantage of you."

"Why did you kiss me?" she managed to ask.

"I've been wanting to kiss you again ever since that day in the parlor."

"Why?"

"Because I like kissing you," Holt said.

"But you don't like me."

"What makes you think that?"

"We're always arguing."

"That doesn't mean I don't like you or want to kiss you."

"Why?" She sounded like a child, repeating the same word over and over again, but she wanted to know. She *needed* to know.

"Do you have to have answers for everything?"

"For this I do."

His hold on her had eased when he broke the kiss, but now it tightened again. Somehow her arms had found their way around his neck.

"You're a very attractive woman," Holt said. "I've thought so from the first time I saw you."

"Do you kiss all the attractive women you meet?" It was a stupid question, but she was feeling a bit stupid right then.

"No."

"They why did you kiss me?"

He chuckled softly. "For a woman with her arms around my neck, you sure are full of questions."

"I've never had my arms around a man's neck before. No man has ever kissed me like you did. Why did you want to?" She looked into his eyes, hoping to find answers there to her questions.

"Partly from impulse. Partly because you looked so vulnerable I couldn't resist."

She didn't know if she liked his answer. She was willing to give Holt the benefit of the doubt, but she wasn't going to accept being kissed because he thought she was needy. She wanted to be kissed for herself.

"I thought men only kissed their wives, or women they planned to marry. Honorable men, that is," she added, thinking of Beau Stregghorn.

"In Vermont, many men don't even do that," Holt said. "I find the Southern practice of kissing friends, especially when they're as pretty as you, more appealing."

"So you don't have to love a woman to kiss her."

"No."

318

"Not even on the mouth?"

"Not even then."

"So I could kiss you and not create a scandal?"

"Do you want to kiss me?"

She wanted to say yes, but she couldn't quite bring herself to do it. "I don't have any experience. I wouldn't know how to do it."

"You don't need much experience. Children learn to do it."

She didn't want childish kisses. She didn't want a purely friendly kiss any more than she wanted to be slobbered over by a philanderer like Beau Stregghorn. She wanted a kiss that would swallow her up and convince her that her dream of being loved wasn't hopeless, that a man could love her with all the deathless passion her mother and father had shared. She wanted a kiss that convinced her she could be loved even though she wasn't as beautiful as Vivian. She wanted a kiss that convinced her that her long wait had not been in vain, that her mother had spoken truly when she said Felicity was born to love. She wanted a kiss that would wipe away all the pain and rejection, the fear that no one would ever love her, the sleepless and tear-filled nights when the longing hurt so much it was like a physical pain. She wanted a kiss that would wipe out the memory of all those empty years. She wanted a kiss that would transform her whole existence.

And she wanted it from Holt.

"Will you teach me?" That was about as forward as she could be.

"You have to help," Holt said. "It won't work if I do everything."

"What should I do?"

"Go with your instincts."

Without giving her mind time to think, she pulled his head down toward her, stood on tiptoes, and kissed him squarely on the mouth.

Holt seemed to know exactly what she wanted. His lips gently covered her mouth. She was shocked at her own eagerness to respond to the touch of his lips. Parting her lips, she raised herself to meet him in the kiss. The touch of his lips was a delicious sensation that sent spirals of ecstasy through her. She returned Holt's kiss with reckless abandon. Apparently, kissing was best without any attempt at control.

Holt's response was instantaneous.

His gentle kiss turned hungry, demanding, insistent. His mouth covered hers hungrily, devouring its softness. The strong hardness of his lips sent the pit of her stomach into a wild swirl. She found herself rising on her tiptoes, trying to increase the pressure of the kiss. Her universe narrowed until it contained no one but the two of them. She felt shock when Holt broke away.

Raising his mouth from hers, he gazed into her eyes. "Not bad for a beginner," he said after his breath slowed.

She didn't want to talk. His kiss had left her mouth burning with an aching need for another kiss. She drew his face to hers in a renewed embrace.

Reclaiming her lips, he crushed her to him. She felt her knees weaken as his mouth devoured hers with a hunger ten times greater than she thought humanly possible. His lips were hard and searching. She had never experienced anything so intense, so earthshaking, so totally involving. It was as though her whole being resided in the lips that touched Holt's mouth. All her physical energy, all her emotional strength was directed to the same end — diving without restraint into a kiss that felt as though it united them as one.

When his tongue forced its way into her mouth, the shock was enormous, but the effect was profound. She realized she was in love with this man and wanted nothing more than to remain in his arms forever. Gasping in horror at her realization, Felicity abruptly broke their kiss.

"What's wrong?" Holt asked without releasing her from his embrace.

Felicity couldn't tell him. It was all she could do not to struggle wildly to break his embrace. "I've never done anything like this," she said. "It's a shock."

"You didn't seem shocked. You wanted to kiss me as much as I wanted to kiss you."

"That's what shocked me," she confessed. "I

never thought of myself as a loose woman."

Her remark surprised a crack of laughter out of Holt. "You'd have to do a lot more to be considered a loose woman."

"This is plenty for me. Not to mention that I've been standing here shamelessly allowing you to kiss me —"

"And kissing me back," Holt added.

"— while my father lies asleep in bed not six feet away."

"I don't think he would be too upset."

"I should hope he *would* be upset to see his daughter acting like an abandoned hussy."

"Let me tell you what a real abandoned hussy would have done."

"I don't want to know," Felicity said, trying to break from his embrace. "I feel embarrassed enough already."

"Why? You haven't done anything unusual."

"I don't know what kind of women you've met, but no woman I know would stand around kissing a near stranger when she should be watching her sick father."

"I'm not a stranger, and we did nothing to be embarrassed about, even if your father were awake and watching."

The thought made Felicity shiver. "Have you ever stood around kissing Vivian like that?"

The laughter and warmth left Holt's face. He released her.

"No."

"If you don't think it's right to behave like

this with the woman you intend to marry, then it certainly isn't right to behave like this with me."

She didn't understand his reaction. He didn't exactly turn cold, but he was distant, closed. The feeling of connection that had existed between them just moments before had completely vanished.

"Are you sure you can't go back to sleep?" he asked.

"Even more so now."

"Then I'll take advantage of your offer."

She wanted to ask him what was wrong, what she had said that had caused such a drastic change in him. His expression was so odd, she was almost afraid, but she couldn't stop the words. She had to know. "What did I say wrong?"

"Nothing."

"I must have. You've turned cold."

He hesitated. "You asked me if I'd ever kissed Vivian as I'd kissed you. I just realized I've never kissed her *at all.*"

Holt knew he'd dumbfounded Felicity when he said he'd never kissed Vivian, but that was nothing compared to his own reaction. How could he believe he was in love with a woman he'd never kissed? More stunning still, he couldn't recall ever wanting to kiss Vivian the way he'd just kissed Felicity. She wasn't the only one who wouldn't get any sleep tonight.

He had to have some answers, and he had to have them right now.

His relationship with Vivian had begun eleven years ago when his uncle introduced her to him as his ward. He was nineteen, she was eleven. She was beautiful and charming even then. Whenever his uncle came into Charlottesville from Price's Nob, she would hold Holt's hand, hug him, and give him a big kiss on the cheek when it was time to leave. He'd fallen under her spell immediately.

She loved to tease him about what they'd do when she was old enough to marry him. No matter how many handsome young men she met, she insisted she liked Holt best of all. He supposed that was when the idea of marrying her started to take shape in his mind.

The Christmas Vivian was fifteen, while his aunt carried Vivian off to look for material for a new Christmas dress, Holt's uncle said he wanted to have a serious talk about Vivian's future. He had explained how he and his wife loved Vivian as their own child. He said it was his fondest hope that Holt would marry Vivian. He promised to leave Price's Nob to Holt so he could be sure Vivian would be provided for.

It had seemed the most natural thing in the world for Holt to promise to marry Vivian. He'd never been attracted to any other woman, but at fifteen Vivian was too young to be married. A year later, Holt's mother had fallen very ill and he had gone back to Vermont. He knew the moment he saw his uncle after his return that something was wrong.

His uncle handed him the note that said Vivian had married Abe Calvert and had gone to live with his family in Texas. She swore she'd never love anybody as much as she loved him, but begged him not to follow her. She said she liked Abe a lot and was certain they could be happy together.

His uncle followed her to Texas and came back to report that Vivian seemed happy with her new life. The letter Vivian sent to Holt expressed her undying love and promised once again she would never forget him.

Holt had been certain that all his hopes for a happy life were blighted forever.

When the talk of war started, he ignored it. If the Southern states wanted to secede, he didn't see why they shouldn't. But when the casualty lists for the first battle came out, sprinkled with the names of several of his college classmates, he knew he couldn't remain on the sidelines. He volunteered for the Confederacy to help save the lives of his friends. By the time the focus of the war changed, he was already with the Night Riders and couldn't consider deserting them.

He saw the notice of Abe Calvert's death on the casualty lists for the battle of Chancellorsville. Holt's uncle died a year later, leaving Holt to inherit a ruined Price's Nob. When the war ended, he came to Texas to look for Vivian. Never once did he question that he loved her and wanted to marry her.

Why hadn't he wanted to kiss her all those years ago? Had he considered himself too old, Vivian too young? Their relationship had been more like that of brother and sister, yet he'd always been sure he wanted to marry her and take care of her. He was stunned to discover he hadn't thought of kissing her that night when she appeared at Gloria Webster's party. He definitely wanted to kiss Felicity again. Why? The answer was important.

When had his feelings changed from those of a green and inexperienced young man dazzled by a beautiful child to those of a grown man who wanted to make a beautiful woman his wife, the mother of his children, the architect of his home, the companion of his old age.

Even though he knew Vivian had a son, he couldn't think of her as a mother. He pictured her at parties, beautifully dressed, vibrant, with men crowded around her. He couldn't visualize her sitting up at night with her father while he suffered through alcohol withdrawal. He was no more successful imagining her as a companion of his old age. Vivian would hate old age and struggle against it.

He *could* imagine Felicity as a wife, mother, and creator of a home that was a refuge for her family. He could see her caring for every aspect of her family's life, because he'd already seen her do that for her father, encouraging him in his dreams and comforting him in his sorrows. He could easily imagine her enjoying a quiet evening at home, a companionable walk, going to bed early.

So how could he love a woman who wasn't anything like what he wanted in a wife?

Because he'd fallen in love with a dream. Because he'd let himself feel responsible for her, because once the idea of marriage had been placed in his head, nothing had come along to dislodge it. But now he had met Felicity, and she had awakened emotions and feelings he'd never experienced with Vivian. He didn't know how far his feelings for Felicity had progressed, but he knew they were the kind of emotions that could grow into love.

He wouldn't turn his back on Vivian, but how could he handle two women in his life? He'd already proved he couldn't handle one.

"You ought to go for a walk," Felicity said to her father. "It's better than being cooped up inside all afternoon."

"If I left this house alone, I'd head straight for a bar," her father said.

"I'll go with you."

"Thanks, but I'm staying put. I don't want anybody to see me shaking like I've got one foot in the grave. My tongue quivers so badly, I'm practically unintelligible. I'm sweating, and my mind is so fuzzy, I probably wouldn't recognize half the people I know."

Felicity's heart went out to her father, but there was nothing she could do. "I know it's bad now, but Holt says it ought to start getting better in a few days. If you could just —"

Her father dropped a small china bird he'd been fingering nervously. It hit the floor and shattered.

"See what I mean? I can't even hold on to a stupid bird."

"It's not important. I never did like it."

"That's not the point. I can't do anything. I'm useless. I'm worse than useless. You'd be better off without me."

Felicity guided her father to a chair. She knew he'd only remain seated a few minutes. "Don't talk nonsense. What would I do without you?"

"Find yourself a nice husband, settle down, and raise a family."

"I still have plenty of time for that."

"You're twenty-six, Felicity. Everybody considers you an old maid, and it's all my fault. I'd hoped maybe you'd like Holt enough to marry him. He's a nice man."

"He's in love with another woman."

"I'm not so sure. I think if you —"

"I'm not going to try to take Holt from Vivian Calvert. You've never seen her, but it's hard to imagine anyone could be that beautiful."

"Holt's interested in more than beauty."

"Right now he's interested in sleeping."

She had been surprised when Holt had come down that morning looking as if he hadn't slept. He'd mumbled something about having things on his mind. She figured he was feeling guilty about kissing her and had lain awake half the night figuring out how to tell her it didn't mean anything, that he couldn't understand how he could have done anything so foolish when he was in love with Vivian. They had no patients until the afternoon, so Felicity had insisted Holt go back to bed.

She'd been relieved when he took her suggestion. She was feeling more than uncomfortable about last night. She was feeling guilty . . . and horrified. She could have stopped him — it wouldn't have taken more than a word. Instead, she had kissed him back with a passion she didn't know she possessed. Well-bred Southern ladies didn't throw themselves at a man — even when the man was their husband. Gentlemen expected a certain decorum from a lady. She didn't know where her decorum was hiding, but it certainly hadn't made an appearance last night. She could hardly believe she had stood kissing a man in her father's bedroom while he lay sleeping nearby!

But she was more horrified to realize she had fallen in love with Holt. That was insanity in so many ways, she didn't even want to think about it. Once her father got over the worst of his withdrawal, she would insist that Holt move back to Mrs. Bennett's house. The minute she felt her father was safely out of the woods, she'd insist that Holt set up his own practice if he wanted to continue in medicine. She didn't dare let herself be around him more than was absolutely essential.

"He looked worse than I did this morning," her father said. "You two don't have to keep sitting up with me."

"I think he's worried about other things."

"What?"

"He doesn't confide in me, but I imagine finding Vivian has given him a lot to think about."

"Like how to get out of marrying her."

"That's not fair, Papa. You've never even met her."

Her father got up and began to move around the room, trailing his fingers along the backs of chairs, toying with the fringe of a throw on the back of the sofa, twisting his hands together to keep from touching anything breakable. "I've heard what you've said about her. She's not the right woman for Holt. A woman that beautiful will never think of anybody but herself."

"That's not true of every woman. Some people have been kind enough to say I'm beautiful, and I worry about you all the time."

"Honey, you're my own daughter and I love you dearly, but you're lovely, not beautiful. There's an essential difference. Men like talking to you, being with you, enjoying your company, but they don't follow you around like they're in a trance."

"I wouldn't want them to."

Her father put down a small glass dish with shaky hands. "That's the difference. A beautiful woman would. That's how she'd judge her worth. I'm glad you're not beautiful that way. Too much external beauty can rot the soul."

From what she'd seen of Vivian, Felicity suspected her father was right, at least in this instance.

"True beauty comes from love, and love comes from within," her father said. "If it's true that beauty is as beauty does, you're the most beautiful woman in the world."

A knock at the front door shortened the hug Felicity gave her father. She was tempted not to answer, but it might be a medical emergency. She was shocked to open the door and see Vivian Calvert and one of the men she'd seen in Vivian's court.

"I've come to see Holt," Vivian announced and entered without waiting for an invitation. "I haven't seen him in three days. Is he sick?"

"This isn't a good time for me to entertain guests," Felicity said as the young man followed Vivian into the house.

"You don't have to entertain me," Vivian said. "Just tell Holt I'm here."

"He's asleep."

"I *knew* he was sick!" she said, satisfied in her assumption.

"My father hasn't been feeling well. Holt was

up part of the night with him."

Vivian had been moving toward the parlor, but she stopped. "Is he sick?"

"No."

"Come on, Edward," she said to her companion as she moved toward the parlor once again. "We can plan your party while I wait for Holt to get dressed."

Apparently, Felicity's company was neither needed nor desired.

"Who's that man?" Vivian asked. She'd stopped just inside the parlor doorway.

"That's my father, Dr. Moore. Papa, this is Holt's friend, Vivian Calvert. I'm sorry. I don't know the gentleman."

"Edward Spiers," the man said, extending his hand to her father, who moved from his position behind the sofa to shake the young man's hand, then retreated once more.

"Tell Holt to hurry," Vivian said. "Edward is taking me for a ride in his new carriage."

"I'll see if he wants to come down."

"He will," Vivian said, and settled herself in the sofa, indicating to Edward that he should sit next to her.

Felicity didn't want to wake Holt, but obviously Vivian didn't expect anything else. Besides, Holt would probably be angry if he missed seeing Vivian. "Papa, would you like a nap?"

"I want to talk to your father," Vivian said. "I've got a little boy who's always having headaches, and nobody can find anything wrong with him."

"You ought to ask Holt," Felicity said.

"Holt's good at cutting people up," Vivian said. "He doesn't know anything about children."

Felicity decided she'd better leave the room before she said something extremely rude. Holt did have more experience as a surgeon than a family doctor, but talking about him like that would hurt him deeply. The more she thought about Vivian's remark, the angrier she got. By the time she reached Holt's bedroom, she was so incensed, she had to pause and force herself to calm down. She knocked lightly on the door.

"What is it?" Holt's response came so quickly, she knew he hadn't been asleep.

"Vivian is here. I told her you were resting, but she insisted that I wake you. I'll tell her you can't come down, if you like."

"No, I'll come down. Give me a few minutes to dress."

"Are you sure? I know you're tired."

"No more than you are."

"You're done with your last patient after five. I could ask her to come back then."

She heard Holt laugh. "No one has ever told Vivian to go away and come back later. She'd be sure you were joking."

He was probably right, but Felicity supposed she couldn't put all the blame on Vivian. If men insisted on treating her like a princess with practically imperial rights, you couldn't blame her for taking advantage.

"I'll tell her you'll be down in a few minutes."

Holt didn't answer, so she started back downstairs. She didn't want to return to the parlor. She could imagine Vivian plying her father with all kinds of questions and not understanding the answers. She probably didn't set eyes on her son for more than a few minutes a day.

Felicity told herself that was unkind. She'd never seen Vivian outside the context of a party. She didn't really know anything about the woman, and to be casting aspersions on her motherhood was extremely unfair. She was acting like a jealous shrew, which was exactly the kind of woman Felicity didn't want to be. She paused a few minutes at the foot of the stairs to get her emotions under control. Taking a deep breath, she walked into the parlor in time to see her father slowly slide from a chair onto the floor.

"He was just sitting there," Vivian said; "then he just stopped talking. I think he's dead."

"Holt!" Felicity screamed as she ran to her father and sank by his side. "I need you!"

Chapter Twenty

Holt had put on his shirt and pants and was about to put on his shoes when he heard Felicity's scream. His reaction was instinctive and instantaneous. He dropped his shoes, crossed the room at a run, jerked open the door, raced down the short hall, and took the stairs three or four at a time. As he hit the floor, he heard his name again.

"Holt!"

He sprinted to the parlor to see Felicity bending over her father, whose body was experiencing light spasms.

"I was asking him some questions about my son," Vivian said as Holt hastened to Dr. Moore's side. "He suddenly got this funny look, uttered a queer little moan, and slid to the floor."

"What's wrong with him?" Felicity asked Holt. "He acts like he's having a seizure, but he's not epileptic."

"It is a seizure. The first thing we have to do is move the furniture out of the way so he can't hurt himself," Holt said.

"Get up!" Felicity ordered Vivian. "Help me move the sofa," she said to Edward. When Vivian didn't move, Felicity grabbed her hand and pulled her to her feet. "Move out of the way. Take the other end and move it toward the doorway," she said to Edward. The startled man obeyed without question.

Holt moved a chair and table against the wall. Felicity and Edward moved the remaining chair and hassock, then turned to the coffee table.

"Now what do we do?" Felicity asked.

"We need to turn him on his side."

It wasn't difficult to roll her father on his side, but it was virtually impossible to keep him there. The spasms increased in strength until it was all Holt could do to keep him in position.

"Don't just stand there," Felicity said to Edward. "Holt needs help."

Edward dropped to the floor opposite Holt. Between the two of them, they steadied her father enough to keep him on his side.

"Is he going to die?" Vivian asked.

"I expect he'll come out of it in a little while," Holt said. "Meanwhile, we have to be careful to watch his breathing. I need to make sure he doesn't swallow his tongue or choke on anything that might come up from his stomach. Vivian, throw me a pillow. I need something to put under his head."

"I'll get it," Felicity said.

"You can bring me a blanket. We need to keep him warm to avoid the possibility of his going into shock."

Holt took the pillow Vivian handed him and placed it under Dr. Moore's head, keeping his face to the side. Felicity was back within moments with a light blanket, which they spread over him. Holt checked Dr. Moore's mouth to be sure he hadn't swallowed his tongue, but his breathing was unimpaired.

"What do we do now?" Felicity asked.

"We wait," Holt said.

No one spoke, all of them staring at Dr. Moore, but it was Felicity's expression that would remain etched in Holt's memory for a long time. He had seen fear expressed in a thousand different ways, but none more heart-rending. It had gouged deep lines in her face until she looked exhausted from the effort to sustain her courage. He wanted to reach out and enfold her in his arms, to comfort her, to make her feel safe, but he couldn't turn his attention from Dr. Moore.

"He's going to be fine," he said to Felicity. "These seizures don't usually last long."

"Nothing like this has ever happened before," she said, her voice sounding hollow, unlike itself. "Is there anything you can do?"

"No."

The spasms gradually became weaker, giving Holt time to remember that Vivian and her young man were still in the room. Edward — he thought that was the correct name — remained kneeling directly across Dr. Moore from him, ready to help if the spasms should get worse. Vivian remained standing against the wall, her expression one of strong distaste.

"He's drunk," she said.

"He's not drunk," Holt corrected. "He's an alcoholic."

"You can't fool me with words," Vivian said. "Sometimes my father drank so much, he'd pass out for a whole day. Then when he woke up, he'd go into spasms just like that if he didn't get something to drink."

Holt was tempted to stuff a pillow in Vivian's mouth. She seemed unaware of the effect her words were having on Felicity, but Holt knew that each word cut with the sharpness of a knife. He'd heard them said about his own father, could remember the meanness of the children who used his father's weakness to taunt him, could remember the desire to disappear and never be seen again.

But he knew that Felicity would never consider disappearing. No matter how much the words or actions of people hurt her, she would use her own body to shield her father from the cruelties and insults.

She was better than he was, Holt thought. Stronger, too.

"People ought to be told," Vivian said.

"People know," Holt said. "We've all come together to help him conquer the problem."

"It will happen again," Vivian said. "People like him can't help themselves."

"Just because your father and mine were powerless to overcome their weakness doesn't mean other people can't," Holt said.

"My father *will* succeed," Felicity said. "I won't leave his side until I'm perfectly certain he's well again."

"Good," Vivian said. She appeared to shake the gravity of the scene from her mind as easily as a dog would shake water from his coat. "I haven't seen you," she said to Holt. "You haven't been to any parties."

"I've been helping Felicity look after her father," Holt said.

"Surely Miss Moore would sit with her father so you could go out and enjoy yourself."

"I'd be happy to assume the entire responsibility for my father," Felicity said.

"There," Vivian said with a brilliant smile. "Now you can come to Mary Elliot's party tonight. She tells me she's invited you."

"I won't be going to any parties until Dr. Moore is better." The spasms had ceased, but the doctor hadn't regained consciousness.

"But if his daughter is willing to take care of him, there's no reason —"

"There's every reason," Holt replied before she could say more. "Besides, I wouldn't be in a party mood worrying about him."

"But he's a stranger," Vivian said. "Why would you be worried about him?"

"Because he's my friend," Holt said. "Besides, I promised, and I don't break a promise."

"But —"

"The doctor appears to be coming around," Edward said. "I'm sure he'll be a lot more comfortable without strangers here."

"He won't know where he is or who we are," Vivian snapped.

Felicity had dropped to the floor next to her father, anxiety pinching her face. "He doesn't look awake to me," she said.

"I saw some movement of his eyelids," Holt said.

"I haven't had a chance to talk to Holt," Vivian said to Edward.

"I'll try to see you some afternoon," Holt said without taking his eyes off the doctor.

"I may not be at home," Vivian said petulantly. "I can't sit around waiting for you to show up."

"Then I'll see you when I can."

"Will you see them to the door?" Felicity asked Holt.

"We can find our way out," Edward said.

Holt knew it was rude to leave guests to show themselves out, but he was nettled at Vivian for what she'd said about the doctor. He could understand why she would never forgive her own father for leaving her an orphan, but he couldn't understand why she didn't realize it would hurt Felicity just as much to have someone refer to her father as a drunk.

"She's angry with you," Felicity said after Vivian had practically flounced out of the room.

"She'll have forgotten about it by tomorrow."

"I doubt it. She feels slighted that you paid

attention to another woman. She's a woman, and I know how we think."

"Your father is coming around."

Felicity forgot Vivian. "What should I do?"

"Continue to make him as comfortable as possible. He probably won't know where he is or what happened. He might not even know who we are, but he'll be back to his normal self in a few hours."

"A few hours! You have patients to see."

"I'll tell them to come back tomorrow."

"I'll take care of my father. You take care of the patients."

"You might need some help."

"If you'll tell me what to expect and what to do, I'll be fine."

Holt felt hurt that she was so anxious to get him out of the room. Was she this upset about the kisses they'd shared last night? "Don't drive me away," he said. "I want to help."

"You have helped. You are helping."

"I don't mean just by seeing patients. I mean by being here with your father. With you."

"Why?"

She wasn't merely asking the obvious question. There was something fearful about the way she looked at him.

"Partly because he wouldn't be in this condition if I hadn't forced it upon him. More than that, I like your father. He's an excellent doctor and a fine man. I want to do everything I can for him. And I want to help you. You've had to shoulder too much responsibility for too long. You love your father — he's all you have in the world, the only person who loves you. You also feel guilty for protecting him so he could drink and grow worse. You're frantic at the thought of losing him. I know how you feel, how helpless, how afraid. I want to be with you, to let you know you're not alone."

"Thank you, but I can handle it."

"For God's sake, Felicity, let me help. I won't tell anybody what I see."

She looked up, her expression that of a person whose most fearful secret has been dragged out into the open.

"Don't look so surprised. I know why you've been trying to get rid of me ever since I got here. You've been afraid to let anyone know your secret. You've kept everyone at a distance. Why did you think we would betray you? Why did you think we wouldn't understand?"

"You didn't."

"Not at first, but I changed after I understood the situation better. So will the others. You've got to be bone tired, not to mention exhausted from worrying. Your friends would like to help. You need time to relax and enjoy yourself, to think of yourself first, to remember you're a young and attractive woman. That's part of the reason Mrs. Bennett volunteered to sit with your father. She likes him, and she wanted to give you a chance to have a few hours to yourself. That's part of the reason

342

Charlotte invited you to the party and I insisted you go with me."

"Is that why you kissed me last night — to help me believe I was still young and attractive? You should have known that wouldn't work. I've seen Vivian."

"Last night had nothing to do with Vivian."

"That's what I thought. We're so different, you don't even see us as belonging in the same picture."

"That's not what I meant."

"Vivian is the beautiful, charming creature you put on a pedestal and want for your own. I'm the doctor's very ordinary old-maid daughter who needs cheering up once in a while. You figured a few kisses ought to do the trick."

Holt had been feeling guilty about kissing Felicity the night before. The kisses had unleashed a passion in him so strong, so different from anything he'd ever experienced, it shocked him. He realized they had had very much the same effect on Felicity.

"I know you're upset over your father, but that's no reason to come up with such a ridiculous —"

"Now I'm ridiculous — probably hysterical as well."

"You're neither, but you're very upset, and it's affecting your thinking."

"It is *not* affecting my thinking. I'm a rational woman who's always been able to handle herself under any circumstances."

"And you probably could handle your father being ill if that were the only thing bothering you."

"There's nothing else."

"There's last night."

"Last night was a mistake."

"Then why is it bothering you?"

Felicity took a deep breath as though calming her nerves — or steeling them in preparation for something unpleasant. "You don't know what I feel about last night."

"Then tell me."

"No."

"Then I'll tell you what *I* feel."

"My father is waking up. I don't have time to listen."

"It won't take long. I feel confused. I thought I knew what love was, but I never felt for Vivian what I felt for you last night. Then when you asked me if I'd ever kissed her, I realized I never *wanted* to kiss her the way I kissed you. Like I want to kiss you again."

"It's never going to happen again."

"You want to kiss me again."

"No, I don't."

"You think you don't because you're afraid. I won't kiss you again until I get some things straight in my mind. But I will kiss you again, and you're going to want me to do it."

He didn't know why he said that. He'd spent half the night telling himself he'd make sure it didn't happen again. Now he'd just promised Felicity that it would. She'd probably kick him out of the house before supper.

The doctor was regaining consciousness, so they didn't have an opportunity to ask the questions that hung in the air between them. Holt decided that was probably best. They each had a lot to think about before they took the next step.

He already knew there would be a *next step*.

"You've been avoiding me," Holt said to Felicity.

"How could I? Except when you visit patients, we've been in this house together for four days."

"You know what I mean."

She did, and she intended to make sure she didn't end up alone with him. Holt wanted to talk to her, but she knew he couldn't have anything to say that she wanted to hear.

"Take a walk with me," he said.

"I can't leave Mrs. Bennett alone with Papa."

"Of course you can. He's happier with her than with us. You need to get out of the house, do something completely different."

"Such as listen to your explanation of what happened in Papa's bedroom?"

"Why are you afraid to use the word *kiss*?"

"Because a kiss is different from what happened between us."

"There can be all kinds of reasons for a kiss,

but a kiss is still a kiss."

"We obviously don't have the same definition."

"Tell me yours."

"It won't make any difference."

"Try me."

She might as well get it over with. She knew they had to talk, but she'd hoped it would be later, when her mind and heart were more in agreement, but maybe it was better to get it over with now. Once things were settled, she ought to be able to regain her peace of mind.

"Okay," she said.

"Let's walk. The exercise will do you good."

Holt steered her toward the beach several blocks away. The night air was cool and humid. She expected they'd have rain before morning. The moon was so bright, the grass and trees seemed to shimmer in its cool, white light. The tree frogs were making a terrible racket, another indication that rain was on the way.

They didn't speak at first, just walked together. They passed a few people, but as they came closer to the beach where the houses were farther apart, they had the pathway to themselves.

"Do you come to the beach often?" Holt asked.

"I don't like being away from the house so long." Beaches were for lovers, families with young children, or old folks with time on their hands. She didn't fit into any of those categories.

346

"I grew up far from the sea. It's always held a fascination for me," he said.

Having reached the end of the road, they followed a path through the stunted oaks and sea grass until they reached a bench someone had built on a small dune.

"Let's sit for a bit," Felicity said. "It's very peaceful," she said after they had both seated themselves. "It's hard to believe the sea can turn into a monster during a storm."

Waves of barely six inches kissed the shore before flowing slowly back to be swallowed up by the next surge. Sand crabs, acting very much like children, ran along the beach, retreating before the incoming wave, then racing forward to search for bits of food. The muted sound of the surf and the soft night air helped to unravel some of the knots inside her. Maybe she should come down to the shore more often. She hadn't felt so relaxed in a long time.

But sitting there enjoying the moonlight and the cool breeze wasn't clearing away the confusion between them. "What are you going to do when Papa is better and doesn't need you anymore?" she asked.

"I haven't thought that far ahead," Holt said. "I can still learn a lot working with him."

"You haven't asked my opinion, but I think you ought to leave as soon as you can. Not because I want to get rid of you. You ought to go back to Virginia and set up a medical practice there. You were born to be a doctor."

"Why do you say that?"

"Because you love it just as much as Papa. I see you together, talking, consulting, looking up answers in his books, and you're completely engrossed. You can do it for hours. If I didn't run them out, you'd keep your patients twice as long as necessary. I never saw anybody so thorough or conscientious."

"I'm just trying to do the best I can. Any doctor would."

"No, they wouldn't. You do it because you love what you do, love your patients, love learning. Papa and I have talked about it. He agrees."

Holt stared off into the distance. The moonlight reflected on the water.

"I know you've been trying to decide what to do with yourself. Perhaps you even consider yourself a failure."

"I hated being a surgeon."

"You don't hate medicine. You hate seeing people die. You love making people well. I know you don't think so right now, but you'll never be happy if you do something else. You didn't succeed at those other things because they weren't right for you."

He still didn't answer.

"Will you think about what I said?"

"Why don't you want me to stay here if I decide to remain in medicine? Your father and I complement each other."

"I don't want Papa to start depending on

348

you. There's not enough work here to support two doctors — certainly not one who has a society wife to provide for. I don't know any dress shops that would accept a side of bacon as partial payment for a gown."

Silence.

"Have you asked Vivian to marry you?"

"No."

"Does she know you want to marry her?"

"She has known since she was sixteen."

"If I was in love with a man, I'd never marry anyone else. If he didn't come back, I'd follow him."

"The war was coming. I expect she was afraid."

Felicity didn't find that an adequate reason. She knew sixteen-year-old women who had been left to take care of farms while their husbands were away, some of whom didn't come back. Only a spoiled, pampered beauty would be afraid when she was the ward of a rich plantation owner.

"How old is her son?"

"Five."

"What's he like?"

"He's a handsome boy but very quiet. Vivian says he takes after his father."

"Do you like him?"

"Yes."

"Do you want children?"

"Yes."

"Does Vivian?"

"I don't know."

From what she'd seen, Vivian didn't appear very maternal. Felicity was certain Vivian wouldn't enjoy losing her figure and having to remain confined for months on end.

"You could move to the fashionable part of town. They don't have a good doctor. At the rate Galveston's growing, you could soon be a rich man."

"I'm happy where I am."

"Well, you can't stay, so you have to find someplace to go."

"Maybe I'll move back to Mrs. Bennett's."

Felicity whipped around to face him. "I've already told you there isn't enough work to support two doctors. You have to leave, Holt. There's nothing for you here."

"Are you sure?"

"Absolutely."

She hoped he would believe her and leave. He might like her and want to kiss her often, but Vivian had become enshrined in his mind years ago and nothing could dislodge her. It was possible that Vivian wouldn't marry him, that he would ultimately marry someone else, but there would always be three people in that marriage. Felicity knew she couldn't live like that. She had known for several days now that she wanted to marry Holt, but she knew just as positively that she had to have all his heart or do without it altogether.

She stood. "It's time to start back."

"We've hardly been here five minutes."

"There's nothing more to say."

"You're wrong. We haven't even begun to say the things that need to be said, that we *must* say to each other. But this isn't the time. There are things that need to be done first."

"Holt, I don't know what you're talking about, but —"

His arms were around her so quickly she was lost before she even had a chance to resist.

"You know exactly what I'm talking about, but you're afraid to admit it. Well, I'm not. I've got some things I have to straighten out, but I'm not afraid. I don't care about being rich. I don't care who likes me or who doesn't. But I do care about you and your father. I've also got to do something about Vivian being involved with Laveau. It's an ugly knot. I don't know how to unravel it yet, but I will. And when I do, we're going to talk in a way you can't ignore."

Then he kissed her.

Chapter Twenty-one

No warning, no invitation, no chance to refuse. Crushing her to him, he pressed his mouth to hers. His mouth covered hers hungrily, but this kiss was nothing like before. This kiss was punishing and angry, demanding rather than asking, taking rather than waiting to be given, hard rather than gentle, passionate rather than sensual. It was as if a smoldering heat somewhere deep inside Holt had burst forth without warning to consume him, to make him dominate her in a way he had never attempted before.

Holt's fierce energy fueled her own anger. She resented that she couldn't have what she wanted. The fulfilment of her dream seemed so close yet unquestionably out of reach that she wanted to strike out at someone. She was angry he would treat her so roughly despite her repeated wish to be left alone. But rather than hit him or attempt to break from his embrace — the choices any sensible woman would have made — she found herself returning his kisses with equal ferocity.

She couldn't explain why she should choose that method to punish him, but it seemed the only way to erase the terrible pain that burned in her chest somewhere just behind her heart.

The harder she kissed him, the deeper her fingers sank into the flesh of his arms, the more she wanted to punish him. It was his fault she had fallen in love with a man who was in love with another woman. It was his fault he had shown her what life could be like when loved and protected by a man stronger than the troubles that surrounded her. It was his fault nothing in her life would ever be the same again.

So she punished him still more, kissing him harder, forcing her tongue into his mouth until she had ravished every corner, every secret chamber. In a show of strength, she pressed her body hard against him, forcing him to press back just as hard. She refused to be intimidated by the strength of his arms or the power of his thighs as they pressed against her with what under any other circumstances would have been daunting intimacy. She would not yield.

Holt broke the kiss as abruptly as he began, his eyes wide with surprise. "I thought you didn't want me."

"I don't, but I refuse to let you think you have only to kiss me and I will fall into your arms."

She didn't like the smile that began to curve his lips. She hated it when somebody knew something she didn't, but that was exactly what it looked like.

"I always thought you were one tough woman."

She wasn't sure she wouldn't rather have been spoiled and soft like Vivian, but she hadn't been given that choice. "I am. I got along before you came. I'll get along just fine after you're gone."

"You can't wait to get rid of me, can you?"

Something was wrong. She didn't know what was going through his mind, but she couldn't think of any scenario that would account for his smile. "If you have to go, I don't see any reason to postpone it. It would just make things harder in the end."

"And what am I supposed to do?"

"Go to Vivian. That's why you came to Texas, isn't it?"

"Yes, it's why I came. And you're right. I do have to go to Vivian."

It was obvious Vivian was still angry with Holt. She paced the room like a caged animal, the material of her silk skirts and stiff petticoats rustling noisily as she executed sharp turns around furniture, the heels of her slippers alternating between dull thuds and loud clumps as she moved back and forth between carpeted and wood floors. The room was sparsely furnished, but the appointments were expensive and in good taste.

"You can't expect me to sit at home waiting for you," she said angrily.

"I just said you must have a very busy social life, since it took four trips to find you at home."

"You sound like you disapprove."

"It's not up to me to approve or disapprove of anything you do. It's your life, not mine."

Holt had finally realized that as much as he felt responsible for Vivian, he had no right to tell her what to do. Or criticize anything she did. He was surprised how relieved he felt.

Vivian eyed him with suspicion. "That's not what you used to say."

"You were young, and I fell into the habit of thinking of myself as your adviser. You're a grown woman now, a mother. What you do with your life is up to you."

"You used to think yourself more than a guardian."

"You mean I was besotted with you," Holt said with a laugh that came with surprising ease. "I thought you were the most beautiful creature ever created. I couldn't think of any better fate than to take care of you for the rest of my life."

"And you don't want to take care of me now?"

She was flirting now, not as overtly as she did with her callow admirers, but with an intimacy that could only exist between two people who'd known each other a long time. Only Holt hadn't known Vivian at all. He'd allowed her beauty to spur his imagination to create a woman so close to perfect as to be inhuman. But that kiss in Felicity's father's bedroom had opened his eyes to things he must have been a fool to miss.

"I still want you to be safe and happy," he said. "I always will. You're one of my oldest friends."

"You make me sound like an old woman," she said with asperity.

"Sit down and stop pacing. You make me feel tired."

"You wouldn't if you hadn't been playing nursemaid for the last week."

He used to laugh with her when she made comments like that. And when he couldn't laugh he blamed her lack of understanding on her youth. Now he couldn't do either.

"Dr. Moore is going through alcohol withdrawal. I couldn't leave him to do it alone."

"He has a daughter to look after him."

"I want to help. They're important to me."

He thought she was going to pout. He used to tease her, make jokes, keep talking until he prodded her into sunny spirits again. Today he felt impatient.

After a moment, she sighed and said with only a slight pout, "Let's not talk about them anymore. You've got to come out of hiding. There are dozens of people who want to meet you."

"I'm sure Laveau diViere isn't one of them."

Her expression changed to mulish stubbornness. "You're not going to tell me again he's a traitor, are you?"

"It's true."

"I told you nobody cares about that anymore."

"He works for the Reconstruction. I doubt most Texans trust him."

"He has friends all over Galveston."

"I'm sure he does, but Laveau is a liar and a thief as well as a traitor. He tried to kill one of my friends while he slept. Just last year he shot two men while trying to rob a bank. I heard some talk about blackmail. I've recently heard of some thefts. It wouldn't surprise me if Laveau is involved. He's done both before." Holt would continue going to parties if it would help him catch Laveau. He was certain Laveau was involved in the blackmail. He needed to protect Vivian as much as he wanted to find evidence he could use against Laveau. "You've got to stop seeing Laveau. Someday he'll hang."

Vivian had turned white. "You have no right to tell me who I can and can't like."

"I'm just trying to look out for you. Laveau is evil. He's —"

"You're just jealous."

"What?"

"You're telling lies about Laveau because you're jealous."

"Why would I be jealous?"

"Because I married Abe Calvert instead of you. I know you loved me and wanted to marry me."

"Vivian, that was a long time ago. We were practically kids."

"You weren't. You were a grown man, and you were crazy in love with me. That's why you came to Texas — to look for me, to make me marry you."

"Yes, I did come to Texas hoping to marry you, but —"

"You can't force me to marry you. You'll be poor your whole life. I won't be poor. I won't!"

Holt didn't understand how Vivian could think he could force her to marry him. Even less did he understand her apparent panic.

"You've never been poor," he said.

"Living in a wealthy household doesn't make you rich. You don't know what it's like not to have a penny of your own, to have to be grateful for every morsel of food, every piece of clothing, the roof over your head."

"Uncle William adored you. He would have given you anything within his power."

"You don't understand. Nothing was mine."

"No, I don't understand," Holt said. "You appeared so happy, I thought you had everything you wanted."

"They even sold my clothes when my father died. I won't let that happen to me again. I won't!"

"I promised my uncle I'd take care of you, but —"

"What can you do for me? You don't have any money."

"I don't need a lot of money to be happy."

"Well, I do. I won't spend my life having ba-

358

bies, worrying about what to cook for dinner, and cleaning up behind some man who gets drunk with his friends every evening. And I'm not going to marry some doctor who's only interested in taking care of people who can't pay him. I want to go to parties, wear pretty dresses, and have a big house."

"I only wanted to help. I feel responsible for you."

"Well, don't," she said, flouncing away from him. "I can take care of myself. I appreciate your concern," she said, suddenly changing her attitude to one of assumed maturity, "but you don't need to worry about me. As you said, I'm a grown woman. I'm responsible for my own actions. So I release you forever from feeling you have any responsibility toward me."

"My uncle asked me —"

"It would have been different if Price's Nob hadn't been destroyed, but it has, so you have no way to take care of me. And I don't want you to try. I *forbid* you to try ever again. Now you must go. I have to get ready to go out." She swooped down on him and gave him a kiss on the cheek. "You really are very sweet. I'll always love you."

Two realizations hit him simultaneously. Vivian didn't mean the same thing he did when she used the word *love*. What she meant was a tepid emotion that she only acknowledged when it was convenient.

The second realization was more important.

He didn't feel responsible for her anymore. He would always have a soft spot in his heart for her, but he wasn't responsible for her life. She had lifted a huge burden from his shoulders. He felt so relieved, so light of heart, he had to restrain himself from releasing a huge sigh of relief.

He stood. "I'm glad things are going well for you. I won't hold you up. One last word of warning. Watch out for Laveau diViere. Sooner or later he'll turn on you."

He didn't give Vivian a chance to defend Laveau. He left the house quickly, practically running into the street. He was free! Free! For the first time he could remember, his life was his own. There was no one who could lay claim to it.

He couldn't wait to tell Felicity.

Felicity was sure that if she didn't get out of her room, she would go crazy. She retreated there to escape being alone with Holt. She ought to say *hide,* because that's what she was doing. She was acting like a foolish girl, but she couldn't help herself. Being around Holt and knowing he was in love with another woman was more than she could endure. She didn't understand how after years of being perfectly capable of controlling her reactions to every man she met, she should be completely incapable of doing so with Holt.

The long evenings she'd spent in her room

alone had been torture. She could force herself to do handwork — trim handkerchiefs, embroider pillowcases, crochet a baby's cap, even work on a patchwork quilt — but she couldn't study any of her father's medical books. Before she finished a single page, she would be daydreaming, Holt having completely consumed her thoughts. Reciting to herself why she couldn't have him hadn't kept him from invading her dreams as well. Holt had become something of an obsession with her. Obsessions had to be confronted before they could be defeated, so she gave herself free rein to confront Holt, to come face to face with the very temptation that tormented her relentlessly.

The first component of her obsession was that he liked her. She hadn't believed it for a long time, but she had to accept it because he stayed when it would have been much easier to leave. But lots of people liked her, and she liked lots of people. That was okay. It wasn't threatening.

The second component was he liked her enough to want to kiss her. That was more dangerous, but she wasn't experienced with kissing. Maybe there were all kinds of kisses — friendship kisses, I-like-you kisses, I-love-you kisses, even kisses of pure passion that had nothing to do with love. If she was going to figure out how to handle the situation, she ought to sample Holt's kisses until she knew what kind they were. A kiss of pure passion might be dangerous in one way, but it didn't have to lead to a broken heart.

Holt's kisses certainly seemed to be more than friendship or I-like-you. They couldn't be I-love-you kisses, because he didn't love her, so they must be kisses of pure passion. That made her nervous, but it also excited her. She'd never aroused passion in anyone before. It gave her a sense of power to know she had the ability to influence the actions of a man like Holt. It also gave her a great deal of pleasure.

The third component of her obsession was believing he could find her physically attractive. Felicity had lived her whole life under the shadow of a mother who was so beautiful, her father had become an alcoholic so he could stand the pain of having lost her. Felicity knew she wasn't beautiful enough to inspire that kind of adoration. She wasn't sure she wanted to be, but she had always wanted to feel that a man could find her attractive, might even think she was pretty. Holt had repeatedly said she was pretty, and proved it by his continued attraction to her.

The fourth component of her obsession was that he wanted to make love to her. Just the thought sent the blood thrumming in her veins. She'd never considered letting a man make love to her until she met the man she was born to love. She had always known she would know him when she found him. What she hadn't anticipated was that he might not love her. But she couldn't control herself when it came to Holt. She had let him kiss her three times. Worse, she had kissed him back and was aching to do it again!

There was no one she could talk to, no one to help solve the riddle of her behavior.

She had heard Holt leave the house earlier, so she ventured out of her room. But that wasn't the answer. Everywhere she went, something reminded her of Holt. The spot in the parlor where he first kissed her. The consulting room where she helped him with his operations. The kitchen where he ate his meals. The library where he and her father consulted their medical books. The house felt as much his as hers. On impulse, she decided to go outside. She chose the back yard. She needed privacy.

She could probably count on one hand the times she'd been in the yard at night, but the gentle rustle of the leaves overhead was soothing. The distant sounds of ships in the bay gave her a sense of place, of belonging, yet being apart. Lights from neighboring houses glowed warm and quiet through the trees. The soft night air caressed her skin with gentle coolness. The deep shadows were like a protective mantle thrown over her, the moon and stars like friends come to sit with her. She wandered over to a chair under a live oak and sank down into it. Two small red eyes stared at her out of the shadows. Moments later a mother opossum waddled across a corner of the yard, several babies clinging to her fur.

Felicity heard the bellow of a bull alligator in the distance, and shivers ran down her spine. She was glad their house was several streets over from the edge of the island. But not even the awareness of alligators had the power to disturb the calm that gradually fell over her. She hadn't felt this peaceful in days. Weeks. Since Holt arrived.

"I read somewhere that a woman looks especially beautiful in the moonlight. I never believed it until now."

Felicity tried to deny the excitement that caused her heart to beat so hard it was almost painful, but it was useless. When it came to her reaction to Holt, logic and self-control flew out the window.

"That's because the shadows make it harder to see the imperfections," she answered. "It's a lot like being in love."

"That's a particularly cynical point of view."

"But realistic."

She continued to stare into the shadows under the trees. She didn't have to turn around to see Holt. His image never left her mind.

"I'm glad you finally decided to come out of your room," Holt said. "It's not good to be closed up so much."

"I've had a lot of thinking to do."

"Was any of it about me?"

"Some."

"Want to tell me what you decided?"

"I've decided it's not a good idea for a man who's in love with one woman to go around kissing other women."

"I've kissed only one *other woman*."

"That's an even worse idea."

"Why?"

"Because that woman might think you meant something special by singling her out."

"And if I did?"

"She'd be making a mistake."

"People can change their minds."

He couldn't know how much she wanted to believe that, but she knew about men who became hypnotized by beautiful women. She looked up to see Holt standing just a few feet from her.

"I won't pretend I didn't enjoy kissing you," she said. "I won't pretend I don't like you. Even though some of the things you've done have made me extremely angry, I believe you're a fine, honorable man. You'll make Vivian a wonderful husband."

"Vivian doesn't want to marry me. Besides, I don't love her."

Holt's own words had given him away, Felicity thought. His first statement was that Vivian didn't want to marry him. That he didn't love her followed. *It didn't precede.* If it had, Felicity might have reacted differently.

"I don't know what you and Vivian said to each other, but six crucial years have gone by during which you were separated. It's only natural that you would have a lot of catching up to do."

"I don't think I ever loved her. I think I fell in love with the *idea* of her."

That was even worse. Men could let go of reality, but an ideal would stay in their hearts and minds forever.

But it wasn't just a question of Holt's feelings. Felicity knew that Vivian would flirt with other men, she might even marry another man, but Holt would be her constant, her shield against disaster, the one man she knew she could depend on when she had nowhere else to turn. Even if Holt didn't love her, he would feel he had to keep her safe. Vivian would use this feeling to keep him tied to her. She'd never let him go.

"Maybe you're right," she said to Holt, "but it's not important. You're bound to her, whether you want to be or not."

"You can't know that."

"My father fell in love with the ideal of my mother more than her reality. Her death nearly destroyed him."

"I'm not blind to Vivian's faults."

"They haven't changed the way you feel about her."

"You don't know how I feel. You haven't given me a chance to tell you."

"Can you tell me you love me?"

"No, but —"

"Can you tell me you'll never see Vivian again?"

"Of course not, but —"

"Then you can't tell me anything that won't hurt us both."

Holt had kept his distance, apparently determined to convince her he was calm and rational, that he had his feelings under control, but now he closed the distance between them, gripped her hands which she had clasped tightly together in her lap, and pulled her to her feet.

"Neither of us knows what can happen until we give it a chance," he said. "I can't make any promises, but —"

"I don't want any promises."

"— neither do I want closed doors."

She tried to pull her hands away, but his grip was too firm. "I've thought it all out. There's no point in opening doors or looking around corners. You and Vivian need to decide what you're going to do now that you've found each other. My father and I have to decide what to do once he's well."

"Aren't you even interested in what could happen between us?"

"There is no *us*. We're just two people whose paths crossed briefly."

"I don't believe that. I don't think you do, either."

He pulled her into his arms. She wanted to fight him but knew it would be useless. It was better to show no resistance, to prove that his words had no effect on her.

"I've never wanted to kiss anybody like I want to kiss you," Holt said.

"Only because I'm not an ice princess. I'm real, human, ordinary, but you can't have the ice princess *and* the peasant girl."

"You're not a peasant girl, and I don't want an ice princess. I never did."

"You may think it's possible for you to fall in love with me, but I don't love you."

"You don't know what can happen."

"I've seen you with Vivian, heard you talk about her. There is nothing here for either of us."

"You're wrong."

She had been expecting him to kiss her, had steeled herself against it. His touch had always destroyed her resistance, but she was determined it would be different this time. She refused to react to the pressure of his mouth on hers, to the sensations of his body pressed against her from breast to thigh. She had to ball her hands into tight fists to keep from putting her arms around his neck. She had to force her jaw to go slack to keep from kissing him back. She had to go rigid from top to bottom to keep from pressing herself against him.

She had nothing left to keep one tear from running down each cheek.

He broke the kiss, released her, and stepped back.

"You're not going to give us a chance, are you?"

368

"There is no chance."

"You could be wrong."

She didn't respond.

He took her hands in his. He was gentle this time. "I know you've always felt that every time you reach out for love it's snatched away from you. You've been hurt badly, but you can't let disappointment cause you to close yourself off from people. A lot of us care for you in different ways. You've also felt alone. It frightened you so badly, you tried to stop feeling. I did the same thing. I don't know how long it will take me to learn to let myself feel, to discover what is *real* about myself and what I made up for protection, but I'm going to do it, because I can't really begin to live my life, to enjoy being alive, until I do. When I learn how, I'm going to teach you. You may never come to love me, but neither of us is going to go through life only half alive."

He leaned forward and kissed her gently. "You deserve much more than that. And so do I." His lips formed a smile that was purely mechanical. "Enjoy the night. Sometimes I think it can be even more beautiful than the day."

Then he backed away. He continued backwards until he was halfway across the yard. Then he turned and walked away without looking back.

Felicity remained unmoving until she heard the back door close. Then the energy left her body with such suddenness, she practically col-

369

lapsed into her chair. Refusing him had to be the hardest thing she'd ever done. She sincerely hoped he wouldn't try again. She didn't have the strength to resist him a second time.

"I didn't know your father was ill until Vivian commented on it," Lillie Hart said. "I'd have come by earlier if I'd known."

Felicity had been very surprised when Lillie Hart and Charlotte Albright dropped in for a visit.

"There's no reason you should have known. We haven't told anyone."

"I certainly understand. It can be a terrible inconvenience to have people popping in all the time. Company makes for a great deal of extra work."

Felicity had liked Lillie from the moment she met her, but she was surprised that anyone would know a visit to express concern and support could be a burden instead of a help.

"We have been rather busy. Even with Holt helping, we've been getting more and more patients."

"That's good."

"It's certainly good that more of them can pay with cash. I know times are hard, but it's very difficult to buy medical supplies with a sack of cornmeal or several dozen eggs."

"I should think so," Lillie said, laughing. "I could just see Clifford's face if anyone presented him with a sack of cornmeal. He probably wouldn't know what it was."

Felicity didn't know why she was discussing such a topic with a woman who obviously *didn't* have trouble making ends meet, but she was glad for Lillie's company. Charlotte had gone off for a short visit with her mother before returning to pick up Lillie. Lillie said her husband had the carriage today, so she'd have been on foot if Charlotte hadn't offered to take her.

"We used to have a difficult time ourselves," Lillie said, lowering her voice as though she were sharing a confidence. "That's why we moved to Galveston. Clifford said if he had to die of starvation, he'd rather not do it in front of our friends."

"I thought you'd always been well off."

"Clifford wasn't rich even before the war. Daddy didn't want me to marry him. He said business wasn't a proper occupation for a gentleman, but I held out until he gave in. I'm grateful for all the business Vivian has helped Clifford find," Lillie said. "I'm glad she lives with us. It's not suitable for a single woman to live alone."

"A woman of Vivian's beauty is going to attract great attention no matter what she does."

"I know. And Holt is no different from the rest. I used to think he was in love with you, but you were right. I think he wants to marry Vivian."

Chapter Twenty-two

"He's been at her side nearly every night this week," Lillie said. "I know she thinks of him as a big brother, someone to look out for her and give her advice, but when he looks at her, his mind seems to be in another world. I plan to do everything I can to convince Vivian to marry Holt. He's the only person who seems to have any influence over her. Maybe he can induce her to have nothing to do with that awful Mr. diViere."

Felicity had to struggle to keep her face from reflecting any of the emotions that boiled inside her. She didn't want anyone to guess she was in love with Holt. He had told her he was going to as many parties as possible in hopes of finding information against Laveau. Felicity had tried hard to rid herself of the fear that Vivian still retained her hold on him, but Lillie's comments made that nearly impossible.

"Holt would make any woman a fine husband," Felicity said.

She had welcomed Lillie's visit, but now she was eager for Charlotte's return. She didn't know how much longer she could preserve her appearance of indifference. She was relieved when the door opened and Holt and her father entered the room. She looked closely at her father, but he appeared in good spirits. Since recovering from his seizure, he had made good progress. He had been spending nearly every evening with Mrs. Bennett.

"You didn't tell me we had a visitor," her father said.

"This is Lillie Hart," Felicity said. "She and Charlotte came by to see how you're doing."

"I'm getting along just fine," her father said. "I'd get along even better if I had more visits from pretty women."

Felicity didn't understand her father. He'd never shown any interest in women since her mother's death, and he never flirted. During the last week he had started to do both. Felicity wondered if Holt had told him it was a good way to expand his practice.

"You're embarrassing her," Felicity said to her father. What she really meant was he was embarrassing his daughter.

"Nonsense," her father said. "The only good thing about being old and fat is being free to indulge in a harmless flirtation with a pretty young woman without having her husband challenge me to a duel at daybreak."

"I'd get up and give you a hug," Lillie said, "but I'm feeling exhausted. This tiredness is so annoying. Clifford is quite out of patience with me."

Her father moved to the sofa and sat down next to Lillie, his brow creased. "Have you been feeling like this for very long?"

"Maybe a week," Lillie said, "but I'm sure it's nothing more than a momentary indisposition."

"Holt, come look at this young woman's complexion and tell me what you think."

"If you're not careful, you'll end up being poked and prodded," Felicity said. "That's what you get for telling a doctor you aren't feeling well."

"It's really nothing," Lillie insisted.

"Have you suffered any chills, fever, or sweating?" Holt asked.

"Well, yes, but nothing very bad."

"What do you think?" Dr. Moore asked Holt.

"I agree," Holt said.

"Agree about what?" Lillie asked fearfully.

"I think you have malaria," Dr. Moore said.

"A mild case," Holt said, "but definitely malaria."

"I can't possibly have anything like that," Lillie insisted. "I saw the doctor just yesterday, and he said it was only a momentary indisposition."

"I think you should get a second opinion," Holt said.

"She just got a second and third opinion," Felicity pointed out.

"I meant from one of her own doctors."

"You mean from one of the doctors who must know more than either of you because he charges more," Felicity snapped.

"I mean a doctor she trusts," Holt said.

"I trust you," Lillie said to Holt. "My brother said army doctors saw malaria all the time."

"Dr. Moore noticed it first," Holt said. "I just confirmed his diagnosis."

"What should I do?" Lillie asked.

"I'd like you to come to my consulting room. Holt and I need to ask a few questions before we decide."

"Am I going to die? Clifford said lots of soldiers died from malaria."

"You're not going to die," Holt said. "You'll probably hardly even know you have it."

Lillie turned to Felicity, a look akin to fear on her face.

"I'll explain to Charlotte when she gets back," Felicity said. "Holt can go home with you to explain everything to your husband."

"Thank you," Lillie said.

"There's no need to be frightened," Dr. Moore said, taking Lillie's hand in a fatherly manner. "We're going to give you some medicine that'll have you feeling much better in a day or two."

"Is it really only a mild case?" Felicity whispered to Holt.

"Yes, but her doctor should have picked it up. Your father would never have missed it, not even if he'd had too much to drink."

"I can't thank you enough for what you've done for my wife," Clifford Hart said to Holt. "She could have died, and I'd never have known she was sick."

"I doubt she would have died," Holt assured him, "but she would have continued to be sick. Without medical attention, there could have been some very serious consequences."

"I saw enough of malaria during the war to know what could have happened," Hart said. "That's why I'm so thankful you recognized it."

"Dr. Moore saw it first," Holt said. "Make sure her doctor sees her regularly until the symptoms disappear."

"You mean you won't see her?" Hart asked, startled.

"I'm not her doctor."

"Of course you are. You don't think I'd send her back to that fool who nearly let her die, do you?"

"If you're sure you want me to undertake her care."

"I don't want anyone else. Can you come by tomorrow?"

"I don't know. Felicity keeps the schedule, and we've been rather busy."

"If need be, I'll bring her around to see you. Now I want to go to Lillie. Since you're old friends, I won't feel I'm being rude if I leave you with Vivian."

Vivian didn't look exactly pleased with the arrangement. "I can't stay long. I've got to get dressed. I'm going out."

"It doesn't matter," Holt replied. "I have to get back. We have patients to see."

"I don't see why you bother helping that old man. He can take care of his own patients. They won't know if he gets things wrong."

"I'm learning a lot from him," Holt said. He was getting tired of defending Dr. Moore to Vivian. "He's the one who noticed Lillie's malaria."

"You could have done it."

"The point is, he saw it when her doctor didn't."

"That's all the more reason you should forget about him. Set up your own practice. Lillie won't stop talking about what you've done. She's a silly female, but she can bring you a lot of patients." She smiled provocatively. "I can bring you even more. You could be a rich man in a few years."

"I don't want to be rich. I already have —"

"You don't want to be rich? Are you crazy?"

Holt wondered if everyone felt disillusioned, cynical, and a little bit stupid when someone they adored proved to be unworthy. Felicity had seen through Vivian right away. It had taken him ten years.

"I'm more interested in making people well," Holt said.

"Because your father was a drunk and you could never make him well, you want to help the rest of the world."

"That may be some of it, but I like what I do."

And he *did* like what he was doing. His experiences in the war had been hard on his soul. He hadn't had the time or experience to put things in perspective, to realize there was good to counter the bad. Felicity was right. He was born to be a doctor, not a planter, cowboy, merchant, or businessman. A doctor.

"*My* father's drinking taught to me to look out for myself first," Vivian said.

"You've always had someone to take care of you. I imagine you always will."

"I thought *you* wanted to take care of me. I didn't realize an old man had become more important to you than I am."

If Holt hadn't been so disappointed, he would have laughed at the comic picture Vivian made. He didn't know how her court of admirers felt about her antics to keep them in constant attendance, but she was like a little girl who pouted and threatened a tantrum when she didn't get what she wanted. He had been blind. He wondered how many people had laughed behind his back at the spectacle of an adult making a fool of himself over a girl who was barely more than a child. He blushed inwardly at the memory.

How could he have spent so many years believing he was in love with a woman he didn't even know? It had taken Felicity to teach him what love really meant. He had loved with his eyes and his head, maybe even with his sense of responsibility, but he hadn't loved with his heart. He had been afraid to let himself feel, afraid it would hurt again like it had hurt when his father preferred alcohol to his family, when his mother blamed him for his father's death.

Now he knew what it was like to let down the barriers and let himself feel. He liked it so much, he couldn't imagine going back. It was a gift he wanted to give Felicity. She had been just as afraid of her emotions, just as bound up in her sense of duty. Neither one of them had known what it was like to have feelings that were uncontrollable, feelings that were so powerful they couldn't be destroyed. Felicity was still afraid. So was he, but he couldn't turn back. He had to see where this new path would lead.

"People are important in different ways," he said to Vivian, "but that doesn't make one more important than the other. Now I've got to be going. I have other patients to see."

"Promise you'll be at the Ravenwoods' party tomorrow night."

"I can't promise about the party, but I will see you again tomorrow. Your brother-in-law insists I'm now Lillie's doctor."

Holt's stride slowed as he neared the house. His feet made little sound on the sandy path. The sun had gone down hours ago, but his eyes were so accustomed to the night, he had no trouble seeing the houses that lined the road on either side or the lights that glowed from the windows. Only the shadows under some of the trees with low-hanging branches concealed anything from his gaze. He could hear the sounds of a few of the older children still playing outside — the voice of a mother calling her daughter inside — but it was late and most children would already be in bed. In other houses, people would be gathered in the parlor or on the porch talking, sharing the events of the day. Signs of life, warmth, and happiness flowed from these homes like light through their windows.

The windows in Dr. Moore's house were dark because nobody was home, he assumed.

Holt didn't look forward to entering an empty house. He had had a long day of seeing patients in the office and two home visits in the evening. He was pleased the practice had picked up some new clients — Lillie Hart had been singing his praises to all her friends — but while the wealthy patients paid in very welcome cash, he found some of them extremely difficult to deal with. They wanted to tell him what was wrong and prescribe what medicine he ought to give them. Making it clear that he was the doctor and would do all the diagnosing as well as prescribing had cost him a client tonight. He didn't mind the loss of the client, just the waste of time.

As a consequence, he was in a bad mood. He didn't want to go out again, but he wanted someone to talk to. It couldn't be Vivian. She would most certainly be at a party. She considered the evening a failure if she had to stay home. Besides, he didn't want to see Vivian. The last time they talked, they'd gotten into a heated argument over Laveau.

Holt didn't want to go out at all. Even though he was developing friendships, he didn't enjoy parties very much. He was sure Laveau was involved in the blackmail and the thefts he'd heard of, but he hadn't been able to get any leads on the blackmail, and the police hadn't found any new evidence about the thefts.

Dr. Moore wouldn't be home until well past midnight. He had taken Mrs. Bennett to visit her daughter in Houston. Mrs. Bennett wouldn't travel alone, and her daughter had small children. Dr. Moore said it was ridiculous for them to live so close and rarely see each other. He insisted it was an even exchange for all the time she'd spent entertaining him.

Then there was Felicity. She had gone to act as midwife at a birthing. Very few doctors were called on to help with childbirth — it was considered a woman's job. And from what he'd been told, Felicity was the best midwife in Galveston.

That didn't surprise him. Felicity was a very intelligent woman with a natural desire to help people. But unlike many people, she'd bolstered that desire with systematic and prolonged study. Holt suspected she knew more medicine than many practicing doctors her age, but she'd been forced into medicine in order to protect her father. She'd convinced herself she was doing what she wanted, but she wasn't happy, and to Holt that was a sign something was wrong.

They met a dozen times each day, but she'd cut herself off from him nearly as effectively as if they lived in separate houses. Holt operated on the theory that the harder a person worked to pretend something didn't matter, the more it really did matter. The pervasiveness of her new attitude proved to Holt she was struggling hard to keep some kind of strong emotion under control.

He opened the gate and crossed the short distance to the house. His doctor's bag felt twice as heavy as it had when he left the house. He'd be relieved to put it down. He tried to open the door before he remembered he had to unlock it first. His parents had never locked their house. Neither did Cade. It was hard to remember that people in Galveston did.

The house seemed unnaturally quiet; his footsteps sounded unnaturally loud. He put his bag down and was reaching for the lamp on a table in the hallway when he thought he heard someone crying. He stood still and listened carefully but heard nothing. He'd almost convinced himself he'd made a mistake when he heard it again. The sound was coming from upstairs.

It was a woman crying.

He climbed the stairs two at a time. The sounds were coming from Felicity's bedroom. He knocked on the door. "Felicity, are you all right?"

He got no response. Just silence.

"I know you're in there, and I know you're crying. Is there anything I can do to help?"

"No."

But that one word was followed by audible sobs. Holt opened the door and went in.

Accustomed as he was to the plain and demure dresses she wore, he was unprepared for the blaze of color in Felicity's bedroom. Whether it was red, blue, yellow, or green, the colors were rich and vibrant. The pattern of the wallpaper was tiny knots of royal blue ribbon against a cream background. Lemon yellow curtains framed the windows. Felicity was lying on a bed covered by a spread elaborately embroidered with deep red rosebuds. A trellis of green leaves formed a decorative border. Holt crossed the room quickly and dropped down on the bed.

"Why are you crying?" he asked.

She buried her face in the pillow and cried harder.

"Tell me."

"There's nothing you can do. There's nothing anybody can do."

"Try me."

"You can't help. You're not God."

That was certainly true, but it ratcheted the

383

level of potential trouble up several notches. He took her left hand, carefully unballed her fist, and pressed it between his palms. "You might feel better if you talked about it — got it out of your system."

She jerked her hand away. Holt figured something had gone wrong with the birth. He had almost no experience with birthing babies, but he knew there were hundreds of things that could go wrong. A large number of women died in childbirth.

He took her by the shoulders and lifted her up. "I don't know what happened, but I'm sure it wasn't your fault. I refuse to let you blame yourself."

She turned her tear-stained face in his direction. "The baby died. Whose fault could it be?"

She tried to bury her face in the pillow again, but he wouldn't let her. He twisted around until he had positioned himself between her and the head of the bed. She couldn't lie back down without lying against him.

"Tell me about it," he said.

"It won't change anything."

"I know, but you might feel better."

She kept her head bowed so he couldn't see her face. He moved a little closer until he could gently place her head on his shoulder. She resisted briefly, then suddenly threw her arms around him and started crying all over again. Holt could feel the tears soaking through his shirt, but he didn't move. He was sure she hadn't let herself cry about anything since she was a child.

"This was Mrs. Marfa's first baby. She was terrified, because her mother died in childbirth. I'd been talking to her for weeks, explaining everything so she wouldn't be afraid. I promised to be with her."

Gradually Felicity poured out the story of a breach birth. The husband hadn't called Felicity until his wife had been in labor a whole day. By then the woman was nearly exhausted and the baby in danger. Turning the baby before the mother's strength ran out was a painful process, and the woman's screams frightened the husband, who called in a doctor. He convinced the husband that Felicity didn't know what she was doing, that the baby should be taken at once with forceps or the mother and baby would die. Despite Felicity's attempts to persuade him she could turn the baby more safely, the doctor pressed ahead. He bungled the birth, and the baby died. Both parents were hysterical. The doctor blamed Felicity for not calling him in immediately.

"What should have been a beautiful experience turned into a nightmare."

"You think you'll get used to it, but you never do," Holt said. "Is this the first time you've lost a patient?"

"No, but it's the first time I lost one because of an incompetent doctor." She looked directly at him. "I smelled alcohol on his breath."

Holt had to stop himself from asking the man's name. There would be time for that later. Right now he needed to comfort Felicity.

"As long as you know you did your best, you have no reason to blame yourself. Don't let anyone else blame you, either."

"I don't want to be a midwife if this is going to happen. I can't stand it."

"You don't have to do anything you don't want to do."

"But there has to be somebody to help women like Mrs. Marfa."

"Maybe you can teach women like her the importance of good medical care."

"You think so?"

"You can do anything you want. You're a re-markable woman."

She had stopped crying and was resting her head on his shoulder. "You didn't always think that."

"I haven't always been very smart."

She chuckled. "I didn't think I'd ever hear you say that."

"I didn't think I'd ever say it. I had to be right all the time because I'd already been wrong enough for a lifetime."

She sat up, looked at him with tear-filled eyes. "I can't believe that." She wiped her eyes with her hands. He pulled out his handkerchief.

"Here, let me."

"You probably hate crying women. Most men do."

"I think you're beautiful, even when you cry."

"You can't like having me soak your shirt."

"It's worth it if it makes you feel better."

"You have a way of making people believe that things aren't really so bad, that they will get better."

Nobody had ever said that to Holt. Most of his life, he'd been blamed for things that went wrong. Even with Vivian, his uncle said she wouldn't have run off with Abe Calvert if Holt had been there to talk her out of it.

"Do you really mean that?"

She sat up so she could look him in the eye. "Of course I do. Why wouldn't I?"

"Because I've been a thorn in your side ever since I got here. You've told me time and time again that you can't wait until I leave your house."

"You forced me to face some uncomfortable truths, but I've always liked you. You're always putting yourself on the line for other people. You didn't *have* to care enough about my father or his patients to insist that he be sober. You didn't *have* to care enough to help my father with his practice and sit up with him and help him through the worst of his withdrawal. You cared enough about me to make me see what I was doing to Papa and myself. But there's one thing I've discovered about you that I don't like."

One step forward, one step back. He and Felicity had been at loggerheads from the beginning.

"You're so busy taking care of other people, you haven't done anything to create your own happiness."

"You're not one to talk."

"I know. I think we ought to make a pact right now."

He felt a little uneasy. Every time someone extracted a promise from him, he ended up regretting it.

"First is a declaration. We deserve to be happy. There's no reason why being concerned about others should mean we can't be happy, too."

"I agree."

"The second is a plan of action. From now on, we're going to concentrate on discovering what makes us happy. Once we know, we're going to do something about it."

"I'm ahead of you there. I already know what will make me happy."

"What?"

"Kissing you."

He took her face in his hands and kissed her. She hesitated at first, then allowed herself to be drawn into the kiss. The hunger Holt had held in check burst forth with such vigor, he had to restrain himself from taking Felicity's mouth in an all-out assault. Her defenses were down. He didn't want to take unfair advantage, but he couldn't waste the opportunity to do what he'd only been able to do in his dreams — kiss her until she believed he could truly like her better than any other woman.

Chapter Twenty-three

Felicity didn't allow herself to think of any of the hundred or so reasons she shouldn't be sitting on her bed with Holt's arms around her, yielding to the temptation to let him kiss her until she could think of no one but the two of them. It seemed that all her life she'd done what she ought to do, what it was her *duty* to do. Just this once she made up her mind to do what she wanted. She would deal with the consequences later.

She would have plenty of time after Holt was gone.

Casting aside all inhibitions, all restraints, she allowed herself to enjoy Holt's embrace. It felt so wonderful to have a strong man's arms around her. She didn't feel alone. She didn't feel she was holding back the tide by herself, that no one else saw or cared about the danger. Holt knew, he understood, he would help her as long as she wanted.

And she did want.

She liked the feel of his lips on her mouth. They were strong, masculine, inviting without demanding. When he buried his face in her neck, she felt shivers run all through her body. She didn't know what she'd thought a man did with his hands when he held a woman in his arms — she'd assumed they were just sort of there. She was wrong. Holt's hands seemed to touch every part of her back from her shoulders to her waist. Her skin became so sensitive, it began to compete with his kisses for her attention.

Shock rocketed through her body when his tongue parted her lips and forced its way into her mouth. It swaggered around in her mouth like a marauder, searching out her sweetness with unerring accuracy. Rising as though from a deep sleep, her tongue danced with his, then ventured into his mouth.

Holt had said he thought she was pretty, but she didn't believe he could mean it, not after Vivian. But he had come to her room to comfort her. He was holding her, kissing her, giving the impression of a man who liked what he was doing. Surely he wouldn't be doing it if he didn't find her attractive.

"Do you think I'm pretty?" she asked.

"I already told you I do."

"You were trying to persuade me to go to the party with you then. Do you *really* think I'm pretty?"

"Have you forgotten Beau Stregghorn?"

"I don't count him. He'd probably make eyes at any willing female."

"You're pretty even in those dreadfully plain dresses you insist upon wearing. Your skin looks nearly white in contrast to your hair. Your eyes are like near-black pools that hold their secrets close. As for your lips, well, I think they're perfect for kissing. I've dreamed about them more nights than I care to admit."

She sat up. "You dreamed about me?" No one had ever done that. It was like getting a Christmas present on a perfectly ordinary day. "Not about me telling you to leave, I hope."

He smiled. "A far more pleasant way than that."

"What way?"

"I don't think I'd better tell you just yet. You might want to slap me."

She pulled out of his embrace, lay back on the bed, and looked up into his eyes. They were inky black, but they seemed to glow, even sparkle. There was nothing sinister or threatening about them. There was warmth, welcome.

"Maybe you should show me," she said. She didn't know what he intended to do, but she desperately wanted to believe that somebody wanted her for herself. Not for what she could do.

Leaning over her, he framed her face with his hands. "I could look at you like this all evening."

It was a good beginning, but she wanted more.

"You have the kind of face a man could look on day after day and find something new each time."

It still wasn't what she wanted. "How can

that be true if my face doesn't change?"

"Because your face is a direct reflection of your character, the person you are, what you're feeling inside. As you grow and change, so does your face."

Okay, that sounded nice, but still it didn't hit the mark. She had to admit she was looking for something frivolous, something silly like *Your eyes make me think of twinkling stars. Your skin is as soft as white velvet. Your kisses are sweeter than honey.*

"But that's not really why I like being with you so much," he continued. "There's something that happens to me when you're around that's never happened before. I don't know why, but I feel more alive. I feel eager, expectant, as if something wonderful is going to happen at any minute. There's something about you no one else has."

She wanted to tell him he affected her very much the same way. From the first, even when she was angry and so afraid she wanted him to leave immediately, there'd been something about him that had made her want him to stay.

"Papa says some people have an attraction between them that's so strong they can't resist it. Do you believe that?"

"I can believe they don't *want* to resist it." He leaned down and feathered kisses across her mouth. "That's the way I feel about you."

Felicity put her arms around his neck and pulled him down next to her. She knew it wasn't wise, that she might be sorry tomorrow, but she decided to let tomorrow take care of itself.

"I don't want to resist, either." She didn't know how she got the courage to say that, but she was glad she had. She would never have another man in her life like Holt.

Holt didn't need a second invitation. He covered her mouth and eyes with clusters of kisses that were gentle and fleeting. It was like being kissed by butterflies. But when he kissed her ears, it wasn't the same at all. Where he'd been unbelievably gentle before, now he was teasing, nipping her earlobe, dipping his tongue into the shell of her ear, then trailing kisses down the side of her neck before beginning another assault on her ear.

Felicity felt as if she would melt from sheer pleasure. The pleasure was even greater when he unbuttoned the top of her dress until he could pull it off her shoulders. She had felt herself stiffen until his lips touched her shoulders. The shivers that raced through her body were amplified when he started to trace patterns there with the tip of his moist tongue.

She took his face in her hands and pulled him up so she could kiss him. "I never dreamed that anyone could make me feel so wonderful," she said.

"This is only the beginning," Holt said.

They kissed again, long and languorous kisses that made her wish they could go on forever. But even as she was imagining being able to kiss Holt like this forever, he opened her dress until he exposed the tops of her breasts. He trailed kisses across the side of her mouth, down her neck, across her shoulders, and across the tops of her breasts. Holt was right. It had been only the beginning. She'd never experienced anything like this.

Felicity had never had any really close friends, but she was aware that some women claimed they were so strongly affected by their senses they sometimes couldn't control their actions, couldn't make themselves do what they knew was best. She'd always considered this nonsense. No intelligent person would allow herself to be ruled by anything but her brain. To do so was merely seeking an excuse for weakness of character. She had already accepted that the heart could overrule the brain. How else could she have fallen in love with Holt? Now it looked as though she was about to learn a lesson that women had known since the beginning of time.

Her body was the repository of a wealth of sensations so vast she would never be able to experience them all. Nor control them.

She was unable to lie still. She writhed under the assault of sensations electrifying her body. She'd never been so acutely aware of any part of her body in her entire life. Not even pain could compare to the impact made by the feeling of Holt's lips on her breasts. She couldn't think of anything else. Didn't *want* to think of anything else. Every sensation became more intense when Holt loosened her shift and exposed her breasts to his warm, soft lips. When his hot, moist tongue touched her firm nipple, she thought she would rise off the bed.

Felicity's body went rigid. She was sure her gasp was loud enough to be heard by half the neighbors, but she didn't care. She couldn't have stopped it if she had wanted to. She was completely, utterly in the throes of sensations so new, so strong, and so vital, she was helpless to control her body. She could only react with shock, surprise, and pleasure to each new one. When Holt began to suckle her nipple, she realized there was no end to the sensations she could experience. Each one seemed like the ultimate, so keen, so excruciatingly pleasurable that it was impossible to experience anything more intense. Yet each new feeling increased the potency of her pleasure even more than the last. When he nipped her nipple with his teeth, she knew she couldn't stand any more.

"Stop!" she said. "I can't stand it."

But he didn't stop, and she was grateful, for she knew she didn't mean it.

"Holt, you've got to stop. I'll go crazy."

Even though she knew she would be in agony if he *did* stop, she couldn't control the words coming out of her mouth. She had become two beings, each locked in a struggle with the other for control of her body.

Holt released her nipple. "Do you really want me to stop?"

"Yes," she said as her body arched upward and she took his face between her hands and forced his mouth back to her nipple. "You're driving me crazy. I don't think I can stand it any longer." She directed his attention to her other nipple. When he seemed to hesitate, she pulled him tight against her. It was agony, but it was an agony she couldn't resist.

Felicity's attention was so tightly focused on what Holt was doing to her breasts, she didn't realize that one hand had moved beneath her dress until she felt his fingers on her upper thigh. Her attention was torn between two parts of her body, between two different sensations, between two different messages being shouted from her brain. She felt herself hesitate, felt some of the heat in her body start to cool. Then she felt a new and unfamiliar sensation in her belly, the sensation of heat pooling, growing warmer, slowly spreading out to encompass more of her, gradually taking away any desire to resist.

Even as Holt's hand drew near her inner self, she felt her body slowly begin to relax, to open to receive him. It wasn't a shock when his fingers entered her. It was new, unknown, but it wasn't unanticipated. Her body and soul knew this was what she wanted, that this was a necessary part of the feelings they had for each other. But when his fingers found and began to gently rub the most sensitive spot of all, she was unable to contain herself.

She heard herself groan as the waves of pleasure grew more intense and washed over more and more of her body. Her body writhed, arched, and pushed itself against Holt's hand in its need to satisfy the hunger that gnawed at her. But nothing seemed to satisfy it. The harder she tried, the greater the need became, until she thought she would die from it. Surely no human body was supposed to endure such a struggle. She heard herself cry out, but she formed no words of protest, nothing to tell him she had never realized that great pleasure could be great agony at the same time. Her body strove for release, for escape, unable to decide between the two. Then when she was certain she could stand no more, her pleasure peaked in a flood of exquisite sensation.

But there was only a moment's release. Even as Felicity felt the tension retreat from the unbearable heights of moments ago, she felt Holt entering her, stretching her, filling her beyond what she'd thought was possible. Almost immediately the tension reversed itself and started to build once again. As Holt moved within her, she felt a different kind of connection. She felt closer to him, like they belonged together. She put her arms around him and drew him close. He gathered her in his embrace, kissed her with such passion she felt consumed by him.

She wanted to be lost in his embrace, to be

enfolded by him, to be part of him so they could never be torn apart. As the tension in her body increased, as her body rose to meet him, becoming an equal participant in taking pleasure and giving pleasure, she felt she'd finally reached a place where life would begin to give her the kind of happiness and fulfillment she'd dreamed of. Anything was possible as long as she was in Holt's arms.

Felicity lay awake, unable to sleep. Next to her, Holt lay sprawled across the bed, only part of his naked body covered by the sheet. Even in the dark, she pulled the sheet up to cover her breasts. No matter how wonderful the night had been, no matter how much she'd like to do it all over again, she couldn't quite be comfortable in bed nude without something covering her body.

She could hardly believe the events of this night. Holt had stayed with her, making love to her twice more, making sweeter love in between when he held her and told her how much his feelings for her had changed his life, had enabled him to see everything he'd done in a different perspective.

He hadn't said he wanted to marry her, he hadn't said he'd be faithful for the rest of his life, but he couldn't be talking about anything else. She finally believed that Holt loved her as much as she loved him.

Yes, she loved him. She was no longer afraid

she'd wake up and find it had all been a dream. Neither of them had the answers just yet to all the questions that faced them, but they'd figure it out between them.

They had to, because they were in love.

She couldn't believe how wonderful it felt. Much more wonderful than she'd ever hoped. She didn't fear she'd become so obsessed with him she'd go crazy if anything ever happened to him. She didn't fear he would take over her life and tell her what to do. She didn't fear he would ignore her abilities or undervalue them. She looked ahead to a future that was going to unravel all the troubles in her life. She reached over and shook Holt.

"What?" he said, his eyes still closed, his voice thick with sleep.

"It's time to get up."

He reached for her. "I'd rather stay here."

"Me, too, but I have to fix breakfast, and you have to get back to your room before my father wakes up."

Holt opened one eye. "You think he'd disapprove?"

"He's been trying to get me to marry you for weeks, but I expect he'd like to see the wedding before the consummation."

The second eye popped open at the mention of the word *wedding*. "I see what you mean." He looked around for his clothes. "We made a mess."

"Neither of us was thinking about neatness."

She shivered when Holt planted a kiss on her belly.

"I'd much rather think about you," he said.

"So would I, but you have to put on your clothes and go to your room."

"It seems pointless to put them on just to take them off again."

"Would you rather risk Papa seeing you leaving my room naked?"

"That might be hard to explain."

"On the contrary. I think it would be very easy."

"Okay. You're throwing me out. That's fine as long as you let me come back again."

"We have lots of things we need to talk about, lots of things we need to decide."

She wouldn't allow herself to think how much she wanted him back in her arms. She knew she loved Holt, but they had made no promises to each other. She didn't want to think about Vivian, but she knew that nothing could progress to the next stage as long as that woman was in his life.

Holt pulled on his pants, then leaned over and kissed her. "You know I'm not going to be able to keep my hands off you, don't you?"

"Everyone thinks you're going to marry Vivian. You can't be in love with both of us at the same time."

"I'm not going to marry Vivian," Holt said, reaching for the rest of his clothes. "I did offer to marry her and take her back to Virginia, but only because I thought it was my duty. She doesn't want to marry me, because I will always be poor. When I told her I felt responsible for her, that I'd promised to take care of her, she practically ordered me not to worry about her ever again. So you see, I'm only thinking about one woman, and I'm with her right now."

Felicity was ready to confess that she was a selfish woman. She probably ought to be thankful that Holt had finally overcome his fascination with Vivian, but that wasn't enough. She wanted it all — the love, the passion, the confession that she was the only woman in the world he had ever truly loved, the only one he *could* ever love. A woman who was truly born to love shouldn't be expected to settle for less.

It's time to face reality. You've lived in a fantasy world too long. Nobody is born to be loved. This may be the best you'll ever have. Don't throw it away for a fantasy.

She knew that was good advice, but she didn't know if she could follow it.

Felicity didn't know what to think when she opened the door to find two policemen on the porch. One of them was Billy Privett, a man she'd known for several years. "Hi, Billy," she said. "Do you need to see the doctor?"

"This isn't a personal call," the other man said. "I'm Captain Lytle. We're here on business. Is Holt Price staying here?" he asked.

"Yes."

"I want to talk to him."

"He's seeing a patient right now."

"We can wait."

"Come in. I'll let him know you're here." Felicity decided to put them in the parlor. She didn't want them upsetting patients. She'd hardly come back after speaking to Holt when she had to answer the front door again. It was Mrs. Bennett.

"I saw two policemen come in. Is there some trouble?"

"I don't know. They want to see Holt."

"What about?"

"I don't know."

"I'll ask them."

She marched into the parlor and did just that.

"There have been some robberies recently," Captain Lytle said. "We're questioning everyone who's been in the houses involved."

"You're wasting your time here," Mrs. Bennett said. "You won't find a more honest and upstanding man than Dr. Price."

"That's not the information we received."

Charlotte had mentioned some recent robberies, but Felicity hadn't thought much about them. Considering how destitute some people were, she wasn't surprised that some of the incredibly ostentatious homes on Broadway would be burgled. Some of the dresses she'd seen cost enough to feed a whole family for a month.

"And just what information might that be?" Mrs. Bennett asked. "And more to the point, who gave it to you?"

"I can't divulge that information," the captain said.

"Well, you'd better be divulging it," Mrs. Bennett said. "The doctor has been talking to me about taking rooms in my house. I have a right to know whether I'm in danger of being murdered in my bed."

"We're only investigating theft," Captain Lytle said. "We know nothing of any murders he may have committed."

Felicity had to fight down an urge to slip out of the room to warn Holt. She was certain he had nothing to do with the robberies, but she didn't know if he could convince the captain of that. But she had waited too long. Holt had entered the parlor.

"Good afternoon," he said. "I was wondering how long it would be before you came to see me."

The policemen looked as startled as Felicity felt.

"Let me guess," Holt said. "Someone has given you information suggesting that I might be responsible for the robberies that have occurred recently."

"How could you know that?" Captain Lytle asked. "The ladies here never left the room."

"I also know who gave you the information," Holt said. "Laveau diViere."

The captain broke out into a cold sweat. "Either someone has been telling what they had no business telling, or you're a mighty cool customer."

"Why didn't someone from the army come?" Holt asked.

"They were going to, but this is a civil matter. And civil matters are supposed to be handled by the local police."

Felicity got the impression that Captain Lytle had had to fight hard for the honor of arresting Holt. Though she was relieved the army hadn't come to her door, she was still worried. Why would Mr. diViere say Holt was stealing, and how could Holt know he would say it?

"Let me tell you a little story," Holt said.

"I'm not here to listen to stories," the captain said. "I'm here about the robberies."

"The story is about the robberies," Holt said.

"Okay," the captain said reluctantly. "But if you're just playing for time —"

"If you want to arrest me after you've heard what I have to say, I'll go with you," Holt said. "But it's only fair to warn you that you'll be facing some mighty angry ex-soldiers."

"I don't pay attention to threats," the captain said. "I fought in the Mexican War."

"Good," Holt said. "You're going to need every bit of your courage if you want to bring this particular criminal to justice."

"And what criminal would that be?"

"Laveau diViere. Let me tell you about him."

So Holt told him about the betrayal of his troop, the rustling of cattle, and the attempted robbery of a bank.

"Why should I believe this? Mr. diViere is a trusted member of the Reconstruction government. Why would he steal?"

"Because he hates all Texans. In case you didn't know, his father and grandfather fought for Mexico in 1836 and 1848."

Captain Lytle looked thunderstruck. "Are you sure this is true?"

"Yes."

"Does the Union Army know?"

"I doubt it, but it's easy to prove."

Felicity could tell the wheels were turning in the captain's head.

"There's more to this, isn't there?" he said.

Holt smiled. "You're very perceptive."

"Don't flatter me. What do you know?"

"Not as much as I would like. When I came to Galveston, I heard whispers that Laveau knew more than he should and was taking advantage of it. I haven't been able to learn much, but it wasn't hard to guess. Laveau has tried blackmail before. It seems he finds bits of information — perhaps that a wealthy businessman has a connection with the Confederacy he's managed to hide — and agrees not to make this information public for a monetary consideration. Laveau knows I can prove he's a thief and a liar. I didn't know what he would do, but I was sure he'd soon come up with a way to discredit me. When you showed up asking about these robberies, I figured Laveau was behind it. They started after I got here. And I'll bet ten to one I've been to a party in every house that was robbed."

The captain nodded. "So you're saying Mr. diViere committed these robberies?"

"I doubt it. Blackmail affords more room for financial gain with comparatively little risk. I expect he's hired someone to do the break-ins for him."

Captain Lytle didn't look happy. "Anybody could make that kind of accusation. Why should I believe you?"

"Because he's an honorable man," Mrs. Bennett said.

"That may be as you say, but I need some proof. Mr. diViere is a man of considerable standing in Galveston."

"What you mean is he's got the Union Army and the Reconstruction government behind him," Mrs. Bennett said.

Captain Lytle held his tongue, but Felicity guessed he'd very much like to bring down one of the Army and Reconstruction government's favorite citizens. They had been very heavy-handed with the civil government.

"What do you suggest I do?" Captain Lytle asked Holt.

"Put a watch on the biggest houses on Broadway that haven't been burgled. Sooner or later someone will attempt to break in.

Follow the culprit and you'll capture the thief and possibly recover the previously stolen items."

"Supposing I had enough men to watch every house — which I don't. How is this supposed to implicate Mr. diViere?"

"I'm sure a little of the right kind of pressure would induce the thief to divulge the name of the man who hired him."

"That's as may be," Captain Lytle said, "but you're under suspicion. I have to search this house."

"Are you implying that I'm involved in thievery?" Dr. Moore asked. He'd entered the parlor in time to hear the last sentence.

"I'm not implying anything," Captain Lytle said, "but I have my orders, and my orders are to search this house."

"You might as well search my house, too," Mrs. Bennett said. "Dr. Price stayed with me for a time. I'm a poor widow. I can always use extra money."

Captain Lytle looked thoroughly beleaguered, but he was dogged about his duty. He and Billy Privett spent more than an hour searching each house.

"It's time for a war council," Mrs. Bennett said after they'd gone. "We can't leave the initiative to the enemy."

"What can we do?" Dr. Moore asked.

"We have to look for someone who could be hired to rob houses," Holt said. "And someone who's being blackmailed and is willing to report it."

"I can help with the thief," Mrs. Bennett said. "One of my sons works at the docks. If anybody knows about thieves, it's the dock workers."

"I'll ask Charlotte to help find out who's being blackmailed," Felicity said. "I'm sure Lillie will help, too. Then you and Papa can talk the person into reporting it to the police."

"I'll stick to Vivian," Holt said. "The men around her are often careless about what they say."

Felicity didn't like Holt having anything to do with Vivian, but that course of action had as much chance of success as any.

"Thanks for believing in me," Holt said to Mrs. Bennett.

"What's to believe in?" she asked. "With the three of us looking over your shoulder, you couldn't have sneaked as much as a teaspoon past us. Besides, you're one of those people who's compulsive about telling the truth. I hope you don't ever find out anything on me."

"So you see why you have to help me," Felicity said to Charlotte and Lillie. "If we can't prove Holt is innocent, he could go to jail."

"The Union Army would probably hang him because he was a Confederate solider," Lillie said.

That was not what Felicity wanted to hear.

"I'll do what I can," Charlotte said, "but my husband might order me to stop. He says there's no way to fight the Reconstruction and the Army."

"We don't want to fight them," Felicity said, "just find out who Mr. diViere has been blackmailing."

"How can we be sure he's blackmailing people if nobody will speak up?" Charlotte asked.

"I don't know who's doing it, but I do know somebody is blackmailing people," Lillie said. "I overheard one of Clifford's clients telling him about it. He was worried it might happen to him."

"But if they're willing to pay money to keep their secrets, how are we going to persuade them to go to the authorities?" Charlotte asked.

"That's where the men take over." Felicity said. "Our job is to find at least one person who's being blackmailed."

"How do we do that?" Charlotte asked.

"Have you noticed dramatic changes in anyone recently?" Felicity asked. "Someone who used to be happy and carefree but who's now nervous or seems constantly upset or on the verge of tears?"

"Maybe somebody who's wearing the same dress to parties," Lillie said. "Or has stopped coming to parties."

"That's Megan Fraser to a tee," Charlotte said. "Mavis and I were just remarking on it two days ago."

"We have to talk to her," Felicity said.

"Which one of us will go?" Lillie asked.

"All of us," Felicity replied.

Megan looked startled when the three women were shown into her sitting room. "I wasn't expecting company," she said, looking flustered.

"This isn't a social visit," Felicity said. "We've come on business."

Megan looked even more confused. "I know nothing about business. I leave that to my husband."

Charlotte sat down next to Megan on the sofa. Felicity and Lillie took seats across from her. "This business concerns your whole family," Felicity said. "Is your husband being blackmailed?"

For a moment Felicity thought Megan would faint. Many women feigned exaggerated reactions when they wanted to avoid facing a difficult situation, but there didn't seem to be anything false about Megan's white complexion or look of fear.

"I don't know what you're talking about," Megan managed to say at last. "We have nothing to hide."

Charlotte took her hand and held it tightly. "We all have things to hide, especially from the Reconstruction government," she said. "You don't have to be afraid of us. We want to help you."

"I really don't know what you're talking about," Megan insisted. "Who could be blackmailing us?"

"Laveau diViere," Felicity said.

"I've heard things from other people," Lillie said. "You're not the only one he's blackmailing."

"I told you nobody's blackmailing us," Megan said. "I don't know where you got such an idea."

"From watching you," Charlotte said. "You're not the happy, contented woman you used to be."

"Things have been a little difficult with the business lately."

"That's not true," Charlotte said. "Just a few days ago my husband was saying your husband's business is the most successful in Galveston. He was speculating on when you'd start building your own mansion on Broadway. You already own one of the biggest lots."

"Your family must have already outgrown this house," Felicity said.

"I must insist that you stop talking like this," Megan said, looking like a cornered animal seeking desperately for a way to escape. "I don't know what gave you the idea —"

"He's blackmailing other people," Lillie repeated.

"And unless we can stop him, he's going to keep on until he ruins you," Felicity said.

"Why do you care?" Megan asked, angrily

turning on Felicity. "You haven't spoken to me for years."

"After Papa lost his money, a lot of people stopped talking to us and inviting us to parties," Felicity said. "I assumed no one wanted to have anything to do with us. I didn't realize that some people just didn't know what to say. I was angry and felt rejected, so I refused all overtures. I'm sorry for my mistake and want to make up for it, but I'm here today for selfish reasons. Mr. diViere has accused Dr. Price of being behind a recent string of thefts."

"Why should Laveau do something like that?" Megan asked.

"He knows Holt can expose him," Felicity said, "so he's trying to discredit Holt." Felicity told her what Holt said Laveau had done in the past. By the time she finished, Megan looked ready to faint.

"Something's wrong," Lillie said. "You've got to tell us, Megan."

"It's Richard," Megan said. "He's got a gun. He says he's going to kill diViere."

"Now you know everything," Richard Fraser said to Captain Lytle. "I'd rather be ruined by you than by that son-of-a-bitch."

Alerted by Felicity to Richard's intentions, Holt and Clifford Hart had been able to persuade Richard to tell Lytle that Laveau was demanding a partnership in his company for his continued silence. Holt had convinced Richard that Laveau wouldn't be satisfied until he had stripped Richard and his wife of everything they owned.

"I will need everything you've told me in writing," Captain Lytle said.

"Give me pen and paper," Richard said. "I'd rather get it over and done with now."

"I'm sorry I didn't believe you," Captain Lytle said to Holt once Richard was occupied, "but he's a very important man."

"I understand that."

"Do you think you can convince more people to come forward?"

"I'd rather capture Laveau without ruining innocent people."

"How do you propose we do that?"

"Mrs. Bennett — you remember meeting her at Dr. Moore's house — has learned through her son that a couple of dock workers have been flashing around more money than they could earn honestly. Have someone follow them. Don't arrest them until you find out where they're hiding what they steal. Under pressure I'm sure they'll implicate Laveau."

"It may still be impossible to prove his connection to the thefts."

"If it is, I have friends coming to Galveston with enough evidence of rustling and robbery to convict him in any court."

"He's one of the two men Mrs. Bennett's son pointed out to me," Holt said to Captain Lytle.

"The other is at the bar getting beer."

"They don't look like thieves," Lytle said.

"Laveau would never use obvious thieves. They'd be too easy to spot."

Holt had taken Lytle to a rough, all-night bar down by the docks on Galveston Bay. It wasn't the place where he wanted to spend his evening, but so far the captain had been unwilling to assign men to the investigation. If they were going to catch Laveau, Holt would have to do some of the legwork himself.

"You really think he's behind the thefts?" Captain Lytle asked.

"Why else would he lodge a complaint against me?"

"Because you're the thief?"

"They're not staying to drink their beer," Holt said. "We've got to follow them."

"I don't have any men with me."

"Then we'll have to do it ourselves."

"I'll get one of these fellas to take a message to the station."

"We don't have time," Holt said.

"You follow them. I'll catch up."

Holt had never intended to trail the thieves by himself. He was a doctor. He hadn't been trained to fight. He had waited in camp for people to bring him the wounded. Nate and Rafe were the ones best suited for this kind of work. They could follow a rattlesnake across rock. He couldn't capture the thieves by himself. They were both bigger than he was.

And of course he didn't have a gun. It wasn't his habit to go around Galveston with one strapped to his waist. He would have been arrested.

He didn't have any problem following the men. It was past midnight and almost no one was on the streets. Holt stayed well back and hugged the shadows. He followed them east along 21st Street. They cut across the square and headed north on McKinney Street, one street over from Broadway. Holt went below the square and turned up William Street. Two blocks later he turned up 19th Street, then headed north on McKinney. He figured they were going to approach the targeted house from the rear.

They were going to rob Gloria Webster's house. She and her husband were at a party which would probably last two or three more hours. Holt cut through between houses, hoping he would see Captain Lytle or one of his men coming up Broadway, but the street was empty. Unwilling to wait longer and risk missing the thieves when they left, he raced back between houses, keeping the rear of the Webster mansion in view. It wasn't long before the thieves came out. They didn't hurry or look around as if they were afraid of being seen.

Holt didn't know what they had taken, but it had to be small. They weren't carrying sacks, and he couldn't see any bulges under their shirts. Convinced they really had stolen something, he followed as they hurried back toward the docks. He figured they planned to use their beers as proof they had spent the evening drinking.

Holt was having difficulty following them without being seen. He kept looking around hoping to see Captain Lytle, but not one policeman was in sight. The two thieves stopped at a small warehouse close to the bar and went inside. Holt got closer. Still, he didn't see any policemen. What was he going to do when the thieves came out? He couldn't stop two huge men by himself. But if he didn't stop them, there would be no way to connect them with the robberies.

Just then he saw Captain Lytle and two other policemen enter the street two blocks away. Holt waved frantically, trying to attract their attention. He wasn't sure they had seen him when the warehouse door opened and the thieves came out. There was no way for Holt to hide. They saw him immediately.

"What are you doing here?" one of them asked.

"I gotta pee," Holt said, pretending to be drunk. "Gotta pee real bad."

He didn't know if they believed him, but he turned away, pretending he was about to relieve himself against the side of the warehouse.

"Hey, don't piss on the building," one of them said. "Piss in the street if you gotta."

His partner grabbed his arm to get his attention. "What're all them policemen doing out this time of night?"

Holt looked up. Captain Lytle and his men were running toward them, but they were still a block away.

"Let's get outta here," one man said.

Holt knew he couldn't let them escape. Once out of sight, they could disappear among the docks. They could be on the mainland in minutes or away in a ship within hours. With a fatalistic sigh, Holt threw himself at one of the thieves. The attack caught the man by surprise and he went down. Hoping his luck would hold, Holt dived at the legs of the other thief, who was already running away. Both men went down in a heap, Holt ending up on the bottom.

"Cut the son-of-a-bitch's throat," the other thief shouted.

Holt managed to throw off his opponent and scrambled to his feet. The thieves broke into a run. "I know you've been breaking into the houses on Broadway," Holt shouted after them. "I know what you look like. You'll never get away."

His taunting delayed them just long enough for Captain Lytle and his men to arrive. It took all four of them to wrestle the men to the ground and hold them long enough for more policemen to arrive. By the time the thieves had been subdued and tied up, a small crowd had gathered.

"Now let's see what you've got in this warehouse," Captain Lytle said, his bruised and battered face transformed by a triumphant smile.

They were about to sit down to lunch the next day when they heard a banging on the front door.

"I'll get it," Felicity said. "If it's a patient, I'll have him come back unless it's an emergency."

Moments later, Felicity returned to the kitchen followed by a tearful Vivian.

"I've got to talk to Holt," Vivian said through her tears. "Privately."

"Use the consulting room," Dr. Moore said.

Holt had seen Vivian cry before. Tears were one of the most powerful weapons a beautiful woman could employ. Vivian rarely used them, but she always used them well. He had a feeling these tears weren't entirely genuine, but he couldn't be sure. There was a look of fear, of desperation in Vivian's eyes he'd never see before.

"What's so important that it's driven you out of your bedroom before noon?"

"I've come to ask you to marry me and take me back to Virginia."

Chapter Twenty-four

Holt settled her in the consulting room and closed the door. "What made you change your mind?" he asked. He knew Vivian well enough to know she wouldn't have changed her mind unless something terrible had happened.

"I just realized I have always loved you. If you want to go back to Virginia, I'll go with you."

She threw herself at him, clasped her arms around his neck, and kissed him on the mouth. Holt couldn't help thinking it ironic. At any moment in the last six years he'd have given his right arm to hear her say she'd made a mistake when she married Abe Calvert, that she loved him and wanted him to carry her away to a secret place where they would be alone for the rest of their lives.

But that time was past. He'd come to a better understanding of himself. A better understanding of Vivian. He removed her arms from around his neck and put enough distance between them so he could look into her eyes. There had been a time when he wanted nothing more than to get lost in them. Now not even glistening tears could make him prefer Vivian's blue eyes to Felicity's dark brown ones.

"Look at me," Holt said when Vivian lowered her gaze. "Just a few days ago you were furious I would even suggest that you go back to Virginia. You practically threw me out of the house. Now you want me to believe you've changed your mind?"

"I was upset," Vivian said. She raised her gaze and looked him straight in the eye. "I was jealous of the attention you paid *that woman*. You know I've always loved you. I've told you so for years."

If Holt hadn't been in love with someone else, he might have fallen for her story. She looked so sincere, so helpless, so fragile, no red-blooded male could resist the chance to do anything he could to make her happy. Tears only enhanced her appeal.

She attempted to put her arms back around his neck and fall into his embrace, but he held her at a distance.

"I can't marry you, Vivian. I love someone else."

"Why are you being so mean to me?"

"I'm just telling you the truth. And I want the truth from you."

She broke his hold on her wrists and backed away angrily. "I've always told you the truth."

"Maybe, but you've also left a lot of it out. This time I want to know everything."

"If I tell you, will you promise to take me to Virginia right away? Uncle William promised you would always take care of me."

"Just tell me why you've changed your mind."

"It's your fault, really."

"What are you talking about?"

"Laveau. You told everybody he was a traitor and a murderer."

"He is." He wanted to tell her about the capture of the thieves, but he couldn't until they implicated Laveau.

"Now everybody blames me for inviting him to parties. They say I can't ever come into their homes again. There — now you know the truth."

She buried her face in her hands, but Holt resisted the impulse to take her in his arms. He was happy that people had finally turned their backs on Laveau, but he didn't understand why this should have caused Vivian to be ostracized.

"I don't understand why they blame you," Holt said.

"Well, they do."

The more he thought about it, the more he was certain he wasn't getting the whole story. "There's more, isn't there?"

"What makes you say that?"

"You're a beautiful woman. If it were merely a matter of social standing, you'd turn up your nose at the women and concentrate on the men. Before long, you'd be invited back into society, if for no other reason than because you'd bring the single men with you."

Vivian beamed. "You think I'm that beautiful?"

"You know you are. What could be so terrible that you can't bend people to your will anymore?"

"If they don't want me, I don't want to go to their parties," she said, tossing her head.

"Come off it, Vivian. This is me you're talking to. You live for parties. What's so dreadful to make you consider hiding away on a country farm?"

"Why won't you believe I love you?"

"Because I know you don't love anybody as much as you love money, position, and power over men. I'm only a poor doctor, remember, who doesn't care about position or money."

"I don't care about those things anymore. Besides, we can live in Richmond, where you will have a lot more patients."

She hadn't set foot outside of Galveston and she was already moving him to Richmond. Next it would be Philadelphia or New York. "Tell me what *really* happened."

Vivian looked mulish.

"Either tell me or leave. I've got patients to see."

"A person would think your patients are more important to you than I am."

"My patients tell me the truth. All of it."

For a moment Vivian glared at him. He was certain she was calculating exactly how much she could tell without telling all. She was probably also wondering whether she hadn't acted hastily and might be able to overcome the problem in some other way. She suddenly flashed a brilliant smile.

"I was too mortified to tell you, but I guess you'll find out anyway. I can't believe I could be so mistaken in a man."

"What did Laveau do?"

"He has been blackmailing people. He finds out who has something to hide and threatens to turn his victims in to the Reconstruction."

The door had opened before Vivian finished speaking. Her sister-in-law entered the room, followed by Felicity. "That's not exactly what people are saying," Lillie Hart said.

Vivian turned white when she saw her sister-in-law, but she quickly regained her composure. "Lillie, what are you doing here?"

"When I learned you weren't packing but had left the house, I figured you would come here to the only man who believes you're a decent woman."

"Holt loves me, and I love him. He's going to marry me and take me back to Virginia."

"That may be his intention, but I believe he has a right to know the kind of woman you are before he marries you."

"They're only lies, Lillie. Nobody can prove a thing."

"Nobody would hold it against Vivian if she'd been taken in by Laveau like the rest of us," Lillie said, turning to Holt. "What has caused Galveston to close its doors to her, and prompted my husband to order her to leave our house immediately, is the knowledge that she gave information to diViere and received payment for it."

"That's not true!" Vivian cried. "You can't prove it."

Holt looked at Vivian in disbelief. She'd never been poor, never wanted for anything. He couldn't believe she would betray her friends for money. He turned to her, hoping she'd say something to prove she hadn't done such a terrible thing. There was fear in her eyes, but behind it rage blazed too strongly to be missed.

"Surely you don't believe her instead of me," Vivian said.

"Why shouldn't I?"

"Because it's not true."

The door had opened again to allow Laveau diViere and Dr. Moore to enter the room.

"I'm sorry to have to contradict you, my sweet," Laveau said, "but it is true."

What had begun as a simple situation was assuming nightmarish proportions. Here, within his grasp, was the man who'd betrayed his fellow soldiers three years ago, the man responsible for so much needless death. Holt was tempted to shoot him, but he didn't want to be hanged for murder. He was willing to sacrifice a lot of things to bring Laveau to justice, but not his future with Felicity.

Holt looked at the people in the room, tried

to ascertain the state of mind of each by his or her expression. Laveau appeared completely calm, undisturbed by the fact that he'd been caught in blackmail. Maybe after betrayal, theft, murder, and rustling, blackmail seemed comparatively harmless. He seemed amused by Vivian's nearly hysterical accusation that he'd drawn an innocent woman into this net, then forced her to help him blackmail the very people whose acceptance meant everything to her.

Lillie Hart's expression was harder to interpret. It seemed to be a combination of shock that a person could be as evil as Laveau, surprise that Vivian had lost control of the situation, and probably a little bit of satisfaction that Vivian had finally been shown to have clay feet.

Felicity's expression was easy to understand. Pain. Devastation. Something must have happened while he was talking to Vivian. He wanted to clear up this mess and send everybody home so he could find out what had upset her so much. He never wanted to see her so unhappy again.

Dr. Moore appeared to be the only impartial observer in the room, watching everyone with wide-eyed curiosity. It was probably the only time in the last thirteen years he wasn't thinking of whiskey.

"You've finally gone too far," Holt said to Laveau, breaking in on Vivian. "You stop at nothing to achieve your ends."

"I certainly don't stop to allow myself to be caught on the losing side," Laveau said.

His voice had lost its liquid smoothness, had turned harsh, the words propelled with great force from his mouth. His mask of sophisticated pretense slipped to reveal the hatred boiling inside him. Even his physical stance changed to one of open hostility.

"And in the process you sacrificed your honor and integrity," Holt said.

Laveau laughed. "You act as if lost honor is gone forever. You naive fool. Honor can be bought and sold just like anything else."

"Not among honorable people."

Laveau sneered. "You're a bigger fool than I thought. You'd risk everything, even your life, for this woman," he said, pointing an accusing finger at Vivian. "A woman who'd make a whore of herself for money."

It was more than Holt could stand to see Laveau untouched after blatantly flouting the laws of man, of common decency, of basic morality that governed the civilized world. Not only had he remained beyond the reach of justice, he mocked its very existence. Laveau's handsome, sneering face caused something inside Holt to snap.

He launched himself at Laveau.

It wasn't much of a fight. Two punches and Laveau sank to the floor, his face bloodied and two buttons popped loose from his vest. Holt stepped back, surprised and a bit embarrassed at his uncontrolled temper.

"That's what I expected from you," Laveau said. He wiped his mouth with the back of his hand, looked at the blood, and smiled. "You always have to do things according to the code of gentlemanly behavior." He stood up, took out his handkerchief, and wiped the blood from his hand. "You never have learned how to deal with your opponents properly." He touched the handkerchief to his mouth and winced with pain.

"And how is that?" Holt asked.

"It's embarrassing to lose a fight," Laveau said, restoring his handkerchief to his pocket, "but even winning can be ineffective. You have to deal with your opponent in a manner that makes certain he won't come back again to trouble you." Without warning he drew a pistol from his inner pocket and fired. "Anything else is a waste of time."

Holt saw the pistol, heard the deafening sound of the shot before he felt the pain. But his thoughts were far from his own hurt. They were focused on Felicity's shock and horror at what had happened. And the knowledge that just when he had found love, he was going to lose it. He reached out to her, his final words an inaudible whisper.

I love you.

After hearing Vivian beg Holt to marry her, Felicity knew her chance for happiness had vanished once again. No man could refuse Vivian, especially not a man who'd been in love with her for years. Felicity had been in a kind of fog, unable to think, unable to move, even unable to explain to her father what had happened. She didn't know how she managed to open the door and invite Lillie Hart into the house, or how she found herself in the room with Vivian and Holt. She felt as though someone else was moving her body about like a chess piece. When she heard the pistol shot, saw the small hole appear in Holt's chest, everything fell away. She was at Holt's side before his body slumped to the floor.

"Papa!" she cried as she ripped open Holt's shirt to expose the wound. Her father was on his knees next to Holt almost before the word left her mouth. "You've got to get the bullet out."

"It won't do any good if he's dead," her father said, his fingers on the vein in Holt's throat.

He couldn't be dead. As much as it would break her heart, she'd rather see him go back to Vivian than be dead. But to die at the hands of a cowardly traitor! She pushed her father's hand aside. "Let me," she said. She started to tell everyone in the room to be quiet, but all noise had ceased. She moved her fingertips along Holt's neck, searching desperately for signs of even a weak pulse. All the time her lips were moving in silent prayer.

Suddenly her fingers stopped. Her lips froze. Her entire concentration was on confirming what she had just felt . . . a faint pulse. She was afraid she felt the pulse because she wanted it so desperately. But when she felt it again, so weak she could barely perceive it, she knew she wasn't mistaken.

"He's alive."

"Are you sure?"

"Yes."

"I'll send for a doctor."

"We don't have time. You have to operate."

"You know I'm not a surgeon like Holt. I'm afraid —"

"I don't want to hear excuses," she shouted, for the first time not bothering to be careful of her father's feelings. "Holt says you know more medicine than he does." She grabbed her father's wrist. "All my life I've taken care of you. I've cooked your meals, cleaned your house, helped with patients, made excuses when you weren't fit to see them, put you to bed when you were too drunk to do it yourself. I'm twenty-six years old and I have nothing because I gave everything up for you. *Everything!* Finally I ask one thing of you and you tell me you can't because you're afraid?"

"Felicity, darling, it's not that I don't want to. I —"

"If Holt dies because you were too cowardly even to try to save his life, I'll walk out of this house and never speak to you again as long as I live."

"You can't mean that."

"Before Mama died, she told me I had to take care of you. For thirteen years I have. Now it's your turn to do something for me."

Her father gazed deep into her eyes. Something he saw there must have helped him make up his mind. He responded with a decisiveness that was new for him. "Okay, but you'll have to help."

Felicity's gaze rarely moved from Holt for the last three days. Mrs. Bennett prepared delicious meals, but Felicity ate the little food she could force herself to swallow sitting in a chair next to his bed. She slept there as well, even though her body was now so stiff she could hardly move. She watched, waited, prayed for a sign that his body was winning the battle against the bullet wound, that he would regain consciousness and his full health.

To become Vivian's husband.

She had been a fool to believe Holt could love her. Vivian was a goddess, the kind of woman men put on a pedestal, the kind of woman men never forget even when they marry another woman. Holt could love Felicity for the very reason that she *was* attainable.

She couldn't live with that. It would have to be all or nothing.

Yet when she looked at him lying in the bed,

naked to the waist except for the bandage across his chest, she wondered how she could face the rest of her life knowing she wouldn't see him again, that he would never kiss her, hold her in his arms and make love to her. Afer being shown heaven for one brief moment, she was starving for more. Did she have the strength to turn away because crumbs were all she was offered?

She tried to push the questions out of her mind. She'd gone over them a thousand times in the last three days. Holt didn't love her as much as he loved Vivian. But every time she convinced herself of that, she would look at him lying there, beautiful and helpless, and everything would change. She couldn't give him up to Vivian. Somehow she had to —

A soft knock at the door preceded her father's entry into the room. He approached the bed, looked at Holt. "Has he shown any signs of regaining consciousness?"

She shook her head.

He sighed. "I did the best I could, but it was a bad wound. I thought he was going to die."

"Holt couldn't have done any better."

"There's someone downstairs to see you."

"I don't want to see anybody."

"I'll sit with him."

"I told you, I don't want to see anybody."

"I think you'll change your mind when you see who it is."

"I'm not dressed for company."

"They won't care."

But she would, Felicity thought, as she changed her dress, combed her hair, and made herself presentable. She wanted to refuse to see whoever this was, but she could tell when her father got stubborn. She would make it as quick as possible. But when she reached the parlor to see a room full of men and two women seated on the sofa — a young one with a baby in her arms and an old one who glared fiercely at everyone in the room — she knew immediately who they were.

"You're Holt's friends, aren't you? The ones he worked with on the ranch."

"I'm Cade Wheeler and this is my wife, Pilar." The beautiful woman with black hair smiled.

"I'd get up, but I don't want to wake the baby," she said.

"And I am Donna Isabella Cordoba diViere," the fierce woman said. "Pilar is my grand-daughter." Felicity thought her expression softened slightly. "And that is my great-grandson."

"Are those his friends?" she asked, indicating the other men. "The ones he fought with in Virginia?" Felicity asked. She recognized Broc. Holt had described his scarring.

"I'm Nate Dolan," one man said.

"Broc Kincaid."

"Ivan Nikolai."

"Rafe Jerry."

"He wrote us that he'd found Laveau

diViere," Cade said. "We came as soon as we could. Your father told us what happened. Do you know what happened to Laveau?"

"He left while we were still in shock. When the rumors started flying that Richard Fraser was going to inform against him, he emptied his accounts. Apparently he stayed in town only long enough to try to kill Holt." After he fled, the thieves admitted that Laveau had hired them.

"He has a habit of doing that," Cade said.

"And of getting away before we can catch him," Nate Dolan said. Felicity thought he looked particularly angry.

"We want to help," Cade said.

"Thanks, but that's not necessary," Felicity said. "My father and I can take care of Holt."

"We're not leaving until he's better," Pilar said. "We love him as much as you do."

"He intends to marry Vivian Calvert. He knew her in Virginia when she was a girl. His uncle —"

"We know all about Vivian," Broc said. "He talked about her all the time."

Exactly what Felicity didn't want to hear. She guessed she'd never stopped hoping.

"Men don't always know what they want until they see it," Pilar said. She handed the baby to her grandmother. "I'm sure you'd rather not have your house invaded by strangers, but Holt is a part of our family. We can't leave until we know he's going to recover.

Owen would be here, but his wife is expecting their first child. Every one of these men has tended wounds and knows what to do. I'll help you set up a schedule."

"If you don't, we're liable to cause so much trouble, they'll run us out of Galveston," Broc said.

"The only reason I'd leave now is to go after Laveau," Nate said.

Felicity felt overwhelmed. She also felt too exhausted to resist. They could do anything they wanted, but she intended to sit with Holt.

"You look exhausted," Pilar said. "Why don't you let me help you to bed?"

"I'm not sleepy."

"You're ready to drop where you stand," Pilar said. "Come on. You can tell me everything I need to know to take care of Holt. This will give me a chance to pay him back for taking such good care of me when I had my son."

"He's a big baby," Felicity said.

"Like his father."

Felicity wondered how big Holt's son would be. She told herself to stop it. She would never know. She had every intention of politely refusing Pilar's help, but it wasn't long before she found herself letting Pilar prepare her for bed. And all the while, she was talking about Holt, telling her everything to watch for, then telling her all about Vivian. The last thing she remembered before giving in to the weight of exhaustion was telling Pilar how Holt had sat up with her father through the worst stages of alcohol withdrawal.

"Holt has always had this compulsion to take care of people," Pilar said. "Oddly enough, it's that very compulsion that has caused him to keep everybody at a distance. I think you're the first person to get close to him."

"He said he loved me," Felicity murmured. "But he's going to marry Vivian."

"We'll see," Pilar said.

Holt didn't understand how he could be a disembodied spirit. He felt as if he were suspended in water. He would float near the surface where he could see light and faces staring back at him. Then he would sink into black depths where he saw and felt nothing. Was he dreaming? Was he dead? Nothing made any sense. What had happened to him?

It was too hard to think. Every time he came close to grasping a thought, it slipped away from him. It was important that he see someone, that he say something, but he couldn't remember who it was or what he wanted to say. It was important to remember how he got here, but he couldn't remember that, either.

The light was brighter today. As he floated near the surface, he saw a woman's face. It looked familiar, but he couldn't tell who it was. He tried to speak. He could feel his lips moving, but no sound came out. He was getting closer and closer to the light. He tried harder and harder to reach the light, to speak. He tried to lift his hand, to reach out to her, but his arm was too heavy. He felt something touch his hand. He tried to squeeze back, felt the slight contraction in his grip. He felt an answering pressure. He tried harder to break through the murkiness that swam above him. He felt weak, powerless, but he wouldn't give up. The grip on his hand felt stronger. He squeezed back.

"Holt."

The soft sound came from a distance. He didn't understand it.

"Holt, can you hear me? Can you feel my hand?"

He could almost understand. He could almost see her features. He could almost see through the haze. Then everything cleared and he found himself looking up into Felicity's worried face.

"Yes, I can hear you and feel your hand." He didn't understand why his voice sounded weak, breathy, the words halting.

She broke into a smile. "Thank God. There were times when I was afraid I'd never hear your voice again."

"What happened?"

"You were shot. You've been unconscious for a week."

"All those faces, those other people. Who are they?"

"They're your friends."

"Is it Vivian?" He wasn't entirely sure who Vivian was.

"You can see her when you're better," Felicity said. "Now you need to rest. Your friends will all want to see you as soon as you're strong enough." She released his hand and rose.

"I've got to talk to you."

"We'll talk later. You need your rest." She moved toward the door.

"But I need to talk now."

"Just rest." She opened the door. "We can talk later."

She left the room and closed the door behind her.

Chapter Twenty-five

"She won't see you," Pilar said to Holt. "I've done everything but drag her in by force."

He started to get up, but he didn't have the strength. Pilar pushed him back down.

"You're not getting up. If you keeping trying, I'll have Broc tie you to the bed."

"He's sadistic."

"He's determined you're not going to get up until you're well. Now behave yourself, or I'll tell Vivian she can't see you today."

Holt had cursed his weakness, and Laveau for being the cause of it, until he couldn't summon the energy to do it anymore. He didn't want to see Vivian, but he would because it was a duty he'd taken on years ago.

"Is she here now?"

"Yes."

"Tell her to come up. I might as well get this over with."

"An extraordinarily beautiful woman is coming to see you, and you don't look happy. Are you sure you're really alive?"

Holt laughed. "You'll see when the right beautiful woman comes through that door."

Felicity was considering whether to leave the shade of a grove of live oaks for the safety of a black willow. She would be practically invisible among the trailing limbs. She was aware that people came to the porch often to check on her. She had begun to feel like a cornered mouse. Everybody was trying to get her to see Holt now that he was conscious, but she had refused. Her resolution had sagged several times during the last three days, but knowing he'd asked about Vivian practically the moment he regained consciousness had stiffened her flagging resolve.

Her father was seeing more patients than ever, was in wonderful spirits, and spent nearly every evening with Mrs. Bennett. He was like a new man. Apparently, operating successfully on Holt had bolstered his confidence.

Felicity felt she'd been cut adrift. All her life she'd had her father to take care of, to look after, to protect. Now he didn't need her any longer. She was free to pursue her own happiness, but now that was an impossibility. She would never love anybody the way she loved Holt.

But that didn't mean she would play second fiddle to Vivian. She had seen Vivian leave earlier looking angry enough to cut out the heart of the first person who crossed her. She wondered what that could signify.

Felicity knew the moment she saw Nate and Broc come out of the house and start toward her like two soldiers in lock step that they had something in mind she wasn't going to like. She briefly considering running away, but in addition to being undignified, it would be useless. She had no doubt these men would pursue her with ungentlemanly persistence.

"Holt wants to see you," Broc said.

"I don't want to see him."

"We have orders to take you to him," Nate said.

"I don't want to be rough on a woman," Broc said, "but Holt's helped all of us at one time or another. We owe him."

"So you're delivering me to him like some kind of sacrifice."

Nate smiled. "He just wants a chance to talk to you. Once he's done, you can do whatever you want."

Okay, she'd let him have his say. All she needed was the courage to walk away one more time.

"Okay," she said, getting to her feet. "Take me to him."

"You're not a prisoner, ma'am," Nate said.

"What do you call it when you make a woman go where she doesn't want to go?"

"Try to consider it friendly persuasion," Broc said.

Pilar was waiting for them when they reached the door to Holt's room. "If you show him that face, you'll set his recovery back a week," she said.

"I'm not happy about this."

"He's a good man. Don't make it any harder

on him. He's still very weak."

That wasn't fair. Pilar knew that was the one thing that could make Felicity abandon her defiant stance. "Are you going in with me?"

"He wants to see you alone."

She would have preferred company, but Holt wouldn't be able to talk forever. She only had to remain strong for a little while. Then she could go back to her room and cry herself to sleep. Pilar opened the door. Felicity took a deep breath and entered Holt's room.

Everything looked the same. She could believe she'd only left for a few minutes, not three days. "Hi," she said. "Glad to see you're finally conscious."

"Why wouldn't you come see me?"

Holt always did believe in getting straight to the crux of the matter. Apparently they didn't believe in small talk in Vermont. "There didn't seem any point in it."

"What do you mean *there didn't seem any point in it?* Hell, I want to marry you. That ought to be something to the point, even in Texas."

Felicity grabbed the back of the chair to steady herself. "I don't know about Vermont or Virginia, but I do know that in Texas they frown on a man being married to two women. Even the Reconstruction government would have trouble explaining that."

"I don't want to marry two women. I'll have enough trouble being married to one. You're not an easy woman to understand."

"You don't have to understand me — just Vivian."

"I understand her perfectly."

"Good. If that's all you wanted to say —"

"I haven't even started on what I wanted to say. Will you sit down? You know I can't sit up without somebody rushing in to push me back down again."

"You shouldn't try to sit up. You're too weak. You nearly died."

"If you don't sit down and let me finish, you're going to finish me off."

She didn't want to sit down. She wanted to run out of the room, but she was certain Pilar, Broc, and Nate would force her to return. "What is it you want to say?"

"I want to talk to you about Vivian."

She got up. "I don't want to hear about your wedding plans."

"If you don't sit down and *stay* in that chair, I swear I'll have Broc and Nate tie you to it."

She figured they'd be just loyal enough to Holt to do it. She sat.

"All my life it seems I've been bound by some duty I couldn't escape," Holt said. "First it was my duty to take care of my father when he was drunk. Then everyone blamed me for his death. My mother said I wasn't welcome in her house anymore. I suppose I still feel that I could have done more. I even became a doctor because I thought by helping other people I could make up for not having been able to help my father. My uncle said he would leave me Price's Nob, but in exchange I was to take care of Vivian. I obligingly fell in love with her, but she married someone else, and my uncle blamed me for that. He said Vivian wouldn't have run away with Abe Calvert if I'd been there."

He looked exhausted. Felicity wanted to tell him not to talk any more, but she knew he wouldn't rest easy until he'd said what he had to say.

"It seems I've spent my whole life being responsible for things I couldn't control, holding fast to a duty that forced me to ignore my own happiness. I got angry with you because I saw you doing the same thing. When I watched your father fight his alcoholism, I realized it is possible for people to change if they want it badly enough. And if they don't, they can't hold anybody else responsible for their own failures. I'm finally free of the guilt of my father's death. He didn't want to change. He didn't care how much suffering he caused. My staying wouldn't have prevented his death."

She wondered if that meant he could now go back to Vermont.

"I still felt I had a duty to Vivian. But after I found her, it soon became clear she wasn't the woman I believed her to be. A few weeks ago I foolishly offered to marry her and take her back to Virginia. Fortunately, she refused me."

"But she asked you again. I heard her."

Holt smiled. "That'll teach you to listen to only part of a conversation. You should have listened to the rest. I told her I was in love with someone else."

Felicity was glad she was sitting down. The strength went out of her body.

"Today I told her that the land would be fertile again someday, but I didn't want Price's Nob. I'll put it in trust for her son."

"What did she say?" She didn't really care about Vivian anymore. She just wanted to know what he was going to do.

Holt laughed, then grimaced at the discomfort it caused. "Most of it was extremely rude, but I don't care. I'm free. Well, not really. I've got myself all tied up again."

"How?"

"Well, you see, I'm in love with a woman who doesn't believe I love her. I admit I didn't do a good job of it in the beginning — actually, I did about as badly as it's possible to do — but I'm willing to do anything I can to make up for it if she'll only give me a chance. I considered having my friends tie her up and bring her to me, but Pilar said that wouldn't make a very good impression."

"Pilar's not always right. Sometimes people have to be forced to do what they really want to do," she said.

"Do you know anybody like that?"

"One person. She thought it was her duty to

take care of her father, to protect him from the world. Then when a man came along who forced her to admit she was wrong, she got angry. When he said he loved her, she couldn't believe him. She didn't realize that although a beautiful woman already filled his mind, his heart was empty."

"Do you think she realizes it now?" he asked.

"She's hoping his heart will soon be filled with somebody new."

"Only if that somebody is you."

She wanted to believe him, but still something held her back. "Are you sure you love me?"

"Why is that so hard to believe?"

"Because I want it so much."

"I never thought I'd be flat on my back unable even to sit up when I proposed marriage to the woman I love, but if you'll come a little closer, I want to tell you that I feel the same way. And if you don't kiss me — God, I can't believe I'm having to beg a woman to kiss me! — I'm going to die anyway."

"You're too weak."

"I'll risk it."

"Your friends will be furious with me."

"They'll never know."

"Of course we will," Broc said from the hallway. "Why do you think I've been killing my knees watching through this keyhole? Kiss him and put me out of my misery."

"See, we're all dependent on you."

Felicity grinned and got up. But rather than kiss Holt, she took a napkin from the table next to the bed and stuffed it into the keyhole.

"Broc's not going to be happy," Holt said.

"Let Broc find his own woman."

"Are you really *my* woman?"

"Just try to get rid of me."

A week later Holt was strong enough to come downstairs. He was delighted to be able to spend the evening in the parlor with Felicity, Mrs. Bennett, and Dr. Moore. "I was getting awfully tired of those same four walls," he said. His friends had left two days earlier. Cade said if they stayed any longer, rustlers would steal all their cows. Holt was sorry to see them go, but it was nice to have Felicity to himself. Broc had started flirting with her just to give Holt something to complain about.

"You're just in time to hear our important announcement," Dr. Moore said.

"What announcement?" Felicity asked.

"He's decided to set himself up as a society doctor and leave me high and dry," Holt teased.

"Not that," Dr. Moore said. Holt had decided he wanted to stay in Galveston and work with Dr. Moore. "We're going to become so successful we can charge outrageous fees and become rich."

"That way we can afford to treat our regular patients for sides of bacon, baskets of eggs, and sacks of pecans."

Felicity was glad Holt had decided to remain in Galveston and work with her father. She couldn't have wished for anything better. Vivian had eloped with one of her suitors and gone to St. Louis. Felicity hoped she'd passed out of their lives forever. Everything was turning out perfectly until her father said he had an announcement to make. He *never* made announcements.

"What is your announcement, Papa?"

"First I have a question. Would you mind having a double wedding?"

Holt's crack of laughter startled her. "What are you talking about?" she asked. "What does Holt think is so funny?"

"Not funny," Holt said. "I'm so pleased, I could bust."

"Pleased about what?" Felicity asked.

"Are you going to tell her or am I?" Holt asked.

"I am," Mrs. Bennett said. "Your father has asked me to marry him, and I've said I would. It was his idea to have a double wedding. I told him a young woman ought to have her own wedding, but I don't mind if you don't."

Felicity was speechless. She knew her mouth was moving, but no words came out.

"You aren't upset, are you?" her father asked.

"She's so happy, she can't think of a word to say," Holt said.

That wasn't true. She could think of hundreds of words to say, none of which she'd utter even after the shock wore off. She'd thought her father was so slavishly devoted to his wife's memory, he could never marry again. If her father could fall in love again, truly anything was possible.

"Of course I'm happy," she finally managed to say. "It's just that I'm surprised. You've been so careful, I had no idea."

"You've been a little preoccupied the last several days," Mrs. Bennett said.

"I plan to see that she's *very* preoccupied for the next several years," Holt said. "And that's just the beginning. By then I ought to know how to do it up good and proper."

It really was just the beginning. Everything in her life had been a prelude to this moment. The fulfillment of her mother's promise that she was born to love. She wished her mother were here now. She'd tell her there was something even better — that *to love and be loved* was the best of all.

UNF*CK
YOURSELF

ABOUT THE AUTHOR

GARY JOHN BISHOP

Born and raised in Glasgow, Scotland, Gary moved to the US in 1997. This opened up his pathway to the world of personal development, specifically to ontology and phenomenology in which he was rigorously trained for a number of years before becoming a senior program director with one of the world's leading personal development companies. After years of facilitating programs to thousands of people all over the world and later studying and being influenced by the philosophies of Martin Heidegger, Hans-Georg Gadamer and Edmund Husserl, Gary is producing his own brand of "urban philosophy." His lifelong commitment to shifting people's ability to exert real change in their lives drives him each and every day. He has a no-frills, no-bullshit approach that has brought him an ever-increasing following, drawn to the simplicity and real-world use of his work. He resides in Florida with his wife and three sons.

CONNECT
@GARYJOHNBISHOP
GARYJOHNBISHOP.COM

UNF*CK
YOURSELF

Get Out of Your Head and Into Your Life

GARY JOHN BISHOP

First published in Great Britain in 2016

This edition published in 2017 by Yellow Kite
An imprint of Hodder & Stoughton
An Hachette UK company

16

A CIP catalogue record for this title is available from the British Library

Trade paperback ISBN 978 1 473 67156 0
eBook ISBN 978 1 473 67158 4

Printed and bound in India by Manipal Technologies Limited, Manipal

Hodder & Stoughton policy is to use papers that are natural, renewable
and recyclable products and made from wood grown in sustainable
forests. The logging and manufacturing processes are expected to
conform to the environmental regulations of the country of origin.

Yellow Kite
Hodder & Stoughton Ltd
Carmelite House
50 Victoria Embankment
London EC4Y 0DZ

www.yellowkitebooks.co.uk
www.hodder.co.uk

This book is dedicated to my three sisters, Paula, Elizabeth, and Sandra, my mother Agnes, and father Patrick. We grew together, we cried together, we stood together, and we fought together. I am who I am because of you.

I acknowledge the downbeat and trodden, the single mothers and unemployed fathers, the dreamers and wannabes; I am you, and you can do it.

Contents

In the beginning...

"This is a conversational slap from the universe to wake you up to your true potential, to unfuck yourself and get spectacularly into your life."

CHAPTER 1

Have you ever felt like a hamster on a wheel, furiously churning your way through life but somehow going nowhere?

All the while you're caught in a loop of constant internal chatter and judgement that never stops, a little voice telling you that you're lazy or stupid or not good enough. You won't even notice the degree to which you believe it or are drained by it, you'll just be spending your day working to overcome the stresses and strains, trying to live your life and at various points facing the resignation that if you can't get your ass off this damned wheel maybe you are never going to get to where you want in life—maybe that happiness you're after or that weight you want to lose or that career or relationship you crave will remain just out of reach.

These pages are dedicated to those that experience that self-defeating monolog—the endless stream of doubt and subterfuge that limits and taints everyday life. This is a conversational slap from the universe to wake you up to your true potential, to unfuck yourself and get spectacularly into your life.

Let's get this thing started in the right place. There are two kinds of talk you engage in every day: talking to others and talking to yourself. You might be one of those that insist, "I don't talk to myself!" But, in fact, most of the conversations you have on any given day are with yourself—all "enjoyed" in the solitude and privacy of your own head.

Whether you're introverted or extroverted, creative or practical, you spend huge swathes of your time talking to…YOU! You do it while exercising, working, eating, reading, writing, walking, texting, crying, arguing, negotiating, planning, praying, meditating, having sex (on your own and with others)—you name it. And yes, you even do it in your sleep.

You're actually doing it right now.

Don't worry, it doesn't mean you're crazy. Or, perhaps it means we're all a little crazy. Either way, we all do it, so settle in and welcome to the freak show.

Studies show that we have over fifty thousand thoughts per day. Think of all the things you say to yourself that you'd rather not or that you try to overcome or defeat. While we have little or no say in those automatic and reactionary thoughts, we have a massive say in which of those same thoughts we attach significance to. They don't come pre-loaded!

The latest in neuroscience and psychology adds weight to the idea that the *kind* of talk you engage in has a profound impact on the quality of your life. Professor Will Hart of the University of Alabama, US, conducted four experiments in which participants either recalled or experienced a positive, negative, or neutral event. They found that people who described the neutral event in ways that suggested it was ongoing actually felt more positive, and when they described a negative event in the same way, they experienced more negativity. In simple terms, the language you use to describe your circumstances determines how you see, experience and participate in them and dramatically affects how you deal with your life and confront problems both big and small.

The connection between what we say and how we feel has been known for hundreds if not thousands of years. Philosophers like Ludwig Wittgenstein, Martin Heidegger and Hans-Georg Gadamer all knew of the importance and significance of language in our lives. Wittgenstein said, "...the harmony between thought and reality can be found in the grammar of the language."

The good news is, studies have continually found that positive self-talk can dramatically improve mood, boost confidence, increase productivity, and more. Much more. In fact, as evidenced by Professor Hart and his studies, it can be one of the key components to a happy, successful life.

The bad news is, the reverse is also true: Negative self-talk can not only put us in a bad mood, it can also leave us feeling helpless. It can make small problems seem bigger and even create problems where none existed before. Here's the breaking news, your self-talk is fucking you over, and in ways you can't even begin to imagine.

With all of this in mind, let's get one thing clear: Even though this is a book about using the right language to improve your life, I'm NOT suggesting you suddenly take on positive thinking or personal affirmations. Those subjects have been done to death with varying degrees of success and are certainly not what we'll be doing here.

I won't ask you to tell yourself you're a tiger as a way to unleash your inner animal. Firstly, you're not a tiger and secondly, well, you're not a tiger. This all may work for some people, but I'm much too Scottish for that. To me, being told to do these sorts of things feels like being force-fed a bucket of maple syrup liberally sprinkled with bits of last year's candy canes. Thanks but eh, no thanks.

For all my "positives" out there, sorry but we're taking this baby in another direction! This book is designed to give you an authentic leg-up—one that feels genuine and right for you and can propel you into greater levels of your true potential.

THE DIFFERENCE BETWEEN SUCCESS AND FAILURE

"If human emotions largely result from thinking, then one may appreciably control one's feelings by

*controlling one's thoughts—or by
changing the internalized sentences,
or self-talk, with which one largely
created the feeling in the first place."*
—Albert Ellis

Albert Ellis is one of the forefathers of modern psychology. He found that how we think and talk about our experiences shifts the way we feel about them. In short, our thoughts are bedfellows with our emotions.

Ellis also found that the way we think can often be completely irrational.

Consider how many times you've told yourself something like, "I'm so stupid," "I always mess things up," "My life is over," or some negative description of an event like, "This is the worst thing that's ever happened to me."

Raise your hand if you've ever completely over-reacted to something that, in hindsight, barely registered on the important-o-meter? OK, put your hand down, people are watching and you're starting to look a bit silly. If you look back you'll see that in the instant before that seemingly random over-reaction, you had a flash of outrageous self-talk, **BANG!**...and off you go with your good self.

Some of the things we say and do aren't always particularly rational but we seem to say and do them anyway! In addition, we never really see what we are leaving ourselves with or the emotional residue of engaging in even the mildest of negative self-talk.

You see, it's not always dramatic self-talk, sometimes it's subtle but equally disempowering. If you're working on something, you might think, **"This is so hard. What if I don't finish in time?"** or worry about all the different ways you can "mess up," which leaves you in an anxious or worried state. Sometimes negative self-talk leads to anger, sadness, or frustration that manifests in different or seemingly unrelated situations.

This kind of self-talk doesn't make your life any easier. The more you tell yourself how hard something is, the harder it will actually seem. Unfortunately, since we are constantly listening to a steady stream of our automatic inner thoughts and have become so accustomed to the critical voice in our heads, we often don't realize how negative thoughts impact our mood and behavior and, as a result, we end up doing—or not doing—things our rational minds want us to do.

For a simple example, take a moment to think about the daily chores you dread the most, all because you've built them up in your mind to be something worse than they really are. We sometimes avoid simple things like folding laundry and unloading the dishwasher, when those tasks actually take very little time and effort. With enough of these little persistent items hanging around it's easy to collapse them in with the bigger, more important things until we find ourselves overwhelmed or exhausted by life.

Why do we "resist" certain things in our lives? We have a personal conversation about those kinds of tasks that is firmly rooted in some negative opinion. Look in your own life for your "stuck-ness" and you'll see what I mean. You have a pretty serious self-talk blockage!

HOW LANGUAGE CHANGES OUR LIVES

The way we talk doesn't only affect us in the moment. It can seep into our subconscious and become internalized, changing our thoughts and behavior in the long term.

In real everyday terms, the way we talk to ourselves and others instantly shapes how we perceive life, and that same perception directly impacts our behavior right there in the moment. Ignore your perceptions at your peril! Even worse, live with the illusion that you don't have perceptions!

If you're sometimes talking about how "unfair" life is, you'll start to act according to that view, perceiving slights where none exist or, as studies have shown, putting less effort into your work because you've already determined it won't accomplish anything. The unfair view will quickly become your reality.

On the other hand, the person who views success as if it were just around the corner will not only work his butt off to achieve it but be energized and alive to it and all the while acting on that fundamental view of success. To be clear, believing you will be successful is only one, albeit important, part of success. By the same token, there is a way to accomplish great things without that belief, although the ride will be a bit rougher!

If you're worried that you don't have that kind of personal belief, READ ON!

Marcus Aurelius, the Stoic philosopher turned Roman Emperor, said, "Here is the rule to remember in the future, when anything tempts you to feel bitter: not 'This is a misfortune,' but 'To bear this worthily is good fortune.'" It's entirely within our power to determine how we think about and talk about our problems. They can be a nuisance or a stepping stone. They can hold us down or lift us up.

In fact, Stoic philosophers like Aurelius believed that outside events hold no power over us at all. We create our own reality with our minds.

"Reject your sense of injury and the injury itself disappears."
–Marcus Aurelius

Take some time here to ponder that statement.

How willing are you to consider that your life is the way it is, not because of the weight of your circumstances or situation, but rather the weight of self-talk that pulls you down? That what you think you can and cannot do is influenced much more directly by some subconscious response than the reality of life itself?

If you keep looking out there, outside of yourself, to your circumstances and feverishly working to get out of them you'll keep getting the same response. No power, no joy, no vitality. At best it's a seesaw of

"It's not that you have to find the answer, you are the answer."

success and disappointment, happiness and despair. Sometimes your circumstances just don't change, sometimes they stagnate and crystallize. What if that thing you're working toward, that thing you are sure will make you happier or more confident, doesn't happen? What then? Even if it does arrive someday, what happens to your life between now and *that* day?

This book will require you to seek the answer, not out there, but *inside* of yourself. It's not that you have to *find* the answer, you *are* the answer. As I've said to my clients many, many times, people spend their lives waiting for the cavalry, all the while never realizing *they* are the cavalry. Your life is waiting on you to finally show up.

RETRAIN YOUR BRAIN—ONE WORD AT A TIME

All this talk about our subconscious isn't just a bunch of psychobabble.

Scientists have discovered that our thoughts can actually change the physical structure of our brains. This phenomenon, neuroplasticity, is revolutionizing the way we think about the human mind.

As we go through life learning and experiencing new things, our brains are constantly arranging and rearranging the neural pathways that control how we think and behave. The best part is, we direct our thoughts in a way that consciously modifies these pathways for ourselves. And the easiest way to shape those thoughts is through conscious, decisive self-talk—the kind of talk that "cuts through" and takes control of your life.

Just like we build habits by repeating an action until it becomes "automatic," we can use strong, assertive language over time to create lasting change in our lives. It's more than just happy thoughts (don't break out the Champagne just yet)—you're affecting your brain's very biology.

We can determine our emotions by steering our thoughts. We can shape those thoughts by being conscious of and diligent about our words and the kind of language we engage in. A lot of this will come down to your basic tolerance of your current mindset and your willingness to change it.

It all starts by making a conscious choice to talk in a way that's helpful rather than harmful. By using the right kind of language and framing our problems in a more readily accessible light, we can quite literally change the way we see and interact with the world. All that stuff you've heard and read about "creating your own reality?" It's not only possible but millions of people the world over are already doing it! And the best part is, they're not only creating it, they are in fact acting on it and living it.

Remember, no matter how difficult, challenging, or pressing life's circumstances can be, how you fundamentally relate to and engage with those circumstances will have the biggest say in how they turn out. Again, the answer is inside you rather than outside you.

How we talk about, think about, and therefore perceive our surroundings is the very foundation for our reality. Create the reality you want to live in by beginning the process of having the kind of conversations, with yourself and others, that actually shape that reality.

A simple way that I reframe my own everyday "problems" is by relating to them as opportunities. They instantly become items in my life that I use to educate and expand myself. I become curious and engaged with them rather than my usual default annoyed and frustrated self!

ASSERTIVE VS NARRATIVE

How the heck does someone create their own reality? By shifting your self-talk from being a streaming narrative (where you talk *about* yourself, others, and life, a dialog of opinion and judgement) to being **assertive**, where you cast all of the default "noise" aside and assert your power right here and now.

One of the first mistakes we make is when we talk about what we are *going* to do or who we *will* be. Don't even get me started on "should," or "try!" Subconsciously we are already determining when that will be happening and it's certainly not in this moment of time.

One of the reasons why we so often abandon New Year's resolutions is because they usually use language to describe what we are "going" to do, i.e. later. All too often they begin with what we're *not* going to do, which leaves us enthusiastic at the beginning but out of juice when faced with the inevitable moment when reality takes a swing at our face. You'll be standing there alone in the giant hole in your life, left open by that behavior you are apparently "stopping." Those are the moments in life where your internal dialog runs riot! What if you've promised yourself to lose weight and are craving pizza or if you promised to save some money but that jacket you just can't live without is suddenly on sale? How does one deal with *those* moments when the enthusiasm wanes and those old thought patterns re-emerge? What are you going to do ***instead***?

Assertive self-talk is when you stake a claim for this moment of time, right here and now. When you start to talk in terms of "I am…" or "I embrace…" or "I accept…" or "I assert…," all of which are powerful and commanding uses of language rather than the narrative of "I will…" or "I'm going to…"

The physiological and psychological impact of using in-the-moment, assertive language is not only powerful, it has a very real in-the-moment effect. There's a massive difference between, "I am relentless" and, "I will be relentless." One of those statements intervenes in this moment of your life, the other lives more like a description of what's to come rather than what's here. All of this will require you to try out assertive speaking in your daily life and catch yourself when you're using the more general, narrative kind of speaking.

USING THIS BOOK

In this book you'll find my handpicked selection of personal assertions to empower, enliven, uplift, and embolden you to take action in your day-to-day life.

You'll also see quotes from famous historical figures, philosophers, and snippets of scientific findings, all of which are there to add weight to my approach but not to prove it. While all of this is well and good, the only real way to read and interact with this book is to explore it for yourself and try on what I am saying. Take the time to think, ponder, and experiment for yourself. There is no greater knowledge than the knowledge you have verified for yourself, in your own experience.

If you take on the following pages as a personal experiment rather than an assessment of the content, you just may end up experiencing the most radical, life-changing exercise you have ever engaged with. Some of this will confront, annoy, jar, and exasperate you. Fine, get over yourself and read on. Like a good movie, it all comes together in the end!

If you're easily offended, stop reading now and re-gift this to someone in your life that you think might benefit from it.

I hope that this book will help you understand the complexity and power of self-talk and how to use it as a force for good in your life. While we are not going to delve into the creative and destructive forces of language, you'll get a sense of the ways in which your life experiences are formed and shaped in your everyday thoughts and internal conversations.

These pages will require you to think—to cognitively connect your language and your feelings in a real and conscious way with your everyday life, to explore the vast landscapes of life that present themselves when you begin to understand the magical connection between how you speak and how you feel.

I recommend reading the book in its entirety with Post-it notes, a highlighter, or any other method you can use to flag the parts that ring your particular bell. That being said, I have designed this book to be as accessible and useful to as many people as possible. Each chapter, though part of the whole, stands on its own, so you should dip in and out of it as much as you like. Use this book up, trawl through the words for what you need to make the difference in your life until its pages are tired and weary from your appetite for change.

In the day-to-day living of your life, you probably won't need to keep poking your nose in here forever (although you might, and that's OK), so the real intention here is for you to use these ideas as a starting point whenever you are stuck or in need of rejuvenation.

At *those* times, dive right in, drink from these pages, and unleash the kind of you that the world has yet to see!

Enjoy.

02

"I am willing."

"Stop blaming luck. Stop blaming other people. Stop pointing to outside influences or circumstances."

CHAPTER 2

You have the life you're willing to put up with.

Think about it. What are the problems, those heinous, dark shadows currently spoiling the warmth and happiness of your otherwise blissful life?

Do you hate your job? Are you in a bad relationship? Is there something wrong with your health? Fine, get a new job. End the relationship. Change your diet and exercise or locate the kind of help you need. Seems simple, doesn't it? Even the things you seemingly had no say in, like the death of a loved one or losing your business, you have a MASSIVE say in the way you live your life in the aftermath of those events.

If you're not willing to take the actions to change your situation—in other words, if you're **willing to put up with** your situation—then, whether you like it or not, that is the life you have chosen.

Before you think "but..." or start to get your knickers in a twist...let me say one more thing: By defending your circumstances as they are right now, you are actually **making a case** for being where you are. Give it up.

No buts. You can't afford them. They're excess baggage on a trip that requires you to travel light.

> *"Circumstances don't make the man; they only reveal him to himself."*
> *—Epictetus*

As Epictetus suggests, the true measure of who you are won't be found in your circumstances but rather the way in which you respond to them. To start this new process, you must first stop another one.

> *Stop blaming luck.*
> *Stop blaming other people.*
> *Stop pointing to outside influences or circumstances.*
> *Stop blaming your childhood or neighborhood.*

This approach is fundamental to everything that I talk about in these pages. You cannot, I repeat CANNOT dwell in any blame game in your life. Even blaming yourself is completely useless. Of course you'll face situations that you seemingly can't control. You may even face tragic circumstances, like disability, disease, or the death of a loved one.

But there is *always* something you can do to impact those circumstances, even if you've had them for years and still can't see a way. But first, you must be willing. To fully embrace my approach, you must first accept that while there are things that have happened in your life that you had no say in, you are 100% responsible for what you do with your life in the aftermath of those events. Always, every time, no excuses.

The dictionary describes willingness as "The quality or state of being prepared; readiness."

In other words, willingness is a state in which we can engage with life and see a situation from a new perspective. It starts with you and ends with you. No one can make you willing, and you cannot move forward until you are willing to make the next move.

When you are finally willing, you can literally experience that willingness, that innate freedom that courses through your veins, and similarly when you are not, the kind of primordial stuck-ness that halts and presses down on you like some invisible weight on your chest.

Believe me, I hear you, "I am willing but..." Every time you add the "but" to the end of that statement, you turn yourself into the victim. In my many years as a coach and mentor, I have heard as many complex life situations as there are, from the darkest of pasts to the weight and gravity of the present, or crippling fear of the future, I have heard them over and over and over again.

You have to hear what I am saying in the way that it's intended. I'm not saying these things to inflame you. Well, maybe I am but the intention is to inflame you to your own potential, to realize your own greatness, not just to piss you off!

Imagine for a moment that willingness is missing in your life. Not some wispy, sheepish willingness but rather a bold willingness, the kind of willing state where you are ready for what's next and ready to act on it. Willingness to change, willingness to let go, willingness to accept. Real, magical, inspired willingness.

FINDING THE DOOR.

*"Fate leads the willing and drags
along the reluctant."*
—Seneca

Either you control your destiny, or your destiny will
control you. Life won't stop for your pauses and
procrastinations. It won't stop for your confusion or
fear. It will continue right along without you. Whether
you play an active part or not, the show will go on.

That's why one of the first personal assertions I teach
to my clients is: **"I am willing."**

Before you can say that to yourself honestly, you must
first ask yourself the question, "Am I willing?" That
question demands an answer. It can't just be left there
in the nothingness of the universe. Am I willing? It pulls
for a response. Am I willing? Its power is irresistible; I
cannot escape its press for truth.

> *Am I willing to go to the gym?*
> *Am I willing to work on that project I've been
> putting off?*
> *Am I willing to face my social fears?*
> *Am I willing to ask for a raise or quit this
> shitty job?*

"Life won't stop for your pauses and procrastinations. It won't stop for your confusion or fear. It will continue right along without you."

In short, are you willing to stop living the life you have and start living the life you're after? It ALL begins with the emergence of willingness, that liquid, constantly expanding and contracting state where life springs and cedes—and all of it is within you at the flick of a linguistic switch.

We often view ourselves as procrastinators or lazy or unmotivated. When in reality, we're simply unwilling. We put things off or avoid them completely because we tell ourselves we just don't want to do it or that we *can't* do it.

Instead of viewing this behavior as a character flaw, let's create a sense of willingness where there is apparently none. A spark of potential, if you like. You are a master generator of this state of openness and potential. Once upon a time in your life, this state was easy to access, enlivened by the vigor of youth or the curiosity of childhood. Somehow, over the years, you lost touch with this magical state.

The famous philosopher and political scientist Niccolò Machiavelli once said,

> *"Where the willingness is great, the difficulties cannot be great."*
> —*Niccolò Machiavelli*

Consider that for a second. It does not matter what you're facing in life, which obstacle you're trying to overcome—if you are willing to generate that *state* of willingness, that's your doorway to making the effort, taking the steps, dealing with the setbacks, and ultimately creating the progress and change in your life that you're seeking.

That's why such a simple statement—"I *am* willing"—is so profound. You become enlivened and empowered by its promise, open to its allure.

I ask again: Are you willing?

WHEN THE DOOR IS CLOSED

Maybe you are in fact, **unwilling**. In many cases, that may actually be the best answer you can give.

Sometimes declaring your unwillingness can be just as powerful as declaring willingness.

Are you willing to live with a body that's unhealthy? No. Are you willing to continue living paycheck to paycheck? No. Are you willing to put up with unworkable, unsustainable relationships? No.

I AM UNWILLING!

Unwillingness ignites resolve and determination. It provides an access to taking a robust and urgent approach to your situation. When you are unwilling it often represents a line in the sand, beyond which point you are no longer willing to go.

Only when you're *unwilling* to continue just simply existing, feeling unsatisfied and unfulfilled, will you make the effort necessary to make a change. Only when you're *unwilling* to put up with the bullshit any longer will you grab your shovel and start digging.

At times there is no greater motivation to change than the unwillingness to do "this" any longer. Which one works for you in your life currently? I am willing or I am unwilling? Can you see how being unwilling can potentially be just as powerful as being willing?

Depending on the circumstance, some of us feel more empowered by the assertion, "I am willing," while for others declaring, "I am unwilling" gives them strength and resolve. You might find yourself motivated by both equally depending on the situation.

Whichever category you fall into, you can not only shift the personal assertion, you can reframe the way you approach your problems.

For example, are you willing to find a new job? Yes. "I am willing." Are you willing to stay in a job you hate? No. "I am unwilling." Both assertions can be just as effective. It's up to you to determine which one fits your persona and situation. Which one "does it" for you?

THE POWER OF PURPOSE

There's another way for your unwillingness to free you from the hamster wheel because sometimes it doesn't matter what you ask yourself or how many times you've said it, you just can't muster the willingness long enough to change anything. You might well be one of life's great starters-but-not-finishers. At the end of it all, you might have to face the cold reality that you have been all too willing to remain the same. You have been unwilling to fundamentally change your life and lose that weight for good, that somewhere in there you are OK with living this way. I mean, come on, you must be or you would have changed it by now! At some level you must have some tolerance to having your life turn out like this.

That's actually OK. Getting straight with yourself about having made the decision to stay where you are can be just as powerful as the decision to move. Why? Because sometimes recognizing that you willingly put yourself in a place where you are unhappy is often all the impetus required to make an opening for real and lasting change. This has to be done without blaming yourself and turning yourself into a victim of some internal blip or character "flaw." In the moment you realize you have cognitively and systematically put yourself here, guess what? That's right, you can cognitively and systematically get yourself out! This is also the foundation of granting yourself the grace of acceptance, of embracing what has been, and daring yourself to reach for an unimaginable future.

> *"He is a wise man who does not grieve for the things which he has not, but rejoices for those which he has."*
> *–Epictetus*

By stating and facing your unwillingness to change, you can take stock of yourself and your life and begin to create a sliver of light for you to at least start. The secret is, once you've separated the task (or whatever it is you are dealing with) from the drama of the past, you may find yourself more open to tackling it. You'll be able to get past the emotional swirl and straight to the heart of the issue itself.

REACHING FOR THE STARS WITH SHORT ARMS

Some goals simply aren't connected to our reality. Don't get me wrong, I am all for reaching for the stars and striving for things that seem impossible. For instance, we'd probably all like to be filthy rich. But are you *willing* to do what it takes to make that much money? Are you willing to work 60, 70, or 80 hours of your week or skip vacations to do the work that needs to get done? Are you willing to take on more responsibility and, importantly, risk it all? Have you, in reality, confronted and dealt with what becoming filthy rich might really demand of you? The seemingly endless drain on your life and mind space? Our society has produced such a headlong rush to be the wealthiest, the smartest, the prettiest, the best dressed, the funniest, or the strongest, and somewhere in there we have lost the ability to just be ourselves, free to breathe life and choose our own path rather than carry the burden of social or familial expectation. What does all that produce? Well, a lot of disappointed and unfulfilled human beings, that's for sure.

That doesn't mean you should stop pursuing amazing life goals if that's what you really want. It also doesn't mean you should let yourself stagnate and stop improving either. There's nothing inherently wrong in working long hours and sacrificing your quality of life, and some people might be perfectly content doing so in order to make the income or get the career they want. But so many of us have actually forgotten why we are pursuing what we are pursuing in the first place.

All too often, we focus solely on what we don't have, even though deep down we don't really need it or perhaps even want it. When I lay these things out, you might be nodding your head. "He's right, I don't need to be a millionaire" or "I don't even really want six-pack abs."

Which of course is all fine until the next time you see that nice car and think, "Why don't I have that?" or when you look at the cover of a magazine and wonder, "Why don't I look like that?" or "Why aren't my clothes that nice?" Making sure we're striving for what we *really* want requires a constant check-in with ourselves. It's not a one-and-done deal.

If you really want those things, then go get them! Begin today, lay out your strategy, deal with your reality and, most importantly, take the actions required and take them often!

But if you're not willing to work an extra 10 or 20 hours a week just to drive to work in a BMW instead of a Honda, give up the complete waste of precious headspace to yearn for it. Stop pretending to yourself. Deal with your unwillingness to take on the kind of actions accomplishing those things would require and accept that you have been bullshitting yourself. You'll have a lot more capacity for loving the life you actually do have and will create some room to begin striving for the things you actually want in life.

"I am unwilling" to give up all of my favorite foods just to have the body I did when I was 20. "I am unwilling" to trade time with my family for an extra zero on my paycheck.

Face your reality. Once you adopt the mindset of "I am unwilling," you will no longer be filled with guilt, resentment, or regret every time you see something you think you "want." You'll be in a place where you are connected to and in tune with your real life and, if you really want to pursue those things in the future, you'll be able to locate yourself from that reality and plot your road to accomplish them.

CHART YOUR PATH

One of the beautiful things about really taking a hard look at your life and goals is that doing so forces you to re-evaluate the path that leads to them.

Is exercising 30 minutes a day *really* as impossible as your mind has built it up to be? Sure, you're going to get a little sweaty and tired but you can throw on your favorite music to help the time go by faster. And, even though it might start out painfully, you'll eventually get used to that and grow stronger.

What's the worst thing that can happen if you offer your idea in that meeting? It gets shot down? So what? Even if you're faced with bigger tasks—MUCH bigger tasks like years of back taxes, a hoarder's paradise of a garage, telling the truth to someone you've been lying to—the path to change starts with that same glimmer of willingness.

Bear in mind we all tend to build things up in our minds to be a lot bigger than they really are. Telling the truth becomes a trek to the Sahara Desert and back. If that's the case for you, try breaking the task down into smaller declarations of willingness to "stand up," "get out of bed," "open my email," etc.

Of course you might well be dealing with something much bigger than these examples but even when you ramp it up, the same model works exceptionally well. Let's say you have been holding onto a dark secret. Maybe you're ashamed or guilty or resentful. Perhaps this is something that could change your life in a significant way. "Am I willing to tell the truth to that person I've been lying to?" When you frame it this way, coming clean becomes an occasion to talk, listen, and then deal with the consequences. You might be dreading it but you can do it. It's not the task that's important, it's the life that's available *after* that's at stake here. When you are free to be open and available, with nothing held back, no lies, no withholds or half-truths, you really are your most expressive, most alive self.

Most of the time, the task we're actually facing is a lot simpler than we think it is. The problem is, we usually don't take the time to really look at it. Some of the things we face certainly can be challenging, but at the same time what's on the other side of those challenges is a life of our dreams. A life where we are willing and open and inspired to take it on.

Make that assertion, "I am willing."

PLANT YOUR FLAG

When you start to view the world through the lens of what you're willing and unwilling to pursue, rather than what it seems you want and don't want, things start to become a lot clearer.

Instead of wasting time worrying about the things other people have, you'll start focusing on what's really important to you and your life. You'll realize that once you replace envy, lust, and desire with a willingness to change your life for the better, things really start to take shape.

When we understand what we are genuinely willing to do, we take back control over the subconscious thoughts and feelings that previously directed our behavior away from where we truly wanted to go. You have the ability to determine what your truth is, not from some subconscious glitch that keeps popping up from the past but instead from your cognitive and conscious self, from the power of intervening on behalf of yourself. Willingness is a truth, a true beauty that only you can generate. No longer will thoughts like "I am a failure because I'm not a millionaire" or "I am lazy because I'm not a size 6," have the power to make you feel like crap because you will have owned your choices.

Once you frame the obstacles in your life as a matter of "willing" and "unwilling"—instead of weighing yourself down with negative opinions of yourself and your circumstances—you can break through the self-imposed barriers that are truly holding you back. You can see through the distractions of self-talk and drama.

You'll realize that when you're willing to do what it takes, nothing else matters. You won't put off the things you're truly willing to do. You won't neglect the responsibilities you took on because you will feel the strong sense of willingness to do them.

Willingness. It's the lifeblood of the new, the infinite well of possibility and potential, a state where new futures arise and a whole new you can begin.

Ask yourself, "Am I willing?" over and over until you can hear it, first thing in the morning, last thing at night, while you're driving, while in the shower, "Am I willing?" Ask, ask, ask until a resounding YES echoes through your consciousness. I AM WILLING!

I ask you again: Are you willing?

"I am wired to win."

"The truth
of it is,
you are
winning at
the life you
have."

What if I told you that even when you think you're losing in life, you're actually winning? That **everything** that happens is really a victory?

It's true. And that's not just some feel-good self-help mumbo jumbo or a sales line that I'm feeding you.

You are a champion. You've knocked out goal after goal, cruising to an undefeated record. Everything you set your mind to comes true.

You're probably starting to think I've lost my mind or maybe even that you've lost yours! Perhaps you're convinced I'm talking to someone else—anyone *but* you. Let me explain before we both end up like a couple of basket cases.

Imagine this scenario: For what seems like all of your life you've been searching for love, that one special person to share your life with. But up to this point, it hasn't happened. (Remember, this is an example, you can use any area of your own life where you have experienced being stuck in a cycle.) You've met people, had relationships, but all of them ended somewhere short of "forever." You and "the one" just never materialized. The fairy tale inevitably came to an end, often a very familiar kind of end.

After a while, you start losing hope. You start to wonder whether you will ever meet the person of your dreams. Maybe you and relationships just aren't *meant* to be?

> *"Will anyone ever love me?"*
> *"Am I worthy of being loved?"*
> *"Why do I always seem to attract the same types of people?"*

You look back at your childhood, to times when you didn't feel loved enough. Or periods of adolescence where you felt like an outsider. Or past relationships that played out like a scene from the movie *Groundhog Day* except with different players each time. So frustrating!

Then one day, you meet someone. You go on a few dates and find out you really enjoy each other's company. Things are coming along nicely as the days stretch into weeks and the weeks into months.

Eventually that day comes where you can't help yourselves and you exchange your first "I love yous."

Not only are you in love, but you start to wonder, "Could *they* be 'the one?' Could this be it?" Wheeeeee! The bliss, excitement, and possibility are invigorating and enlivening.

At some point, however, the dark clouds of doubt start rolling in, it starts in small ways that grow first slowly and then all at once until the storm finally breaks loose. No sooner are you "in love" than you start to fall out, waaaaaaay out. The smallest things turn to arguments. The chemistry slowly evaporates until your relationship is a desert, barren and dry, and you are left with the soul-destroying basics of just trying to get along. Ugh. Not again.

At some point you both can see it's not working—
perhaps you reach a breaking point and have one (or
a number) of those nasty fallings out. Maybe it just
slowly dies until you eventually decide to pull the plug.
Either way, you eventually go your separate ways. Oh
well. You're hurt, crushed, but somehow resolute that
in the end things will turn out for you. Someday.

Except they *did*. Even though it may look and feel like
a loss, this was in fact a glorious, resounding win. A
victory from the Gods. HURRAH!

The truth of it is, you are winning at the life you *have*.

What if I don't want this life? Fine; but this is the one
you're currently winning at.

BUILDING THE MYSTERY

How could I possibly call a failed relationship a win?

Well, I'm not about to tell you how you're better off
without certain people in your life. I'm not going to
assure you that you're a special little snowflake who
will find the perfect person "when you're ready."
I'm not going to buy into the self-righteous bumper
stickers and internet memes that tell you how great

you are and that everyone else is the problem. You and I both know that when it comes down to it, that's just not accurate.

Nope. You won at that failed relationship because you achieved exactly what you set out to accomplish in the first place. From the very first "hello." "But, but, but my partner wasn't stepping up, THEY ruined it!" I got that, but what if you subconsciously picked that person in the first place? The kind of ideal character to recreate the same vignettes of life over and over and over?

What if you are actually driven to prove the notion that no one will ever love you? What if it was planted there as a subconscious reaction to a turbulent childhood, bad breakups, or the like? And what if, with this pattern buried deep in your subconscious, you actively and deliberately undermined the success of your own relationship?

You became sensitive to problems where there were apparently none. You started picking at, getting annoyed by, and blowing up at the tiniest of things. Over time you proved your point and the relationship reached its obvious, final, and natural conclusion. What if *this* is what you have become wired to win at?

You were convinced you weren't worthy of a loving relationship, so you systematically set out to prove it and you succeeded. Congratulations!

If you think this is starting to make you sound like a hopeless sado-masochist, don't worry. There is a silver lining in all of this.

You may not relate to the example I described above. Maybe you're happily married to the love of your life. Or perhaps you're beating off eligible suitors with a giant stick. Look at your own "dark spots," the parts of your life where you are most ineffective, where it seems like you *have* lost or are currently losing.

You see, our thoughts are so powerful that they are constantly pushing you toward your goals, even when you don't realize what those goals actually are! Your brain is wired to win.

It doesn't just apply to your relationships. This dynamic is at play in your career, your fitness, your finances, and everything else you do. You are hardwired to win.

That brings us to our next assertion: ***"I am wired to win."***

You're always winning because your brain is wired to win. The trouble comes when what you really want—on a

"For the most part, you're basically on autopilot, mindlessly gouging your way through life's predictable muddy field."

subconscious level—and what you say you want are different, sometimes radically so.

RULER OF YOUR DOMAIN

In his research, Dr. Bruce Lipton, the famous stem cell and DNA scientist, found that 95% of what we do in our day-to-day life is controlled by our subconscious. Think about that for a moment. That means that out of all the things you say or do, only a tiny fraction of them are said or done with a true sense of volition.

Think of all those times you lost track of time, drove home and couldn't remember a single thing about the journey, or forgot what day it was. For the most part, you're basically on autopilot, mindlessly gouging your way through life's predictable muddy field.

The path you follow through life is the one dictated by your deepest, most inconspicuous thoughts. Your brain is constantly pushing you along that path, whether it's the one you would consciously choose to take or not.

Can't seem to increase your income? Can't seem to lose weight? Have you considered the subconscious, concealed beliefs about your income and your weight that may be driving your action (or lack of it)? You automatically relate to yourself as belonging to a certain economic class, with a certain level of fitness, and your actions serve to keep you in place, right where you're most familiar to yourself.

I like to say that we win in domains or worlds. Let's say you make £30,000 per year. That's a domain. All of the planning, strategy, and thinking you do to make that money constitute that domain.

Believe it or not, it's not necessarily any harder to make £60k than it is £30k. You may think it is, but that's not an absolute. Whether you work for £25/hour or £50/hour, 40 hours of work is still 40 hours of actual work. While it's important to identify what you're working on and whether you are being productive instead of just busy, sometimes it really is a question of getting yourself into another domain. How does one do that? Firstly, you have to uncover and realize the ways in which you have limited yourself. The kind of "absolutes" that you are currently unaware of. In short, the conclusions that you have come to about yourself, others, and life itself. Those conclusions are the limit of your potential. It's only when you have broken through those conclusions and can experience a life outside of your current existence that you start to understand the power of this phenomenon.

While I appreciate that seems like an overly simplistic view of life, it's a view that can open you up to whole other worlds of accomplishment, although that's a conversation for another time. In this instance, take the case that your life is split up into particular domains that you are existing in and winning at.

The point is, you're winning in whichever domain you are playing in. You're wired to win in that domain. What it takes to move out of that domain is going to require some significant changes to your automatic thoughts.

FIND YOUR WINNING EDGE

Still not convinced? It's time to turn the mirror on yourself and find out exactly where your wins are coming from.

Look at your problem areas. Where in your life are you struggling most? Is it your career? Is it a negative habit? Is it your diet?

Maybe you're constantly putting off work until the last minute. You'll wait and wait until you absolutely can't wait any longer, then bust out the project once the pressure of a strict deadline is looming over you.

We are always winning at proving something. In the case above, you win at proving either you have no time or that you are a procrastinator or a loser by getting things done at the very last minute. Or maybe it's something else. The key here is to question yourself, look at your actions. What is the real point of all of this? What is it that you get to be right about when all is said and done?

Just like I demonstrated in the opening example about romantic relationships, we hold a certain belief about ourselves or life in general that we prove right time and time again through our everyday actions. Those beliefs uncannily turn out to be deadly accurate in our reality. Spinning your wheels? What are you out to prove there?

"I'm not worthy of love," "I'm not smart," "I'm a failure," "I'm not as capable as I used to be." With these kinds of repeats stuck in your subconscious, is it any wonder that you are masterful in consistently proving them right? To succeed in another, more positive way, you'd have to prove those firmly held beliefs WRONG! For your persona, that's a ground-shaking idea that is almost too much to bear. It would in fact unsettle the very foundations of who you have become!

Many of my clients, I have found, have one particular thing in common: the subconscious desire to prove that their parents did a bad job raising them. This can manifest in so many different ways, some being worse than others. Some are subtle, others obvious, while all are very potent.

You might try to prove that your parents failed to raise you well by treating your body like crap, getting arrested, becoming addicted to drugs or alcohol, dropping out of school, consistently failing in relationships, chronic financial crises, or any one of a number of seemingly random paths we get ourselves lost in. They can drop all the way down to simply being disconnected or lost in the pressures of work as an adult.

All of these are real-life examples that some of my clients discovered about themselves that ultimately "proved" that one or both of their parents failed to do their job, that their experiences as children did not adequately prepare them for adulthood. This belief, conveniently, also allows for a ready-made explanation as to why they did what they did and why they, from time to time, acted like complete assholes to others in *their* life.

Can you see ways in which you do this in your own life? Think of the problem areas in your life. Now think about them in terms of what you are winning at. What do you see there?

If you're struggling to get work done, perhaps you believe that you're incapable or lazy. You prove that idea every single time you pause or procrastinate. You're proving to yourself and others that you really are that person. Why do we do such things? We are survival machines and what better way to survive what's to come than by reliving what has been, after all, it got you this far regardless of how bad or negative it has been. You have survived.

Don't limit yourself to the examples I'm giving. They're just that: examples. You could be winning at something completely different. Take some time for introspection. If need be, write down the patterns you are seeing. Put the pieces of the jigsaw together.

Maybe you had great parents but still find yourself incapable of committing to one person. Could it be because you believe your significant other couldn't possibly live up to the example you were raised with?

The point is we all have these items.

Search out and connect all the different situations that came into play in your life. Take note of all the times you broke your promise to diet, save your money, or speak your mind. Consider how many days you skipped the gym. Think about how you went shopping instead of to the bank. Pick one and see if you can discover the "win." The amount of times you argued or lost your temper when you know you shouldn't have. What is it all pointing to?

Whatever the domain you're winning in, you'll start to realize something: you're really good at it.

You can avoid those dirty dishes in the sink for days. You'll use every plate, cup, and piece of cutlery in the house and then you start getting creative until you're eating cereal out of a handy Tupperware container using a wooden baking spoon. Holy crap, a life hack, take a picture and get it on your Pinterest page!

It's actually rather impressive in a weird kind of way.

Once you've taken the time to analyze your own life through this lens, you'll start to see that what I'm saying is true. You really are wired to win. You really can (and do) achieve the things you set your mind to.

"It is the power of the mind to be unconquerable."

—*Seneca*

Right now, your mind is unconquerable when it comes to proving that you're not worthy of love, that you're lazy, or that you'll always be out of shape or never have any money.

But if we change our thinking a little, we can use our mind's unconquerable nature to act on all the positive goals and dreams we hold for ourselves. *We are wired to win*—we just have to point ourselves in the right direction so we can win at something we consciously choose.

CREATING A GAME PLAN

"The happiness of your life depends upon the quality of your thoughts. Therefore, guard accordingly, and take care that you entertain no notions unsuitable to virtue and reasonable nature."

—*Marcus Aurelius*

We've talked about the enormous role our subconscious plays in everything we do. Even if we consciously made the right decisions at every opportunity, it would still only account for a fraction of our daily life.

The personal assertion, "I am wired to win," will support you in realizing how truly powerful you and your mind are. But you still need a game plan.

That means we have to start filling our "bucket" with the right ideas. Here's a good way to start.

Think about the thing or things you'd like to change in your life. They could be related to the problem areas you looked at earlier, or they could be something completely different.

Where would you really like to see progress? What do you really want to accomplish?

Take that goal and break it down. What exact steps do you need to take to achieve it? What are the milestones you need to set out to identify your progress?

If you want to lose weight, think about how you'll need to change your diet, get more exercise, and generally adopt more healthful, nurturing habits. Go through the daily kind of actions you'll need to practice. Get it in reality.

Don't stop there. Consider the changes in mindset you'll need to make during and after your quest to become more fit. You have to be relentless in the pursuit of your goal, particularly when those automatic past-based conversations start to become louder in your head.

Once you've faced your problems head on, how will your sense of self change? When you're the fit and healthy person you want to be, how will your beliefs about yourself be different? What will *that* life look like? I would warn against the idea that you'll suddenly be awesome. Your future is not the answer to your present.

As we've discussed, subconscious thoughts are deeply ingrained in your psyche, so it can take a lot of thinking, imagination, and commitment to transform these invisible yet powerful thoughts into ones that better align with your stated goals. As with every page here, make the time to take your time.

If you look at the problem areas you came up with before, you might be able to connect to an emotionally charged event somewhere in your life that helped set them in your mind, perhaps in the form of infidelity in a relationship, childhood bullying, parents that never quite lived up to your wants and needs, public embarrassment, or major career failures.

But the more you think about your future and what you really want to accomplish, the deeper those thought processes will work their way into your mind and take hold. Remember, when you explore and discover what it is you've really been winning at, it's not about fighting against or resisting those thoughts and actions but rather changing direction and setting yourself new goals and outcomes. This must be the kind of work that raises your awareness and throws up red flags for when you are getting off course. The better you understand your patterns, the better shot you have in altering them.

When you have set out the goals that you are claiming as yours in life and, more importantly, relentlessly taking the actions to produce results, it's only a matter of when.

We are wired to win. You are wired to win. Define your game, embrace the challenge, and strive to understand yourself in deeper and more meaningful ways.

True understanding of yourself and your personal constraints allows for ever-unfolding degrees of freedom and success. The more aware you become of your hardwiring, the more space and opportunity become available in those areas.

Step out there. Trust yourself; give yourself fully to your vast capacity for victory. Set yourself the challenge of winning in new and exciting ways. Demand greatness of yourself and repeat after me: "I am wired to win."

"I got this."

"I got this."

"Everyone
has their
problems,
and life
isn't always
perfect. It
never will be."

CHAPTER 4

Ugh.

There comes a time in all of our lives when we're feeling a little down, a little defeated. When it seems like nothing is going our way. It's not like we've completely given up (although sometimes we have), but at the same time, the struggle is very real.

You could be facing a massive problem: You got laid off. Your spouse filed for divorce. You wrecked your car. Or maybe all three at the same time. So much for that lucky charm, huh?

Or it could be something less serious: You lost your favorite shirt. Your dog used your mail for a toy. You didn't get much sleep last night. You burned dinner.

The thing is, the negative experiences we have rarely stay contained to that one issue. They **spread**. Like a toxic chemical, those experiences seep into all aspects of our lives.

For example, if you're having financial trouble, you'll either consciously or subconsciously stress about it at dinner, which means you don't enjoy your meal. You start feeling on edge around family. You feel resentful toward your spouse and distant from your children. You're annoyed when your dog barks or when your neighbors make too much noise. Little things like traffic and long queues begin prompting your frustration.

It's like your *whole* life is tainted, as your smaller problems leak into the bigger picture. Like a coffee spill on your desk, small problems quickly spread and create bigger ones. As the spilled liquid relentlessly heads for your laptop, phone, and stack of bills, you hopelessly pad at the random chaos with your napkin in some forlorn attempt at denying the disaster, creating an even bigger mess.

That little mess can influence all areas of your life until your emotions surrounding that one area become the lens through which you see everything.

You end up thinking...

"Life is too hard."
"I'll never make it through this."
"Everyone's a jerk."
"I'm done with this shit."

None of these sentiments reflect reality (no matter what you might currently think), but rather your perception of your reality. Unfortunately, knowing this makes no difference whatsoever when you're stuck right bang in the middle of it all. And, of course, all of this only makes things somehow even worse. A negative experience of yourself and/or your life doesn't help you overcome what you're dealing with, let alone enjoy your life.

To deal with this, we need to shift how we view our problems and the world and adopt a new, powerfully optimistic, and grounded approach.

That's why my next personal assertion is, *"I got this."*

PUTTING PROBLEMS IN PERSPECTIVE

"If all our misfortunes were laid in one common heap whence everyone must take an equal portion, most people would be content to take their own and depart."
—Socrates

Everyone has their problems, and life isn't always perfect. It never will be. It wasn't 2,400 years ago, when Socrates was around, and it certainly isn't today.

But if we're being brutally honest with ourselves, we'll realize that our own problems are pretty insignificant compared to the rest of the world's. Really. Think about it.

If you're reading this, chances are your life isn't as hard as a child in Somalia or an Untouchable in India. Chances are your problems are pretty small in comparison to the ones people had when Socrates was born in 470 BC, before modern medicine or electricity or cars or laws to protect public safety existed.

You don't have to travel across the globe or back in time for a comparison either. Travel to the other side of your town or look around your office or neighbourhood,

"Get connected to your reality, your real life instead of your emotionally soaked self-talk narrative about your life."

and you're almost guaranteed to find plenty of people with worse problems than yours. You might not see it but it's the same for all of us. We only see the highlight reels of others' lives while being continually reminded of our own behind the scenes.

If you're rolling your eyes and wondering, "How does any of that help me solve my problems?" I'll tell you: it doesn't. None of this will change the tire on your car for you or deposit another thousand pounds into your bank account.

Now, just for a moment of your significant existence, stop picking fluff out of your belly button and look around you. Get connected to your reality, your real life instead of your emotionally soaked self-talk narrative about your life.

What this will do is help you put things in some kind of reality-based perspective. This will serve to help you face life and all of its problems with a powerful attitude, to starve the creeping specter of negativity that can and does catch us in its grip. If *everyone* around you is dealing with their issues—even those that are worse than yours—then you certainly can.

But I get it. Even as I say all of this, we both know that when disaster strikes, it's challenging to stay levelheaded. Our problems are still real, they still hurt, and they can still result in our emotions getting the better of us.

When you start having those crappy feelings, take a step back. Way back. No, back further than that, MUCH further than that. Keep going…see if you can picture your life for what it really is.

You have to start here with your imagination.

Firstly, I advise my clients to start by looking at their entire life. Imagine it in front of you like a railroad track, running to the left and right as far as the eye can see.

Of course, the tracks aren't just sitting in the middle of a void. They cut through countryside and cities, under tunnels and over bridges, across stretches of ocean, around towering mountains and plunging canyons. Picture the magnitude and magical variety of the surroundings.

Now look waaaay down those tracks to the left. This is your past. This is where you came from, the ground you've already covered in your journey through life.

Follow the tracks down and far into the distance. As you walk, you'll see your entire life—everything that's ever happened to you—expanding in front of you.

Take the time to think about the most memorable experiences from your life.

Perhaps you recall walking down the aisle with the love of your life. Maybe it's the birth of your first child and the feeling of holding them in your arms. Would you trade that for anything?

Go back to that family vacation you took in the Caribbean, spending a few days in paradise.

How about when you bought your first house? Or when you landed that job you wanted? Whatever your past, savor the memory of each and every wonderful experience.

Depending on where you are today, you've got dozens or hundreds of great experiences to look back on: graduations, promotions, awards, parties, and relationships. Remember the little things like childhood memories that cradle and comfort you, or those memorable tastes, sights, and sounds that embrace you in their familiarity and inspire feelings of warmth and joy. Open up and allow yourself the good grace of those times.

But don't just limit it to the sugary goodness either. Think about the bad, too.

Recall all the times where you struggled, suffered setbacks, or got knocked down. The arguments, the breakups, the speeding tickets, or the late bills.

Do you remember that time when your parents caught you sneaking out and grounded you? If you experienced a tough childhood, let all of that in here. How about the time you forgot to pay your electricity bill and you had to spend the night reading by candlelight?

Or when you had surgery and had to spend days lying in a hospital bed? Or when you broke up with someone and felt depressed for weeks? Let all of it in, from the most tragic and traumatic to the merely irritating, annoying, or regretful.

Remember all the problems you faced—and eventually overcame. A lot of them may be very similar to what you're dealing with today.

You probably felt a lot of the same emotions back then, too. You thought you'd never get over your ex, that you'd never find a better job, or that you wouldn't live through the humiliation of some situation. But you did. You raised up and kicked on and, looking back, some of those problems might even seem a little silly now.

Can you believe how upset you were when you got a
D on your maths test in school? Or how bad you felt
when you never got a second date with that girl or guy
you liked?

Even the more serious problems probably seem a lot
different today. After all, you did make it through them,
and they helped shape and form who you are today.

LOOKING TO THE FUTURE

Now that you've traveled to the end of the track in
one direction, it's time to turn around and head the
other way.

To the right—if you haven't figured it out—is your
future. Here's where you'll find the things to come, all
of the experiences and events awaiting you in life.

New relationships with people you've yet to meet.
Places to visit that you've never been. Doing the things
you've always wanted to try.

You'll get to experience the spine-tingling rush that
comes when you first kiss someone you're really
attracted to. Or the connection, satisfaction, and
peace of growing old with the person you love.

Maybe you'll have children and watch them grow up, graduate with honors, score the winning goal, or perform in the school play. In no time at all they'll be introducing you to the love of *their* life. And then will come trips to the movies or Disney World with your grandkids.

There are reams of untapped potential and opportunities waiting in your future—whether it's a major life event or a night of laughing with your best friends. The future can have truly great things in store for you.

Of course, it won't all be puppies and rainbows, but you already know that. There will be trials and tribulations. Disappointments, defeats, fights, and fears. Don't stop there, keep looking ALL the way to the end, the ultimate end. That's right, this life will come to a close, your life force will cease to exist on this physical plane, your experience of being you will conclude: Think about the day you're going to die. I know it's unpleasant, but it's going to happen, so why not accept it now?

In this life, you'll sometimes have to do things you don't want to, with people you don't like, and in places you don't care for. People will leave your life as quickly and easily as they come into it. You'll lose money, things will break, and your dog will die.

But you'll get through it all, the good and the bad, just like you did in the past. You'll stand there like the champion you are because they're all just yet another passing scene in the movie that is your life's story.

A SEA OF SOMETHINGS

"It is during our darkest moments that we must focus to see the light."
—Aristotle

The purpose of this exercise is to get you to start putting things back into perspective. As you examine all the things you've experienced and all the things you've yet to experience, take a moment to examine what you are currently dealing with today. Everything on your plate at this point in time is just **another something in a sea of somethings**.

Your boat hasn't and won't sink so easily. There may be some waves, you might go through some storms, and you'll probably end up seasick from time to time, but your journey across that ocean we call life will continue.

But just like a captain facing a major squall, you can't let yourself be tossed about. You have to step up and steer your life back in the direction you want it to go. So your journey wasn't as smooth as you wanted it to be. Does that mean you're just going to let yourself get blown off course? I didn't think so. And you definitely shouldn't let what happens in one area of life affect your outlook on the whole. You just can't afford to allow your struggles at work to make you miserable at home or let your relationship troubles affect your mood at the office.

Face your problems as they come, one by one, give them the attention they need, and move on. Bundling them all together into a morass of confusion and letting them overwhelm you just won't help. It takes precision, patience, and discipline of thought. Work through each item pragmatically and with a solution in mind. Remember, *everything* is solvable, and if you can't see a solution, it only means you haven't worked it out yet.

Often the reason you can't see the solution is because you're too close to the problem. Zoom out a little, zoom out A LOT, and look at the big picture. This is a similar phenomenon to what psychologists call "cognitive restructuring"—shifting the way in which your problems are presenting themselves in your life.

Our minds naturally play tricks on us, twisting and distorting our thoughts in ways that are not always rational. Even though we'd like to think we're always logical, we're not. We're at the mercy of cognitive biases, emotions, and misconceptions, and most of it is completely unseen by us.

> *"That's one of the peculiar things about bad moods—we often fool ourselves and create misery by telling ourselves things that simply are not true."*
> *–David D. Burns*

Sometimes we're too close, too involved in it to even realize. It's up to us to slow down, take a step back, and understand what's really going on. And if things are still out of focus, take another step back. And another. And another.

Ask yourself, "What's *really* going on here?" until you experience your problems cleanly, clearly, and free of that emotional anchor. Persist until you can see the whole course of your life and realize that your current problems are just another bump in the road.

YOU GOT THIS

When you've finally put things into perspective, you'll come to your assertion: "I got this." You'll start to really believe it, experience it, and live *from* it.

You can handle this. It's not going to kill you. Your life isn't over. You've got plenty more left in the tank. Plenty.

"I got this" doesn't mean you have the perfect solution. It just means you have your hands on the wheel, you have a say in this, just like you've had a say all along. I mean come on, you *live* for this shit!

It's not always pretty. It's not always fun but you've got this. I'm not just saying this to paper over the cracks or to make you feel a little better for a split second. Look at your track record; you've *really* got this! You'll make it work, just like you always have. You had it then and you got it now.

Get in touch with who you **really** are and say it.

I got this. I got this. I got this.

05

"I embrace the uncertainty."

"Uncertainty is where new happens."

CHAPTER 5

You're an addict.

You're out of control and so dependent on your drug of choice, you don't even realize how it's affecting your life. You have a gnawing craving and that craving is for prediction.

Will it rain tomorrow? How will my stock perform? Who will win the election? You're constantly looking ahead, trying to figure out what's going to happen before it actually does.

Why?

Certainty. We seek the certain and avoid the uncertain. We want to know what to expect, where to go, and what to wear. We want to be prepared. We want to be safe. It's far beyond a want though, it's more like that addiction. We're sizing people up before we even know them, predicting their character in seconds. We buy the goods and brand names we're used to even though there are plenty of alternatives. We take supplements and vitamins to prevent an illness we don't yet have, date people for months, sometimes years, to make *sure* of our future, to make sure that it turns out in a way that we can predict. Give me that certainty, certainty, certainty!

We all know the bumper stickers and internet memes that praise risk takers and urge us to embrace uncertainty. We even know that our openness to taking risks directly correlates with our potential for fortune and possibility, yet many of us still stay inside our own little organized, certain world.

And there's a reason for that. Until fairly recently, the world was a much scarier place for the likes of you and me. Every step into the unknown was a dance with death. Life was one big game of Russian roulette. Literally every day, you would have been on the dinner menu for an assortment of beasts and creatures, or among the poor suckers that walked blindly into the path of Mother Nature's dark sense of humor.

Lucky for us, the world isn't nearly as scary as it was thousands of years ago (although not quite a utopian safe zone). Life has become much safer, unbelievably so, in fact. Medicine and technology get better by the day; violent crime, although rampant in our news outlets, is in fact a rarity in the everyday life of your average citizen in a Western country.

Sure, there are still deadly diseases and the threat of random acts of violence or catastrophe, but the chances of you catching a mystery zombie virus or being swept up with Dorothy and Toto to a fantastical Hollywood dreamland are, I'm happy to say, slim.

Here's some other startling news: Chances are you're not going to suddenly die on the way to the corner shop, your boss isn't *actually* going to kill you if you ask for a raise, and, believe it or not, asking someone out will not result in your pants mysteriously falling to the floor, painfully exposing your SpongeBob SquarePants underwear and bringing about your early demise via acute terminal embarrassment with the laughter of everyone in Starbucks ringing in your ears as you depart this mortal coil.

In other words, our aversion to risk, which was once necessary, no longer is. Those same survival instincts that once kept us alive can now be the very thing that keeps us from actually living.

A PARADIGM OF POTENTIAL

Our obsession with certainty can be tragic and counterproductive for two reasons.

First, uncertainty is where things happen. Uncertainty is your personal pathway to opportunity. It's the environment in which you grow, experience new things, and produce new, unprecedented results. Uncertainty is where *new* happens.

> *"The desire for safety stands against every great and noble enterprise."*
> –Tacitus

When you stick to what you're comfortable with, doing the same things you've always done, you're in effect living in the past—not moving forward. You're repeating things and behaviors that at one time in your life were risky, since you didn't know what they would lead to, but have since turned into routine.

Think about it: How can you go to new places if you never leave the house? How can you make friends and start romances without meeting new people? How can you do anything new by doing what you've always done?

You can't. The truth is you can't even predict what the people you know will do, let alone the people you don't know. Whether it's the checkout line or a night-club or the bank, social situations are inevitably filled with uncertainty. Jeez, half of the time you can't even predict your own thoughts and feelings! Think of the many times you've rushed to judge and then later changed your mind.

How will you ever get a raise if you don't take the risk of asking? How will you get ahead in your career if you're always holding on to certainty and comfort?

You won't. Success is never certain. It never comes without risk. Even if you're the smartest or the hardest working, there's no guarantee of anything.

The people who go on to do great things in their lives know this. They also embrace it.

"In any moment of decision, the best thing you can do is the right thing, the next best thing is the wrong thing, and the worst thing you can do is nothing."

—Theodore Roosevelt

Reflect on that Teddy Roosevelt quote for a minute here. Missing the target isn't the worst thing you can do. Not taking the shot is.

You may look at successful people and think they've always had it figured out. Many of them seem to have a kind of confidence, charisma, or talent that makes everything they do seem easy. They certainly seem to have something you don't, but believe me, their rise to the top was anything but certain or easy. Most of them doubted it every single day, sometimes hundreds of times per day. That's right, they sat there, just like you are right now, wondering how they would make it, whether it was all worthwhile, or whether they had what it takes.

There were days when they doubted what they were doing. Where they thought, "This is never going to work." Many found themselves on the verge of giving up at numerous occasions along the way.

They didn't succeed because they were certain they were going to succeed; they succeeded because they didn't let uncertainty stop them. They did it anyway. They ignored their doubts and kept pushing forward. They were relentless when the only thing they had to fuel them was relentlessness.

Give some thought to all the people who have achieved something great, only to quickly fade into obscurity. I'm sure you can think of a few, whether they're entertainers or business people or athletes.

In my career I've coached many "successful" people who came to me because their lives had gone flat, and they had become uninspired and tepid. What happened? For many of them, they got comfortable. For years, they had pushed their comfort zones to get where they wanted to be. But as soon as they chose certainty over uncertainty, they stopped achieving. They hit a wall.

Why does it happen? Because when you've accomplished one of your goals, when you're rich and successful, the future naturally *seems* a little more certain. I'm sure we'd all feel a little more secure with a million bucks or so in the bank.

But that mindset shift is exactly what creates the environment for our ultimate undoing. When we're no longer uncertain about money, the desire—the need, even—to pursue it recedes. When we're no longer uncertain about success, our ambition can blunt or mellow. We get to wallow in our bloated illusion of certainty. Eventually we get to do that thing called "settle." We settle for certainty.

That's the kind of power that uncertainty has in our lives. It can make us or break us. It can make us rich or make us poor. It can be the key to our success or drive us in the other direction.

For many people, it ends up being both.

CHASING WHAT DOESN'T EXIST

The funny thing is, no matter how much you chase certainty, you'll never really be able to hold it or retain it. That's because it doesn't exist. The universe will always send us little reminders of its chaos and power, and no one is exempt from the prompting.

Nothing is certain. You could go to sleep tonight and never wake up. You could get in your car and never make it to work. Certainty is a complete illusion. Voodoo.

Some of you might find this terrible to think about, but it's true. No matter how hard we may try, we can never predict exactly what life will bring. Our plans will falter at some point eventually.

By running from uncertainty in search of certainty, we're actually rejecting the one thing in life that is guaranteed in favor of something that's nothing more than a fantasy.

"All I know," Socrates once said, "is that I know nothing." Many wise people understand this. In fact, they owe their wisdom to that very realization—that they don't actually know a damn thing.

Because when we think we know everything, we inadvertently turn ourselves away from the unknown and, by default, whole new realms of success. The person who accepts how unpredictable and uncertain life is has no choice but to embrace it.

They're not afraid of the uncertain; it's just a part of life. They don't seek out certainty because they know it doesn't really exist. They are also the kind of people who are aware of and open to the real magic and miracles of life and what can be accomplished.

One of the pillars of philosophy is the examination of how we know what we know. How can we prove that what we believe is true? In most cases, we can't.

In reality, even many of the things we think of as hard facts aren't. They're half-truths. They're assumptions. They're misinterpretations. They're guesses. They're based on cognitive biases, faulty information, or conditioning. Use science as an example. What we believed 5, 10, or 20 years ago has since been disproved. We have made radical leaps in understanding and those leaps are continuing every day. What we know today will one day be looked upon as archaic and outdated. Consider that those same limits of understanding are everywhere in your life.

If we can't even be certain about what we "know" today, how can we know what will happen tomorrow?

As you've probably noticed, when you do try to stay in your comfort zone, you never truly feel comfortable. There's always that nagging feeling that you could be doing more. There's always that desire for a life that's better than the one you have now.

The more we try to stay comfortable today, the more uncomfortable we'll be tomorrow. There really is no destination, there is only exploring, exploring, and exploring.

"If you want to win, you have to be willing to be judged by others."

STEP FORWARD AND BE JUDGED

Like plenty of other things in our lives, part of our aversion to uncertainty comes from our fear of being judged by others. We are, in a very real way, afraid of what the tribe thinks and the prospect of being thrown out into the mystery and uncertainty of the wild.

If we put ourselves in uncomfortable situations, maybe we'll look awkward. People will think we're "weird."

If we push our limits and try to achieve new things, maybe we'll fail. People will think we're a "failure."

> *"If you want to improve, be content to be thought foolish and stupid."*
> *—Epictetus*

You're never going to achieve your true potential if you're hooked by what other people think. In fact, you could change your life overnight if you simply abandoned the notion that other people's opinions matter. Life goes on, opinion heavy or opinion light.

That doesn't mean you should go off and become a brazen sociopath and completely disregard what others think. But if you want to win, you have to be willing to be judged by others and not let it get to you. If you want to do something truly great, you'll have to accept that some people are going to think you're delusional or an idiot or righteous.

The person who avoids the uncertain doesn't do this. They're too afraid of being judged. They're too afraid to look foolish or stupid. They are stopped, one foot nailed to the floor, by an illusion.

EMBRACING THE UNCERTAIN

This can all come as quite a shock. Some of you are probably squirming in your chair as you read this.

That's because you're rejecting and avoiding uncertainty. You're afraid of it. You're trying to control and know things that you simply can't know or control. You're caught up in the La-La land that we are all born into and can never quite seem to get out of.

The good news is, it doesn't have to be that way.

That's why I want you to shift your thinking. Embrace the uncertainty. That's your personal assertion: ***"I embrace the uncertainty."*** Meet it head on. Cherish it. Enjoy it.

Remember, all of the successes, all of the experiences, all of the things you've always dreamed of are waiting for you in uncertainty. Once you accept this, it's not as scary as before. Sure, you might still be nervous about what will happen, but you'll also be hopeful and excited at the prospect of what may come.

While the unknown can hold plenty of bad things, it also holds everything good as well. It's overflowing with opportunity and progress.

I challenge you to go out today and take the bull by the horns and embrace your own uncertainty. Do the things you normally wouldn't. Shake up that daily routine. Dare to dream, dare to risk, and startle your life into life.

Start with simple things. Take a different route to work. Instead of bringing your lunch or eating at the same few places, try somewhere you've never been. Start a conversation with the waiter or cashier. Smile and say hello to the people you pass on the street, or give them a friendly nod. Talk to that girl or guy who caught your eye.

Or maybe you're a natural extrovert who does all of that already. What are the things that make you uncomfortable? What are the things you'd like to do but avoid because of uncertainty?

Do them. Starting now. There's no better time than this moment. Develop and grow that muscle to be with the uncertain in life. To be with the glory of life itself, unconstrained by your own limits and opinions.

Don't stop there. Instead of simply stretching your comfort zones, let's blow the thing up completely. Try acting in a way you'd never think about acting. Doing something completely out of character would be a great start. Embrace that uncertainty and strike a blow for your future!

OPPORTUNITY HUNTING

Embracing uncertainty has the power to transform your life, from your personal relationships to your career. It can help you get in shape, make more money, or find your future spouse.

You'll no longer be hiding from life, you'll be living it, drinking from it, and enlivened by it.

When you stop searching for certainty, when you quit trying to make sense of everything, a lot of your stress will simply melt away. There really is nothing to figure out. If you took the time to be with what I'm saying, you'd realize that what causes most of your worry is trying to predict the future and then refusing to accept things when they don't or aren't going to go your way.

Life is an adventure. It's absolutely filled with opportunity. But it's up to you to embrace those opportunities fully and completely in all of their majestic, unnerving, and invigorating uncertainty.

Focus on the things you can control and release yourself from worrying about what you can't, like the weather, the Dow Jones, or what your neighbor thinks about your haircut.

"I embrace the uncertainty." This one simple statement can completely change the way you live, moment to moment. The only thing that's guaranteed in life is that it's uncertain. The only thing we know is that we know nothing.

Go ahead, say it, embrace it: "I embrace the uncertainty."

"I am not my thoughts; I am what I do."

"You are
not defined
by what's
inside your
head. You
are what
you do. Your
actions."

CHAPTER 6

"Change your thoughts, change your life."

I was scrolling through Facebook recently when I came across this little gem. It had more likes than Justin Bieber and comments up the yin yang.

As I sat there in my crimson smoking jacket and pale yellow cravat, I pondered its philosophical weight while sipping softly at the edges of my evening crème de menthe. (OK, I was wearing an old AC/DC T-shirt and sweatpants and drinking coffee, but you get the picture.) After a moment, I thought to myself, "What a complete pile of bullshit that is."

Imagine this: You're at work, you've got something to do, but you're dreading it, just not "feeling it" today. You glance at the clock. 10:34. Ah well, at least it's not long until lunch.

"Hmm, what will I eat today? Oh, I've been wanting to try that new place down the street. My coworker said it's really good. But I really should stick to my budget..."

You suddenly snap back to reality and find yourself staring at the blinking cursor on your computer screen.

"Wow, I suck at this. I'm just not up for it today. I need some energy."

Before you know it, you've opened your browser and are scrolling through one of your favorite time-wasting sites.

"Wowzer! Hover shoes! I could really use some of those!"

Quick step back to reality. You check your email. A message from your credit card company. "I'm in so much debt. I'm never going to get out of this mess. No hover shoes or lunch out for me."

A notification from that online dating site you signed up for a few weeks ago. "I'll never find someone. My love life is a disaster. Maybe relationships and I just don't match."

Someone walks past your desk. You frantically click your mouse and mash on the keyboard, feigning busyness for the unsuspecting intruder. "Whew, that was close!"

Look at the clock again. 11:13. Another half an hour wasted. "I should really get to work...right after I..."

Is any of this sounding familiar? Maybe you don't work in an office, but you can still relate to that feeling of dread that hits when you're faced with something you've been resisting. Like you'd rather do anything than the task at hand. That "to-do" list quickly becomes a "don't-wanna-do" list.

Even if you're married or already in a relationship, you might also identify with those feelings of undesirability. Your thoughts about your situation may have become more consuming and debilitating than everything else. When you have become so distracted from what your relationship is supposed to be about, so embroiled in the should/shouldn'ts, could/couldn'ts and who's right or wrong, you often wonder why the hell you're still in it at all.

The truth is, we all do this from time to time. Even the most driven, most successful, and wisest among us have these kinds of thoughts.

So what is it that separates those successful people from you and me? They understand (consciously or otherwise) one simple thing: What they think and what they do don't always have to align.

YOU ARE NOT YOUR THOUGHTS

You are not your thoughts. You are not defined by what's inside your head. You are what you do. Your actions.

> *"Great thoughts speak only to the thoughtful mind, but great actions speak to all mankind."*
> *—Theodore Roosevelt*

Most of us let our internal condition weigh heavily on what we do. But the truly great performers are great precisely because they've learned to experience those feelings while sidestepping the inclination to act upon them.

It's not that they never doubt themselves or never have a desire to procrastinate or avoid a particular situation. It's not that they always "feel" like doing what they should.

They simply focus and lean in. They act anyway.

It'd be great if we could simply decide to never have a negative thought, but when it comes down to it, that's just not realistic. I know, I know, my positive-thinking peeps are losing their minds at this statement but here's something for even those people to consider. Haven't you wondered why you came up with positivity as an answer to your life in the first place? Have you ever noticed how you are when impacted or surrounded by apparently negative people or situations? That's right, even you get gripped by the old negative hand now and again no matter how you might try and avoid it.

The truth is, it's difficult to have a say in, let alone control, what you think about. Especially because, as we've established elsewhere in this book, we're not even aware of the majority of the things we think about.

We have just as many pointless, irrelevant thoughts as important ones. Then there are those default thoughts that pop into your head day in and day out. Thoughts of unworthiness, being judged, not belonging, or some lack of competence. All of this while going to work, paying your bills, going to the grocery store, or driving your car!

Many of the things I teach my clients involve changing the way you approach and look at life. But these are long-term solutions. Ultimately my goal is to help you shift your subconscious. And that, my dears, is like turning a battleship. It takes time.

No matter how hard you try, you're going to have the occasional negative thought. Maybe more than occasionally. Maybe every day. Maybe hundreds of times per day.

You're going to have days where you don't want to get out of bed, where you don't want to go to work, where you don't want to take care of your responsibilities. But you do. Every day you engage in activities that you don't *really* want to do. That means you already have a muscle for having thoughts and acting independently of them.

As I consistently say to my clients, you don't have to feel like today is your day, you just have to act like it is.

Sure, it never hurts to be in the right kind of mood or mindset, but if we sit around waiting to be in the perfect mood, we're just never going to get started.

I've come across literally thousands of people in my career who have spent their lives waiting to feel or

"You don't have to feel like today is your day, you just have to act like it is."

think differently. And while inspiration or motivation may strike once in a while, they are fickle friends and can't be depended on to show up whenever you need them.

> *"We become just by performing just actions, temperate by performing temperate actions, brave by performing brave actions."*
> —Aristotle

You change your life by doing, not by thinking about doing. In fact, when you become closely associated with the actions you are taking, something magical starts to become apparent.

Thoughts without actions are just that, thoughts. Your negative thoughts about yourself, others, or your circumstances will have no impact on your success as long as you leave them where they lie.

HOW DOING CHANGES YOUR THINKING

The benefits of doing are two-fold.

Doing gets you doing what you need to do, of course. But it is, ironically, also the quickest way to change your thoughts.

There are a couple of reasons for this. We know your thoughts can become your reality. And when your reality is one of acting on the things that are in your best interests, your thoughts will actually shift to match that. Think about this: Your thoughts (and the resulting feelings) are not always aligned with what is in the best interests of your life, your health, your finances, or your potential. Many times those same thoughts and feelings are pulling you away from your potential. Things like doubt, fear, procrastination, or frustration rule the day instead of the kind of positive action that will actually forward your life.

If you always attack the task at hand without hesitation, what will you think the next time you have something important to do? Your thoughts start to become intuitive action over time until you start to act independently of your negative thoughts time after time after time. Are you going to think about yourself and what you lack, or are you going to deal with the actions presenting themselves right there in that moment of time?

Haven't you ever noticed, when you're fully immersed in something, all of your problems or negative conversations seem to disappear? When you are cognitively and genuinely engaged in a practice or project, that internal chatter gets quieter and quieter. The golfers, tennis players, meditators, knitters, musicians, artists, and runners among us know exactly what I am talking about. Athletes call this "the zone." And the good news is, you can get better at getting in the zone, too!

When you can focus your attention on the action at hand, eventually your consciousness starts to get the idea.

Each time you do it, you build your experience of self-confidence and trust in yourself. All of that impacts the long-term way in which you think.

So what's the second way that actions influence our thoughts?

Remember when I said your thoughts can become your reality? That's true. While your thoughts can become your reality, it's *only* through your actions that your thoughts actually *become your life*. Until then, they are only thoughts.

Sometimes our mind is like the equivalent of a funhouse mirror, distorting and contorting and blurring our lives and our potential.

Our minds often have an unrealistic perception of the world, peppered with interpretation, misunderstanding, automatic behaviors and opinions, and cultural and familial programming all laid on top of our lives like designs on a giant sheet of tracing paper. The more we strive to get our reality to match this design, the more we struggle.

The gap between how life *is* and how we *think* life is, is often the black hole in which we fruitlessly labor.

We think things are worse or better, harder or easier than they actually are from this cacophony of background noise and judgement.

Consider this: You just messed something important up. Immediately thoughts like "I'm so stupid" and "I always screw things up" randomly pop into your head.

All this means is that your reaction to one situation is out of sync with the whole. Just like when you whine (yes, you whine) about how "impossible" what you need to do is. Your brain starts to follow that line of thought all the way down the rabbit hole!

Fortunately, by accepting and including your thoughts as just a small part of the whole and getting down to taking actions, you'll slowly start to realize just how out of touch you've been all along.

This method is actually similar to one used by psychiatrists giving therapy to their patients. That's because it works. By challenging our thoughts with actions and exposing ourselves to the situations we resist, we train our brains to see the world more cognitively. We get accustomed to living life "as is" rather than how we think it is!

The next time you're feeling or experiencing any sort of negative or diminishing thought that disempowers you, move on immediately. Act independently of that thought. More specifically, act in a way that's in your best interests rather than in a way that is dominated by how you automatically think and feel. Each time will be better than the last until your mind wakes up and realizes, "Hey, I can do this. I'm learning!"

ACTION GREASES THE WHEEL OF LIFE

"Inaction breeds doubt and fear. Action breeds confidence and courage. If you want to conquer fear, do not sit home and think about it. Go out and get busy."

—Dale Carnegie

I like what Carnegie says here. When we choose action instead of inaction, when we act beyond our automatic thoughts, something interesting happens: we start to forget about the things that are bothering us.

Simply put, when we act, we just don't have time for anything else! It's hard to focus on your internal worrying and naysaying when you're busy getting things done. It's all about momentum. Once you've started rolling, it's easier to stay moving. That road that looked so long and intimidating before starts to blur as you speed along it.

But you've got to put your key in the ignition, crank 'er up, and put the car in drive first. The car isn't going to start itself and then wait patiently for you in the driveway.

When you think about it, that's basically what most of us do. We want to be driven. We think a more productive mood will chauffeur us through life, a confident mood will make things easier or more do-able. But if you want to get to where you're going, you'll have to take the wheel.

You have to buckle in and stomp hard on that gas pedal, whether you're ready to or not.

Today, I want you to do something different than what you normally do. I want you to act in a way that's independent of your typical negative or unproductive thoughts. Act on the moment and in line with what the item in front of your face demands of you. Fuck how you feel, ACT!

Don't wait for the mood to strike. Don't get stuck looking for that magic feeling that will do the work for you.

Simply act. Put aside your thoughts and move.

It's not about psyching yourself up. It's not about getting everything aligned just right. Just act. Do it.

Not in a minute. Not after this show is over. Now.

Of course, your mind will always try to rationalize *not* acting. It'll remind you of all the other things you could be doing. It'll dredge up all your recent stresses and doubts.

But don't act on your thoughts. Act on what's in front of you.

Change your life by changing your actions. That's the only way.

Still need more motivation? Think about the greatest people you know of, either personally or by reputation. Do you consider their thoughts? Or do you remember their actions?

Do you think Gandhi or Rosa Parks or Abraham Lincoln were never gripped by thoughts of doubt, fear, or uncertainty?

How about Nikola Tesla or Steve Jobs? Do you seriously think those people woke up every day in the perfect mood with "Everything's Coming Up Roses" playing in their heads? HELL NO! They were wracked by the same kind of shit you are, but they acted ANYWAY. They rolled up whatever was in their way, set it aside, and strode out into the unknown. It wasn't a passive endeavor. Their greatness didn't just miraculously float out into the ether for us to consume. If they hadn't taken action, we'd never have known what their passions were in the first place. We'd never have witnessed their greatness or wisdom.

They toiled, doubted, and had sleepless nights, they worried and battled and ground it out until their lives and their work finally aligned.

I mean, come on, chances are you can think of plenty of people, past and present, who appeared to have "good thoughts" but never accomplished much. That's what we become when we're more worried about how we think than what we do.

On the other hand, think of how many people with negative thoughts have gone on to become wildly successful. All the legendary musicians with drug problems. All the pro athletes with anger management issues. The models with unhealthy body images. The millionaires with scarcity mindsets.

I could go on and on. The point is, positive thinking isn't a predictor of accomplishment any more than negative thinking indicates failure. All of the people described above acted independently of their internal condition. You can too.

It's all about action. Going out there, doing it, and taking all your negative bullshit along for the ride. It's never going to get any better, any easier, or any more understandable. This is it, life is now and you're never going to have a better moment than this.

Don't know what to do or where to start? Good, that's your first action. Find out, understand. Trawl the internet, read books, ask questions, take courses, seek advice, do whatever you need to do to unfuck yourself and get into your life.

Get up on your feet and get going.

> *"Action may not bring happiness, but there is no happiness without action."*
>
> Benjamin Disraeli

SEPARATING YOUR THOUGHTS FROM WHO YOU ARE

"I am not my thoughts; I am what I do."

That's your newest personal assertion, the phrase that sums it all up. Go ahead, try it out. "I am not my thoughts; I am what I do."

You are not your thoughts. They're just a bunch of random things running through your head. Many of them you have no control over.

Eventually we'd all like to have better, more positive thoughts. But sitting there isn't going to make it happen.

It's when we challenge our bodies and minds, when we experience, when we face our fears, when we accomplish—even when we fail—that we truly change who we are.

You could be the smartest person in the world, but that doesn't mean a thing if you don't take action.

Remember that the next time you're not "feeling it." When you're not in the mood to go to work or take a significant step in life. When you're doubting yourself too much to get started.

Forget all of it. Just take that first step. And the next one. And the next one.

You are not your thoughts. Act. You are what you do.

"I am relentless."

"Our biggest successes are born out of discomfort, uncertainty, and risk."

CHAPTER 7

Think back to some of your biggest successes in life.

Maybe you made a really big sale, started a new business, or bought a house. Maybe you got married to the love of your life or went back to school or completed a marathon. It could be anything you're truly proud of.

How the hell did you achieve it?

Well, you probably weren't sitting on the couch pondering your navel. Chances are you weren't wrapped up in the humdrum of your everyday existence either, or mentally calculating the sharp rise in the price of milk since 1977.

So what was it?

I may not be able to guess exactly what you were doing, but I can be certain of one thing: you were uncomfortable. Put a slightly different way, you were most likely operating outside of your "comfort zone."

From the nervousness and doubt we feel when we take risks in our careers to the muscle soreness and shortness of breath we experience pumping out another five minutes on the treadmill, our biggest successes are born out of discomfort, uncertainty, and risk.

> *"Nothing in the world is worth having or worth doing unless it means effort, pain, difficulty."*
> *—Theodore Roosevelt*

In fact, the greater the degree of discomfort you experience, the greater the difficulty, the greater the sense of personal accomplishment that comes after.

And that's exactly why great accomplishments and extraordinary successes are so rare. Because most people don't like being uncomfortable.

BEING RELENTLESS

Anytime you're working to achieve something, you're going against the current. Often the opinion of the people around you is trying to push and pull you away from your destination.

They'll say you can't do it, you're making a mistake, it's impossible, you'll fail. The more unique and out-of-the-box your endeavor is, the stronger the push back can be. Why? Well, mostly because the other people in your life have gotten used to relating to you as a specific "kind" of person. So any time you attempt to break out of that mold, you're not only messing with your own world, you're also messing with theirs.

And the resistance doesn't just come from other people; it comes from your own mind too. Both your conscious and subconscious thoughts can work against you to stop your dreams right in their tracks.

It could be outright negative—"That's impossible. Why even try?" Or it could be subtler.

"Wouldn't it be a lot better to just sleep in instead of getting an early jump on things at the office?" "That game on your phone is so much more fun than working."

You could overcome these distractions and objections, of course, as we discussed in the previous chapter. But there comes a point on your journey where you sometimes lose track of where you are. You become so locked up in the daily humdrum that you've completely wandered off the path and into the middle of the fucking jungle, and you are now meandering around with no map, no water, and no clue.

Are you going in the right direction? How long until you get there? How much more of this can you take? Maybe it's over here. No wait, maybe it's this way.

And when you inevitably stumble or encounter some sort of obstacle, you question the journey at all. Maybe it's even time to turn back.

At this point, when you don't know whether you're up or down, how far you have to go or how far you've come, there's only one thing that can keep you going.

That thing is relentlessness. The momentum to keep moving and moving, no matter what happens.

It doesn't matter if you're "feeling it," it doesn't matter if you're gripped by doubt and worry.

Here's the deal, true relentlessness comes when the only thing you have left is relentlessness. When it seems all is lost and all hope and evidence for success has long since vanished, relentlessness is the fuel that drives you through.

IT'S ONLY TRUE IF YOU AGREE

The most successful among us got to where they are today because they transcended obstacles.

But that's easier said than done. It's one thing to say "never give up" (I fucking hate bumper-sticker slogans), but quite another to actually put relentlessness into your life's most worthy causes.

Listen, when it comes down to it, the world doesn't stop you from succeeding; you're not that big of a deal. The universe is neither conspiring for nor against you, and the only thing that stops you is when you buy into the notion that you are stopped. Then, my friend, you really *are* stopped. Until then, it's on like freaking Donkey Kong.

> *"It is the mark of an educated mind to be able to entertain a thought without accepting it."*
> —Aristotle

Think about all of the things that have been accomplished in human history that were once considered "impossible." If you told someone from the 1850s that you could fly from California to China in a hollow metal tube filled with hundreds of people, they'd have more than likely sent you to the local insane asylum for the rest of your days.

But the Wright brothers didn't accept that flight was impossible. They simply didn't accept that thought—even though there was no historical evidence to prove that human flight *was* possible.

Even though they had no physical proof and it had never been done before, they were determined to make it happen and they were relentless in its pursuit.

Now compare that to your own problems. If you're like most people, your goals probably aren't nearly as ambitious as inventing the first airplane.

You probably just want to make more money, face your fears, find your soul mate, lose some weight, or strike a blow for a better life—things that have been done millions of times before, and will be done again and again in the future, by people just as capable as you.

"Sometimes you just have to grind it out, stake your claim, and hustle for what you want."

These goals ARE possible. However, don't be fooled by the self-help bullshit that tells you, "You deserve it!" Because you don't. No one does. That conversation will leave you waiting and wanting and, eventually, a complete victim to your own life. Sometimes you just have to grind it out, stake your claim, and hustle for what you want. You will need to quite literally **make** it happen.

So when someone looks at you and says, "You'll never make a million pounds" or your brain is telling you, "It's impossible for you to lose a hundred pounds," you have two choices. You could succumb to the notion that you don't know what you're doing, that you lack the resources, that you don't have what it takes, or that you or your life needs to be fixed before you can do those things. And then you can quit.

Or you can disagree. You can absolutely refuse to accept it and reach for your greatness. You can say, "No, you're wrong, and I'm going to prove it."

The impossible only becomes possible in the moment you believe it is.

*"We would accomplish more things
if we did not think of them as
impossible."*

−Vince Lombardi

Here's the crazy thing: You can never really prove
what's possible or impossible.

You could throw yourself at something a thousand
times, failing miserably on every attempt, and yet
succeed on attempt #1,001.

The truth is, you can never really know. We never really
have all the facts. As humans, we still only understand
a tiny fraction of our own minds, let alone the world
or the oceans or space or technology. If someone tells
you they have all the answers, call them out on that
bullshit. The truth is they're winging it just like you, just
like everyone else. Answers? Gimme a freaking break!

So if we can't even say for certain that it's impossible to
put a man on Mars, how can any of us know what we're
really capable of in the day-to-day living of our lives?

We can't. The only question is whether you agree with
what you can and cannot do. An opinion only becomes
true when you accept it and stop acting on your
potential.

My own life is an example of what's possible when you live life beyond your own beliefs and the views of others. I was a pretty average student at school, but I've gone on to travel the world and coach thousands and thousands of people. I've guided doctors, lawyers, politicians, actors, celebrities, athletes, CEOs—hell, I've even coached Catholic priests in Ireland and Buddhist monks in Thailand!

There's a wondrous, magical life out there waiting for you in the unknown and while it's not all cherry pies and bubblegum, there is a reality that you can accomplish that's far beyond the one you're currently wasting away in.

BLAZING THE RELENTLESS TRAIL

To see this idea of relentlessness in action, let's look at a major success story that you and I are likely to be familiar with: Arnold Schwarzenegger.

Arnold was born to relatively poor parents in a small town in Austria, just a couple of years after the end of World War II. Yet young Arnold dreamed of going to America and acting in movies. What do you think his parents thought of that dream? What do you think his fellow Austrian townsfolk told him about his ambitions or whispered behind his back?

Remember, we're not talking about today, where we have television and internet and smartphones and anyone with a wireless connection can become a celebrity. Back then, most households didn't even have a TV.

"America" was a nebulous, fantastical concept for Arnold and the people he grew up with—a place they had only seen in pictures or movies.

So you can pretty much guarantee that everyone he knew thought there was no chance he'd ever realize his dream, and if he had accepted that at any point, their words would have come true.

If he had agreed that he couldn't become a world-famous bodybuilder, it would've been true. If he had agreed that he couldn't move to America, he wouldn't have. If he had accepted that he'd never make it into movies or he'd never be a star actor or he couldn't become Governor of California, he would have quit.

But he never agreed with what the world or other people told him about what was and wasn't possible.

He was relentless. He spent hours in the gym every day, pushing his body. He practiced his bodybuilding poses. He read books. He learned business. He auditioned for movie roles.

Relentlessly. Giving up or changing plans simply wasn't an option.

And if you look at his path, you can learn something valuable about relentlessness: sometimes, it's all you have.

Before Arnold, no Austrian bodybuilder had ever gone on to become an A-list action star in the United States, let alone be elected Governor of California. You can be sure he spent a good part of his life and career not really knowing where he was going. There aren't any road signs when you're trekking through uncharted territory, it's all discovery and exploration. You are blazing a trail, not following one.

When you find yourself in that situation, all you can do is focus on and deal with what's directly in front of you. You just put one foot in front of the other, taking things on as they present themselves.

Even Arnold, who had a big, grand vision, ultimately achieved it by taking one step at a time.

He'd go to the gym and start working his biceps. He'd focus on each movement, each rise and fall of the dumbbell, rep after rep after rep, feeling his muscles flex and tear and grow.

Then when he was done with biceps, he'd move on to shoulders. And then back. And then glutes. And then quads. And then calves.

As he worked each respective muscle group, he gave it his full attention. And then it was on to the next one, moment by moment by moment.

When he had worked each muscle, each body part, to exhaustion, he went home. But there he was the next day, doing it all over again. Relentlessly.

Look more recently at people like Malala Yousafzai who stands for the rights of women and children in Afghanistan or Michael Phelps and his record-breaking athletic accomplishments, or Jessica Cox, born without arms and currently flying commercial airlines.

Are you getting the picture here?

The key to becoming relentless is to focus on the problem in front of you. Give it your full attention. Become someone who progresses even when all seems lost.

The answer is always out there; all you need to do is find it.

Then you can move forward to your next obstacle. And you give that obstacle your full attention until it's taken care of. Then there's the next and the next and the next.

By doing this, you never have to wonder where you're going. You're not worried about how many miles you have left to walk. You become someone who loves obstacles rather than avoids them because obstacles are your keys to success and growth. You simply take one step at a time.

And if you come upon something that's blocking your path, you find a way to get over it or get around it. Then you keep walking.

Relentlessness doesn't mean charging into the fray headfirst, swinging and flailing your arms every which way. It's focused, determined action. Again and again and again.

You're not bashing your fist against a brick wall until it's bloody and bruised. You're using your hammer and chisel to slowly, methodically chip away at it, piece by piece, until eventually there's a hole.

And then the hole gets bigger. And bigger. And before you know it, you're like Alice stepping through the looking glass to a whole new world.

YOU ARE RELENTLESS

When you're not sure if you're following the right path, when you've been knocked down a few too many times, it's completely fine to get discouraged; hell, even defeated. What's not OK is to stop.

Because you can always lean on relentlessness. When you have nothing else, you have relentlessness.

Rather than worrying about whether you should keep going or turn back, press on relentlessly. Relentlessness has one direction, and that's forward. It only has one option, and that's to keep the momentum going.

There is no giving up. There is no quitting. There is no changing of plans.

Relentless is the bodybuilder who goes to the gym for hours every day. Relentless is the prospective entrepreneur who has been ridiculed or rejected for their completely original idea but keeps pitching it anyway. Relentless is the overweight mother who feels like she's never going to get there. Relentless is the newly minted college graduate at the bottom of the corporate ladder barely making enough to pay her rent and yet staying at the office later than anyone else just to learn as much as she can. Relentless is you.

Anyone who's ever gone to the gym knows that the results aren't immediate. You don't spend 30 minutes on the treadmill and look like a new person.

But that doesn't mean what you're doing isn't working. You're making progress. With each exercise, each step, each movement, each action, you get a little better, a little closer.

Until one day you look in the mirror and think, "Wow!"

It's the same thing with your business or your health or your career or your relationships. Even when you don't see anything happening, it is. Even when you're not quite hitting the mark, you're making progress.

Until one day you look at your bank balance or your new job or your children or your new house and think, "Wow!"

That's why you have to keep going. Relentlessly.

Because when you're trekking through the jungle, you don't know if you're three days from civilization or 30 minutes. All you can do is walk. The only way out is forward.

Sit up, straighten your spine, and repeat after me: "I am relentless."

08

"I expect nothing and accept everything."

"Stop doing all that shit you know you shouldn't be doing and start doing all the shit you know you should be doing."

CHAPTER 8

Firstly, do not be deceived by the title of this chapter. There is something truly amazing for you to discover in the following pages.

Imagine this.

You've always dreamed of starting your own business—being your own boss, controlling your own schedule, and building something you can be proud of, something you can point to as a major life accomplishment.

Through a combination of hard work, determination, and solid planning, you've managed to organize your life in such a way that this dream of yours can now become a reality.

You've already come up with a great business idea, hired a company to create a cool logo and branding, and now it's time to get to work. Here's where the fun begins...

You'll need a store, of course. And that's the first task you tackle, spending the next week driving around town, scouting locations and negotiating with real estate agents.

It's not easy, but you finally find what you think is a pretty good location, for a pretty good price. There was another place you really had your eye on, but you couldn't make it work within the budget.

There are a few other things to get taken care of, like property insurance, a business license, and setting up your taxes. Even though you've yet to make a penny, you've already had to hire an accountant to help you sort through those complicated business taxes.

Oh well, on to the next project. Your store will need furniture and other necessary equipment, so you shop around to get a rate on that. Another thing off the checklist.

Obviously you'll need someone to work there, too. Time to hire some employees. Check.

It's all going pretty well until…BOOM! That deal you had fought for and ground out to secure the unique product you were planning to sell fell through and now you have to look for alternatives. SHIT!

Your heart sinks and breathing shallows as you frantically search out wholesalers, importers, manufacturers— anyone who can help—and start asking for quotes.

The only problem is, the new prices you're being quoted are way beyond your pricing model. How can you make this thing work? You tirelessly continue searching but keep coming up zero after zero after zero. This is fast becoming a disaster!

You've already invested massive amounts of time and resources into this and now you've hit a big fat road block. You're realizing now that you should have seen this coming. This is business; stuff is bound to go wrong. The cascading stream of doubt and second-guessing washes through your brain with a heavy rinse cycle of reality.

"Dammit, this was going too smoothly; I just **knew** something like this would happen!"

This feeling builds and grows until it starts to pull you under. Setting up a business means risking everything you've ever worked for. Is it even worth it? You've got bills for the love of God!

Now that you **really** think about it, you've spent more time working on this project than you did at your last job. A LOT more. I mean, come on, it's been day and night with hardly a breath. You have less control of your time than you ever did before. Your every thought, second, and penny has been geared toward this thing. Why did you ever think it was better to work for yourself?

This isn't what you signed up for, is it? Maybe this whole thing was a mistake. You're starting to feel a little darker and more depressed while you start to confront the gut-churning possibility that you might lose all that investment and wind up having to crawl back to your old boss to ask if you can return to your old job.

WHOOOAAAAA!

Easy tiger! Before we get ahead of ourselves, let's take a step back.

EXPECTING THE EXPECTED

What's really going on here?

It's simple. You, like everybody else, are weighed down by expectation.

I'm not talking about the usual kind of everyday expectations you're aware of. It's also not like we're literally saying to ourselves, "I expect this" or "I expected that" in a conscious way. It's something that's happening just below the surface, where you'll only see it if you take the time to look closely.

No, I'm talking about the ugly, undermining, hidden, and treacherous expectations that dwell in the wings and under the stage of your Broadway blockbuster. The kind of expectations you didn't even know you had until they came out of nowhere and blindsided you and sucked the air from your lungs.

When you and I take on a life-changing project, we prepare for it from what we know. That includes items from our own experience, what we've read, heard, and imagined. We start to picture it in our minds. We research, we ask others for their opinions, and consume reams of information. We begin to assemble an idea of what this will look like and how we're going to get there. That image in our heads becomes the template from which we work and plan.

What we **don't** see is that we're also setting up a world of hidden expectations—the cracks and crevices hidden in the foundation of our best-laid plans that can kill off a potential idea before it really gets going. In our business example, our budding entrepreneur "didn't expect" to lose his deal for that product, and while losing the deal was bad enough, the interruption to his expectation was actually the biggest blow to his aspirations.

How do you know if you have hidden expectations in your life? If you have places in your life where you experience disappointment, resentment, regret, suppression, anger, lethargy—essentially anywhere you are deflated or have some loss of your personal chutzpah or any other suppressive emotion—you have these expectations. Any place where you're just not *yourself*, if you look at these places long enough, you'll see the reality of that area of your life is some way short of the scenario you had anticipated in your mind's eye. If you have upset in your marriage, you'll see a gap between your expectation of how it was "supposed" to be and how it, in fact, is. For others, it might be their finances, their weight loss, their new job, etc.

Your powerlessness is directly correlated to the gap between your hidden expectations and your reality. The greater the gap between them, the worse you'll actually feel.

I read somewhere that the root cause of upset in marriage is **unmet** expectation.

I think it goes out further, much further. I say the problem is expectation itself. I contend that the upsets strewn throughout your entire life are a product of thousands of unspoken or unrecognized expectations that cast a giant shadow across your life experience, causing great stress when you're trying to make life fit with your expectations and great disappointment when life doesn't match up to them.

Here's what else they do, they actually get in the way of our **real** lives, our real issues, and items that require attention. They are like a mirage that diverts us from our genuine power and clouds our ability to take pronounced, decisive action. In short, you end up working on your expectations and having life line up with **them** rather than taking the actions that would positively impact your situation. This "sidetracking" draws all of your power away from what's actually going to improve your life or accomplish your goal, down a pathway of no power, no results, and wasted time.

CUTTING OUT THE MIDDLE MAN OF EXPECTATION

Now that we've busted our problems with expectations wide open, you'll start to realize something. And that's that many of the difficulties and complications in your life are the direct result of expectations that you have or have had.

We've been using an example of a business plan gone wrong, but, in your own life, your failed relationships, dissatisfaction with work, and abandoned diets can be traced right back to expectation. How many times have you said to yourself, "This isn't how I thought it would be?"

What about the last time you were angry with someone? Can you remember it?

Take a moment to examine that situation and you'll soon realize that your anger was a product of expectations. The gap between how it is and how it should have been. You harbor an unspoken expectation that people in your life will be agreeable, you expect them to tell the truth and follow through on any agreements you have with them. Expect, expect, expect. And when people don't match those expectations? Oh boy!

"This is all great and good, Mr. Scottish-man but how in the hell do I uncover *my* hidden expectations?"

Easy. Pick an area of your life in which things aren't going as well as you'd like them to, maybe even somewhere in your life that sucks right now. Take a pen and piece of paper and write out how that area was "supposed" to turn out. How had you planned it?

How should this have gone? You might have to use your imagination and sense of wonder to get in touch with how the future looked from back there. Get in touch with the hope and positivity of that area and where it was supposed to head. Describe it in as much detail as you can possible recall.

Next, on a separate piece of paper, write down how this area *actually* looks. Again, make this an exhaustive description not just "it sucks." Get into detail about why it is the way it is and what you now have to deal with. How do you feel now that this part of your life did not meet your expectations?

Now, look at both pieces of paper side by side. Your pain, anguish, disappointment (or whatever your thing is) is greater in the areas where the gap is widest between what you expected and what you actually have. In there are your hidden expectations. Do the work here until you fully uncover the expectations you had inadvertently set yourself up for.

Good, now look again. In what way does how you feel about this make a difference to your reality? Does it make it any better? Does it solve your issue? Hell no, it makes no positive difference whatso-freakin-ever! It even makes it WORSE!

Your problems don't derail you, your hidden expectations do!

The point here is that the "expectation" of how life should be doesn't do you any good. You're actually more winded by the whack your expectations took than the situation itself, and that's the deal with expectations; they blow things out of proportion and dilute your power to deal with issues effectively and powerfully. Listen, it's not like I'm saying something radically new here, the notion of "letting go" of expectations has been around for thousands of years, although in our culture (that of the West) it's a practice very few engage in.

Here's the coaching: CUT IT OUT! Let go of those expectations NOW!

It's much more powerful to come to terms with life's unpredictability and to engage with your circumstances for what they are than get bogged down by your refusal to let go of unnecessary or unproductive expectations.

The world revolves around change. Birth and death, growth and destruction, rise and fall, summer and winter. It's never the same from one day to another no matter how much it might seem that it is.

> *"No man ever steps in the same river twice..."*
> *—Heraclitus*

Our minds would love to predict and plan for everything that's going to happen. But it's simply not possible. And these expectations not only have a negative effect on our emotional state, they actually leave us less powerful than we really could be.

It's so much more effective to simply take things as they present themselves, to live in the moment (like there's another moment you could live in) and solve issues and items as they arise, than to constantly expect.

It's not that I'm anti-planning, I most certainly am not, but the stone-cold attachment to the plan (and all the expectation therein) is a little like falling out of a rowing boat and continuing to row, even though you have no oars and no boat under you anymore. Your plan (and image) of how this should have gone is no longer relevant but yet you still struggle to reconcile the space between your expectations and reality.

Life can be like that at times. On some occasions you have to realize that the game has changed (sometimes dramatically so) and you need to pivot. Deal with your reality.

Wake up, you're in the water. Stop waving your arms about and paddle to shore dammit!

LIFE IS MORE OF A DANCE THAN A MARCH

Our mind has all kinds of automatic thought processes that we don't even know are going on. Expectations are just one of them, albeit an important one.

Here's the harsh truth about how our brain works.

We all like to believe in something called "free will."
It's one of those concepts that really speaks to who
we are as human beings. I mean, let's be honest, if we
don't have free will, what in the hell do we have?

We value the notion that we freely choose what we do,
and when to do it. We want to feel that we control our
own fate and shape our own destiny.

But when our minds are ruled by these automatic
thought processes, do we really have free will? Many
would argue that we don't. Listen, the bottom line is
that you have to stop doing all that shit you know you
shouldn't be doing and start doing all the shit you
know you should be doing. All of it.

This free will stuff isn't so easy now is it!?

> *"No man is free who is not master*
> *of himself."*
> *–Epictetus*

Because, as we've talked about throughout this book,
even when you feel yourself making a conscious
decision, there are a series of unconscious thought
processes that are driving that choice. Things you
don't even see or acknowledge.

People are much more irrational and illogical than we realize. In many cases, our subconscious is the puppet master that truly pulls the strings.

Fortunately, you can take back your freedom to choose. And that's by understanding how your mind works, seeing what it's doing as it does it, and being able to use that information to cognitively choose something else. To make conscious that which is currently unconscious.

Expectations are just one of these things.

WHEN LIFE IS APPROPRIATE

"I expect nothing and accept everything." This is your final personal assertion.

Let me get clear about this one. This is not some meek, weak submission to life. No, this is the statement of a masterful celebrant of success, someone who cannot be dominated by anyone or anything.

When you expect nothing, you're living in the moment. You're not worrying about the future or rejecting the past. You're simply embracing your situation as it comes. When you accept everything, that doesn't mean you are OK with it or that you agree with it, but simply that you are owning it and in charge of it. Remember, you can always change something when you can take ownership and responsibility for it. Sometimes it's the single most effective way of resolving your "stuff." Own it!

> *"Don't seek to have events happen as you wish, but wish them to happen as they do happen, and all will be well with you."*
> *—Epictetus*

The next time you catch yourself getting brought down by your expectations, shift things in a different direction. Instead of getting your knickers in a twist about how things didn't turn out the way you wanted or expected them to, simply accept them for what they are. In that moment you are now freed up to deal with them.

"This is appropriate." When you're having growing pains at your new job, take a step back and realize how appropriate that really is. Of course a new job is going to take some getting used to, whether it's the tasks you're performing or the people you work with. It's therefore entirely appropriate to make a few mistakes or tread carefully as you try to get to know your new colleagues. The expectations dissolve right there, immediately.

If your relationship is struggling, change your perspective and get the whole picture. What are your expectations?

Many of us expect our partners to be a certain way consistently, or to anticipate our needs and know exactly what we're feeling, as if by magic. But your partner, like you, is an imperfect human with his or her own set of complicated emotions and thoughts. So it's appropriate that they may sometimes be distracted or get short with you after a bad day.

We often expect other people to treat us exactly as we treat them. If we do them a favor, for example, we expect to get the same favor back in return. It becomes an unspoken "debt" of sorts. When we give our partner a foot massage, we expect them to reciprocate either directly or indirectly. Those expectations grow both in weight and complexity in an intimate or romantic relationship.

You won't believe how much your interactions with other people will improve the moment you let go of expecting, the instant you learn to accept things as they happen.

Again, this doesn't mean you need to put up with shitty or abusive relationships. But the only thing more unpredictable than one person is two unpredictable people. If you are in one of those kinds of relationships, it's time for you to invoke the boat analogy. Stop rowing, the game has changed, shift your plan. Your partners, friends, and family members all have their own desires, perceptions, and feelings. While you're thinking one thing, they're more than likely thinking something completely different. That thing that's got you feeling pissed may not have even registered on their radar. They could be completely oblivious to what's going on with you.

Instead of silently expecting something and feeling slighted when it doesn't happen, let go of that expectation. If there's something you want, how about asking for it with no expectation? And when you do something positive or generous, do it because you genuinely want to rather than loading in the added weight of what you expect in return.

That game of tit for tat only hurts you both in the long run.

If it's something serious that consistently challenges the relationship, confront the other party about it. Don't expect them to realize how you feel or, by the same token, expect them to be able to change how you feel. They can't. Only you can do that.

People are always going to lie, steal, cheat, and everything else one can imagine. It's just not connected to reality to live in the expectation that they somehow won't and then throw a hissy fit when they do it anyway. Remember, in those cases, you always end up worse off than they do! Much worse!

You end up sticking yourself with resentment, regret, anger, or frustration. Remember, they're not doing that to you, you're doing that part to yourself! You really can accept things for what they are. It doesn't mean you condone them or that you won't decisively change them, this is about becoming masterful with your mind and your emotional state. It's about quieting the mind and allowing yourself to act with power in the situations of your life rather than succumbing to your internal and external upsets.

EXPECTING NOTHING, ACCEPTING EVERYTHING

None of this means you can't plan, or that I'm telling you to walk through life aimlessly without direction or goals.

But when you make a plan, what do you have to gain from being welded to the expectations inherent in it? Nothing. When you are free from its expectations you are "in a dance" with life where you can simply execute the plan, and deal with what happens.

If it succeeds, you can celebrate. If it fails, you can recalibrate.

Don't **expect** victory or defeat. Plan for victory, learn from defeat. The expectation of people loving you or respecting you is a pointless exercise, too. Be free to love them the way they are and be loved the way that they love you. Free yourself from the burden and melodrama of expectation, let the chips fall where they may.

Love the life you have, not the one you expected to have.

"I expect nothing and accept everything." This simple personal assertion gets you out of your head and

"Stay out of the swamp of mediocrity and drama, reach for your greatest self, your greatest potential, and challenge yourself to live that life every single day of it."

powerfully into your life, out of your thoughts and into your reality. Problems, barriers, disagreements, and disappointments are all part of every human being's life.

Your job is to not get caught up in that crap, to stay out of the swamp of mediocrity and drama, reach for your greatest self, your greatest potential, and challenge yourself to live that life every single day of it.

Your life, your success, your happiness, really is in your own hands. The power to change, the power to let go, be adventurous, and embrace your potential all lies within your reach. Remember, no one can save you, no one can shift you, all of that is your responsibility and what better time to embrace that change than now?

09

Where next?

"It's this simple: In order to improve your internal world, you have to start by taking action in the external world. Get out of your mind and get into your life."

CHAPTER 9

I've given you seven personal assertions.

"I am willing."

"I am wired to win."

"I got this."

"I embrace the uncertainty."

"I am not my thoughts; I am what I do."

"I am relentless."

"I expect nothing and accept everything."

Each of them plays into a theme. You may not immediately see it, but it's there.

If you want your life to be different, you have to make it happen. All of the thinking or meditating or planning or anti-anxiety medication in the world isn't going to improve your life if you're not willing to go out and take action and make changes. You can't sit around waiting for the right mood to strike or for life to play out the way you want it to. Nor can you rely on positive thinking alone to transform things for the better. You have to go out and **do**.

One of the ironic things about developing our minds and our mindsets is that it can actually keep us from acting on the things we need to act on. You can become a personal development drone. You know tons of cool shit but it's made little difference to your life.

We think, "As soon as I get rid of my worry or discomfort, I'll start dating again." Or, "When I find the root of my procrastination or when I find something to motivate me, I'll be completely unleashed and happy." The desire to work on our "procrastination" just leaves us stuck in the cycle of procrastination/not procrastination and keeps us even further from forwarding our actual lives.

We're waiting on that moment or experience when everything in our mind is just perfect. Our thoughts are clear, our emotions are positive, and our anxiety or worry has completely disappeared.

When we **feel** "off," we put our lives off. That's right, you're waiting on a feeling.

Life doesn't work like that. There is no perfect mood. And while you're waiting on it to improve and miraculously make your life better, guess what? Your life isn't getting any better! None of these assertions are going to make your life easy. Hell, for a while, they're more than likely to make your life harder! Nor is it enough to simply internalize them. You need to **act** on them.

It's this simple: In order to improve your internal world, you have to start by taking action in the external world.

Get out of your mind and get into your life.

YOU'RE GOING TO DIE

> "If I take death into my life, acknowledge it, and face it squarely, I will free myself from the anxiety of death and the pettiness of life—and only then will I be free to become myself."
>
> —Martin Heidegger

One day, you're going to die. You're going to stop breathing, become still, and cease to exist. You will exit this physical plane. Whether it's tomorrow or 20 years from now, it's going to happen.

We're all mortal. There's no escaping that fact. You might find discomfort in these words or resist the notion of your demise but if it's truth you're after, that's the one truth you just cannot argue with. You are going to die.

Imagine that you're on your deathbed. You hear the beep...beep...beep of the monitor nearby. Your health is critical, and you've only got a few hours to live. You can feel your heartbeat and energy slide.

As you lie there, you start to look back on your life. You never made the change you wanted. You stayed stuck in that same job, that same relationship, that same overweight body until now, the day you die.

You read books, but you never applied them. You planned diets, but you never followed them. You told yourself what you were going to do, psyched yourself up a thousand times, but you never did it. You started dozens if not hundreds of life-changing escapades and then wilted.

As you lie there in your hospital bed, loved ones cycling in and out over the course of the day, what do you feel?

Regret? Remorse? Sorrow? What would you give if you could go back to this moment—the one in which you're reading this book—and do things differently? If only…

Dammit, WAKE UP! The regret will course through your body, your mind, your heart. It'll be crushing. Unbearable. You're not sure whether to fear death or to welcome it, just so it can take you out of this misery.

Here's the thing: Future you is not going to regret a lack of achievement or the absence of any one thing in your life. The only thing you will regret is not trying. Not pushing through when the going got tough.

Not all mountaineers make the summit, sometimes they turn back, re-tool, keep coming at it. They're just never satisfied with standing at the bottom, hanging out with all the other non-climbers and explaining their lack of ascent. No, they packed up their tent and moved forward, and they will pass from this world knowing they gave every ounce of their effort. That they played full out. They loved the climb.

You won't regret not making a million pounds, you'll regret never starting that business or quitting that lousy job. You won't regret not marrying a supermodel, you'll regret staying in that dead-end relationship when you knew you could do better. You won't regret not looking like a bodybuilder, you'll regret stopping at the drive-thru every night on your way home and living a lie.

And this will happen to you. You will die. You will go through all of that on your own, in the quiet solitude of your own dwindling consciousness.

Unless you take the action that's needed to change, to build the life you want, the life you can be proud of.

STOP BUYING YOURSELF OFF

We're constantly buying ourselves off. We have all kinds of things we tell ourselves about why we "can't."

I can't, I can't, I can't. But you can. These are all just excuses. You promise yourself all kinds of new actions, you put them off with a litany of reasons and end up with nothing more than a growing connection to yourself as a bullshitter!

You're way more likely to sell out on yourself than anyone else!

The only difference between you and the person who's living the life you want is that they're doing it. They've built that life, and they're living it.

They're not smarter, more mindful, stronger, or any of that stuff. They don't have anything you don't. The only difference is that successful people don't wait. They're not waiting for the "right" moment. They don't wait for inspiration to strike or for some cosmic event to force them to action. They get up and they do, and they try, and they fail even before they may feel "ready." They're flying the airplane while they're building it. If it falls out of the sky, they'll piece it back together and try again.

Your internal condition means nothing. It's just another excuse that you give yourself to stay out of the risky zones of life. The problem is, those risky zones ARE life! The rest is just existing.

STOP BLAMING YOUR PAST

For those of you that are blaming your past, thinking that holds you back, I invite you to think again. I invite you to confront the notion that what has been is greater than what can be. We all have pasts, some of them are fucking horrific. SO WHAT!!!!?????

Before you jump furiously on the offended bus, why is it you show more passion for your past than you do your future? You and I both know no one can free you but you. I'm not just another guy with an opinion; I've coached people with pasts that would make your toes curl. They have gone on to live free and happy lives and you can, too.

People become trapped in their past, trapped in their childhood. It's one of the many reasons we tell ourselves that we "can't." It's an easy way to relieve yourself of the responsibility you have for your current circumstances.

But nothing can stop you from moving forward and being great, if that's what you really want. It doesn't matter what happened yesterday or five years ago or when you were at school.

Just like how we improve our internal by moving to the external, we can forget our past by creating a future. Build something big, something bigger than anything you've done.

When what's in front of you is so bright and so satisfying, you won't have time to look behind you. Your eyes and mind will be focused straight ahead.

That will draw you out. A big enough, bright enough, sexy enough future, a future so soaked with potential and possibility that its weight will snap you free from that significant and laborious past.

You may not like everything from your past, but it's helped shape who you are today, good and bad. That's right, there is plenty good about you, and that good is enough to get you what you want. That person is fully capable of living the life they want. Nothing will hold you back, if you want it enough and act on it enough.

TWO STEPS TO FREEDOM

If you're truly ready to take hold of that freedom you've been missing, there are two things you need to do.

1. Stop doing what you're currently doing.

Simple, right? Look at the things that are sourcing your problems, the habits that have put you in the situation you are in.

If you don't get anything done because you're glued to the couch, binge-watching Netflix for hours at a time, or have become a little too attracted to the delicacies of your local McDonald's, stop doing it. No, seriously, STOP. Now.

Don't start listing all the reasons you can't. "But the shows are so good, and I'm so tired after work," or "I need the small pleasures to keep me going."

If you can't even stop watching TV long enough to get your life together, you obviously don't want to change. That's basic shit. It's the bare minimum, to be honest.

So what will it be? Netflix or a better-paying career? Donuts or a body you can be proud of? Video games or a loving relationship?

If eating out every day makes you feel like crap, why are you still doing it?

And every time you think you "can't" stop, that's just another excuse. You can. You can, and you will. Stop buying yourself off. Stop letting your internal condition dominate the quality of your life. Take back the wheel.

If you continue to be led by your emotions, you'll only be left with regret. You'll eventually live that vision, lying on your deathbed and thinking, "What if?" I'm not saying your emotions and feelings aren't important; I'm not asking you to turn into a robot. What I AM saying is you need to get those experiences much further down the ladder of importance and act on what is going to make the biggest difference to your life.

One of the common excuses we feed ourselves is, "I want to change my life but…" while watching hours of TV, eating junk food, reaming our way through Facebook, etc. Be straight with yourself.

YOU DON'T WANT TO CHANGE! If you did, you'd be doing it! Call yourself out on this shit.

Take a long, hard look at your life. Be honest with yourself, identify the behaviors that are holding you back. You need to use every waking hour of your life to further your cause, no excuses. You're not any different or any worse off than anyone else. You're not a fucking special case who needs different rules than anyone else.

You need to make a choice, right now. You're never going to change your life until you get rid of those things. No more excuses.

2. Start taking the actions to propel you forward.

Again, pretty straightforward, right? Changing your life isn't just about NOT doing certain things. You've also got to put in the work and build the positive habits that will pull you in the right direction.

If you want a new job, go out and apply for one. Get out there and network. Search the classifieds, talk to friends, ask for references.

No, I mean really do them. Don't say you will, and then don't. Don't hype yourself up, then push it off until tomorrow.

> *"You are what you do, not what you say you'll do."*
> *–Carl Jung*

Take stock of the things you want to achieve. What do you want to accomplish? What do you need to do to get there? Map out the next step—hold yourself accountable, moment by moment, to those steps.

These two steps, stopping and starting, are naturally linked. Because psychologically, it's hard to just quit something "cold turkey." Especially when it's an addictive habit that affects the very chemistry of our brains, like food or sex or drugs or video games.

Stopping your bad habit doesn't help, unless you replace it with something else, something that actually works in your favor and is an example of the new kind of life you really want to live. It's about systematically replacing the old with the new, forging a new life for yourself—the kind of life you've always wanted.

You have to clear out the bad to make room for the good. Otherwise, you're not going to have enough evidence for that new life. You're building a case for a new life, item by item. The process has to be thorough and decisive or you'll always be held back and slowed down on your journey to change, carrying that dead weight.

Quit the TV, the sea of self-help books that you read and do nothing with, excessive eating, sofa camping, and procrastination. Replace them with tango classes, book clubs, eating for fuel, bicycle riding, and expressing yourself...ANYTHING!

Need support? Get yourself a coach, a good one, the best you can afford. If money's an issue, join my i365 program, a 12-month journey of personal expansion and power. It's on my website and you can participate for less than the cost of a daily cup of coffee. Like I said, NO EXCUSES!

GET OUT OF YOUR HEAD

"Take time to deliberate, but when the time for action comes, stop thinking and go in."
—Napoleon Bonaparte

There's a time for thinking and developing your mind. But ultimately, you've got to step up to the plate and put what you know into action.

All of your assertions play into that. You are willing to take action. And embrace the uncertainty that comes along with it.

"I am relentless" doesn't mean relentlessly thinking or watching TV. It means relentlessly doing. Relentlessly taking action, pursuing your goals, acting and failing, and, ultimately, succeeding.

Nothing that I've shown you will make a single difference in your life, unless you act on it. You have to **make** the difference. Make it happen.

You have to claim your greatness. I'm not going to do it for you. Neither is your mother or your spouse or your neighbor. Confidence won't save you, the future is not suddenly going to improve, your worry isn't going to suddenly disappear, and your new qualifications

"This isn't just about seizing the day, this is about seizing the moment, the hour, the week, the month."

aren't going to make you suddenly assertive or credible. Only you can take a stand for your potential.

Don't just read this, think about it, and then go on about your life doing the same shit over and over. Apply it.

"I'll do it later"—no, do it now.

"I'm not smart enough to do that"—cut it out. Stop honoring that shit and act.

Don't let your mind control you any longer. Stop letting it hold you back with its excuses and distractions and worries.

You are not your thoughts. You are your actions. You are what you do.

And your actions are the only thing separating you from where you are and where you want to be.

This isn't just about seizing the day, this is about seizing the moment, the hour, the week, the month. This is about seizing your fucking life and staking a claim for yourself as though your life depended on it.

Because, the reality is, it does.

yellow
kite

books to help you live a good life

Join the conversation and tell
us how you live a #goodlife

🐦 @yellowkitebooks
f YellowKiteBooks
📌 Yellow Kite Books
📷 YellowKiteBooks